UNALLOCATED

SPACE

A thriller by

JERRY HATCHETT

RED
HOUSE
PUBLISHING

*For my forensicator friends who pursue nefarious bits
and bytes across the ether...*

CHAPTER I

AFGHANISTAN

2002

"Good hell, Flatbread. Who names a horse Johnny?"

I glanced over at Ditto and watched his green self bob up and down in my night vision as his own horse climbed the rocky trail. "You ever been quiet for five minutes in your life, just because?" I said.

"Got a question for you."

Johnny slowed, picked his way through a ten-foot patch of bigger stones, about the size of bowling balls. Maybe if I ignored Ditto he'd clap his trap.

Ditto said, "What you think the public would think of us?"

"Most of 'em would cheer us on, but we'd end up villains anyway."

"How you figure?"

"The media would make us out to be monsters and find a couple dozen Americans who agreed with them and blast it twenty-four-seven."

"Assholes," he said. "Somebody's gotta do it."

I nodded and gave Johnny a nudge to pick it up a bit.

About two hours later, I checked my GPS. We were there. I reined Johnny to an easy stop. There was nothing to tie to in this hellhole of a place, so I looped the reins around his fetlocks as a makeshift hobble that would allow a quick getaway if needed. Ditto did likewise with his mount, whose name changed daily, but I think on this day the mare's name was Wildfire. ("'Cause that's one more awesome damn horse song," according to Ditto.)

We started our hike up the remaining distance, a couple hundred yards to go. It's slow going to check every footstep in advance to be sure you're not stepping on anything that could make a sound, but after a half hour we could see the destination through our goggles. A black hole in the side of the mountain.

I switched my view from infrared to thermal. Scanned the mountain face above the cave opening. Found what I was looking for: a hundred feet up, a smaller hole, leaking enough heat to look like a bonfire through the goggles. "Intel looks good," I whispered.

"No time like right now," Ditto said. "Let's do this thing."

We continued our quiet ascent and in a few minutes we stood outside the cave, me just to the left edge of the six-foot-wide opening, Ditto on the right. It was high enough for us to stand. That helped. I used hand signals for us to move in and we both took a step before Ditto held up a fist.

I froze. He pointed to an electronic device on his chest and we pulled back to our positions flanking the hole.

The gadget was the latest and greatest Blackberry. It could send and receive electronic mail anytime it had a signal, and thanks to an adapter that connected to our satphones, that translated to pretty much anytime and anywhere we had a look at the sky. Ditto's had obviously vibrated. He detached it and flipped up his goggles. I could see its screen glowing a dim green as he read the message. Then he was typing on it with his thumbs. As soon as he stopped, mine vibrated its tickle-buzz across my Kevlar vest. I raised my headset and read the message.

SHIT. AIRSTRIKE IN 7 MIN

Damn. I stowed the Blackberry, dropped my goggles, and raised five fingers to Ditto. We set five-minute timers on our watches and, on my signal, simultaneously started the countdown. No time left for the kind of stealth I preferred. I signaled one more time and we moved inside the cave as quietly as we could while still making haste.

We worked our way through a few small chambers that twisted and turned, and then we could see light ahead in a larger space. At the edge of the opening to that space, we dropped to our bellies, flipped up our NV gear, made a quick scan. Nine assholes inside. The most important one, sitting in front of a laptop with a cable snaking up to the roof of the cavern and disappearing inside a vertical shaft, was on the leftmost wall. The cavern was lit by a couple propane lanterns on stands.

I counted down three fingers to Ditto and it was on. The left side was mine. Our suppressed M4s made quick work of most of them while we had the element of surprise. No idiotic movie spraying on full auto, just quick and efficient double-taps to the head. Seven of them could now have much more intimate conversations with Allah. Two remained, my guy with the laptop—I did not want to kill him yet—and one guy on the right behind a large wooden shipping crate. We stood and entered. I was focused on Computer Guy, but my peripheral vision picked up things going very wrong on the right. Standing from behind the crate and screaming like an animal, Ditto's guy opened up with an AK-47. My partner wasn't fast enough. Ditto's head burst open in a sickening spray of gore. Sonofabitch. I pivoted right and returned the favor to the jihadi. There was no need to check on Ditto.

When I turned back to Computer Guy, he was coming out of his state of shock, his hands over the keyboard. I popped a .223 round into each shoulder and he was no longer concerned with typing. While he wailed, I checked my watch. The firefight had felt like a half hour but my countdown was just moving through 3:18. I was at the computer in three quick steps. I grabbed the guy by his nasty beard and yanked him away from the computer. I took his place on the rock he'd been using as an office chair.

The laptop was asking for a password. In Pashto, I screamed, "What is the password?" to the waste of human flesh on the floor, still wailing and whining and slobbering. He looked at me and shook his head. I shot him in each knee and re-presented the question.

2:59... He was going into shock now, the blubbering giving way to a quiet mewling. He stared at me through wide, unfocused eyes. I had no time for this. My mission was simple. Recover the computer and its password, by any means.

Even if the crypto guys could break through the password at all, that took time. The name of this game was Get the Info Now. Whatever data the laptop held could be useless in two days, much less the two months it might take to crack. I handed him a small notepad and a pen and started screaming, "Write the password! Write the password!" He spit at me.

2:47... Using my tactical knife, I split his pants open at the crotch. No underwear, and the stench of the filthy bastard's genitals was hellish. I grabbed the head of his penis in my left hand, stretched it up, and put the knife at the base. This takes the defiance out of ninety-nine percent of all men on the planet.

2:35... This one-percenter spit at me again and started screaming about Allah. I drew the knife lightly across, enough to bring plenty of blood but not enough to cut it off; the blood loss would be too quick for my needs. He continued to pontificate on Allah.

2:28... Time for the one-hundred-percent solution. I reached around to my pack, dropped a zipper on its bottom right, and reached inside. From a rubberized compartment, I pulled a small dead pig. I rammed my knife into its heart and pulled it out, now smeared with porcine blood.

2:07... Exaltation of his god ended and he stared at the knife. I put it to his throat and said, "Write the password or I'll send you to hell right now. No paradise. No wine. No virgins."

When he finished writing, I keyed in the password and the laptop opened to a screen of email addresses and phone numbers. Damn skippy. I turned back to the guy and slit his throat. After cutting the line that fed from the laptop up into the shaft, I pulled its battery and stowed the computer in my backpack, then left the way we had come, this time at a dead run.

1:31... Just inside the cave entrance, I dropped a laser designator to light the way for the missiles, then hustled back down the trail as fast as I could go without stumbling and tripping on the endless rocks. A sprained ankle right now would be a mortal wound.

0:30... I reached the horses. Unhobbled Ditto's mare first, pointed her downhill, slapped her ass. She bolted. With the mission complete, the sight of Ditto's head bursting like a melon started cycling through my mind. I unwound the reins from Johnny's fetlocks and leapt into the saddle, reined him around to head back down the mountain, then kickstarted him with my heels. "Go, Johnny! Go!" He launched. In my mind, poor Ditto's head exploded again.

0:10... The wind was an icy razor on my face. The countdown expired, and I knew I had ninety seconds max before the F-18s brought hell. Johnny was hauling ass, but we weren't far enough away from the cave for my comfort. It turned out to be closer to thirty seconds. I saw four little spits of fire in the sky ahead as the missiles dropped from their moorings on the F-18s, then ignited and streaked toward the laser designator, just as we reached the base of the mountain. The ground leveled out, and Johnny needed no encouragement. He was a magnificent creature with somewhere to go. We went.

The explosions at our backs lit the valley before us as the world roared. I felt heat and pressure a few seconds later, but that's it. I applied the brakes and Johnny stopped. We turned around and watched the cave spit fire from its maw and a column of sparks from the vent hole above it.

I patted Johnny on the neck, his taut hide drenched with sweat in the cold Afghan night and radiating the smell of proud horse. Then I leaned left and stretched way forward in the saddle so I could look him in the eye. "Buddy," I said, "I'll get you out of this miserable excuse of a country someday, and we'll never have to do this kind of shit again. I promise."

Johnny snorted.

CHAPTER 2

LAS VEGAS

NOW

I HAD SEEN PICTURES. Read all about it. Even saw an episode about it on a reality show about amazing something or other. High-res and high-def did nothing to prepare me for the real thing. 'Amazing' didn't come close. It was shocking.

SPACE, not just the world's largest casino hotel, but the world's largest man-made structure. The company was my newest client; their high-dollar slot machines were paying out huge jackpots more often than they should, and the company suspected foul play. Hence the arrival of yours truly, owner and sole employee of Sam Flatt Digital Forensics.

The property loomed on the far south end of the neon canyon called Las Vegas Boulevard, a.k.a. the Strip, like an unearthly presence. Which was exactly the point: The illusion was that of a space station, and its realism made the rest of Vegas's architectural wonders look like kitschy little toys from a dollar store. When the limo was a couple miles from it, already it looked enormous. I don't know how many hundreds of acres it covered, but the whole thing was bathed in a bluish light that heightened the surreality of the scene. Tiny white strobes flashed at random across the whole thing, both on the structures and in the air.

A huge white glass dome housed the casino and anchored the center of the spread. From the center of the dome, a 185-floor round hotel climbed the night sky, a gleaming white shaft peppered sparsely with dark windows among glossy white ones. On the ground, five spokes connected to and radiated out from the dome's perimeter. Each of these spokes terminated in a structure that was itself some noteworthy attraction. On the north spoke, the largest mall in the country. Others ended variously in everything from entertainment complexes to a NASA museum with a retired space shuttle. In a city full of spectacles, SPACE was the one to end them all.

When the driver turned into the complex, I saw that the twinkling strobes in the air weren't mounted on anything. They were tiny flashing orbs that were flying themselves around like mechanized fireflies. Wow. We arrived at the portico, and I stepped out of the car without waiting for anyone to open the door. The hot night air hit me, felt like I'd opened the door on an oven. The difference between its dryness and the soggy heat back home in Houston was immediately apparent.

Outside the car, I was greeted by an attendant in white coveralls emblazoned front and back with the

SPACE logo. "Mr. Flatt," the attendant said when I exited the car, "welcome to SPACE. I'm James Nichols and I'll be your host while you're here." I shook his hand. "If you'll come with me, I'll get you settled in and have your luggage brought up."

I followed him through an entrance fashioned like an air lock. Twenty feet inside, we boarded an escalator with clear steps. At the top of its long climb, we stepped onto a people mover, also with a transparent floor, that arced up and over the casino floor. Above us, the massive dome looked to be one giant video screen. Its realistic panorama of the space environment combined with the nearly invisible conveyor we were riding created a convincing illusion of floating through space between components of a space station. Well, except for the hundreds of gaming tables and thousands of slot and poker machines below us. After a lengthy ride we arrived at an elevated platform at the top center of the dome. That platform turned out to be the hotel lobby. Nichols ignored the desk and headed straight for a bank of elevators. The acceleration was unlike anything I'd experienced in an elevator, my ears popping as the floor numbers whizzed by. I felt it slowing and watched the display as the number settled on 140.

My suite looked like something straight from the future, all softly glowing glass and plush furnishings. I had expected a much more modest room but I have a bit of a thing about small spaces so I was glad to see the spacious accommodations. As Nichols was showing me around, my bags arrived. When I tried to tip the bellhop, he nodded and said, "Thank you, sir, but that won't be necessary," and backed out of the room.

"What's up with that?" I said.

"You're our guest, Mr. Flatt. Nothing here will cost

you anything, unless you want to gamble." He smiled and said, "That's on your dime. By the way, here's your credential bracelet." He handed me a thin rubbery bracelet, bright blue. "It functions as your key. Just wear it and it does the rest." I thanked him and he left.

Even the water in the shower glowed along a blue-to-red spectrum depending on temperature. Clean and fresh in a hotel robe, I stood at the window with my phone and touched the icon to initiate a video chat with my daughter. Ally's mom, my ex, had moved them here a few years ago, after the divorce, when a good job came up in her field. Ally's mom is an event planner who sets up conferences and conventions and such, and Vegas is a hotbed for that industry. I objected to the move, but it did no good. Abby Lowenstein Flatt is a stubborn and formidable woman, and I wasn't willing to create great strife between the two of us. We compromised: I wouldn't fight the move, and she wouldn't gripe about my unconventional lifestyle when Ally came to visit me back in Texas. It worked.

When Ally answered, I held the phone against the glass so the camera faced out at the amazing view. "Guess where I am?" I said.

"Hmmm, lots of lights," Ally said. "Oh my gosh, you're here, Daddy? In Las Vegas?"

"Yup."

"Why didn't you tell me you were coming?"

"Case just popped up this morning."

"Where are you staying?"

I braced myself. "SPACE."

"Daddy! You know I wanna see that place, and Mom won't take me! When can I come? Say I can come!"

"I don't know, sweetie. Not sure a casino is the best

place for a fourteen-year-old, but I'll talk it over with your mom."

"Promise?"

"Promise."

We chatted a few minutes more and said good-night.

I stood at the window and marveled at the north-facing view, Las Vegas spread before me like a bejeweled domain. If only I had known what I was standing on top of.

CHAPTER 3

SPACE

LAWYERS HAVE A BAD REP. Many times it's an unfair stereotype. Sometimes it's not. Case in point was my meeting the next morning, which featured a couple lawyer examples. Jacob Allen was general counsel for SPACE Corporation and we met in his office. It was the first room I'd encountered that wasn't technofuturistic. Instead, Allen was obviously enamored with the traditions of law. Situated on the hotel tower's third floor, the office was all dark wood and tufted leather and old books. Allen was a human version of a Bassett hound, sad-eyed and droopy in his vested suit, and seemed a pretty nice guy.

He didn't small talk, got right to the case details. "What do you know about EGMs?"

"Don't know the term," I said.

"Electronic gaming machines. Slots, poker?"

"Not a lot. At the gambling game, you guys win. And I'm a sore loser."

He smiled. "Suffice to say there's a reason why we have ten times as many machines as tables: They're profitable. Very. Today's EGMs are all electronic, really just computers. Instead of adjusting mechanical parts to tweak payout rates, we just change some computer settings."

I said, "While I have some idea of what you're talking about, pretend I don't. What's a payout rate?"

"By law in Nevada, a slot has to have an RTP of at least seventy-five percent. So over time—and it can be a long time—a machine has to 'return to players' at least seventy-five percent of what's put into it. Make sense?"

"Perfect."

"In reality, the only machines with rates that low are the ones in airports, convenience stores, McDonald's, and a few gimmick machines in casinos. It's a competitive area and the average RTP in this town is about ninety-five percent. But here's the problem. Over the past several weeks, a number of our high-stakes machines have been paying out anywhere from ninety-eight to ninety-nine. Considering the amount of money fed into a thousand-dollar-a-pull machine, you can understand that this is resulting in a significant loss of profit."

I nodded. "You want me to find out who's doing the tweaking."

"Exactly," he said. He pushed a small binder across his desk to me. "This will get you up to speed on the general process of managing these machines."

I picked up the binder, opened it, flipped through its pages of diagrams, procedures, personnel.

"So, does this sound like something you can do?" he said.

"It's computer data. It's what I do."

"Excellent. If you look at the people in that binder, you'll see a summary for a former employee named Christine Gamboa." I found the page and he continued. "Miss Gamboa was an executive host when she came here, meaning she took care of certain VIP clients, the kind who play blackjack at twenty-five thousand per hand, slots at a thousand a pull. She's brilliant, has a graduate degree from CalTech in some kind of computer science. Not quite a year ago, she asked to be transferred to the technology department. We jumped at it and in no time she was running the unit in charge of programming EGMs. Two weeks ago, she bolted for a competitor, Renaissance. No trouble here, no warning signs, and no notice, just didn't show up for work one morning."

"She get a better position there?" I said.

"No. She went back to hosting. Makes no sense."

"Interesting," I said. "I assume you have her devices on hand for me to examine."

"Of course."

On the other end of the lawyer personality spectrum was Brandy Palmer, the outside counsel leading this charge. She was the high-powered titular head of Palmer & Bradford, a smallish forty-lawyer litigation firm known for its aggressive posture and unwillingness to lose. About fifty, she was dressed and smelled expensive. A slim brunette with curves, she had probably been a knockout as a young adult, but years of being a bitch had taken its toll. So far today, she always looked like she'd just bitten into a rotten pickle and sounded like a bulldozer.

"We'll need the results by the end of the week," she said.

I stopped taking notes. "Ms. Palmer, that's unlikely in the extreme."

"Why's that?"

"This is a complex investigation involving, what, a hundred or more machines, not to mention Gamboa's devices? I could get lucky and find a smoking gun right away, but it could also take weeks. Just the way it is."

"The local forensic guy I use is willing to do what it takes to get the results I need. When I need them." She cut eyes at Allen. "And at half your rate, Mr. Flatt."

"Then use him," I said. "It's just millions at stake, after all. Maybe Mr. Allen should hire himself a cut-rate attorney, too. I'm sure he can find one around Fremont Street at a fraction of your rate."

I swear I saw smoke coming from her ears. "How. Dare. You," she said.

After folding up my notebook and stowing my pen, I stood, looked at Allen, and said, "Thanks for the trip, but I'm busy enough that I can reject cases I don't like. And this one? I don't—"

"Please sit down, Mr. Flatt. You are the digital forensic expert on this case."

"Jake," she said, "since when do you choose my experts?"

"This is an internal investigation. It may develop into litigation, but it's not there yet. That makes the expert my choice, Brandy."

She grunted, her lips drawn into a tight little wad that looked a lot like an anus.

I took a couple deep breaths and said, "Okay. If we can get my letter of engagement signed and retainer paid, I'll get started. But I have no patience for bullshit like this." I pointed at Palmer to be really clear.

Palmer started up out of her chair but eased back into it after a look from Jacobs.

Allen said, "My admin will take care of that right now. Your host—Nichols, I think?—will get you set up in a workplace and have the computers brought to you." He looked at Palmer. "And there won't be any more... bullshit." Looking back at me now. "Anything else?"

"Nope," I said.

I left Jacob Allen's office and Nichols took me to a mid-sized conference room where my equipment was waiting. Correction: Staying true to SPACEtalk, he took me to a conference chamber on the fifth floor. Apparently there are no rooms in space. By the time I had my gear arranged and powered up, the retainer was in my checking account and Christine Gamboa's full personnel file had arrived in my inbox from human resources. The letter of engagement hadn't arrived yet but since the money had, work could begin.

The front page of Gamboa's file was a headshot of an absurdly beautiful woman. Glossy black hair and a mild Eurasian look with impossible green eyes. Twenty-six years old, never married. Master's degree from CalTech in Applied and Computational Mathematics—and she chose to take a job as a glorified escort? And then to work on slot machines? And back to escort? The rest of her file was more of the same: She was a brilliant and beautiful girl without a hint of trouble in her background. One of life's winners.

About the time I finished perusing her file, a courier arrived with her devices. It was a typical high-end corporate spread: desktop PC, laptop, iPad and iPhone. It took about twenty minutes to get forensic copies of all her data started. With that process chugging along, I opened the binder Allen had given me and dug into the scintillating world of electronic gaming machines. Okay, it wasn't scintillating. Behind the flashing lights and cool sounds, it was all about a bunch of little computers that generated random numbers in a very careful way. An hour into it my eyes were glazing over and my stomach was screaming for input.

James Ever-Present Nichols was outside the door. "Hey, Jimbo," I said. "You guys have anything to eat around here?"

He took me to the Rings of Saturn, a big round buffet from which I ate a stupid amount of really good food. All terrestrial fare, best I could tell, but with creative names like Renduvian Rolls and Spironicus Spaghetti. At the exit, the doors whooshed open as I approached, Star Trek style, no doubt a function of the "credential bracelet" on my wrist. "Please tell me there's a holodeck," I said to Nichols.

"Sort of," he said.

"No crap?"

"Yeah, a virtual video game like you've never seen. We can go if you like."

"Definitely," I said, "But later."

The forensic copying was done when we got back from lunch, so I fired up the initial processing of the evidence, a bunch of techno-crunching that prepares the data for my hardcore examination. While that ran, I dug into the initial analysis of the oh-so-lovely Miss Gamboa's data. It took about two minutes to encounter the first red flag. She, or someone, had formatted the hard drives on both her computers. Silly people, especially computer-oriented people like her who should know better. Lesson number one? If you want to destroy data, find out how. Don't pull stunts like this that do nothing but make you look guilty. And stupid.

Fifteen minutes later, I had recovered the data she thought she deleted. The techno-crunching that was still running would recover far more, but for now I had enough to start getting an idea of who Cyber-Christine Gamboa was. On the surface, she was just a good-looking girl living the high life in Sin City. Like every woman on the planet with a smartphone, she loved taking selfies. Especially in her car. Why do they do this? I have no idea. She Facebooked and tweeted and Instagrammed and saved thousands of pictures to her boards on Pinterest. She texted a lot but thankfully she did so with real words, not "ur" and b4" and "bff" and other crap that make grown people look like twelve-year-olds.

She also bought enough books from Amazon to stock a library, but it would be an e-library. Kindle. She favored thrillers, which gave us something in common. Maybe when this was over I'd ask her out, if I hadn't helped put her in prison by then. Or even if I had, maybe we could have a prison romance. I'd write her beautiful letters and we'd have a darling little jailhouse wedding, and then would come the conjugal visits. Or maybe she'd tell me to go conjugate myself.

Quicken was her tool of choice for financial management, and it was there that red flags started pinging like the Whack-a-Mole at a county fair. Holy crap.

CHAPTER 4

McCARRAN INTERNATIONAL AIRPORT
LAS VEGAS

Christine Gamboa

CHRISTINE PINNED THE RENAISSANCE LOGO to her dress, checked her hair and makeup, then stepped from the limousine and walked to the bottom of the stairway, where she waited for the door of the private jet to open. When she heard the door being released from inside, she assumed her most radiant and expectant smile. The door opened and her client for the next couple of days appeared. Alexander "Sasha" Maslov was in his sixties, a thick and sturdy Ukrainian—or was that Russian now?—who had made a fortune in what he described to others as "an old family business in Crimea." She knew better.

When he saw Christine, his big Slavic face morphed

from scowl to delight. "Chrissy!" He came down the stairs two at a time, wrapped her in a hug and kissed her on the lips.

"Sasha!" she said.

"Let us go now and you can to tell me all about your new job, Kohana."

In the limo, Maslov poured two glasses of pepper vodka and handed one to Christine. Despite the rule that she couldn't drink on the job, she had learned long ago it was best to have at least one drink with him even if they were headed to her workplace. The way she saw it, it was better to break a few rules than offend a client. Especially this one. She raised her glass to his with a solid clink and threw back the amber liquid, fighting not to gasp as the liquid fire hit her throat and stomach.

Maslov drank his, then roared with approving laughter at her accomplishment. "I think you learn to love my drinks!"

She smiled and blinked away the tears, shook her head to try to clear the buzz that had already hit. "I do it only for you, Sasha. Only you."

"Yes, and this is why you are my favorite Kohana!"

Christine bit her bottom lip and gave him a pouty look. "Favorite Kohana, huh? I bet you have these 'special girlfriends' stashed everywhere, you big charmer."

"Ah, but none like you, my love. Now, you must to tell me about your new job. I liked very much when you wore the outer space jumping suit, you know this?"

"Yes, I know you liked the jumpsuit, but I missed working with people, got tired of staring at computers all day. Renaissance is nice. They pay a little more and they give me three days a week off instead of one."

"Wonderful. Wonderful. I want Kohana to be well rested when I come. And this time, this is the time when you will finally to marry me, yes?"

"We'll see, Sasha."

He roared again and poured himself another drink. "Yes, we will. We will to see."

Once they arrived at Renaissance, they went straight to the high stakes gaming area, where Maslov played blackjack for hours, all joviality, win or lose. He put away enough pepper vodka to float a boat but never seemed intoxicated. Loose, yes. Drunk, no. Christine stayed nearby to meet any requests; clients like Maslov didn't wait for cocktail waitresses to come around taking requests. Whatever he was drinking or smoking—with him it was always pepper vodka and a particular Cuban cigar—stayed fresh and at hand. She also kept up with how his gambling was going, not because she was required to, but because knowing made it far easier to know whether or not to mention it later.

This had been a good night. She guessed he finished about fifty thousand to the good. In the elevator to his suite, she said, "How'd you do?"

"Wonderful night, Kohana, just wonderful. Sasha won many American dollars this night."

Later, in Maslov's suite, Christine watched as Sasha got up from the lavish bed and walked toward the suite's living area. She stood from the bed and pulled on a hotel robe, then followed. He stood at the glass wall that looked out over the north side of the SPACE campus and the city beyond. She wondered what someone like Sasha saw there. A playground to be raided? A criminal kingdom to rule? And what was she to him and his organization? Princess? Concubine? Or just a loose end?

CHAPTER 5

SPACE

TIME HAD FADED AWAY, as it often does once I dig into a case. I was combing and analyzing, studying the digital breadcrumbs that would tell me who Christine Gamboa was and hopefully what she had e-done. Computers that were nothing more than a novelty a generation ago are today's life recorders and it was time for some playback on Christine. I walked the halls outside my workroom enough to be sure no one else was still working nearby, then set up my little-yet-kickbutt wireless speaker, connected my phone, and cranked up a long, shuffled playlist.

She had made good money at SPACE—about one-fifty a year during her time as an executive host, ten grand more when she moved in with the brainiacs—but she spent a lot, too. Drove a 7-series BMW, lived in a pricey apartment, dressed expensively, and had an affinity for purses that cost a stupid amount. Her lifestyle was enough to max out her budget and then some. I assumed she picked up some pretty nice tips as a host, but it was hard to imagine enough tips for her to have anything meaningful left over. So how was it that she had over four hundred thousand in her personal checking account?

I dug into her Quicken data but it was no help in figuring out where the money came from. She had only been using the program for seven months, and she had logged a balance forward in her checking account of $453,269.22 when she first set up Quicken. That number was now down to $405,200.86, so in seven months she had spent almost fifty grand of the mystery cash, plus every penny of her salary.

I spent some time going through her spending in more detail, taking notes as I went. Twelve grand on purses. Thousand-dollar bedsheets. Over two thousand a month payment on the BMW, and thirty-nine hundred rent on the apartment. An addiction to the latest and greatest of all things Apple, including an iPhone and iPad, curious since she already had both those items furnished by SPACE. And on and on it went. It was like an episode of Lifestyles of the Rich and Famous. Except she wasn't famous and didn't make enough money to be rich. It sure wasn't family money; according to the background report in her employment file, her parents eked out a living in a small grocery store they owned in rural Arizona.

A knock on the door made me jump. It cracked and Nichols stuck his head in. "Need anything?" He looked awake but looking that way was his job and I understood the real question.

I checked the time on my computer and saw that it was 2:26 a.m. "Am I wearing you out, Jimbo?"

It took a moment for the "Jimbo" to register, then he said, "Oh, no. No. I just thought you might need something."

The head disappeared and the door closed. I did the math and realized it was 4:26 a.m. back home in Houston, decided to call it a night myself. I engaged the lock screen on my examination computer and stepped through the door. "How late can I get breakfast around here?" I said.

"Up to you," Nichols said.

"Excellent. See you here tomorrow about ten?"

"Sure, sounds great."

I thought maybe Nichols would get the hint that I didn't need him to walk me to my room. Didn't work. After a couple miles of walking in SPACE, I stood at my room door and said, "Good-night, Jimbo."

"Good-night."

When I shut the water off in the shower, I heard my phone ringing. I walked naked and dripping to the work-desk in the suite's living room and glanced at the screen as the phone rang and vibrated against the hard surface. The caller ID said PRIVATE CALLER. Who in hell would call me at three o'clock in the morning? I picked it up and touched to answer. "Hello?"

"Is this Mr. Flatt?"

"It is."

"Mr. Flatt, my name is Courtney Meyer. I'm a special agent with the FBI, calling from New York."

"Okay," I said. The feebs are never just agents. Always special. "What can I do for you?"

"First, I need to tell you that this call is being recorded. Second, I need your assurance of confidentiality before proceeding with the conversation. Do I have that assurance?"

"It's what, almost six a.m. in New York?"

"I wanted to call when I thought it most likely you'd be alone. Is that the case?"

What the hell? "Yes, Agent, I'm alone. What's this about?" I had worked on a few cases over the years that had FBI involvement, always on the other side. Nothing recent, though, and certainly nothing active.

"I need your agreement to keep this confidential," Meyer said.

"You have it. It's late, so please get to the point."

"We need your assistance on a case."

This was getting stranger by the moment. One thing the Bureau boys and girls never ask for, no matter how badly they might need it, is outside forensic assistance. They'd let a serial killer go before admitting they couldn't get evidence off his computer. "Sorry, I'm tied up on a major case right now."

"We know. You're working for the SPACE casino in Nevada. That's what we need your help with."

I thought about that for a moment, and when it still didn't make the first lick of sense, I touched the phone into speaker mode, laid it on the desk, and said, "Hold on a sec." I continued to mull as I walked to the bathroom and grabbed a towel from the rack. I toweled my hair, face, and neck as I walked back to the living room. When I got there, I said, "Not sure how or why you'd know what case I'm working, but I can't imagine how I can help you."

"I'll remind you that this is extremely confidential, and—"

I cut her off: "You said that already, and I agreed already. Get to the point, please."

"I—we—need you to keep us apprised of progress on the forensic investigation you're conducting."

Like hell. I drew a breath to respond, then did a slow count to ten, willing calm into my soul in the face of this idiocy.

"Mr. Flatt?" she said.

"Agent," I said, "that—"

"It's Special Agent Meyer. M-E-Y-E-R."

"Whatever. Look, you harp to me about the need for confidentiality, then ask me to break confidentiality with my client, with whom I've signed a very strong and very clear confidentiality agreement? Gotta tell you, not gonna happen, not without my client authorizing it. In fact, I don't want to hear any more, don't want to be in a position where you tell me information my client has a contractual expectation for me to tell them."

"You cannot mention this to your client in any way."

"And why exactly do you want these updates from me?"

"I'm not at liberty to discuss that."

"Then we're done."

"No, Mr. Flatt. We're not done."

I laughed out loud. "Good-night, Special Agent Meyer, M-E-Y-E-R." I reached toward the phone, aiming for the END CALL icon.

"Hang up on me and you will regret it, Mr. Flatt."

This bitch was starting to piss me off. I pulled my finger back from the phone. "Are you threatening me, ma'am?"

"I'm warning you, sir."

"You know one of the things I hate most on this earth?" I said.

"I know virtually all there is to know about you."

That was worth another laugh, but I held back. "Arrogance. You call me in the middle of the night with something this ridiculous and think I'm just gonna fall in line? In addition to the legality and ethics, you know how many cases I'd get once it got out that I divulged client information to law enforcement? Do you have any idea how freaking crazy you sound?"

"You would be better served to think about how 'crazy' it is to antagonize the Federal Bureau of Investigation."

Enough. "And you'd be better served to put the crack-pipe down and back slowly away. Stuff'll kill you in the end, you know."

This time I touched END CALL.

CHAPTER 6

KIEV, UKRAINE

THE MAN WAS OLD, his face a leathery map of a hundred creases, but his step was lively and his eyes bright as he strolled generally south along the tree-lined street, keeping to the shade amid the dazzling sunny day. Though he had been but a child, he remembered when Khreshchatyk Street looked very different, more in keeping with traditional Ukrainian architecture, even though it had been heavily influenced by the Russian bastards, first the czarists and later the Bolsheviks. He remembered it becoming a cratered strip of rubble at the hands of the Soviet bastards who planted mines all along it and detonated them by radio control once the Nazi bastards arrived in 1941. He remembered the rebuilding after the Great Patriotic War that eventually transformed it into the beautiful kilometer it almost still was. Almost, because once the Soviet Union fell apart and Ukraine declared its independence in 1991, the influence of the West had been a slow but steady rot. Where proud old businesses once stood, today's storefronts on the grand street showed names like Gucci and DKNY and Chanel. And TGIF. What the fuck was that? Italian. American. French. Bastards all.

At the end of the street, he made his way inside the sprawl of Bessarabska Market, where he took his time and eventually filled a small basket with fruits and vegetables from the various stalls. He paid for some of the goods. He offered to pay for all, but many merchants recognized him and refused his grivna. To these he nodded his appreciation instead.

Basket in hand, he left the market and headed back the way he had come. Halfway up Khreshchatyk, he came to his apartment building on the left side of the street. Many of his colleagues and competitors, especially the young snots, had made their way to the suburbs of Kiev where they built ridiculous houses. He had no need to prove himself. No need to scream to the world, "Look at me!" No, he had grown up in the Center, and it was there that he would live until he breathed his last. He turned into a small alley, punched his code into the gate, then walked around the back of the building. There he keyed in another code to enter the building, and stepped inside.

Outside, the building was an old, beautifully maintained example of architecture that inspired the soul. Once through the door, the building had enjoyed the most basic of maintenance and no renovation since its construction in 1949. This was Kiev. This was Ukraine. Who wanted to spend money on things few would ever see and nobody gave a shit about? He had installed an elevator in the 1990s so he wouldn't have to listen to the whining from the paying tenants, but he had never been inside it. Stairs were good for a man, body and soul. When the staircase reached its last landing, he inserted his massive key into a state-of-the-art security lock, rotated it to the click, then twisted the handle and stepped inside.

The interior of the apartment yielded another transition. Unlike the building's stately outer appearance, and even more unlike the dreary old common areas outside his door, the apartment was meticulously maintained and filled with lavish Ukrainian antiques. He put away the fruits and vegetables, then crossed the big open room from the kitchen area to the living area. After easing down onto a pillowy leather sofa, he picked up a remote control and switched on the electronics which enabled him to monitor his business interests around the world. Some of this monitoring took the form of stock quotes and such, but more interesting were the cameras that allowed him to literally see and hear inside his businesses. He was particularly concerned about the state of affairs at his Las Vegas operation. Stupid bastards. Navigating menus with the remote, he pulled up one of the cameras of that branch and turned up the volume a bit. He then pushed a button to extend his footrest and recline his end of the sofa, and settled in to observe. He first watched the room of computer workers. They looked busy. Good. He pushed a button on the remote and switched to the view from a very different camera, one whose feed stirred something primal in his aged loins.

CHAPTER 7

SPACE

THE BIZARRE FBI CALL WAS THE FIRST THING on my mind when I woke. Maybe I should have played it a little cooler and tried a little harder to coax some info out of her, something that would let me make sense of something so weird. I Googled Meyer and found nothing particularly useful, just a barebones bio and a few cases in which she was mentioned, all organized crime, typically RICO. Crap. I hadn't done anything wrong, but that didn't mean this woman wouldn't come after me just because I pissed her off. The feds can ruin an innocent man through sheer attrition.

I called a top-shelf private investigator I used from time to time, and asked him to dig up everything he could on her. Then it was time to put Special Agent Meyer out of my mind and get to work.

The IT department at SPACE was the nicest I'd seen. Ever. At the center of a large room of desks and cubicles was an elevated server room they called "the tower." At a glance my guess was that it housed no fewer than fifty racks of servers; it was a glass-walled wonderland of monster computers and blinking lights, the nerve center of the empire. I walked past the cubicles and approached a desk on a raised dais just outside the tower. A balding guy in his thirties, wearing glasses that were a little too hip for his face and a SPACE lab coat, looked down at me from the desk as if I were a peasant drawing near his royal throne.

He said nothing, just arched his eyebrows at me.

I said, "I'm looking for Jerry Rose."

"I'm Dr. Rose."

Dr. Rose? A PhD running IT? Interesting. "Sam Flatt," I said.

He sighed and peered at his screen. "What can I do for you, Mr. Flatt?"

"Jacob Allen told me you were the man to see for access to a few servers."

More peering. "I have your name here as someone I'm to 'aid in data retrieval,' but I assure you no one is going to 'access' my servers."

His servers. I turned and looked at the always-at-the-ready James Nichols, who said, "Tell me what you'd like me to do, Mr. Flatt."

Leaning in so I could whisper in his ear, I said, "Sam. Sam. Sam. No more 'Mr. Flatt,' remember?"

He cracked a small grin and nodded.

I climbed the steps to Rose's desk and extended my hand. "Let's start over. I'm Sam Flatt. I'm here because I've been hired to examine some data that is very important to your employer, my client. We're working for the same boss, and I'd be most grateful for your cooperation."

Rose exhaled through his nose and took my hand in a limp little excuse of a handshake. "I'm very busy, Mr. Flatt, so if you can tell me what data you need—specifically—I'll see what I can do."

In less than a minute, I'd had my fill of this little prick. I walked back down the steps, found an empty chair, carried it up the dais, and plopped it down right beside Rose, who had never even bothered to stand. With forced calm I pulled my laptop from its sheath, found an electrical outlet and got my laptop plugged up. I then plugged it into an empty network jack on the back of his desk and with a flourish hit my power button. When I was up and running, I said, "I'm here to harvest data related to employee two-one-six-eight. I need admin access to the Exchange server that houses that account. I need admin or root to the primary print server for that account, admin or root to the servers containing her network shares, and admin or root to any servers and routers that handle outside traffic for that account."

Rose's face was somewhere between confused and indignant. He looked at me, then at Nichols, and said to Nichols, "This is completely unacceptable!"

Nichols shrugged.

What I wanted to do: Grab the lapels of the weenie's lab coat and shake him till he rattled. Instead, I said, "Dr. Rose. I've told you what I need. Will you arrange that, or not?"

"I most certainly will not."

Looking to Nichols, I said, "Jim, will you please see if Mr. Allen is available?"

He touched an icon on his phone and put it to his ear. A couple seconds later, he said, "Yes, this is Nichols. Can you please tell Mr. Allen we have a situation in IT that requires his attention....Yes, thank you....Hello, Mr. Allen, I'm in IT with Mr. Flatt and he's hit some resistance in getting the access he needs....Yes, sir...thank you." He ended the call and slipped the phone back into his pocket.

Five seconds later, Rose's phone rang. He glanced at its screen, picked up the handset. "This is Dr. Rose."

I don't know what Allen was saying, but Rose's nerdy little face reddened and his nostrils quivered as all defiance drained away. I noticed that the clickety-click of keyboards around the room had gone quiet. We had an audience, and I guessed more than a few of them were enjoying the show. I've spent years dealing with self-important jerks like Rose and their brand of douchebaggery really tries my patience these days. Was I being an asshole myself? Yep. But with guys like this, you have to establish the rules up front. I was here to get to the bottom of a big issue for my client, and I had no intention of wasting time on games every time I needed something.

After maybe a minute, Rose laid the handset back in its cradle. He looked at me with pure hatred, but that was okay because after his best attempt at a Stare of Death, he turned to his screen and started setting up the access I had asked for. I watched his screen and when he finished, I smiled and said, "Thank you, Dr. Rose." Then I moved my chair and turned my laptop so he couldn't watch what I was doing.

A couple hours later, I was back in my ersatz lab. While searches ran against Gamboa's email stores I'd gotten from IT, I dug deeper into the binder, looking for policies and procedures for managing the payout rates on SPACE's machines. I found those things, along with a fifty-something-page report on the company's own investigation of the issue. That investigation, conducted by SPACE's security department, had been thorough and meticulous. They had walked through and documented every step of the process, then turned every employee who had access to the process upside down and inside out. That included Gamboa, although she didn't appear to have received any more scrutiny than anyone else. Then again, she was more interesting now because she had bolted from the company without notice. At the time of the investigation, several months prior, she was just one of several key people with that kind of access. The weenie from IT, Jerry Rose, was mentioned several times in the report as the person who conducted the computer-related aspects of the investigation. Logins, credentials, system access levels, things like that. The investigation found exactly nothing amiss and wrapped up with a line that said, FINDINGS: INCONCLUSIVE. It was signed by the head of security, Hank Dobo.

I closed the binder, leaned back in my chair, and stretched. With my eyes closed, I mentally walked through the process of a SPACE employee making a legitimate adjustment to one of the machines: First, someone in management decides to make the change. A written order is issued via email to the head of the Gaming Technology department. The head does two things: he assigns it to a senior technician and files an electronic request for a witness visit from the gaming commission. The commission responds with a scheduled time, although in practice these commission guys run regular routes to the major casinos and adjustments get handled then. The commission regulator arrives, approves the proposed change. The assigned technician loads the configuration console for the machine, remotely, on the technician's normal workstation. At a casino as modern as SPACE, no one need touch the physical machine. It all happens over the network. After the regulator verifies that no changes have been made to the machine since the last commission inspection, he (or she) watches while the technician implements the change. The regulator records the hash value of the machine's source code—this electronic fingerprint is the equivalent of a tamper-proof seal that will be used next time to verify no alterations have taken place. Finally, the machine is placed back into service with its new RTP setting in place.

So where were the holes in this process? One jumped out immediately. The perpetrator could make the change to the source code, let the bogus code work its black magic, then change the source code back to the approved version, thereby resetting the electronic fingerprint to its proper value before it was inspected again. This seemed way too easy, so I dug into the binder again. After a few minutes of reading, I found the safeguard against this. The Nevada Gaming Act for the 21st Century, passed a year earlier and known as NG21, mandated daily electronic polling of slots by the commission to check for things like this, along with additional random polling. Meaning the gaming commission had computers that did nothing except reach out and electronically quiz slot machines 24/7: "Hi there, can I have your digital fingerprint, please?" Inability to connect to a machine, or a response from a machine with other than the expected hash value, auto-triggered an alarm. It would be easy enough to work around a daily e-check, so the real question was how often did the random checks occur?

Nichols had made a couple calls and got me set up with a live test machine, so I decided to answer the question. I connected to the machine with my laptop and set up a trigger to record each time the machine was contacted by something outside the SPACE network. Common sense told me I shouldn't have to wait long. The best way for the gaming commission to keep tabs on any changes made to these machines would be to contact them often. Given the number of machines in Nevada to query, that may sound like a major task, but reality is, a single computer could ping every machine in the state a thousand times a day as long as a proper connection was in place. I expected a ping within five minutes.

After an hour, I still had nothing. I verified my setup, found no problems. I worked on some other issues while I waited. Two hours. Three. Four. I guess I shouldn't have been surprised by a poorly designed government operation, but in this case, I was. I left the ping monitor running and gave a quiet shout for Nichols.

His head was in the door in seconds, his eyebrows raised.

"I have to run a personal errand that will take a couple hours. When I get back, how about we check out that holodeck?" I said.

He smiled. "You got it."

CHAPTER 8

RENAISSANCE CASINO RESORT
LAS VEGAS

Mikail Sultanovich

MIKAIL HAD FIRST SEEN HER a couple days before, while trailing the Crimean. Since then, not an hour had passed when he didn't think of her. Maybe not even a minute. She was the hottest bitch he had ever seen, and he had seen a lot of hot bitches. More than seen. Bedded. Hundreds of them. Not like this one, though. Her hair. Those green eyes with the little slant. And that ass. The thought of the Crimean slob tapping that, while he wasn't, made his blood boil and his cock stiffen. He couldn't wait to—

The girl was walking away, leaving the Crimean at the blackjack table. The man was his job, but that bucket of fat wasn't going anywhere. He had been at the table for hours. Bastard must have a bladder the size of a melon. Mikail waited until the girl passed the bar where he was sitting, then rose and followed her down a corridor. When she entered the ladies' restroom, he positioned himself for an accidental meeting. It was time for her to meet The Sultan.

Sasha Maslov

Sasha glanced over his shoulder and smiled. Mikail had done exactly as expected and followed Christine down the hall like a mongrel chasing a champion bitch in heat. Sasha stood from the table, flipped a black chip to the dealer and gestured at his chips. "Send to account."

"Thank you, sir," the dealer said with a tip of the head.

After a brisk walk through the casino, Sasha stepped outside and waited only moments beneath the gilded portico before a Renaissance limo pulled up. He opened the door himself and got in before the driver could make it out of the vehicle. "Take me to the outer space."

Christine Gamboa

Christine sat on the counter in the restroom and killed five minutes on Facebook to give Sasha time to make his exit. After touching up her lipstick, she pushed through the heavy door and into the corridor. What a surprise that her admirer happened to be coming down the hallway toward her. When they were three feet apart, he stepped in front of her and, with his hand over his heart, said, "Hello, beautiful. I simply must meet you."

The guy was tall with fair skin and dark hair and features, very Slavic, very good looking. Unfortunately, he also looked like a thug. His shirt was open about three buttons too many, revealing a gold chain as thick as her pinky, buried in thick chest hair. His accent was similar to Sasha's, but much smoother. He had been here a while. He also had to be the dumbest guy on the planet to pick for tailing someone. In addition to leaving his target to follow her, here he was introducing himself, making himself memorable to her. Not that he was invisible to begin with; Sasha had pointed him out two days ago, but still, how dumb could you be?

She gave a small professional smile—she was on the clock, after all—and said, "Hi."

"I am Mikail Sultanovich. Ladies know me as The Sultan."

If not for the importance of her actions to Sasha and the fact that she was representing her employer, she would have burst out laughing. The Sultan? Really? Instead, she said, "It's very nice to meet you, sir. Enjoy your visit to Renaissance." Then she stepped around him and walked away.

Mikail Sultanovich

As he watched her walk away, Mikail wanted her more than ever. She wore a shiny gold dress that hugged her ass just right. He imagined himself unzipping that dress—no, not so gentle with this one. This one would want the dress ripped from her body. If she didn't, oh well. Sometimes people got what they wanted. Sometimes they got what they didn't want. This was life.

Once she turned the corner back into the VIP table area, he waited a couple minutes, then headed back to the bar where he could keep an eye on that fat Crimean bastard. Now that he had stood so close to her, now that he had heard her voice, he hated Maslov because Maslov was getting that ass and he wasn't. Maybe he would gut the fat sonofabitch when this was over. He walked to the bar, sat on the same stool as before, and looked over to the table where—shit, Maslov was gone!

Mikail walked to the edge of the VIP area, leaned against a gold column, and looked as casual as he could while searching the tables and machines for Maslov. He was nowhere. The girl was nowhere. He started walking the aisles of the main floor. Nothing. Shit. Ten minutes he looked, then twenty, but he was nowhere to be seen. Yes, Mikail was definitely going to gut that fat Crimean piece of shit. No doubt about it.

CHAPTER 9

SPACE

IT HAD TAKEN SOME TALKING, but there they were, stepping off the elevator outside Alpha Centaurum, one of SPACE's higher-end restaurants. Ally broke into a run when she saw me and leapt into my arms. I hugged her tight, taking in the wonderful smell of my teenaged baby girl. When I let go, Abby had reached us. I saw her and my heart skipped a beat, as it always had. "Hey, Ab," I said, and gave her a kiss on the cheek.

"Sammy," she said with a tight smile.

"Come on," I said and gestured them into the restaurant. The maitre d' led us to a quiet booth by a glass wall that overlooked the casino.

Ally took the seat closest to the glass. "This is so amazing," she said. "When can I see the rest of it?"

"We'll see," I said, which earned me an instant stink-eye from Abby.

We spent the next ninety minutes eating, talking, and laughing. It felt almost like the old days. Almost. When we were done, I walked them out, down, and through the casino to the front entrance. Abby gave the valet attendant her ticket and in a few minutes he delivered her car. Ally and I hugged again, but Abby got in before I had a chance for any kind of physical goodbye.

"Call me!" Ally said.

"You got it!" I said.

Then they were gone, and watching them leave gave me that same old empty feeling I'd felt too many times before.

The "module transport" whisking us through the spoke from the dome out to the "simulation center" was unlike any other people mover on earth. I don't claim to have been on every people mover around the planet, but trust me, sometimes you know. We didn't stand. We sat in seats that reminded me of modern roller coasters, with a padded lap bar that locked in place. Good thing, since we had to be doing fifty miles an hour and it had not taken long to hit that speed. Quick trip.

As in the central dome, the bracelets, no doubt embedded with RFID chips, worked like magic. Wherever we went, doors opened, turnstiles spun, and SPACE employees greeted us with great enthusiasm. Nichols called this place Sim City. It reminded me of a huge mall, except it was round and looked to have been beamed back from the future like everything else here. In the center, an area half the size of a football field was dotted with fountains of glowing water, trees that didn't look terrestrial, and people of every stripe gawking with open mouths.

Nichols pointed at an area across the way, where a

holographic sign floated in midair. The sign looked like a metallic blue globe wrapped with rotating green text that said MISSION TRAINING CENTER. "Our destination."

"Wow," was all I could manage.

"You a gamer?"

"Not compatible with my lifestyle," I said.

"Figured you for a gadget freak extraordinaire. You telling me you don't have a house full of tech goodies?"

"I don't have a house."

"Apartment dweller, huh?"

"Nope."

Nichols mulled that. "If you don't have a house, and don't have an apartment, where do you live, in the office?"

"Nope."

"Then where?"

"Nowhere," I said.

He stopped walking. "Nowhere?"

"Nowhere. Everywhere. I move around a lot, stay where I have the urge to stay." I resumed walking and he followed.

"So you, what, just drive around from place to place? I don't get it."

"Not exactly. I don't have a car."

"Then what do you have?"

"A horse."

"Horse?" Nichols said.

"His name is Johnny."

Nichols was right: The Mission Training Center was as close as you could get to a holodeck outside Star Fleet. After donning electronic glasses and stretchy sensor suits, we chose our weapons. Not all the games were weapons-based, but it's something I know and I chose what looked and felt like a real M4, fitted with some electronics. Then we stepped into a twenty-by-twenty room with walls full of cameras and sensors and speakers. We went through a five-minute session that explained how to navigate the virtual world, which was basically getting used to walking on a weird pad that we stood on that moved under our feet when we walked and also allowed us to swivel and turn. When the learning was done, Nichols said, "System engage," and we weren't in a little room anymore.

We stood in the center of a cavernous space that reminded me of an aircraft hangar, except in this case it would have been more accurately called a space hangar. A command cluster of holographic screens and controls floated in midair before us. The middle screen showed a woman in a command-style uniform, styled in the SPACE color scheme. She said, "Please select a mission," and a series of video images appeared below her. The acoustics were perfect, sounding exactly as they would if the large space around us had been real.

I looked over the selection of scenarios, then reached out and touched a video of a post-apocalyptic city labeled AFTERMATH: EARTH COLONY 42. I couldn't believe how real my hand and arm looked as they reached out, and the sensor suit even provided a little tactile sizzle to my fingertip when I touched the video. I had no idea such tech even existed.

"Thank you," the synth girl said. "Train as peacekeepers or rebels?"

Nothing appeared for me to touch, so I said, "Rebels."

"Mission will begin in five...four...three...two...one...Begin."

The hangar disappeared. We stood in a street of a decimated but futuristic city that reminded me of New York. I looked down and saw that we were dressed in tattered fatigues. My rifle still looked like an M4, but one that had been futurized. When I looked at Nichols, I couldn't believe my eyes. He looked exactly like himself except for being filthy. I don't mean he looked like a video game version of himself—he looked real. So did the buildings. So did everything. In fact, it even smelled real.

"We need to move," Nichols said.

"You played this one before?"

"They're never exactly the same, but I've played enough scenarios to know that the enemy will appear sooner rather than later."

"Roger that," I said. "Let's find cover."

We jogged toward a shell of a building and I was back in an old familiar element.

USDA FOREIGN AGRICULTURAL OFFICE KABUL, AFGHANISTAN

THEN

The sawed-off little bureaucrat's name was Eugene Hathaway. He reminded me of a banty rooster, all puffed up and pacing back and forth behind the Formica counter while he pointed his finger at me. "Sir," he said, "I don't know any more ways to say it: You're not taking a wild Afghan horse into the country."

"Johnny's not wild. He's an exceptionally well-trained animal who has served the U.S. with far more distinction than you have. Or ever will."

He snorted at that. "That animal will never see the United States of America."

I drew a long, deep breath. Counted to five. "I want to see the law or regulation that gives you the authority to make that decision."

"Hire an attorney to look it up for you. I'm not required to show you anything. You have my decision. Good day." He turned his back to me and started walking away.

The past few months had been pretty rough. Ditto's replacement had died too, and almost got me killed in the process. Now here I stood, listening to a bunch of bluster from this office weenie. "I don't accept your decision," I said.

He stopped, pivoted to face me. After staring at me for a moment, he stomped to the little gate that separated the visitor area of the lobby from the employee area, burst through it, and huffed over to where I was standing, his face red, spidery veins coloring on his greasy nose. "You know what?" he said, spittle hitting my face. "I'm half a mind to order the animal destroyed. How would you like that?" He punctuated the last word by sticking his finger in my face.

To be clear, I don't remember the next few minutes, nothing beyond the feeling of the red fog boiling up in my soul, but I later saw a surveillance recording that captured everything in quite clear video and audio. I grabbed that finger and wrenched it back until it lay flat against the back of his hand. His eyes bulged for a couple seconds, then he started screaming like the bitch he was. We were the only people in the little cinder block building, but hell, it was obvious on the tape that I didn't want to listen to his blubbering. Despite the red fog, I showed restraint because I didn't cock my fist more than twelve inches before hitting him in the mouth. After that, however, things went downhill a bit.

When I yanked on his tie, it came loose. Who the hell wears a clip-on tie in the twenty-first century? He was still screaming, which sprayed me with blood from his busted-up mouth. That pissed me off. I grabbed a snow globe paperweight from the counter—it was a little smaller than a pool ball and had a red-white-and-blue bald eagle inside—and shoved it into his mouth. After tying the clip-on around his head to secure the snow globe, I grabbed him by the shirt with one hand and by the nuts with the other. I picked him up and sat him on the counter.

Then I stood in front of him with my arms crossed and, in a calm voice, said, "Eugene, I respectfully request that you revisit your decision on this matter."

He looked at me like I was crazy, didn't answer.

"Eugene," I said, "I would really like to discuss Johnny's status again. Can we do that, Eugene?"

This time he started nodding, his head bobbing up and down at the speed of light.

I smiled. "Excellent!"

SPACE

NOW

We were about twenty minutes into the game, hunkered down and waiting for our weapons to recharge. Thanks to some real ass-kicking on our part, we had earned a number of privileges. One of those was a stealth mode that rendered our enemies deaf to anything we said or did, so we were able to converse without giving away our position. Nichols said, "Thought you weren't a gamer."

"That's right."

"Never played Call of Duty? This scenario is a lot like it."

"I didn't say I've never played it, but I'm not a gamer. Maybe a couple hours in that game, total."

He shook his head. "That makes you a prodigy in my book. I am a gamer, and Call of Duty is my game."

"It shows," I said. "You're good."

"Yeah. I am. But you have double the kills. How's that possible?"

"There are ways other than video games to learn certain skills."

"So you were, what, some kind of special ops guy who did this for real?" Nichols was now very interested, his virtual head cocked in anticipation.

"Not exactly."

He beckoned for more with his hand. "Then what?"

I winked and said, "A little like this, but definitely not in freaking outer space. Come on, let's kill some virtual assholes."

CHAPTER 10

SPACE

IT MADE NO SENSE. The test machine had been running more than twenty-four hours, yet hadn't registered a single query from the gaming commission. So much for my expectation that each machine would have been polled many times per day. This didn't meet the barest minimum required by the gaming statute, and the failure looked to be on the state, not the casino. I verified my setup again, tested connectivity, found no problems.

After a couple calls by Nichols, I was able to check the polling on all the casino's gaming machines. What I found made me shake my head in bewilderment. None of SPACE's machines—there were more than ten thousand of them—had recorded a single interaction with the gaming commission in the past twenty-four hours. I went deeper. Not a one of them had been touched by commission computers in weeks.

Now I was dumbfounded. I could understand why the casino wouldn't check this kind of activity on a regular basis. But the state gaming commission? No. First, it was law that they had to check it. Second, surely the gaming commission wasn't in the habit of letting casinos run wild with their electronic gaming operation. Based on what I was seeing, SPACE could have all their machines set to pay back 10% instead of 95%, and aside from disgruntled gamblers, who would be the wiser? The amount of money they could make by tweaking even a fraction of their machines to illegal payout rates could be staggering. I doubted anything like that was going on, but with no oversight, it was possible.

"Hey, Jimbo," I said. Nichols was staying in my workroom most of the time now. No need to make the guy hang out in the hallway like a kid in trouble. Besides, I liked him.

"Yeah?"

"You know anything about the regulatory end?"

"Like what?"

I gave him a capsule version of what I'd found—given Nichols's near-constant proximity to me, Jacob Allen had cleared him to be in the loop—and then said, "I'm curious as to whether the gaming commission provides any reports to the casino on stuff like this."

"No idea, but I can find out." The phone came out and he went to work. I've never seen anyone who could accomplish so much on the phone in so little time. A skill that no doubt saw plenty of use when taking care of the rich and famous in his job.

While he worked the phone, I stepped meticulously through my test setup one more time. Raising this issue with the client and then finding out I'd made an error somewhere wasn't acceptable. I make mistakes like every other human on the planet, but when a client is paying me $600 per hour, I make damn sure they're rare. Once again, my setup checked out as perfect.

About five minutes later, Nichols slipped the phone back into his pocket and said, "Check your email."

My computer sounded its new-mail ding before my hand touched the mouse. I double-clicked the new email and it blossomed onto the screen. It was a forward from the gaming commission and it had a spreadsheet attached. I opened the spreadsheet and skimmed it for a couple minutes, then leaned back in my chair.

Now I had that little quiver in my brain that happens when I find something in an investigation, a skittering around the edges of my psyche. After days of finding little, this felt big. SPACE's gaming machines had not been queried by the gaming commission's computers in weeks. Yet according to the report on my screen, a report from the commission, every one of those machines had been queried thousands of times per day for the entire time they had been in use. Either I was wrong when I looked at the machines, or the commission report was wrong. I wasn't wrong; the machines had not been touched. So why did the commission systems think they had?

The P.I. report on Special Agent Courtney Meyer that I had ordered the day before arrived in my email inbox late that afternoon. I spent some time reading it. Ms. Meyer looked to be a pretty standard career FBI agent. Forty-two years old. Penny-ante assignments until five years ago, when she was involved in a major RICO case that netted a half-dozen indictments and a subsequent mashup of pleas and convictions from a bunch of corrupt

New Jersey politicians. That case put her on the feeb map and she'd been a rising star ever since.

Native New Yorker, third generation law enforcement, although Daddy and Granddaddy had both been NYPD. Never married. A smattering of photos from news articles showed an average-looking woman, not ugly but not particularly attractive.

The report was sparse on her recent activity, the only information being that she was thought to have been working on a case involving organized crime in several major U.S. cities that tracked back to foreign origins. Nothing that illuminated specifically why she was poking around SPACE, and nothing to hint at why she would have approached me like a bitch on wheels. My investigation was still in its early stages, but I'd seen nothing to point toward an organized crime connection, which seemed to be her forté.

My gut said I'd eventually find out exactly why she was intruding on my case and in my life, whether I wanted to or not.

CHAPTER 11

SPACE

ONE WEEK LATER

JACOB ALLEN SAT BEHIND HIS DESK, his mouth a little open, looking over his reading glasses at me. "You're sure about this?"

I nodded.

Brandy Palmer kept reading the status report I had prepared for the meeting.

Allen stabbed a button on his phone and his secretary answered. "Yes, sir?"

"Get Jerry Rose in here right now."

Minutes later, Rose arrived. Allen pointed to a chair. "Sit."

Rose looked offended, but he sat, arranging his white lab coat as he did, smoothing its little lapels.

Allen looked at me and said, "Tell him, Sam."

I was sitting on a sofa, opposite end from Palmer. I leaned forward, elbows on knees, looked at Rose, and began. "Every machine here has been compromised. Slots, poker, all of them. They—"

"Nonsense!" Rose said, interrupting. "This is the most secure envir—"

"Shut up and listen, Rose!" Allen said. More pit bull than Bassett hound now.

Rose's face reddened and he drew a breath, but held his tongue when Allen pointed at him and shook his head.

I continued. "You're familiar with how the gaming commission constantly polls the machines to verify the integrity of their code?"

He gave a little snort. "I know my job, Mr. Flatt."

"Well, not a single machine here has been polled by the commission in almost three months." Rose started to rear up again but this time I held up a hand and continued. "The commission computers have been polling, and as far as they and the commission know, all is normal. The problem is that what they've been communicating with is not the thousands of SPACE EGMs, but a single computer."

Rose scrunched up his face, confused.

"Specifically," I said, "they've been polling a computer designated on the SPACE network as VM2467. I'm assuming that's a virtual machine?"

He nodded, and I went on. "That virtual machine is running a database and some really clever routing code. It intercepts each incoming query from the commission computers, decodes the request, then answers. In short, that VM 'pretends' to be whatever slot or poker or whatever machine the commission is polling, and responds with the perfect answer every time."

"How could you possibly know this?" Rose said.

"I've spent the past three days, and most of the nights, tracking it all down. I'm right on this."

"That would require full admin and root on my network, which you don't have, so I don't see—"

My turn to interrupt: "Which I do have, and which I have had since my second day here. I know my job."

He was puffing up again. "You what, broke into my network?"

Allen rejoined the conversation. "He accessed the company's network. With my blessing."

"You're legal counsel," Rose said. "What gave you the right or the authority to interfere in my department?"

"Rose," Allen said, "this happened right under your nose. If you want any chance of keeping your job, any chance of ever working in this industry again, you'll start kissing ass as of this moment. Clear?"

Rose said nothing, but now looked like a leaky balloon. He said, "Why would someone do this?"

"To give themselves free rein over SPACE's electronic gaming environment."

"To what end?" Rose said.

I handed Rose a copy of my report, then said, "To steal millions. And to destroy the company while doing it."

After the meeting with Jacob Allen, I headed back to my workroom with Nichols in tow. I really liked the guy, something that doesn't happen often. I was anxious to see what my latest search had turned up on Gamboa's devices. The past week had been productive, and now I had that fire in my gut. I wanted to nail this thing down, put all the puzzle pieces together.

I had designed a search to comb through Gamboa's network activity, both on the Internet and the internal network, and extract anything unusual. The search was done, so I settled into my chair and started scrolling through the results. Five minutes later, I leaned forward and studied the screen. Then I smiled and slapped the table.

Nichols looked up from his Kindle, which he'd started bringing to work a couple days earlier. "What you got?"

"I have an onion, Mr. Nichols. A lovely and splendiferous onion."

"An onion?" Nichols said. "Color me confused, Sam."

I motioned him over and pointed to a picture of a stylized onion on my screen. "That, my friend, is a very special onion." He arched his eyebrows and I continued. "What you're looking at is an icon for a web browser called Onion, and that browser has been used on this computer before."

"Like Chrome, or Firefox?"

"Sort of, but special. Chrome, Firefox, Internet Explorer, they're all made for browsing the World Wide Web, you know, all those WWW addresses. Onion is made specifically to browse something called the Tor Onion network."

"Never heard of it."

"Most people haven't, because the people who do use it prefer it that way. Techy users may call it Tor, but a lot of people call it the deep web, or the underground web, or dark web. I prefer the term 'dark web' myself."

"Is it legal?"

"Sure, the network itself is legal. And to be fair, many

users are just paranoid about privacy. They don't want people snooping around their online activity. And with Tor, nobody is going to."

"What about the government?"

"Not even them. Breaking Tor encryption so they can snoop on its users is a high priority for the NSA, but they have an uphill climb. If you set it up right, Tor is very secret and very anonymous."

"I see," Nichols said. "I'm assuming it's popular with cyber-criminals, too?"

"Indeed it is," I said. "Hang on a sec, let me show you something." I fired up Onion on my laptop, ran a quick search, and loaded one of the websites identified by the search. Then I spun my laptop around, so Nichols would have a full view, and said, "Feast your eyes on that, Jimmy Boy."

His eyes widened and his mouth dropped open. "Holy crap, this can't be real."

"Wrong," I said.

CHAPTER 12

TUNICA, MISSISSIPPI

Mikail Sultanovich

MIKAIL SULTANOVICH PUSHED BACK from his table at the Blue and White Café. He didn't know if it was a place where you paid at the table or not, and he didn't care. He dropped a twenty and headed out, grabbing a toothpick from the front counter along the way. He got into his car, cranked the engine, and sat there while he dug roast beef from between his teeth and spit it out the window. That done, he backed out, then pulled into traffic headed north on Highway 61. The drive from Las Vegas to Mississippi had been a tough one, but now that he was here and had eaten a proper sit-down meal, it was time to move forward. His fuck of a father would regret the day he tried to have him killed. Dmitry already did. Mikail smiled at the thought.

Forty-five minutes later, he turned into the "deer camp" that sat between the Mississippi River and its levee. Perhaps the long, narrow building set on top of poles had been for deer hunters at some point, but it served a very different purpose now. He hated driving his Bentley on gravel roads and through mudholes, but some things could not be helped when you were running from a father who wanted you dead. After pulling inside the garage and closing its door behind him, he climbed a short set of stairs and stopped at the top long enough to pull his .45 from its holster. He racked a round into the chamber, then opened the door and stepped into a large kitchen. Almost immediately, a Slavic-looking man he knew only as Peter came charging toward him like a bull. Mikail shot him in the throat and moved deeper into the old lodge.

The far end of the kitchen opened into a long corridor that stretched the length of the structure. He stepped through the door and closed it behind him. Then he dropped to one knee and waited, pistol forward and ready. Closed doors lined both sides of the dim hallway. He didn't have to wait long. Within ten seconds, two men entered the corridor from two separate doors, one on the right and one on the left. They never stood a chance. Especially the dumb shit whose pants were still halfway down. Mikail shot them, then waited a couple minutes to see if more men would arrive. None did. He stepped over the first man; he had a bloody and pulpy hole where an eye used to be.

The second man was still very much alive, with blood that looked almost black leaking from his gut. Mikail stood above him and laughed, the big Slavic animal in him rising up. "Hope was good pussy for you! Maybe I shoot your dick off now?"

The man looked terrified and shook his head side to side. "Nyet! Nyet!"

"Okay, okay," Mikail said before he began another laughing jag that went on until he wheezed. After he caught his breath, he shot the man between the eyes and stepped over him.

Continuing down the hall, he glanced at the doors as he went, all of which had locks on the outside. Most of them were locked. Father's goons had been busy. Good. Easier to negotiate when you hold something of great value to the other side.

CHAPTER 13

SPACE

"It looks just like an online store," Nichols said.

"That's exactly what it is," I said.

"How is that possible? If we can see this, anybody can, right?"

I nodded. "Installing the software to access the deep web takes four or five minutes. After that, just do a search like I did, and follow some simple instructions."

He was scrolling through the products, looking at pictures, reading descriptions, shaking his head in disbelief. He clicked into a product listing for 1g Afghan #4 Heroin. At the top of the page was a picture of a block of what looked like heroin. The seller's net name was listed next, along with a price. Then came the features and benefits, listed in nice bullets.

High quality #4. Use with extreme caution.
What you get with me:

-> Free shipping
-> 100% Refund/Reship policy
-> All prices are in Bitcoin
-> Top quality product
-> Big stockpiles of product
-> Timely communication

Please also carefully read my profile before ordering!
These are my Terms and Conditions.

The listing went on to show shipping options and all the other details to be expected with any online product.

"If anyone can see this," he said, "why doesn't the government shut it down?"

"They have shut this one down. Several times. It just pops back up at a new address the next day. These sites are in constant motion, different URL addresses, different servers. It's a shell game and the black hats are very good at it."

"Black hats?"

"Technogeeks on the wrong side of things."

"Ah, got it. Hey, what currency is this in?" He pointed to the price on the screen.

0.164544

"Bitcoin," I said. "A global, digital currency. And if you want it to be, it can be just as anonymous and just as untraceable as these deep web stores."

"I've never heard of that either. If it's global, are you

telling me I can walk into a bank and exchange dollars for bitcoins?"

"Some banks, yes. Not widespread yet in the banking industry. You can buy it at countless online exchanges, though, and not only on the deep web. Plenty of places on the normal web, too. More and more legitimate online vendors are accepting it."

From the look on his face, Nichols was still trying to wrap his head around the whole thing. "So how much does a gram of this Afghan heroin cost in good old American dollars?"

"No clue," I said, "but it's easy enough to find out. Copy that amount to your clipboard, then open a new tab in your browser."

He did.

"Now search for 'bitcoin converter' and you'll get plenty of hits."

He chose a site and plugged in the amount. Using the conversion rate of the moment, the equivalent amount was USD $137.80.

"I'm blown away," he said.

"Well, you didn't expect it to be cheap, did you? After all, it's Afghan number four, whatever the hell that is. With free shipping!"

We laughed and Nichols gave me a knuckle-bump for a good one. He said, "Will you be able to tell what sites Gamboa visited on the deep web?"

"If she set it up right, no, that would be tough."

"You think she set it up right?"

"I hope not."

CHAPTER 14

TENNESSEE AIRSPACE

Max Sultanovich

MAX SAT ALONE IN THE PLUSH CABIN, looking out the
window of the private Falcon as they neared Memphis.
The digital clock at the front of the cabin read 1:56 a.m.,
and he could not believe the number of other airplanes
he could see in the skies around them. It looked like there
could be a hundred of them, all lined up with their lights
blazing, going to the same airport in the middle of the
night. What the hell?

His decades in the Soviet Union had given him a
strong sense of skepticism regarding unusual activity.
Communism was about order and routine. Usual was
tolerable. Unusual meant trouble. He pushed the intercom button on his armrest.

"Yes sir, Mr. Sultanovich?" one of the pilots said.

"Why are so many airplanes around us? Should we land at another place?"

"It's routine, sir. This is the time of night when FedEx planes arrive from around the world."

FedEx. Yes, he knew this company, even used their services sometimes. From the looks of it, they had enough airplanes to make an air force. American bastards.

The intercom sounded again: "Will there be anything else, sir?"

"When will we land?"

"We should touch down in about fifteen minutes."

Max switched the intercom off. He hated long flights for the way they corrupted the timings of his body. He had barely slept in the past eighteen hours, no matter how many times he had tried during the flight. Now here he was in the middle of the night, exhausted and preparing to deal with his lummox of a son. Mikail was difficult enough under the very best of circumstances, and this was far from that. By killing Dmitry, Mikail had put great hardship on the family's business operations. Plus there was the fact that Dmitry had always been more of a son to Max than that cumshot Mikail. Depriving Max of that would be something Mikail would come to regret during the short remainder of his life. Max would see most personally to that.

CHAPTER 15

SPACE

I'VE SEEN IT A HUNDRED TIMES: People who should know better, don't. Gamboa didn't invest the five minutes it would have taken to learn how to properly install and configure the programs for her to access the deep web. If she had, figuring out what she had done on the deep web would have been a nightmare at best, impossible at worst.

As it was, within a half hour I had reconstructed a long list of sites she had visited. Most of them had nonsensical online addresses, which is common. On the World Wide Web, businesses and people want their addresses to be easy to remember, so they're straightforward, like www.google.com. Not so with these businesses. Their addresses are arcane combinations of numbers and letters, and they change a lot, to make it more difficult for law enforcement to trace the site back to a real computer at a physical address.

I worked my way down the list, typing each of the addresses into my own Onion browser. The further I went, the less attractive Gamboa became. A lot of the addresses weren't working anymore, the sites having moved on to new addresses. There were a few porn sites, raunchy but not that different from what's on the normal web. Then came the bad stuff.

The tingle and buzz around my psyche that tells me I'm getting close to the nut of a case, had turned into screaming klaxons. This was an unexpected direction, unrelated to the original thrust of the case, but it was big. Miss Gamboa had spent considerable time on multiple occasions browsing a rape site. There are a lot of fake sites out there on which actors and actresses act out rapes to sate the desires of evil, worthless human beings who get off on seeing women—and sometimes men—brutalized. This site wasn't fake. No tiny disclaimers at the bottom saying "simulation for entertainment purposes only."

On the home page, a column of thumbnail videos ran from top to bottom, each one looping some particular scene over and over. No audio. Beside each thumbnail, a text description explained the content in graphic detail. Once you clicked a thumbnail, the full version of that video loaded. Too much sound. Many of the videos in high-def. All of them disgusting, depraved. I watched one of them start to finish, eighteen minutes of horror. Every time a shot revealed even a slight bit of the rapist's face, I studied it, committing it to memory.

I had spent years remaking myself, mending my psyche, leaving behind the man I was and vowing to never become that man again. Now, looking at this, witnessing the degradation of the innocent at the hands of the brutal, the old Sam was coming to life somewhere deep inside my soul. I tried to tell myself I could control him and the elemental urges he would bring back into the here and now, but at the same time I was telling myself that, I was hoping and praying that I would come face to face with this rapist, this animalistic waste of human flesh.

CHAPTER 16

AFGHANISTAN

THEN

THE METAL BUCKET CREAKS AS IT TIPS in a rusty bail. A fraction of a second later, the cold weight of the water hits the towel over my face. Now it drops through the towel, again, into my mouth, down my windpipe, into my lungs. I think this is the eleventh time, but my count could be off a pour or two in either direction. My back arches and my naked body convulses against the hemp ropes as the pain and wild physiological fear erupt. I think I've felt worse pain, but at this moment I can't remember specifics. I know the savagery of this pain. There is nothing else in the world, nothing else in the universe, nothing else that has ever been or ever will be, except this agony.

Then a tiny light emerges from the darkness. It's not much, but I focus on that pinprick in my screaming mind as it becomes a firefly, a gorgeous and wondrous firefly, one with a cerulean glow instead of yellow-green. And it comes closer and closer as I watch it, and finally it speaks to me in a soothing voice, saying, "You will survive. You will survive. You will survive. You will—"

The water stops and someone lifts the towel away. The firefly of salvation is gone, replaced by eyes of black hatred looking down on me. I gasp in great heaves, trying to get all the oxygen I can into my body before it is again deprived. The Taliban animal above is named Atash Sadati. He has information I need, but things have obviously not gone well to this point, or I wouldn't be on the wrong end of this affair.

Sadati's face is disgusting. It has a half-dozen boils scattered across it, each filled with pus. Who knows what caused the sores, but they're surely exacerbated by the fact that he hasn't had a bath in months. Assholes like him care so little about any standards of civilized human beings that they won't even wash their faces when a water hose is ten feet away. His beard is a collection of filthy, matted clumps, especially around his mouth. A mouth that is too small for his face; it looks like a rectum filled with rotten teeth. Some are completely black with decay. Others are mottled with black among the green shade that comes from years of chewing khat to stay stoned.

"You are not so tough now, fucking American! Not so tough!" His breath is rotten and the spittle that hits my face is a foul slurry out of hell itself.

I say nothing. I have nothing in my heart and soul for him but contempt. Not because he tortures me; I do the same when it's needed. I hate him because he is an abomination, a putrid sub-human who is unworthy of conversation of any kind. I'm not yet near giving up information that will harm my country, but he isn't even worth the oxygen required to tell him a lie. In my mind, to speak to him at all is to grant him some measure of respect, and that I will not do unless it furthers the needs of my mission or somehow provides personal pleasure to me.

"You will talk to me!" He's in a pure rage, unable to believe or comprehend that someone is able to withstand hours of everything he has to offer.

Pure rage is exactly what I want from him right now, because rage doesn't think. It exists and it consumes all else.

His co-animal speaks for the first time in an hour: "Atash, the hour is late. Perhaps we should take him to the camp now and let them have him. Chief Azizi will be very pleased with such a valuable gift."

It never occurs to them that I speak Pashto far better than they speak English.

Sadati explodes. "We will take this fucking American nowhere! Do you hear me, Koshan? Allah willing, this fucking American will tell me what I want to know!"

"Yes, I hear you, Atash. But sometimes we must consider that Allah is not willing at this moment. We do not know his ways."

Now is the unexpected moment that making my first voluntary sound in their presence can benefit me: I loose a burst of laughter. It's not difficult, because this really is some funny shit. Both men stare at me. Ali's face is a study in bewilderment. Sadati is over the edge, apoplectic, veins throbbing, eyes bugged. His hell-zits look like they may burst at any moment.

I seize the moment and drop right down to their elementary level of insults and language. "You assholes are entertaining as hell, you know that?" They look at each other, clearly stunned by my behavior. "For years, I've been listening to you goat herders talk about all the mighty things you're going to do, 'Allah willing.' So I have to wonder, why do you idiots never seem to notice that Allah obviously is not willing?

"You fail at every damn thing you do. You live in caves. Caves! You smell like raw shit. Half of you love to fuck little boys, probably because no woman in her right mind would want anything to do with your pathetic little dicks. Every fight you get in, you get your asses kicked. Doesn't matter who you're fighting: United States. European pussies. Even yourselves. Hell, your bunch can't even handle tiny little Israel. They've kicked your ass so many times it's like a hobby to them."

I pause for just a moment to check their status. They still look stunned, but there's also a difference between the two of them slipping more into play. Ali has a much cooler head; he knows what I'm worth to his superiors, both in money and in prestige. Sadati, however, is a man who burns with hatred and lets it rule him. Fire and ice. Time to bring them together.

I laugh again, and move in for the final push. "The way I see it, there are only two possibilities. First, even Allah doesn't give a flying fuck about your dumb asses. He didn't do a damn thing when Abraham told Ishmael to hit the road, did he? Did he care when Jacob bought Esau's birthright for a damned bowl of soup? Not a bit. And he's not doing a damn thing for you today, is he? Nope. Now the second possibility is the one I personally favor. Want to know what it is?"

Sadati is breathing hard, eyes wide, that nasty little mouth hung open, which makes it about the size of a quarter. His nostrils are quivering and, most importantly, he's opening and closing his hand around the hilt of his pesh-kabz, his tribal fighting knife. Here we go. "I guess the pussycat got your tongues, but I know you boys will want to know this. The second possibility is that Allah, your moon god, doesn't exist at all. He's just—"

Showtime. Sadati lunges toward me, screaming like an animal as he pulls the old knife from his waistband. Ali sees money, power, and probably even his life slipping away. He reaches out and grabs at Sadati. "Atash, no!"

Throughout my rant, I've been working on the rope around my wrists. Since I'm on my back with my hands tied together atop my stomach, it's all been in plain view, but they weren't watching my hands. They were transfixed by the laughter and insults coming from the fucking American. Watching my face. The knot comes loose just as Sadati wheels around toward Ali. My hands are free.

"You cannot do—" Ali starts, but he never gets to finish.

Sadati shoves the curved blade in just below the left side of Ali's ribcage, then shoves it up into the heart. As Ali's eyes widen in shock, Sadati screams, "Fuck you, Koshan! Fuck you! Fuck you! Fuck you!"

I pull the final knot apart and unwrap the rope from my ankles. I roll off the table and move toward Sadati. He doesn't have his back fully to me; he's at more of a forty-five-degree angle. I'm six feet away when he picks me up in his peripheral vision. He spins around to face me, yanking the knife out of Ali as he turns. I'm no more than a foot away as he drives the blade toward me with an underhanded motion. I move in closer, grab his wrist with my right hand and his elbow with my left, then force his knife hand up and back. I wasn't quick enough. A burning sensation rips up the left side of my abdomen as an inch of the knife's tip scores for about six inches.

With the knife now forced back from my torso, I lean my head back, then whip it forward as hard as I can. The head-butt connects, a point just above my hairline driving into Sadati's nose with a crunch I find almost musical. He staggers back a step and tries to back away, but I stay with him. I twist his wrist and the knife falls free. Now it's hand-to-hand, and that means Mr. Atash Sadati is well and truly a dead man walking. The red fog rises in my soul.

CHAPTER 17

SPACE

NOW

I worked my way through the presentation, explaining the deep web to Jacob Allen and Brandy Palmer. Nichols was there in the conference room too, but he'd already heard this whole spiel. I wrapped it up with a trimmed-down version of the same sickening video I had watched earlier. When it finished and faded to black, I touched the END PRESENTATION icon on the control screen that was flush-mounted in the table. The large display panel returned to the SPACE logo, the room lights raised to a pleasant glow, and the electrochromic windows lightened to reveal the bustle of Las Vegas outside.

At least a minute passed in silence before Allen said, "Dear God."

Palmer stood and started pacing back and forth between the conference table and the windows. After a few trips, she stopped and looked at Allen. "Jake, I don't need to tell you how important it is to keep this contained. If this is linked to the company in any way, it—"

"I know, I know," he said, and they looked at each other a long moment. The look was curious, a wordless communication between the two of them. Then Allen said, "Sam, James, not a word of this can get out. Not one word."

Nichols nodded. I did not. Could not. "That's a problem," I said, looking Allen in the eye.

His eyebrows scrunched down, making for a confused look on his droopy face. "Pardon?"

Palmer planted her hands on her hips, a dramatic pose. "What does that mean?"

"The rape videos have to be turned over to the police," I said. "Today."

"Oh, hell no," Palmer said. "They most certainly will not." Now she looked like a bull getting ready to charge.

"Brandy's right," Allen said. "That's unacceptable, Sam."

I said, "Let me be really clear, people: This point is not up for debate. I've uncovered evidence of a crime, numerous crimes, and I'm required both by law and by the ethics of my profession to notify the nearest law enforcement agency, not to mention the moral obligation."

"What moral obligation?" Palmer said.

That pissed me off. "You," I said, "are being either disingenuous, or obtuse. Do you think they let those women go when they were through raping them? No, they didn't. They either killed them, or they still have them."

She stomped to my side of the table in her heels, a little flurry of clicks and clacks on the hard white floor, stopped right beside me, and stuck her finger in my face. "You are completely out of line, in more ways than one."

I drew three deep breaths before responding. "Ms. Palmer, your gender and my sense of chivalry are the only things keeping me from—"

"Whoa, whoa, whoa," Allen said. "Let's take a deep breath, everybody."

"I just had three deep breaths," I said. "And you don't want to know what I did with the last finger somebody stuck in my face."

She dropped her hand and turned to Allen. "Jake, I told you it was a mistake to hire him. His type are all the same."

"My type?" I said.

She was cocked and ready to fire a response when Allen gave her a look that caused her to freeze momentarily, then fume. But she said no more.

Allen said, "Sam, I understand the need to notify police, but I need you to understand that the timing of this is…precarious for the company. Perhaps you can give us a few days?"

"No, Jacob. I can't. There's no time in something like this. I have—no, we have—evidence of multiple felonies. Do you think the police will give a damn why we didn't turn it over as soon as we found it?"

"I believe I can handle the police," he said. "And I'll sign an addendum to your contract that indemnifies you from any fallout. I don't mean to seem callous to this situation, but my legal responsibility is to protect the company. And I think the best way for me to do that right now is to very carefully consider the fallout before any of this is disclosed."

"First, you can't indemnify me against criminal prosecution. Second, what the hell is wrong with you people? You saw that video, and there are a lot more of them. If those animals had you, would you want someone to wait a few days?" He didn't say anything. I had more to say, and did. "Understand this, Jacob. I always maintain maximum confidentiality for my clients, but when I see clear evidence of a crime, that's it. It's out of my hands. It will take me a couple hours to get everything extracted and copied. Once that's done, I'm headed to the police department. Any more questions?"

He looked at me with a sad face, maximum droop, and said nothing.

I closed my laptop, unplugged it, and left the room.

LAS VEGAS POLICE DEPARTMENT DETECTIVES BUREAU

We sat in a cramped office that had to be ninety degrees. Puke-green cinder block walls, no windows, and an old surplus metal office desk without a square inch unused. The detective's name was Ronnie Huddleston. He looked about forty. At least three hundred pounds, with a complicated comb-over unlike anything I'd encountered before. The flushed look of his face suggested a lot of drinking and the puffy eyes told the same story.

Huddleston took the DVD, inserted it into an older Dell tower, and waited until a window appeared listing the contents of the disk.

I leaned over so I could see his screen and said, "The fourth file from the top is pretty representative of the collection."

He made no indication that he heard me, and double-clicked the first file, which was nothing more than a text inventory I'd included of the disk's contents. Huddleston stared at it as if it were a foreign language. After about a minute of that, he turned to me and said, "What is this, exactly?"

"It's a list of the files on the DVD that I put together, an evidence log of sorts."

"You made this DVD?"

"Yeah, I extracted the relevant files from the suspect's hard drive, and put them on that disk for you."

"So these aren't even originals?"

"No," I said, "but they're digital copies, exactly the same content as the originals."

He blew out a dramatic sigh and hit the eject button on the computer's DVD drive. The tray slid out, and he removed the disk and handed it across the desk to me. "This is no use to me, Mr. Flack. I'll have to have the original."

"The name is Flatt. You telling me you're not even going to look at it?"

He spread his arms, puffy palms face up on his desk. Then he smiled. I couldn't help but stare. He had tombstone teeth, bright white and way too big for his mouth. He looked like a grinning mule. It bothered me to look at him. "I appreciate you bringing it, but we can only work with original evidence. You had no way to know that, of course. It's how the law works."

"I have a decent understanding of the law, Detective. I've brought you evidence of dozens of rapes and other felonies, and you refuse to even look at it. Gotta tell you, that's a first."

Another mule smile. He pushed his giant ass up out of the chair. "Thank you for coming, sir. If you'd like to bring the original evidence, we would of course be interested in taking a look."

I stood, snapped the DVD back into its case, closed it. "Did you speak with someone representing my client before I got here?"

He didn't say a word, just stared at me with that disturbing smile. I had a wicked urge to knock those slabs of milk-bone down his throat, but I resisted, turned, and left.

In a cab on the way back to the casino, I worked through the situation in my mind. When Jacob Allen said he could take care of the police, he wasn't joking. The sad-eyed hound dog of a lawyer was obviously wired into the authorities and didn't mind using his connections for his employer. I thought momentarily about calling the heifer from the FBI, but discounted that idea pretty quickly. I knew what she'd do; instead of doing the right thing and jumping on it, she would offer action on the videos in exchange for my feeding her info on my investigation. I couldn't do that, so best to stay off that road altogether. From a legal perspective, I had met my immediate burden by trying to give the evidence to the police.

Some people would say I had met my moral obligation, as well. I was not among such pussified assholes. Women were suffering. If not the women on the videos, if they were dead, more victims had almost certainly taken their place. That could not stand. I would not let it.

CHAPTER 18

SPACE

I EXITED THE CAB ON THE STREET in front of SPACE. That left what looked like a mile of walking still left to get inside, but that was okay. It gave me time to make a phone call I was sure wouldn't be eavesdropped. I had no specific reason to think anyone at SPACE had been listening in as I worked, but my life experience has taught me to assume privacy is rare. Especially when dealing with powerful people you have any conflict at all with; Jacob Allen had just shown me that conflict was indeed in the air. I pulled my phone, lit it up, and touched the #1 speed-dial icon.

"This is Paul Flatt," was, as always, the answer.

"Big Bro," I said.

"Little Bro! You come in out of the woods?"

"Too long ago. On a gig in Vegas right now. I need to pick your legal brain a minute."

"Shoot."

I gave him a condensed version of everything that had happened with the videos on the rape site, from finding them, to the argument with the client, to being blown off by the police. I wrapped it up with, "I need to know what my legal responsibility is. I went to the police, but I know that agency is compromised. What more do I need to do to be in the clear?"

"My first impression? Nothing. Not sure you were legally bound to do what you've already done. That said, I'm a civil attorney in Texas, Little Bro. I'm no expert on the criminal end, and I know zero about Nevada law. Let me research it a bit and I'll call you back, okay?"

"Roger that," I said, and the call was over. I looked at the phone and touched the icon to dial my daughter, then kept walking while it rang. No answer. When it went to voicemail, I left her a simple message: "Love you, sweetie. Let's get together again soon."

After a visit to my room for a quick shower, I headed to my workroom. A few minutes after I got there, Nichols showed up. I looked at him and said, "I didn't ping you. How'd you know I was here?"

He raised his right hand, exposing the bracelet on his wrist, gave it a little shake.

"You tracking me everywhere I go?" I said.

"No no," he said. "The system is set to let me know whenever you enter this room, since it's my job to be here when you're working."

It should have occurred to me earlier that the bracelet might be more than a simple guest ID tool. I wouldn't ignore that possibility again. "And how do you set the system to do that?"

"Don't know. Somebody else does it. Yours was set up that way before you got here. Didn't realize it myself until I got a text the first time I brought you in here."

I nodded. "Cool tech."

"How'd your excursion to the police department go?"

"They blew me off," I said.

He arched his eyebrows.

I said, "Yeah, really."

I was wading through Gamboa's deep web activity again. I had been about two-thirds of the way through it when I hit the rape site earlier, and that had put my exploration on pause. Once more, I encountered a lot of sites that no longer worked, along with more hard porn. Then, when I loaded the third from last site on the list, everything changed.

CHAPTER 19

LAS VEGAS

Christine Gamboa

CHRISTINE GAMBOA WAS ENJOYING a day off from work. Many of the whales she catered to expected her to be there 24/7, but Sasha insisted she take her day off. He was sweet like that, or at least had a little sweetness in him. As a result, she was on her couch, unshowered, unkempt, endlessly browsing Netflix and never choosing anything to actually watch. She was relaxed enough that she was slipping into sleep and didn't realize it, but that all came to a lurching halt—literally—when the klaxon alarm sounded on her iPhone. The sound of the klaxon might have been enough on its own, but it wasn't on its own.

That particular alarm tone meant only one thing: Someone had just accessed one of her trigger sites. They would look like dead sites on the deep web to anyone who loaded them, but each one was really an online trip-wire, designed to notify her immediately if anyone was snooping on her online history. The problem was that she had never accessed any of the deep web sites from anywhere except her SPACE laptop, and she had thoroughly cleaned it before leaving. So how was that possible? It wasn't, but the klaxon was screaming. She killed the sound, then pulled up the encrypted spreadsheet that would tell her which site had tripped the alarm. While she was scrolling through the list and looking for the specific site, the alarm sounded again. She assumed she had touched SNOOZE instead of CANCEL, but when she looked at the phone, she saw that it was a new alarm. Shit. She killed it.

It didn't matter which site. Time to go. The alarm sounded again. She killed all sound on the phone and sprang from the sofa, any hint of relaxation long gone. She didn't walk to her bedroom. She ran. Into the closet, where she had a go-bag ready. To the bathroom for a quick pee. She looked in the mirror on the way out of the toilet closet; she looked like hell. No matter. No time. Back into the closet, where she grabbed a plain pink baseball cap and pulled it down over her mess of hair. Then she headed for the door.

CHAPTER 20

NORTH MISSISSIPPI

Max Sultanovich

HE GAZED OUT THE WINDOW OF THE SEDAN as his driver motored them south on Mississippi's Highway 61, the late afternoon sun flooding the flat farmland and its green crops with soft golden light. Max had never seen so many billboard signs on a rural highway. They never stopped. One bastard casino after another promising easy money to idiots who were stupid enough to believe it. He hated such people who believed they could seize wealth without work. Nothing would please him more than to walk through one of the casinos, killing them at random, just for being too stupid to live. Stab one. Shoot the next. Whatever he wanted. But that was useless dreaming.

"How long?" he said.

"Minutes," the driver said.

Six thousand miles he had come to deal with his own special idiot. He had often wished he could accuse his wife of spreading her legs to someone else when Mikail was conceived. He could not. From the moment of his birth, Mikail had looked like him. The same eyes, same Slavic features, same physique. Somehow a rotten glob of seed had spewed from his dick and produced this burden named Mikail Maximovich Sultanovich. It was a burden he had endured for too many years.

The driver turned right onto a narrow road that seemed to be more holes and bumps than paving. Max turned his gaze forward as the car lurched along toward the setting sun. After more turns, they were on a gravel road, sand and rocks pounding the bottom of the car as they drove. Soon they approached the face of a levee that seemed to go forever to left and right. The road continued up the face of the green hill, then down the back side, but was blocked by a closed gate that looked like it had not been opened in years. The car stopped and the driver said, "Sir? What to do?"

"Wait." Max already had his smartphone in hand, swiping through screens until he found what he was looking for. He touched an icon and a numeric keypad appeared. Once he touched in an eight-digit sequence, the gate swung open. "Go," he said.

The car moved forward with a violent shake as it crossed some kind of barred surface that rattled Max to his bones. Thankfully, it did not last long. They were back on the gravel road, the gate closing smoothly behind them. At the bottom, they turned right, drove for a kilometer or two, then veered left into thick woods. The road continued, and after a few curves, arrived at a long wooden building built on top of poles to elevate it from the ground. On the left end of the building, a garage was built at ground level, beneath the main structure.

"Stop," Max said, pointing to the left end of the building. "There."

The moment the car stopped, three men appeared from behind the building, all carrying weapons.

Max opened the door, stepped out, then stuck his head back inside the car to say, "Stay in car."

The driver nodded and Max closed the door.

When the men reached him, Max spoke, holding up a picture of Mikail. "Go. Bring him to me."

Not one of the three spoke. One nodded, and all turned and walked toward different doors of the building. Front. Rear. Garage.

There were no gunshots, no sounds at all for the next five minutes. Then the men were back. The one who had nodded said, "He is not here. Just women. And some blood on floor."

Max sighed and wondered if his misery with Mikail would ever end. "Find him. Kill him." He got back into his car and motioned for the driver to go.

CHAPTER 21

SPACE

IT'S A RARE OCCURRENCE FOR ME, but the time had come. The rape site. The corporate mind-set that a company is more important than innocent women. Half-ass police. Things like this pile up and feed a darkness inside me that I'd kept at bay for a very long time. I needed a break, needed to drown that darkness in strong drink. Tomorrow I would return to the job I was hired to do with a clearer mind and a more focused soul; and given what I'd found on Gamboa's computer at the end of the workday, I knew I was getting closer to the nut of the original issue, closer to finding out exactly who was stealing my client's money. I felt it. It was big and I was going to blow this thing wide open. Tomorrow.

"Jimmy Boy," I said to Nichols, "know any good places in this town to do some serious drinking?"

He looked at me, a bit blank-faced.

"What?" I said. "Surely you're familiar with the concept?"

"Oh yeah," he said, a little smile breaking out. "Just caught me off guard. You've been pretty...uh...I'll say 'work-centric' since you got here. Can I join you?"

"I insist. One condition, though."

He cocked his head and waited.

"I don't need an assistant, no SPACE escort. I need a drinking buddy. You up for that?"

His smile grew. "Hell, yes."

We started the evening in SPACE. I wanted to roam, check things out, really see the place. Nichols instantly went into tour guide mode and I stopped him a millisecond or two later. "You're not working, Jimmy Boy, so shut up and enjoy the sights as best you can."

"Got it," he said with a smile.

I love everything about space travel, so we got on one of the turbo people movers and got shot through a spoke to SPACE's space museum. After picking up a fresh round of drinks at the first bar we encountered, I headed toward the space shuttle in the middle of the atrium. The atrium was huge. I'm talking at least a half-million square feet, half the size of a typical modern mall. At first glance, the roof appeared to be a one-piece glass dome. It of course wasn't; it was really an assembly of thousands of curved transparent panels, fitted in a framework built from acrylic, also transparent. I stood for a while and looked up and around. The blue glow of the 'spacescape' outside, with the flashing of the tiny flying orbs, was enchanting. Just this thing would be worth a trip to see and behold, as a remarkable piece of engineering. And it was just one of countless marvels in this futuristic wonderland.

The space shuttle in the middle looked antique in this setting. She had flown a lot of missions and had the scars to prove it. Lots of mismatches among the tiles that formed her thermal skin. I'd seen several of the shuttles before, but this was the first time I'd seen one that you could walk up to and touch, walk underneath, study the old tiles scorched from reentry into Earth's atmosphere.

I took a healthy sip of my drink and looked at Nichols. "Amazing machines."

"Bigger than I imagined," he said.

"You haven't been here before?"

He shook his head. "When I first started here, I was sure I'd be spending my evenings here for a month, just walking and looking."

"Like we're doing now."

"Exactly," he said. "But reality set in. I work hard, and when the workday is done, I bail."

"Yeah, I get that. I worked a few years for a big corporate consulting firm. Had an office on the fiftieth floor. New York branch. I had this fantastic view of Manhattan that took my breath, for about a week. Then I didn't even notice it anymore. It was just the office."

He extended a fist for a knuckle-bump. I complied. He looked up at the shuttle. "I don't see how it even flies. Looks like the wings aren't big enough."

"It's really more glider than airplane. Not a great glider at that—there's a reason they call it a flying brick—but it's good enough to get it on the ground in a controlled fashion."

"You an airplane nut?" he said.

"Wouldn't go that far. I do like to fly, though."

"You're a pilot?"

I nodded, took another drink of my Red Bull and vodka.

"Have a plane?" he said.

I nodded again.

"Jet?"

That was worth a laugh. "No, Cessna one-seventy-two. Little four-seater."

"Still cool. So, you don't own a house, you live in the woods with a horse named Bobby—"

"Johnny," I said. "Not Bobby."

"Excuse me, got it. You don't have a house, you live in the woods with a horse named Johnny, you don't own a car, but you do own an airplane."

I extended a fist and said, "Good job, you know everything there is to know about me."

He bumped my knuckles. "I have a feeling that's a long, long way from true."

I smiled and gave him a wink.

After another hour of wandering around SPACE, we decided to leave the future and head out to somewhere more conducive for both of us to relax. It was, after all, still Nichols's workplace. We ended up downtown at the Golden Nugget. It's old, but it's pristinely maintained and elegant with all its beautiful white and gold. We walked, drank, talked, drank, and were both well into a buzz when we decided to have a seat in a lounge area off the casino floor.

I had gathered all kinds of information on Nichols. He was thirty-two, never married, no kids, grew up in Reno and moved to Vegas about ten years ago. Started working the hotel side of the industry, then switched to dealing tables, on to the pit, and finally to the executive host gig, which he called whalesitting and didn't really like. He wanted to go back to the pit, but his whales liked him and management wanted him to stay put.

He said, "So, Sammy Flatt—you mind if I call you Sammy?"

"I like 'Sammy.' Would have preferred that growing up."

"What was it growing up? Sambo?" He burst out laughing, well into the alcohol phase known as 'Unfunny Becomes Hilarious' and enjoying it.

"I wish."

"Uh-oh, I smell something grand. Spill it!"

"Jimmy Boy," I said, "you wouldn't believe me if I told you what my real name is."

"How bad could it be?"

"Bad enough that I filed the paperwork to legally change it on the day I turned eighteen."

"Come on, you gotta tell me now. What is it?"

I took another robust sip, smacked my lips. "My birth name, young James, is Unclavius Samuel Flattbush."

A good fifteen seconds passed with him just staring at me. Then he said, "Ho-ly shit," and took a big gulp of his own drink. "So what did your parents call you?"

I said, "You're kidding, right? My name was Uncla-vius Samuel. What do you think they called me?"

Then he got it and burst out laughing, spraying me with whiskey and Coke. "Uncle Sam! They freaking called you Uncle Sam, didn't they?"

"They were…very patriotic. And hey, I have siblings. I didn't necessarily get the worst of it."

CHAPTER 22

McCARRAN INTERNATIONAL AIRPORT
LAS VEGAS

Christine Gamboa

CHRISTINE'S HEART FELT READY TO LEAP OUT of her chest as she threw some bills at the cab driver and stepped out into the hot night. She had spent the past several hours hopefully creating the illusion of normal activity, running errands, a little shopping, all while trying to ascertain whether she was being followed. She hadn't seen anyone, but she wasn't naive. Yes, she was intelligent and had good, maybe even great, skills of observation. Two dressing room changes into new clothes should help. Using a different mall exit than entrance, and grabbing a cab while her car was parked on the far side of the mall could help. But being on the run and spotting clandestine pursuers wasn't exactly a skill set she possessed.

Her stride was quick and her path direct as she stepped inside McCarran International Airport. She was just one more traveler rushing to make a plane. She hoped. The cab ride had been quick, but it gave her enough time to get the new smartphone set up well enough to buy her ticket. The electronic boarding pass was on its screen and she was ten yards from the TSA podium at the entrance to the security checkpoint. She could hear her pulse in her ears as she held the phone against the scanner and handed her ID to the TSA agent. The agent gave her a perfunctory smile as he took the ID and squinted at it. Then the scanner flashed red and beeped. What the hell?

But she knew. All her clever tactics had been for nothing. The electronic web of the modern world had tracked her. Someone would show up and haul her off and that would be that.

"Ma'am?" the TSA agent said.

Christine jerked her head up. "Sorry, what?"

"Please move ahead."

She looked down at the scanner and saw it had turned green. Oh, thank God. She stowed her ID and phone and moved into the security line. The crowd was light and she was through the security area in three minutes. Now she just had to make it to the gate. Maybe she'd make it after all. They could track her, figure it out soon enough, but if she could pull this off, at least she'd have a little time. She quickened her stride toward the gate.

Five minutes later, she was in the jetway, midway through the line as it crept forward. She was going to make it. When she reached the door and stepped into the plane, her body relaxed. She couldn't wait to get airborne so she could get a drink. As she was making her way through the first class cabin, her heart stopped. There, in the third seat on the right, sat Sasha Maslov, staring right at her. Smiling that smile.

He was in the aisle seat. When she drew even with him, he reached over and patted the window seat. "Come, kohona. This is much better seat than row twenty-seven."

CHAPTER 23

GOLDEN NUGGET CASINO
LAS VEGAS

WE SAT AT A BLACKJACK TABLE, just Nichols, a dour-faced Asian dealer who had to be in her seventies, and me. We were both beyond a little buzzed, and well into the blood alcohol levels at which guys slip into the maudlin lands of lost loves and such. I played basic strategy and knew it well enough that there were no decisions to make while playing. Just stand, hold, split, or double down, based on the combination of your two cards versus the dealer's up-card. Nichols played the same way, but with an impulsive move every now and then that varied from the strategy.

"Married?" Nichols said.

I shook my head and slipped my cards beneath my bet to signal a stand. "Not anymore."

"How long?"

"Married thirteen, divorced five," I said. "You?"

"Nah, never married. Figured it's best to wait till I really settle into a career and stuff."

"Yeah. Maybe I should've done that."

"You move around a lot or something?" Nichols said.

"Something," I said, as the dealer raked in my chips from her twenty-one against my twenty.

"What'd you do before the forensic thing? I've asked a couple times and you just said nothing, didn't answer at all. What's up with that?"

A cocktail waitress arrived with her tray of goodies and put two new shots of tequila before each of us. I picked one of mine up and took care of it, then picked up the other one, along with my chips, and motioned with my head for Nichols to follow. He did.

Out on Fremont Street, we walked beneath the garish animated canopy as it splashed the street with never-ending swaths of color and light.

Nichols said, "Now you gonna tell me what you did before?"

I walked a few steps without answering, then killed the shot of tequila I'd walked out of the casino with. (Rules are made to be broken, remember?) I looked at Nichols, knowing I shouldn't answer his question. But I wanted to answer it. I needed to answer it, had needed to answer it for so many years.

CHAPTER 24

AIRBORNE

Christine Gamboa

THE FLIGHT REACHED ALTITUDE and the seat belt light dinged off. Christine watched as Sasha pulled a flask from his pocket and drew a long sip. She could smell the pepper vodka as he passed the flask to her. She shook her head. "No, thanks."

"Ah, kohona, you—"

"Stop calling me that, Sasha. If I were a 'special girl-friend' you cared about, you wouldn't have been tracking me, wouldn't have been waiting for me on this plane."

"Sasha only want to help you, Chrissy."

"I'm not an idiot."

"Oh no, you are very smart girl. I think maybe too smart, is why you now to run away."

"What does that even mean?"

"Too smart. Know too many things, too many dangerous things. So you try to go."

Christine said, "Whatever you think I know, you're wrong. I don't—"

The look on Maslov's face, which had been amiable and warm until that moment, went cold and hard. "You shut up. You shut up with lies to me!" His voice was quiet, hissing, terrifying.

She wiped her eyes with her sleeve, but said nothing.

"You take our half the million dollars for computer instructions," Maslov said. "Do not to tell me you know nothing. Why you decide to run?"

Christine didn't bother wiping her eyes again, and let the tears stream down her face. She nodded. "I was afraid."

"I think you afraid. And something else, too."

She shook her head.

"I think you thought to stop operation, but you want to get away from SPACE first. No connection. Make hard to figure out it was you who go to police."

This was her nightmare, the worst-case scenario unfolding at 35,000 feet. She stared at the video screen in the seatback in front of her and thought how nice it would be to be as carefree as the sitcom actors looked on that screen. She dried her tears and made a decision to stop the tears. Maybe she couldn't be carefree, but she didn't have to melt into pitiful mush, either. She turned and looked at Sasha. "So what is it you have in mind? How are you here to help me?"

Sweet, cordial Sasha was back. "Right now, no one else knows these things. Only me, me and my loyal people. I think is best to stay this way, yes?"

"And what do you want in return for that?"

No more tears came, but his smile did raise goose-bumps all over her body.

FREMONT STREET
LAS VEGAS

"You gonna answer your drinking buddy or what?" Nichols said, giving me a little spur with his elbow.

"If I tell you, you take it to the grave. I like you, Jimbo, but if you ever breathe a word of this, you will have betrayed me. I don't like betrayal. Deal?"

Nichols gave a little laugh. "Sure, man. I get it. If I tell, you'll have to kill me, right?"

I didn't laugh. "No, I won't kill you. But I will track you down and give you an ass whipping like you've never imagined. I'm serious. No joke."

No more laughing. "Okay, Sam. Never pass my lips. You have my word." He extended his hand and we shook on it.

We were walking past a bench beside the sidewalk. I stopped and sat. Nichols joined me. "I spent seven years working for the government, most of it overseas."

"Military?"

"Yes and no. We were trained by the military, different special ops groups. After the training, which all took place under false names, we disappeared from the books. We didn't exist anymore."

"Like the CIA? You became spies?"

I shook my head. "No. Spies have legends where they're deployed, but they're ultimately still on record with the agency. We weren't. There is no record anywhere that I ever had one minute of affiliation with the United States government. On paper, I was a traveling tech consultant my entire adult life."

"Are you shitting me, man? Sounds like a movie."

I looked at him. "James, do I look like I'm shitting you?"

"No," he said. "You sure don't."

"We were deployed in two-man teams called BAM squads, and we were the ultimate in covert, the blackest of black ops."

"BAM?" Nichols said.

"By. Any. Means. We did the stuff the military isn't allowed to do in today's pussified environment."

"And you did what, exactly?"

"Whatever had to be done."

"Give me an example."

I blew out a long breath, and could still taste the tequila. I had dozens of stories I could tell, but like many men of war, and like many policemen who encounter awful things, I had one story in particular. The one that haunted me. The one I could never push far enough back in my mind, the one I couldn't contain inside my soul. I'd had opportunities to tell it to off-the-books shrinks who work for the government, but never had. Truth is, I never trusted anyone enough to talk about it, especially from the government. Yet here I sat on a public street in Las Vegas, drunk, about to spill it to someone I'd known a couple weeks. Was I crazy? Drunk or not, I knew not to do it. I knew that if it ever got out that I had told anyone, I'd disappear from the earth, and not just from records. I knew all this, but still I started talking.

"My first partner was a guy we called Ditto. On our second mission, we were tasked with grabbing a Taliban asshole from some no-name village, after—"

"Afghanistan? Or Iraq?" Nichols said.

"Afghanistan. We were supposed to grab him, take him outside the village, and find out what he knew about an upcoming attack they had planned against some of our guys. We went in at some ungodly hour in the middle of the night and snatched him from his bed without much of a fight. Took him a couple clicks outside the village, up a hill and into some woods. We started interrogating and he kept insisting we had the wrong man, that he didn't know anything. Which is exactly what about ninety percent of them say. After an hour of beating him and tazing him and burning him with a propane torch, we still had nothing. He was still insisting we had the wrong man. The picture in my pocket made it clear we had exactly the right guy.

"I got tired of his bullshit." I stopped talking, my eyes closed, the scene as vivid in my mind as Fremont Street was right then when my eyes were open.

Nichols sounded scared of the answer, but asked it anyway: "What'd you do?"

"I started by tying him to a tree, standing up with his back to the tree, and plucking out his left eye." Nichols's eyes were huge, the glassy sheen of alcohol fast clearing. "There this guy was, his eye hanging by the optic nerve, screaming like you wouldn't believe. He still didn't break, so I popped out the right one next."

"Ho-ly shit," Nichols said.

"Yeah, it was pretty freaky, but you can usually pop the eyeballs back in and they're fine."

"Well, that's…good to know."

"Then I went for what we were taught as 'the ninety-nine maneuver,' because once you've done enough to make them believe you capable of anything, ninety-nine percent of all guys on the planet fold to this threat."

"Oh hell," Nichols said. "Oh hell, oh hell, oh hell, tell me you didn't—"

"I cut all his clothes off him, stretched his dick out, and put a knife at the base. Told him he had ten seconds to talk, or I'd turn him into a eunuch. I still remember looking at him, seeing his eyeballs hanging on his face and realizing that he had no choice but to watch. His eyes were pointed straight at his crotch and he sure as hell couldn't move them." I stopped talking, my eyes closed again, reliving it for what felt like the millionth time.

Nichols said, "And?"

"I cut his dick off. And the instant the blade was all the way through and his dick came loose in my hand, a round from an AK-47 hit the armor plate on my back. Knocked me down, and I instinctively rolled away when I hit the ground. Good thing, because the fire kept coming from some guy charging through the woods toward us, bellowing like a stuck bull. I found cover behind a fallen tree, and when I looked back at the dickless guy through my night vision, the guy with the rifle was at the tree, hugging him, talking to him."

At this point, Nichols was sober and without words, so I continued.

"I raised my N-V goggles and hit the scene with a flashlight that lit it up like daylight. The new arrival turned toward me and I couldn't believe what I was looking at. He was the guy from the picture in my pocket."

Nichols still said nothing, just gawked at me.

"The guy we'd tortured had been telling the truth all along. We had the wrong guy. We had the twin brother, a brother no one had bothered to mention to us. I screwed up, tortured and killed an innocent man. And that is the one that's haunted me forever."

CHAPTER 25

24-HOUR DINER
LAS VEGAS

THE DRINKING WAS DONE. My cathartic, if shocking, revelations had come to a close. Nichols looked about normal—well, as normal as anyone looks during breakfast at the end of an all-nighter. Thanks to my mistake of looking in a mirror in the bathroom, I knew I looked the same. We drank coffee while we waited for our order to arrive.

"You know what?" Nichols said.

"What?"

"You still never told me what happened with your marriage. Why'd you break up?"

"Lots of reasons, but looking back? When we married, I was a brash, young asshole, way too full of myself. I went and did what I did for my country, and became a screwed-up asshole, during my time over there, and especially the few years after. I was lost, distant to my wife, not there even when I was."

"You guys get along?"

I nodded. "We have a daughter, she's fourteen. We have to get along."

"What're their names?"

"Wife, Abby. Daughter, Allison."

"Abby and Ally, the A-team," Nichols said.

"Yup."

"Where do they live?"

"Here, Vegas."

"Really?"

I nodded.

"Seen them since you got here?"

"Yeah."

"I know you miss your daughter. What about the wife? Miss her?"

"Every day," I said.

"Most guys wouldn't admit missing an ex after so long."

I shrugged. "It is what it is. She was—is—the love of my life. Every day since she left? Feels like I'm living some alternate timeline, a future that was never supposed to happen."

Nichols was looking at me with an odd expression.

"What?" I said.

"I wouldn't have picked you as the sentimental type, is all. Not in a thousand years."

"Sentimental is not a word I'd use to describe myself, Jimbo."

He laughed. "Okay, I'm sure lots of non-sentimental types are sitting around pining for their ex-wives after five years. My bad."

"Smart-ass," I said.

"Just speaking truth, Sam."

"Smart-ass."

The waitress showed up with a wonderful tray full of fried pork and eggs and potatoes and grits and biscuits, and distributed it among us. We had enough grease before us to float a boat. Nichols bit into a biscuit and said through a full mouth, "Got a picture of your daughter?"

I pulled my phone from my pocket, touched and swiped for a few seconds, and handed it over.

"Man," he said. "She's gonna be beautiful. Very exotic looking."

"Thanks," I said, taking the phone back from him. "We adopted her out of a Russian orphanage when she was a little girl." I looked at the picture before putting the phone away, her blond hair, blue eyes, the dimples beside the glowing smile. I smiled back, but only for a moment. Because it only took a moment for the videos to take over my mind, videos of young girls being brutalized, some of whom looked no older than my own daughter. The smart and safe thing for me to do was to focus on the job my client was paying me for, and try to forget the rest, try to leave alone what I had no legal power to do anything about.

I've never been very good at smart and safe.

CHAPTER 26

SPACE

AFTER A FEW HOURS' SLEEP, I was back in my workroom and in high gear on the SPACE investigation. Just before quitting for the day and going out with Nichols the evening before, I had found on Gamboa's computer what I suspected would turn out to be a major piece of evidence. I was wrong. It wasn't just major. It was huge, and I had barely scratched the surface.

The first part of the find was a simple web page on the deep web, a page that was live and operating. No graphics, just a long list of words that stretched up and down the left edge of the page. Midway down the list was the word SPACE. When I clicked it, my browser took me to another page with another simple list, but this time the list was all numbers. And because I had been buried in SPACE's electronic gaming universe for a couple weeks, I recognized the numbers. They were the network identi-

fiers for the EGMs in SPACE's high stakes gaming area.
These were the machines that had been hacked; I felt sure
of it.

I opened the spreadsheet that had been begrudgingly
provided to me by the weenie in charge of IT, Jerry Rose.
Excuse me: Dr. Jerry Rose. I was right. The list of hacked
machines, which I had highlighted in red on the spreadsheet, was a perfect match for the list of numbers I was
looking at on the deep web. I leaned back in my chair,
stretched, and cracked my knuckles. When I glanced
through the glass wall of the conference room into the
anteroom, I saw that my buddy Nichols had dozed off.
Good for him.

Next, I fired up a couple of apps to document everything I was about to do, everything I was about to see.
The first app recorded both my keystrokes and my screen.
The other one captured all the network traffic, every bit
and byte this virtual recreation of Gamboa's machine
would exchange with any other computer or device. With
both of them active, I moved forward. "392" was the first
number on the page, and by looking at the spreadsheet,
I saw that its full identifier was VIP-S-392. This told me:
a) it was a gaming machine in the VIP area; b) it was a
slot machine; and c) its number on the SPACE network
was 392.

I clicked the 392 link. When the 392 page opened,
I smiled and said, "Hello, sugar." I had not seen a page
like this before, but I instantly knew what it was. It was
a configuration page for that machine. From right here,
I could set the machine's payout rate to anything I wanted. I could change the color scheme of its screen and the
sounds it would make. I had complete control. This was
the smoking gun, and it was on the exquisite Miss Gam-

boa's computer. Time for me to visit Jacob Allen with a great big update.

The normally docile lawyer was as animated as I'd ever seen, pacing back and forth behind his desk. For the third or fourth time, he looked at me and said, "You're sure about this?"

I nodded and said, again, "I'm sure. You saw it."

He stopped pacing and sat in his big chair, then finally asked a new question. "Can we be sure it was Gamboa who was manipulating the machines?"

This time I shook my head. "No. What we know at this point is that her computer could be used to manipulate the machines. I can also tell you that the 'C-Gamboa' user account was logged in when these pages were accessed on the deep web. But can I put her physically at the keyboard? No."

"By the way," he said, "I thought you had locked all the machines down so no one could get to them anymore. But you just got to them with her computer. How?"

"My computer and the computers I'm investigating are set up as trusted on the network, so I can thoroughly explore. You can rest easy, though. Aside from my machines and those you personally cleared for access, no one's getting in. The losses have stopped, right?"

"Yes. I just want to be sure they stay stopped."

"They will," I said. "Now we need to figure out the other angle of this scheme."

He nodded and steepled his fingers beneath his chin. "Who was playing the machines while they were rigged."

"Exactly. I haven't had any dealings yet with the non-IT security people, but—"

Allen dismissed it with a little wave. "The security

chief is Hank Dobo. Good guy, been at this game a long time. I'll call him as soon as we're done here."

"It's not really within my purview, but it might be a good idea to put someone on Gamboa. This was a sophisticated scheme and I doubt she was in it alone."

"We've had someone on her for weeks. Unfortunately, they lost track of her."

"When?" I said.

"Last night."

CHAPTER 27

SIMFEROPOL, CRIMEA, UKRAINE

Christine Gamboa

CHRISTINE WAS EXHAUSTED. When her commercial flight from Vegas landed at La Guardia, a limo had been waiting for Sasha and her. She napped while they rode, and when she awoke, they were at a small airport in Teterboro, New Jersey. They boarded a private jet, flew for what felt like forever, landed for fuel, then flew several more hours before landing again. She looked out the small window as they taxied, and knew she was screwed when she noticed that the fuel trucks and luggage tows were lettered with Cyrillic writing. She was in Russia or Ukraine or some such backward-ass country.

"Are we done flying?" she said.

"Almost," Sasha said. "No more airplane. Now we go on helicopter."

"Will you please tell me where we are now?"

"I will to tell you. We in Simferopol. Is in Crimea. Now we go in my house."

The plane came to a stop and the door opened on a rolling stairway. She followed Maslov down and across the tarmac to a helicopter with its blades already slowly turning. He helped her in, then climbed in beside her. The interior was plush, all gold carpet and blue leather and burled wood, and it smelled brand new. When he closed the door, the noise of the helicopter all but disappeared. He tapped the pilot on the shoulder. After a slight vibration, they lifted off the asphalt, tilted forward a bit, then moved forward and up.

Christine looked out the window at the airport below. Its main building was flat, not really large, a white and blue block that looked mundane, industrial, compared to airports in the United States. She wondered if she'd ever see one of those airports again. "How far to your place, Sasha?"

"Soon," he said, already reaching for a bottle of his hideous pepper vodka that was held onto a small shelf by a gold-colored bungee cord.

He wasn't lying. Within minutes, she felt the helicopter slowing, and looked out the window. Whatever she had expected, this wasn't it. They were descending onto the grounds of a mansion, or maybe castle was a better description. She didn't know what time it was here, but it looked to be late in the day. Soft golden sunlight bathed the expanse below them, beautiful green grass dappled with shadows cast by copses of large trees. At the center of the grounds, the house looked more like a royal palace than a place where normal people lived. Then again, who could call Sasha normal?

Once they were on the ground and out of the aircraft, Sasha led her from the concrete landing pad behind the house through a complex of tennis courts, past the biggest swimming pool she'd ever seen, and finally, inside. After passing through a kitchen that could cook for a state dinner, they went down a long and wide corridor and arrived in a living room. Everything there was opulent, a display of grandiosity that exceeded anything Christine had ever seen in someone's home.

Ten feet into the room, Sasha froze. It was abrupt enough that she literally ran into his back. She stepped back and to the side, so she could see what he was looking at. It was a who instead of a what, an elderly man sitting on one of the sofas with his legs crossed. Another man, much younger, but still in his fifties, stood behind the sofa with his hands folded in front of him. The standing man looked like a bodyguard type, a goon. They were still ten or fifteen feet away, but already she could see that the old man on the sofa had bright, piercing eyes, an unnatural light blue. They could have been beautiful in another face. Not this one.

"Max," Sasha said, before launching into a foreign spiel she couldn't understand.

The old man gestured toward a sofa facing him and said, "Both, please sit. And we will speak English. I want your guest to clearly understand what I have to say."

CHAPTER 28

SPACE

BACK IN MY MAKESHIFT LAB, a.k.a. conference room, a.k.a. conference chamber, I dug into the other links on the list of links I had found on the deep web. I had dubbed the page of links "the portal," so I'd have something short and simple to call it going forward. I sure didn't want to be calling it "the list of links I had found on the deep web" a dozen times in every report I wrote for this investigation. The SPACE links were straightforward enough. They linked to the high-stakes EGMs. The other links were more cryptic.

One was labeled "HCTRA," and when I clicked it, I found myself on a black screen filled with ever-changing green numbers. No words, just numbers. Within the context of my hometown, I knew that HCTRA stood for Harris County Toll Road Association. It was the government agency that administered the various toll roads in Houston and the surrounding area. At first, it was hard to fathom that outfit as a hack target. The more I thought about it, though, the more sense it made as a perfect target. The money involved was huge. I Googled up the agency's latest financial report and saw that the toll revenues for the most recent year had been almost six hundred million dollars. That's a number worthy of any hacker's attention.

Even better, that money is taken in a dollar or two at a time, which means hundreds of millions of transactions are involved. You would only need to skim a tiny portion of those transactions, transactions watched over by mainly low-level government employees. Within minutes, I knew exactly how I'd pull off such an operation: EZ TAG.

Forget the paper currency and coins people paid manually at the toll booths. The real money was in the flood of cars with the RFID tags on their windshields that auto-charged their accounts as they flew though the stations without ever slowing down. I went back to the black screen of shifting numbers and started trying to figure out the scheme. I stared until my eyes watered, then set up an app to record the stream of numbers. My plan was to let it collect the numbers overnight, then crunch them the next day and find the trick. But I couldn't. An old school screen of numbers that looked like it was from the eighties was irresistible to a geek like me. It took about an hour. Then I saw it. It was simple. It was brilliant. And someone was stealing an unfathomable amount of money with it.

CHAPTER 29

CRIMEA, UKRAINE

Max Sultanovich

MAX UNCROSSED HIS LEGS and leaned forward, elbows on knees. He stared at Maslov for a moment, then turned his eyes on the woman. It excused nothing, but he understood as soon as he saw her, exactly how it was that his lummox of a son had gotten distracted from following the Crimean. Perhaps he should buy her from Maslov. A diplomatic approach, as it were. But, no. If he wanted the bitch, he would take her. That would be that, and Maslov could go fuck himself.

"I have flown around the world and back," Max said, eyes locked on the woman's. "I am old, and I am tired. I have enough to worry about without you making trouble in my life. If you do not—"

Maslov interrupted, "Max, she—"

Sultanovich shot one look at Maslov, and the fat bastard closed his mouth.

Max continued, eyes back on the woman. "If you do not understand me, girl, if you cause me one more minute of trouble, I will have you put in a gulag with a thousand men who have not seen a woman in years. You will not be so pretty a cunt when you are fucked a hundred times a day."

He watched her eyes go wide and liquid, and fought the urge to smile as tears rolled down her face. She looked to Maslov, as if that tub of fat would or even could help her; the Crimean bastard did not even turn his head to her. Max felt his cock stiffen in his trousers, stiffen like it had not done in years. He felt the whirling lightness in his gut, in his mind. Oh, how he wanted to take her right there while Maslov watched. Perhaps later.

"So tell me, girl, how is my English? Am I communicating clearly for you?"

She wiped at her face, nodded.

"Good," Max said. "Now tell me what you know. Tell it all to me right now."

And she did, for the most part.

CHAPTER 30

MEMPHIS, TENNESSEE

Mikail Sultanovich

HE HAD TO MAKE A PLAN, and soon. After dragging the dead men out of the lodge and into the woods, he had relieved the lodge's safe of its cash. It had a pathetic $12,000 in it, and that wouldn't last long. He had already gone through half of that since going to Memphis to avoid his father. There was no doubt that the old bastard would come for him. It would be better to face the fucker and do away with him, but Mikail wasn't quite ready. It was reasonable to clear the head, to think and prepare for such a thing as killing one's father, right? He could've gotten a cheaper hotel room and laid low, but he had needed to clear his head. He did that by buying a couple grand worth of coke, picking up a pair of whores, and retiring to The Peabody. He thought they might ask him to leave when he and Tiffany and Angel started quacking at the ducks while they made their famous march, but five crisp hundreds had taken care of that.

Now that his dick of a father had not shown back up at the lodge for twenty-four hours, he felt pretty good about going back there, but that was not a long-term plan. The old man would eventually return or, more likely, a small army of his goons would. And they would keep coming until they got him, because the word quit just was not in the old bastard's vocabulary. Maybe it was time for a different kind of thinking. He told the whores to go, stuffed his few things into a plastic laundry bag from the closet in his room, and left The Peabody.

Forty-five minutes later, he drove slowly up to the lodge. He had never understood why they even had this place. If it were up to him, he'd put all these bitches on the streets in Vegas and L.A. and New York as soon as they got them. But his decrepit old father insisted on bringing them here to the backwoods until—how did he put it?—they were "properly broken of spirit and ready to be compliant earners." Dumb shit.

After sitting in his car and watching for five minutes and seeing nothing, he got out and went inside. As soon as he closed the door, he heard beating and banging and shouting coming from many of the rooms. He stomped into the hallway and screamed, "Shut up!"

Some of the bitches did, but some did not. They started shouting about food. Okay, fair enough. He had not thought about food for them since killing all the attendants a day and a half ago. Apparently, his father had missed this issue as well. Pretty funny, really.

"Okay, okay, I will get you food if you will hush your mouths!" The noise stopped. He would find them food, but first things must come first. He pulled the plastic bag from his pocket and looked at his remaining coke. Running low. He opened the bag, held it over his nose and sucked in a good hit, then put it back in his pocket. Not as efficient as running a line, but hey, he was in a hurry.

In the kitchen, he found a lot of food, but it was the kind of food that had to be cooked. He was not cooking shit. He stepped back into the hallway and said, "Who knows how to cook?"

One reply, about halfway down the hall on the right: "I can cook."

He walked to the door, unlocked it, and motioned for the girl to come out. She was maybe eighteen, a brunette with brown eyes, maybe a Mexican, he thought. Like all of them, she was dressed in a blue jumpsuit. He took her to the kitchen, spread his hands to the room, and said, "Cook."

While she got busy in the kitchen, Mikail sat on a stool and watched. The coke felt good, very good. And her ass looked good in the jumpsuit. He watched her, watched that ass, as she moved back and forth, gathering things from the pantry, from the refrigerator. Hit the bag of coke again. Watched it some more. After five minutes, he said, "Take off the clothes."

The girl froze, her back to him. He said it again: "Take. Off. The. Clothes. Bitch."

She reached to her front and he heard the satisfying sound of the zipper as she pulled it down. His coke-jacked senses were running a thousand miles an hour now. He saw everything, heard everything, felt everything. Heard the rustle of the fabric as she pulled the jumpsuit apart and wiggled it off her shoulders. Heard the wonderful, soft friction of fabric on skin as she pulled it down around her knees and stepped out of it.

If her ass was nice in the jumpsuit, it was perfection bare. "Turn around," he said.

The girl turned, and he took in the view. Everything about her was perfect. The face. The little tits with their dime-sized nipples. The patch of dark hair between her legs. He stood, unsnapped his jeans, pulled the zipper down, and let the pants fall to his ankles. He looked her in the eye for several seconds, liked the fear he saw there. He pulled his briefs down, felt his manhood spring free.

"Suck my cock," he said, and sat back onto the stool, leaning backward with his elbows on the counter behind him.

She walked toward him, the steps of her bare feet making the old floorboards creak ever so gently. His heartbeat raced—thump, thump, thump—and his member throbbed in anticipation. This was living, making a beautiful young bitch do what he wanted and what she did not. When she reached him, she bent over without a sound and took him in her mouth. Mikail closed his eyes and leaned his head back. Seconds later, he heard a small sound, one that should have been instantly familiar, but in the ecstasy of the moment, he could not identify it.

Then the pain exploded in his crotch, and in a microsecond, he knew what the sound had been. She had reached behind him and pulled a knife from a wood block. He shrieked and looked down. The girl looked up at him, her face feral, teeth bared. He looked past her face and gasped at what he saw. Her hand still gripped the handle of the knife. She had driven it up into him, under his balls, through the muscles there, and into his insides. Though his balls hid the full view, he could see enough to tell it was stuck in him as far as it would go. While he watched, she grunted and twisted the knife a quarter-turn, then pulled it slowly out. He was now one with the pain. He was pain and pain was him. And smell. He smelled piss and blood draining from him.

She kicked the stool out from under him and he fell, his tailbone cracking as he hit the wooden floor. But a tailbone was nothing, a bite of a bug by comparison. And then, as if by magic, the pain seemed to fade. He felt her doing something else to him but it was like a dream. The bitch let out a roar and held up her hand as if she had just been declared the victor in a great battle. Her hand was bloody and there was something in it. It looked like... a dick. How strange. She lowered her hand and leaned down over him, again doing something to him that he couldn't really discern because now everything was fading. But he did know that he was choking on something, something in his throat. And for just a moment, he knew. After all the times people had tried and failed to kill him, this little girl with the dime-sized nipples had succeeded, and he was going to choke to death, on his own dick. He thought that was pretty funny in a way. And then he thought no more.

CHAPTER 31

SPACE

FINDING THE HACK OF HOUSTON'S TOLL ROAD SYSTEM had expanded my investigative mind on this case in a big way. This wasn't just about hacking a casino. This was an organized operation, massive in scale. By this point, there was little doubt in my mind that when it was all uncovered, this thing would dwarf any nefarious hacking operation that had come before. Well, at least operations outside the NSA. Who knows what all that bunch had pulled off, and they fell squarely into the nefarious column as far as I was concerned.

Houston was one of many. The portal led to connections inside toll road systems all over the country. In each one, the hackers had basically installed taps between the automated car-counting systems, and the database that stored and processed the money transfer from each driver's account into the account of whatever government agency administered the toll roads. These taps siphoned off a tiny percentage of those transfers, but because of the amount of money involved, those siphons were pulling off a staggering amount of funds. I spent a little time trying to figure out where the money was going, but that was going to be a lengthy process because every dollar was riding a pipeline into the deep web, where it was converted to Bitcoin. That would have to wait for later, and most likely for someone other than me to solve. If my client hadn't wanted to get the Las Vegas Police Department involved, they would really freak when all this had to be turned over to an array of federal agencies.

Oh, toll roads weren't the only targets involving government agencies. These guys were running similar hacks on "smart" utility meters, siphoning pennies here and there off payments of water bills, electric bills, gas bills, you name it, but always in systems run by some form of local or state government. Towns or cities that ran their own utilities. Never private electric or gas or water providers. The more I dug, the more incredible it became. On the other hand, the more I thought about it, the more sense it made. Why go after hard targets like banks, or Amazon.com, or other major corporations? Go soft. Smaller government agencies were exactly where you'd find systems without the protections put in place by the Amazons of the world, outfits with huge resources and not beholden to the lowest bidder.

The one outlier in all this? SPACE. Exactly the kind of hard target they appeared to avoid with the rest of their operation. Dr. Jerry Rose may be a dweeb, but for the most part casinos hired some of the top minds available in security, both the electronic and brick-and-mortar flavors. So why go after them? It was a mystery, one that didn't fit. I hate things that don't fit.

I started one of my periodic scans through my email to be sure nothing important had come in, and stopped cold when I saw a subject line that read CONFIDENTIAL AND URGENT: FEDERAL BUREAU OF INVESTIGATION. I opened the email and saw that it was from Courtney Meyer, the FBI agent who had called a few days earlier.

Dear Mr. Flatt,

I would like to apologize for my tone during our earlier conversation. I need your assistance, and my behavior was not conducive to a good working relationship. I hope you will reconsider your position. The matter is of utmost importance.

Sincerely,
Courtney A. Meyer, SA

Given the brevity, I wondered if Ms. Meyer hadn't been coerced into sending that one. She'd been much more verbose while spewing venom and threats, and I suspected that was the real Special Agent Meyer. I typed and sent a quick response thanking her for the email and explaining that, regrettably, I still couldn't cooperate.

I also spent a fair amount of time pondering her request, wondering exactly what she was looking for. Federal involvement made a lot more sense since I'd found the hacking operation, but there was no way to know if she was looking for what I'd found, looking for something altogether different, or fishing in the blind for something—anything—on a suspect she'd been unable to pin down.

One thing was sure: Hearing from her again made me uncomfortable. She was an unknown factor, a wild card who wanted something and thought she was entitled to it, whether I could give it or not. Feebs in that situation have enough power to create trouble. I'd have to think some more on how to handle the *oh-so-Special* Agent Meyer.

CHAPTER 32

CRIMEA, UKRAINE

Sasha Maslov

MAX WAS WAVING AROUND A PIECE OF PAPER as if Sasha could know what was on it. "Why has the income from the casino machines stopped?" He shoved the paper at Sasha.

Sasha took the paper and looked it over. It was a print-out of the computer operation's harvest for the past week. The harvest from SPACE had dropped to zero. "I've been busy, Max. I don't know. Do you need me to investigate?"

"No, I will pursue this," Max said, launching a stream of spittle halfway across the room. "I will handle this."

Sasha nodded, then waited while Sultanovich switched topics. He threatened, humiliated, and ridiculed Christine. In Sasha's view, Maxim Sultanovich was more animal than man. He had known him more than thirty years. In Sasha's line of work, he had seen a lot of cruelty from a lot of sadistic men (and a few women, too), but none like Max. He was a monster, plain and simple, and Sasha had long regretted the day he agreed to partner with him on occasional projects, no matter how much money he made. He wanted to grab the scrawny husk of a man and choke him until he stopped twitching. Not today, however. And not here, not in his home. He would wait, but in the past minutes he had made the decision that enough was enough.

Max finally stopped talking, put his palms on his knees, and pushed himself to his feet. He walked across the room and toward the entrance foyer, his goons tethered to his old carcass like flies hovering over a pile of shit. Sasha did not follow and did not say goodbye. The cordiality and manners would have been wasted. Just before Max reached the door, he turned and motioned for Sasha to come. Sasha went, vowing that his time of being a dog on Max's leash was almost at an end.

When he reached him, Max leaned toward him and in a soft rasp said, *"Vbyty yiyi,"* then stepped through the door one of the goons had opened for him. *Kill her.*

CHAPTER 33

SPACE

IT WAS NEARING 8 P.M. AND I HAD COVERED an awful lot of ground that day, and I did it on little sleep following an all-nighter. My body ached and my mind hurt. I shut down and secured my work, then jumped into my email for a quick check before I headed to my room. I answered the messages that needed it, deleted the junk, and was about to close the lid on the laptop when I noticed a news headline that read NINE WOMEN ESCAPE CAPTIV-ITY NEAR TUNICA CASINOS. I clicked into the message.

> TUNICA, MS - 7:25 PM - In a sensational case sure to attract widespread attention, Tunica County Sheriff, Art Goodman, reports that nine women were rescued today following their escape from captivity in a hunting lodge near Casino Center.

According to Goodman, the identities of the women, who range in age from 16 to 29, are known but being withheld at this time. Sources close to the investigation have said that several of the women are not American, speak little or no English, and appear to have accents consistent with Eastern Europe. It is also believed that at least one of the women is an undocumented Hispanic immigrant.

"The females report that they were held captive in a lodge near the Mississippi River, some for as little as two weeks, and some for as long as two months," Goodman said during a hastily arranged press conference at the Tunica County Courthouse late this afternoon. "We have officers on the scene and I can confirm that early observations seem to support the narrative given to us by the females. I can also confirm multiple fatalities at the scene, presumably of the captors, although we cannot confirm that as of yet. Our investigation is ongoing and will be handled with utmost professionalism."

CHAPTER 34

SPACE

I WOKE UP THE NEXT MORNING with my daughter on my mind. Glanced at the bedside clock: 7:42 a.m. After brushing my teeth and readying myself for the day, I prepped and powered up the little coffeemaker, then grabbed my phone and dialed her number.

"Hello," she said, her sleepy voice music to my ears.

"Hey, baby."

"Daaaaaddy, what time is it?"

"Almost eight, shouldn't you be getting ready for school?"

The coffeemaker gurgled and gasped its aroma into the room while I waited for her to respond. "Ally?" I said.

More awake now: "Dad, it's Saturday."

Crap. I sometimes forget other people don't work, or go to school or whatever, seven days a week like I do when I'm on a case. "Wow, sorry. My days run together when I'm on a case."

I heard a long, exasperated sigh, the kind only teen-age girls can do. "S'okay. What's up?"

"Just wanted to talk to you a minute. You haven't answered my voicemails or texts over the past few days. We okay?"

"Why wouldn't we be?"

"I don't know. You usually answer me, so I wanted to be sure."

"Just busy. I'm in this new school and they're giving us a stupid amount of work to do."

Her new school was a magnet school for gifted math and science students, and I'm sure she wasn't exaggerating about the workload. "How you like it?"

"Fine, lots of nerds."

"Like you?" I said.

"Daddy!"

I laughed. "Hey, just calling it like it is, baby girl. Be happy, nerds make all the money and end up running the world today, especially beautiful ones like you."

"I give that recovery a six," she said.

"Six? At least an eight! Three separate positives."

"No way. You called me a nerd. Seven, tops."

"I can live with that."

"Hey, Daddy?"

"Yup."

"Did you talk to Mom yet? About me getting to see SPACE for real?"

"Not yet, but I will as soon as I wrap up this case. And hey, let's get together again in the next day or two, okay? We'll find something fun that has nothing to do with casinos."

"Sure. When will you finish the case?"

"Not sure, no more than a few weeks."

Another teenage-girl sigh. "O-kay. Listen, I really gotta go to the bathroom."

"Okay, sweetie. You go. I'll talk to you later."

"Love you!"

"I love you too," I said, and ended the call.

Living outdoors most of the time, with a horse and without a car, presents some logistical challenges. Thankfully, I have Charleen "Charlie" Papa to handle these things. She has a little company—little, as in it's just her—that provides "personal concierge" services, helping out folks who don't have the time or means or desire to take care of life's pesky details but who do have the money to hire her. In my case, she serves as quasi-accountant, errand runner, and some other things. I pay her well because I trust her. I dialed her up.

"Velvet Glove," she said when she answered.

"Is this my favorite paid flunky?" I said.

"I'm your girl, handsome. Anything for a buck." She laughed. I laughed. Then she got down to business. "What can I do for you today, Sam?"

"You near a computer?"

"You know it."

"Pull up my accounts."

I listened to her click and type for fifteen seconds or so.

"Done," she said.

"What's the balance in the main business checking account?"

"Let's see, Sammy boy, looks like…a hundred and twenty-four thousand and change."

"Can you get me two bars and put them away?"

"You got it. Anything else?"

"Yeah, can you go to the stables and check on Johnny?"

"Now that's something I'd love to do."

"You rock, Charlie," I said. "Later."

"Damn right I do. See you."

I hung up and touched into the Kitco app I use to track the price of precious metals. I don't trust our currency these days, paper that's backed by nothing, and worse, paper that our government keeps printing with abandon. I also don't like having all my assets tied up in bank accounts that may be vulnerable to the shenanigans of a troublesome FBI agent with her panties in a bunch. If that sounds paranoid, chances are you haven't dealt much with today's federal government.

So I keep most of my money in gold and silver. The two kilobars would set me back about $84,000, leaving me plenty of cash on hand if I had a quick need. Charlie would make the necessary calls and transfers, then take physical possession of the bars and stash them in a safe deposit box for me. Like I said, I trust her. A lot.

Business handled, I left the room and headed for my forensication chamber, ready to chase bits and bytes and the bad guys behind them. The day was just starting and I had already talked to my daughter and arranged for a couple more shiny ingots. This was going to be a good day.

CHAPTER 35

CRIMEA, UKRAINE

Christine Gamboa

CHRISTINE STRETCHED, OPENED HER EYES, and looked at the clock on the nightstand. Thankfully, numbers were the same here. It was almost 3 p.m. She couldn't believe she had slept that long, even though she had been exhausted from the long flight. Even more surprising was the fact that Sasha hadn't expected her to sleep with him. He had shown her where everything was, brought her upstairs to this room, said good-night, and left. She had undressed, gotten into bed, and fallen asleep instantly, not taking time to notice anything about the room.

The bedroom was huge and lavish, like something out of a fairy tale. She had stayed in five-star hotels before, but none compared to this. Her bed, far larger than king size, was covered with a silky blue canopy with metallic gold stripes woven in. Sasha was obviously big on the Ukrainian national colors of blue and gold. She stepped out of the bed and her foot sank into carpet that seemed to caress her feet as she walked to the bathroom. It was an expanse of white marble, lit by gentle indirect lighting hidden in a valance at the top of the walls. On the counter she found a variety of toiletries, everything she could possibly need, and more.

She showered and put on a fresh T-shirt and pair of jeans from the tiny bag she had brought along for her failed escape. No makeup. Nothing or no one here warranted the trouble. When she descended the stairs, she found Sasha in the living room, pacing back and forth with a phone stuck to his ear. She went to the kitchen and put together a plate of fruit, then returned to the living room and curled up on a sofa with her food. After about five minutes, Sasha finished his call and sat down beside her. His face was heavy, his eyes bloodshot.

"You okay?" she said.

"Chrissy," he said, "we must to leave here. We must to leave here now."

She stopped eating. "Why? I thought I'd be safe here."

"You think I was expecting to come home to find Maxim Sultanovich? In Sasha's house? No!"

Now she was worried, because she saw something in his big face she would not have thought possible twenty-four hours earlier: He was scared. "What's going on, Sasha?"

"Maxim is telling me I must to kill you."

Tears flooded her eyes and the few bites of fruit threatened to come back up. She had originally thought Sasha meant to kill her. Then she had started to think she was wrong, starting to believe he really did want to help her, starting to relax, the terror of her situation beginning to wane a bit. Now it all came back in a rush.

"Do not to cry, Chrissy. I will not to kill you. Sasha will not let the old man to kill you. We must to leave. We must to leave now."

CHAPTER 36

SPACE

BY NOON, I HAD IDENTIFIED MOST of the hack targets on the portal. This wasn't a multimillion dollar operation. This was a billion-dollar operation. These people, whoever they were, had systematically identified, cracked, and tapped a staggering array of electronic cash sources. Toll roads. Public utilities. Parking facilities. If there was an enterprise out there built on huge numbers of transactions, an enterprise likely to have vulnerabilities, they had targeted it. Plus SPACE, which was still a solitary outlier. There were a few links that led to things I couldn't yet identify, but I would. For now, it was time to write an update report for Jacob Allen.

I had pondered how to handle the issue of notifying law enforcement. My lawyer brother had called after he researched it, and said he felt confident that I was under no legal obligation to go to law enforcement myself. His suggestion was to notify my client, in writing, of what I'd found, along with a clear suggestion that the authorities should be notified. And that was how I would handle it. I didn't want an unnecessary battle on my hands with my client. More importantly to me, I wanted them to think I had put the rape videos behind me. Let them think that. Let LVPD think that, too. But it wasn't true.

Those videos would not leave me alone. I couldn't get past the idea that these girls were alone, terrified, savaged. What if my own daughter were in a situation like that? The videos haunted my dreams. They haunted my days, hanging back in the black recesses of my soul, niggling at me like a single fly in a large house. Always there. Even when they weren't front and center, they were there, in the blackness, calling me to join them in the shadows.

CHAPTER 37

CRIMEA, UKRAINE

Sasha Maslov

IT HAD TAKEN HOURS FOR HIS PEOPLE to get it, but after trying a hundred times to call Max's son Mikail, Sasha finally had a phone number for Benjamin Zuyev. He was not ideal, but he was all Sasha had if Mikail was missing. According to Sasha's contacts, Zuyev was a wily old Muscovite who had become Max's chief lieutenant in the United States by way of attrition when Mikail killed Dmitry. The contacts all seemed to agree that Zuyev's reputation was one of competence. Sasha dialed the number, then stuck the phone back in its cradle. The sound of the ringing came through the car's speakers. When the call was answered, he said, "Benjamin?"

"Who is this?"

"Benjamin, is Sasha Maslov. Please to speak in English so my companion can to understand."

"I am speaking in English. What you want, Maslov?"

"Benjamin. I believe we can to help each other."

"How?"

"We can to go to FBI, make deal."

Zuyev laughed, a long and guttural affair, before saying, "Have you lost your Ukrainian mind, Maslov? Why would I do that?"

"To live."

"What the hell are you talking about? You really are insane, no?"

"Max ordered Mikail to kill Dmitry," Sasha said, although it was highly unlikely. Max would come closer to killing his own son before Dmitry. "And Benjamin? He has also to ordered him to kill *you*."

Now there was a long pause, then: "I do not believe this."

"Is true, Benjamin."

"Why? Why would Max want me dead?"

"FBI knows about operation. Preparing to arrest everyone. Max wants no one alive to talk, but if we make deal with them, we live and not much time in the prison."

An even longer pause. Sasha looked over at Chrissy and winked again.

"And why you want to help me?" Zuyev said.

"I want to live, and I want my friend to live. Max has to ordered us killed, also. With what I know, and what you know, and what my friend knows, we can to make very good deal. We can to blame Max for everything. He will go to prison forever. We make deal, not much prison."

"I don't believe that is possible."

"You listen to my friend Christine. She is smart, like genius. Okay?"

"I am listening."

CHAPTER 38

SPACE

LIKE EVERYONE ELSE, I'VE SEEN PLENTY of casino security operations on TV and movie screens. Huge walls of monitors in a dark room with an army of eagle-eyed experts watching. Hollywood got it wrong. The security operations center of the largest casino the world had ever known, was maybe half the size of a typical convenience store. Maybe. There were monitors, of course, but not a sea of them. And there were watchers, but here's where you're gonna be tempted not to believe me. I counted seven people, each seated at a computer desk with two monitors. At least there was a wall with one giant screen on it.

Shortly after I arrived, a sturdy man of about fifty with a definite military bearing walked up with his hand extended. "Mr. Flatt, Hank Dobo."

I shook his hand. Hank had a great handshake, strong, just long enough. "Good to meet you. Please call me Sam."

"You got it, Sam." He gestured for me to follow him and said, "Come on, let me show you my little kingdom." He walked through the door from which he had appeared. I followed and he talked as he went. "Figure it'll be easier for me to help you once you understand what we do and how we do it. Okay with you?"

"You bet. Looks fascinating," I said.

"Won't argue with you on that, Sam."

We stepped into what was obviously a server room, and it put Jerry Rose's (impressive) IT fiefdom to shame. This room was huge, and most of it was occupied by a glassed-in area with enough racks of servers and equipment to run a country. Dobo walked up to a glass panel that looked just like all the rest and pressed his splayed hand against it. The entire panel flashed green and slid to the side. A blast of cold air hit us and we stepped inside.

"Now I'm impressed," I said, following him around to the back of the racks.

He pointed at the line of racks, where thousands of cables glowed green as they snaked out of the floor, up the racks, and plugged into the backs of the servers. "Everything feeds in here, all the cameras. Self-monitoring. If there's a problem anywhere—" He walked about twenty feet down the line and pointed at a single cable, glowing red instead of green. "We can pinpoint it at a glance."

"How many cameras are there?"

"Seven thousand and change. All high-def, ten-eighty minimum. About a quarter are four-K." I'm sure I looked bewildered, because Dobo said, "Question?"

"Yeah. I counted seven guys out there watching video. How are they keeping up with a thousand cameras a man?"

He smiled. "We'll get to that." And Hank Dobo kept

walking and talking, and I kept following and listening as he walked me through the techno-flow of his remarkable system. When we arrived back in the operations center, he said, "Here's where the technology really shows off."

"Obviously," I said.

"This is the same basic setup you'll see in just about every up-to-date casino in town. Each technician is responsible for a patrol zone, or group of cameras. Maybe five hundred of the cameras are on the general grounds, meaning they're not in the casino. Typical surveillance. The rest are divided up among the various gaming areas. Our guys watch a rotating sample of cameras, as opposed to sitting and staring at a camera waiting for something to happen."

"Don't you run the risk of missing cheats and such, watching so few of the cameras?" I said.

"We're not watching few. We're watching all of them, just not with human eyeballs. Our algorithms have been fed data on every scheme imaginable, data gathered over decades."

"Like what?"

He tapped one of the technicians on the shoulder and said, "Steve, put an algo-feed on the big screen." Steve tapped a few keys and the view on the monitor wall switched to a high-res view looking straight down onto the playing surface of a blackjack table. Overlaid green circles and squares flitted in and out of existence on the image; they reminded me a lot of the targeting display on modern military aircraft. It's like they were "locking on" to stacks of chips, cards, players' hands, the dealer's hands, all in rapid succession.

Hank Dobo said, "Got anything showing activity?"

Steve scanned one of his monitors. "B-J one-fifty-nine." He hit a few keys and the view changed to a different table. This time not all the targets were green. One stack of chips was ringed by a blinking red circle.

"Wait for it," Dobo said.

The player at that spot placed a bet and the cards came out. He looked at his cards, and then with a lightning move of one of his hands, reached out and pulled most of the chips he had bet back out of the betting circle.

"I'll be damned," I said. "The software knows the game, knows what movements should and shouldn't happen at the various stages of the game."

"Bingo. All the algos are some variation of that, watching for something that's not right. When it finds it and watches enough to verify suspicious activity, it will alert the tech who's watching that zone." No sooner had he said that than one of the computers sounded a little bell, and that same camera view appeared on the monitor of one of the technicians.

"Amazing," I said, and shook my head. "Did the computers or the techs pick up on anything weird for the EGMs and dates I sent you?"

"Not a thing," he said. "I read your report and I've been going through those recordings for the past several nights. Nothing out of the ordinary, but I did compile a list of the players."

"Names?" I said. "How?"

"Well, some names. Pictures of all of them, and our facial recognition database was able to put names with about eighty percent of them. You wanna see the list?"

I nodded, then followed him into a small but well-appointed office. He closed the door, picked up a file folder from his desk. As he handed it to me, he said, "Here you go, Flatbread."

I've developed some pretty good acting chops through the years, because as covert as we were in our missions, we were still around the military all the time. Several times through the years, I've run into someone who said, "Hey, didn't we serve together?" or something like that. It's easy enough to blow that off. But no one, and I mean no one has ever called me "Flatbread" other than other BAM-team members, and that's been a long time. So when Hank Dobo said it, no amount of acting could mask the way time froze for several seconds.

There was no point in acting. I said, "When and where?"

"Remember a mission in a cave, guy with a computer?"

"A lot of them."

"You lost your partner."

I nodded slowly. Remembered exactly which mission now.

"Saw you guys on base beforehand. Your partner was giving you shit in the mess hall about your horse."

I nodded again. "Ditto. Giving me shit about my horse was his favorite thing to do."

Dobo smiled. "I was in one of the F-18s at the end of that thing. Small world, huh?"

I looked him in the eye and said, "Tiny."

CHAPTER 39

**FEDERAL BUREAU OF INVESTIGATION
MANHATTAN FIELD OFFICE
NEW YORK CITY**

Special Agent Courtney Meyer

COURTNEY MEYER WAS AT HER WIT'S END. After eighteen months investigating the Eastern Europe crime family headed up by Maxim Sultanovich, she had exactly nothing. Not just nothing on Sultanovich himself. Nothing on anyone of value. Sure, she could haul in a gaggle of street thugs and threaten, scream, and shout. But it would accomplish nothing. There wasn't a Ukrainian or Russian soldier on the street who wouldn't prefer federal prison over the consequences of betrayal.

Her big RICO case a few years ago had gotten her on the map, given her some juice. But a year and a half of nothing spent a lot of juice. Every investigative trail she followed had eventually hit a dead end. Not because she was wrong. She wasn't. It was the same old story: the bigger the fish, the more money and clout they had, the harder they were to land. People like Sultanovich insulated themselves. They didn't tell underlings, "Hey, go shoot this guy in the head." They said it with a look, a nod. Then those people looked and nodded at someone else. By the time you drilled down to someone dumb enough to open their mouths, they were low-level thugs who mattered little, whose absence from the operation would change nothing. It was an old story in the investigation of organized crime, and it was made even tougher when the bad guys were on the other side of the planet.

Her SAIC, Tom Belt, had supported her all the way, but that too would play out. Belt hadn't made it to the top of such a cherry office by backing losing causes. She needed a break, had to have it.

Meyer leaned back in her chair, hands clasped behind her head. The damn tilt lock on the chair gave way and she tilted so far back she almost fell over.

"Damn it!" she said out loud as she righted herself, then reached beneath the seat of the chair and wiggled the lock back into place. While looking down, she saw that her butt almost filled the width of the chair. *Focus: One problem at a time. Solve the case, then you can address your lard ass.*

The key was Vegas. She knew it, felt it in every bone of her body. Too many Ukes and Russkies in and out of there over the past couple years. And there was the hard link between Sultanovich himself and that casino, SPACE. Yes, she needed Vegas. She needed to know how the casino figured into the equation. Special Agent Courtney Meyer needed Samuel Flatt to cooperate. Her initial, direct approach hadn't worked. Nor had the sappy apology Belt had suggested she send. No surprise there. Time for a new strategy. The chair creaked as she leaned forward and moved back into a work posture. She pulled a drawer open and extracted the file folder labeled FLATT, SAMUEL.

"Let's get more acquainted, Computer Boy," she said as she opened the folder. "Bound to be something here I can use to convince you to do your patriotic duty."

CHAPTER 40

SPACE

BACK IN MY MAKESHIFT LAB, I studied the contents of the folder Hank Dobo had given me. Looked through the names of the high-value slot players he had given me, didn't recognize any of them. I plugged in a flash drive from the folder and started watching video of the people who had won significant jackpots on any of the hacked slots during the timeframe of interest. All the cameras in the high-stakes areas were 4K resolution, so the quality of the video was remarkable. There were several dozen different people, a mix of men and women. Reaction to their wins varied from ecstatic jumping around, to subtle fist pumps.

What was a Hornet driver doing working in casino security? Most of the guys who fly fighter jets are so eaten up with flying that they don't want to do anything else. And they're so good at it, they can get any job they want in the private sector.

I played the video again. And again. And again. After an hour of this, I had something. I'm not a gambler myself—not anymore—but I have some insight into those who are. Frequent gamblers are addicts, always chasing the high of the next win, and this has to be doubly true with those who play for big dollars. Casinos treat these people like kings and queens because they want them to keep gambling. If you keep gambling, the house eventually wins. It's not luck. It's math. The casinos want them to keep gambling, and they do keep gambling. That's why I kept seeing a lot of the same faces on the videos. But there were several I saw only once. Not impossible, but outside the norm. A few people will make a big score and walk away, but most people who hit a $25,000 or $50,000 jackpot on a machine would keep going. They'd want to do it again. And because they sit and feed these machines absurd amounts of money for days on end, they usually do have several big wins.

After all the watching, I focused on three people. One man and two women. Each of them appeared just once. I cobbled together a quick edit of just those three, and put it playing on a loop. The loop was a little under three minutes. I watched it dozens of times. Memorizing. Absorbing. The way they sat. The way they pushed the buttons. Where they put their feet. How they scratched an itch. How they celebrated their wins. I became one with each of them. Then I composed an email to Hank Dobo the Hornet-Driving Casino Security Chief.

Hank, I need some more footage. I've attached a spreadsheet of the dates, times, and machines.

Please pull every angle you have, and please include five minutes before and after each win event.

Thanks,
Sam

CHAPTER 41

OVER THE ATLANTIC

Christine Gamboa

OVER THE PAST TWENTY-FOUR HOURS, Christine had listened and talked through numerous phone calls between Sasha, Zuyev, and her. Their plan for going to the FBI and cutting a deal was coming together. It was complicated, all the schemes and lies the two men had concocted to shift as much blame off themselves as possible and onto Max and his henchmen. Henchmen other than Zuyev and Sasha, anyway. In addition to the lies themselves, Sasha had been busy creating evidence to substantiate the lies. He apparently had a whole network of people willing to create any kind of document imaginable, willing to testify to anything, willing to do anything. She wished she had never met any of them. She wasn't like them. Sure, she took their money. Who wouldn't? But there was a hell of a difference between getting somebody into a computer network, and doing the kinds of things these men did.

She was exhausted from the mental effort of participating, from walking the line between being forthcoming, and being too forthcoming about what she knew. She wanted to pull the window shade down, recline the jet's comfy leather seat, and crash. Sasha, unfortunately, wouldn't shut up.

"Chrissy, you must not to trust Zuyev. He is bad man."

Gee. She would never have guessed. Thank God she had Sasha, such a good man himself, to educate her. "I know, Sasha. I won't."

"You must to never go alone with him."

"I won't."

"I cannot to protect you if you go alone with him."

"I know."

He nodded his big head and said nothing more. Christine pulled her shade down, pressed the button to recline her seat, and pulled the little blanket up under her chin. The ride was smooth, the jet engines just loud enough to provide perfect white noise for sleeping. As she started to drift, she cycled through the things she knew, things she had to remain constantly cognizant of in order to stay safe. Based on what Sasha had told her, Zuyev was a bad man, a brute, a classic thug in every sense of the word. Max was black-souled evil. And Sasha, while a criminal, was a better man than she had given him credit for. He also had no idea what was really going on. He thought he did, but he did not. Zuyev, and hopefully Max, thought she was likewise ignorant to the truth, thought she believed this whole thing to be about breaking into computers and stealing money.

They were wrong.

CHAPTER 42

SPACE

I SHUT DOWN MY WORK COMPUTERS and stood for a few minutes looking out the window of my workroom. It was late in the day and I loved the way sunlight transformed into a soft golden hue and cast shadows with feathery edges. From this perspective, Vegas was beautiful, with its tall buildings bathed in amber, along with the mountains that ringed the valley. When I was done soaking up the peace, I pulled a flash drive from the computer I'd been working on and dropped it into my pocket. Time to visit Hank Dobo again.

After an elevator ride, I walked to the door labeled SOC—I guess they don't want the uninformed to know when they're walking by the Security Operations Center—and watched the glass-looking door handle turn green when I touched it and my bracelet's credentials were accepted. The techs never looked up as I passed through the room on my way to Dobo's office. I rapped on the frame of the open door and he motioned me in.

"Hey, Flatbread," Dobo said, his hand out.

I shook it and said, "If it's all the same to you, how about sticking with 'Sam' instead?"

He shrugged. "What's up?"

Taking the flash drive from my pocket, I handed it across his desk and sat down. "Can you put that flash drive's content on that monitor?" I pointed to a large panel on a side wall.

When he had the video up and running, he said, "What am I looking for?"

"Let it play. I'll narrate." The video started with a still shot that used a split frame to show the two men and one woman who'd attracted my attention during my watcha-thon. "These three faces only appeared once, which made me curious. So I studied them." The video cut to the first guy, switching between camera angles and showing him from a minute before his jackpot to a minute after his little celebration ended. Then parts of it played again, this time slowed down and annotated to highlight certain movements. After that, the view switched to a different man and the same basic sequence repeated itself.

When the sequence finished playing, Dobo paused the video and looked at me. "Sonofabitch. Same guy."

I nodded. "Unless both men just happen to use their middle finger to scratch their left ear in exactly the same way, yep, same guy. Play the rest of it."

Dobo resumed the video and the same thing played out with four more men. "Crap," he said. "Six times he hit us." He paused it again, stood, paced a bit.

"I call him The Itch. He's the most obvious, but when you watch the rest of the video, you'll see that there are two more 'morphlings,' another man and a woman. They were also sharp enough to never give the cameras a great view of their faces, so I'm not sure your facial recognition system will be much use, unless you want to get a graphics expert to try to use all the different angles and partials to compose a frontal view."

He nodded. "I'll work on that."

"Okay," I said. "I'd like to know if you identify them. Keep me posted?"

Dobo said, "I'll do that."

CHAPTER 43

SPACE

BACK IN MY SUITE, I showered and sat down at the glass desk to check my email once more for the night. While the laptop powered up, I ran my finger along the smooth edge of the glass and tried to spot the tech that made just the edge glow in an ever-morphing range of colors. I was ready to stretch out on the bed and find a movie to watch. Then I saw the email at the top of my inbox with the now-familiar subject of CONFIDENTIAL AND URGENT: FEDERAL BUREAU OF INVESTIGATION. I clicked into the message.

Dear Mr. Flatt,

I wish you had reconsidered, but I have no choice but to accept your decision. Thank you for your reply.

Courtney A. Meyer, SA

PS: As an aside, your name happened to come up in a conversation I had today with a friend who works at ICE. He mentioned that there is some kind of irregularity from several years ago concerning the adoption of your daughter. She was from Russia, right? I was surprised to hear of them revisiting something that far back, especially in the context of Child Protective Services and such. It hardly seems fair. Anyway, I pass this along merely as a courtesy. I'm sure you handled everything properly and it's nothing to worry about. Have a wonderful night.

I read it again, my blood sizzling through my veins and arteries, my heart pounding so hard I could feel the pulse in my neck. That bitch. That low-down, bottom-feeding, ass-sucking bitch. I slammed the lid on the laptop and stood, sending the desk chair wheeling across the marble floor before it bounced off the coffee table. After walking to the big window, I stood looking at the expansive view of Vegas for a good ten minutes, my mind working. My first instinct was to call my ex-wife and tell her about it, but it was late and there was no need to ruin her night, too.

She couldn't do anything about this anyway. This was all between me and a petty bitch in Manhattan. I placed my palms flat against the cool glass and willed my heart to slow, taking long deep breaths. Inhale. Exhale. Inhale. Exhale. Back in control, I forced down the urge to call Meyer and explain to her what a life-changing mistake she had made. Always better to show instead of tell.

CHAPTER 44

SPACE

"THIS IS OUTSTANDING WORK," Jacob Allen said after I brought him up to speed the next morning. "I see why you're expensive. I have to say it concerns me that an outside consultant with no experience in casino security found in a day what our people didn't find in weeks."

"Not sure that's fair to Dobo," I said. "Not my call, though."

"How much?"

"According to the logs, over a three-day period, they hit jackpots of almost a million bucks."

"Against what kind of input?"

"That's where it gets really interesting," I said. "Once I had these narrow timeframes to work with, I was able to get far more granular with my digital inspection of the machines. The nut is that the combined input for all these wins was six thousand and change, but—"

"Jesus, Mary, Joseph, and all the apostles! How is that possible?"

"The moment before they pushed the PLAY button on each and every one of these jackpots, that machine was set to a payout rate of virtually one hundred percent. The software won't allow a rate of a hundred percent, but it will allow ninety-nine and a whole bunch of decimal places. A win was all but certain on every occasion. And the moment the win was registered, the machine dropped back down to its normal rate. The ultimate in rigged games."

He sat, shaking his head several times before looking up. "Where are we on identifying these people?"

"That's in Dobo's hands. I'd like to continue my current track of investigation. This is just what I spotted in a day. There could be more."

"You have carte blanche. Proceed how you see fit."

I nodded, thanked him, and left the room.

I spent the rest of the morning back and forth on the phone between Abby, my ex, and Paul, my attorney brother. Abby was completely freaked. Paul was getting up to speed and looking for the right immigration lawyer. I was settling into a mode of quiet determination.

Ally had to be gotten out of the horrible situation she was in back in Russia all those years ago. She was at danger daily of being molested, or sold, or worse. After a year of Russian bureaucracy and bribes and begging going nowhere, I took her from the orphanage in the middle of the night and disappeared. I did what had to be done, because that's who I am. I don't regret it for a moment. Would do it again a thousand times. But now someone was trying to use a bloated bureaucracy to exploit what had happened, to take advantage of the salvation of a little girl. *My* little girl.

After all the info had been exchanged and everyone was up to speed, it was time for me to get back to work at SPACE. I could have an expensive legal battle ahead.

CHAPTER 45

SPACE

By mid-afternoon, I'd found a couple more players and handed them off to Dobo. My eyes were burning from watching video, so I switched my attention to finding out exactly where the machine adjustments had come from. After studying a lot of data, I had ruled out Gamboa's devices. She was somehow involved in all this, no doubt about that, but she wasn't the one tricking out machines to offer near-guaranteed wins at precisely the right moment.

The adjustments were, however, coming from inside the SPACE network, from the same computer every time, and that computer was likely in the same location every time. I knew this because of numerical signatures that are attached to computers and network locations. It was a start.

The problem? According to every bit of data I had from Rose and his IT underlings, the network location of that computer shouldn't exist on the SPACE network. Their network diagrams showed all the various subnets ("roped-off" smaller networks that combined to make up the larger SPACE data network), complete with the appropriate numerical addresses assigned to the devices inside each subnet. For example, each computer had a unique address, as did each EGM, each network printer, each data device of any kind that was connected to the company's network.

But the computer that made the adjustments, which I had taken to calling the "HCC," for "Hackers' Control Computer," had an address that was nowhere to be found among the diagrams. Its address shouldn't even be possible, because it was part of a subnet that, on paper, didn't exist. Imagine you're standing in front of a house at 123 Coyote Avenue, in Acme, Arizona. You know the house and the address exist, because you're looking at it. Yet when you pull out your smartphone and search for the address on Google Maps, Google tells you the address (HCC) doesn't exist. In fact, it tells you that Coyote Avenue (the subnet that HCC sits on) doesn't exist at all. That's where I was.

"Hey, Jimbo?" I said.

Nichols looked up from his Kindle. "Yes, sir?"

"Who could get me a set of architectural drawings for SPACE, all of it?"

He squinted his eyes for a bit. "Bert Addison. His title is Station Manager. Should be your guy."

"Thanks," I said. "Go back to your book." I pulled up a directory from the SPACE Resource Guide on the company intranet, found Addison, and shot him an email. Looks like Jacob Allen had spread the word well on cooperation, because I had a response back in a couple minutes. He wanted to know what kind of drawings I wanted. I told him to give me everything and I'd sort it out. Within five minutes, I had a big .ZIP file full of drawings. Maybe I should have narrowed my request.

It took a while to figure out what I had, and even longer to learn how to interpret the various symbols and labels, but I got to what I wanted, which turned out to be an elevation multiview that showed a wireframe rendering of the physical structure, overlaid with a network diagram. Actually, there were several of these, one for each major component of the SPACE complex. I strongly suspected what I was looking for would be in the central building that housed the casino and hotel, so I started there.

I moved from my laptop to one of my desktop machines, so I'd have a couple large monitors side by side. On the left, I brought up the master network diagram from IT. On the right, the wireframe architectural drawing. Looking back and forth between the two, a coherent mental image came together for where the various network locations were in the physical world. The IT diagram matched up perfectly with the wireframe, which is to say I still had no idea where the Control Computer or its mystery subnet were. I repeated the process for the shopping complex, the space museum, the entertainment area, and every other structure of the physical world of SPACE. Same result.

Back to the beginning. I pulled the wireframe for the casino-hotel back up and adjusted the view so I could see the entire drawing on my screen. Nothing. Well, almost nothing. This tidbit didn't provide me any information about the location of the Control Computer, but it was a curiosity, and when I encounter oddities of any kind in a difficult investigation, I pay attention. At the very bottom of the casino-hotel structure on the wireframe, which I hadn't paid much attention to during my first study of the wireframe, because the basement had little in the way of data networking, a section of the building was highlighted in bright yellow with an overlay of faint, diagonal red lines. By "bottom," I mean below the basement, which put the area at least a couple stories underground. The highlight depicted a pair of rectangular central areas, surrounded by an array of corridors and smaller rooms. One of the corridors connected to a tunnel that angled up to ground level. Emblazoned in bold black text across the highlighted area was a label that said **UNALLOCATED SPACE.**

CHAPTER 46

SPACE

THE WORD PLAY FOR "UNALLOCATED SPACE" in this particular case could go on for a while. The term has a lot of meaning to digital forensic geeks like me, since it's the name of the electronic trash heap on a hard drive or flash drive or whatever. We often pull our juiciest tidbits from this junkyard of bits and bytes. That was true in this case; it was in unallocated space that I found Gamboa's deep web history. Then there was the obvious SPACE connection. And now here was a mysterious area with the label on a SPACE architectural drawing. I don't believe in omens, but as previously mentioned, I do investigate aberrations.

I shot an email over to Station Manager Bert Addison and asked him what the mystery space was for, and if he happened to have any more detail on it. Specifically, data network information. Less than a minute later, the phone on the conference table rang. I answered it, "Sam Flatt."

"Mr. Flatt, this is Bert Addison." His accent was Southern and strong.

"Call me Sam."

"All right. Listen, I wish I could tell you more about the 'unallocated space,' but I can't."

This was the first pushback I had encountered at SPACE in a while. "Will it help if Jacob Allen calls and okays you to tell me about it?"

"Ummm, no. You misunderstand, Sam. I can't tell you about it, because I don't know anything about it."

"You're in charge of this whole physical complex, and you don't know what something is for?" I said.

"Listen, it's not for lack of trying, believe you me. I pitched several hissy fits over that dadgum yellow void— that's what I call it, the yellow void. In the end, I was told I could shut up about it or be on my way."

"Who told you that?"

"Allen. Listen, they may call him just an in-house lawyer, but he's the biggest boss anybody's ever seen here. If you want to know what's what, he's your huckleberry."

I smiled at the colorful language. "Okay, I appreciate your help, Bert. Holler at you later."

After I hung up the phone, I leaned back in my chair and stretched while little red flags pinged up across my mind. I liked Jacob Allen and he had been nothing but helpful to me, but I also couldn't forget the way he shut me down on getting law enforcement involved in those rape videos. Now I was hearing that perhaps Jacob was more influential than a typical in-house counsel. I'd ask him about the unallocated space, but not now. Later.

Jacob Allen had told me I had *carte blanche,* so I felt empowered to dig on my own. If I asked him about the space and he told me directly to stay away from the issue, I'd have no choice but to comply. I had a better idea. It was a long shot, but sometimes long shots come through.

CHAPTER 47

SPACE

WE FIRST CROSSED PATHS at a digital forensics training conference I attended. This particular affair always brings in a big tech name to deliver the keynote address, and that year the big name was Matt Decker, of Decker Digital fame. Decker had gone through a hellish week when the U.S. power grid went down a year or so before, since the grid was controlled by software his company created. In the span of seven days, he had gone from celebrity geek to scapegoat to national hero, and his speech was one of the more interesting ones I'd heard.

I happened to catch him standing alone for a moment at a meet-and-greet after the talk, and decided to introduce myself. We hit it off and ended up hanging out some for a couple days, and it had been right here in Vegas. He's easily the most brilliant geek I've ever met.

I had also discovered during my investigation that his company won the bid for all the network hardware in the SPACE complex, so if anyone had any helpful tricks, Matt Decker should be the man. I wasn't sure he'd remember me, but it was worth a shot so I emailed him.

> Hey Matt,
>
> Remember me? We met in Vegas after one of your talks, and took a helicopter ride out to the Grand Canyon, checked out Hoover Dam and some other stuff. Anyway, I'm back in the desert working a case and would love to pick your brain on something. Understand if you're too busy. Hope all is well.
>
> Sam Flatt

That evening, I was in my room responding to a long list of personal email that had piled up, when my email notifier dinged. When I checked it, I had a response from Decker.

> Sam! Do I remember? How in hell could I forget getting kicked out of Hoover Dam? Great to hear from you, man. I'm in LA at the moment, so if you can hang on til tomorrow, I'll grab a shuttle flight over there. Where are you?

The caller ID said PAUL FLATT and I answered quickly. "Talk to me, bro."

"It ain't good."

My stomach tightened, did a little flip. "I'm listening."

"I found a great immigration lawyer at one of our offices, had a long talk."

"And?"

"I know why you took her out of Russia without the paperwork, and why you snuck her into the country without a visa already in place. I get it, I—"

"A history lesson is not helpful at this point, Paul. I know why I did it, you know why I did it. What does it mean now? That's all I care about."

"The feds could retroactively void the adoption. We might win in court—it's hard to imagine that we wouldn't win and be able to stop the deportation of a fourteen-year-old who's been here since she was five. But they could legally take her from you and put her with CPS during the fight. You work in the court system just like I do, so no need to tell you how long such a battle could last."

"So that's it? No options, nothing we can do to head it off?"

"I'm sorry, Sam."

"Thanks, bro," I said, and ended the call.

I walked to the window and looked out, wishing I'd never heard of SPACE. Then I returned to the desk, got her phone number from the last email she had sent, and dialed Special Agent Courtney Meyer.

She answered in a cheerful tone that made me want to reach through the phone and strangle her. "Good evening, Mr. Flatt! I didn't expect to be hearing from you."

"Bullshit," I said. "I'll send you updates on my case from a secure, anonymous email. Understand this, Ms. Meyer: If you ever let word get out that I'm doing this, I'll make you wish you'd decided to be a sewage worker instead of an FBI agent, and—"

"Don't you *ever* threaten m—"

"Shut your damn mouth and listen, you despicable bitch. And record this if you like, because I don't give a rat's ass who hears it. If anyone remotely connected with the United States government ever comes near my daughter, in any way, I will hunt your ass down and make you suffer like you can't imagine. Then I. Will. Kill. You."

I touched END CALL and laid the phone on the desk.

CHAPTER 48

KIEV, UKRAINE

Max Sultanovich

MAX SAT ON THE SOFA, reading that day's copy of the *Kyiv Post*. Beside him, his six-year-old granddaughter Tatyana sat coloring a picture of a horse outside a barn. He paused his read and watched her, watched the way she carefully replaced one crayon before choosing another. The meticulous way in which she filled in the colors on the page. Her little face was a picture of concentration. She was the one thing Mikail had ever done right, and of course even that was only by chance, a fluke that what was likely the single good sperm in his body happened to be the one to squirm its way inside the egg. With a kiss to the top of Tatyana's head, he returned to his newspaper.

On the front page, below the fold, a headline read, SON OF PROMINENT KYIV BUSINESSMAN DEAD

IN USA. Inserted in the text of the article was a picture of a younger Mikail. Probably his passport photo. Max's first thought was that some American bastard had killed his boy, for which he would require the life of at least that American bastard in return. Yes, he had given an order for Mikail to be killed, but that was different, a matter of fatherly and business prerogative. After mulling the issue and the appropriate retribution for a minute or two, he decided to read the article before thinking on it further. The more he read, the colder the blood ran in his old veins.

The women in Mississippi had escaped. It was a disaster. And his son was killed and he learned about it from a newspaper six thousand miles away? He picked up his phone and dialed Zuyev, the man he had moved from New York to Las Vegas when Mikail killed Dmitry. No answer. Something was very wrong. Zuyev would never not answer his call.

He scrolled through his contacts and dialed another number. When the call was answered, he said, "I must fly to America right now."

CHAPTER 49

SPACE

IN MY ROOM THE NEXT MORNING, I set up the anonymous email to use with Meyer and put together a terse summary of why I'd been hired, some of what I'd done, and some of what I'd found, then sent it and made my way to the workroom.

Matt Decker arrived a little before noon, and Nichols arranged for him to be brought straight to the workroom. I had already spoken with Jacob and gotten clearance to use Matt as a consultant, so we were good to go from a confidentiality perspective. After a little small talk and catching up, I brought him up to speed on my hunt for the location of the hackers and the HCC, my nickname for the Hackers' Control Computer.

"You sure we're allowed to investigate however we like?" Matt said with a crooked smile.

"Positive," I said.

"Then this should be doable. We sold the routers and switches for this place."

"Yes, you did. I saw that before I emailed you."

"Ah, so you just wanted to take advantage of me," he said, smiling.

I shrugged and gave him my best you-got-me smile.

"I pulled the records this morning. They bought the best of everything, which is gonna be very good for you, Uncle Sam."

"Oh no," I said. "You remember."

"Coolest name I ever heard."

"Glad you think so. How do we do this? Gotta tell you, I've already checked everything imaginable via routers and switches."

He pulled up a terminal window and started entering commands. "A lot of our high-end gear has experimental features. We don't document it because we don't want to support it yet, and in a lot of cases, we even cripple it."

I watched everything he did, and it became obvious that he was running commands that were proprietary to the Decker Digital gear. "And what feature are you accessing now?" I said.

"Would on-premises geolocation interest you?"

"No way," I said.

"Our customers with big networks have this problem often enough to be a problem. Networks get set up without proper naming conventions and things get 'lost,' in that they still work but nobody knows what is where. We expect big things when we roll this feature out to market."

"And the devices here have the feature?"

"They're crippled, but every router and switch here has the capability. I'm about to run a script that will turn the feature on in every one of them." He raised his hand

and brought a finger down on the Enter key with flair.

"Unlikely that many of the devices can get a GPS signal in here."

"They don't have to," he said. "At least not many of them. If just a few of them can get a lock, we're golden."

He minimized the terminal window and brought up a blank white page in a web browser. It wasn't blank for long. Little globe icons started appearing in what appeared to be random locations on the page. After a couple minutes, the page had the icons scattered left to right and top to bottom.

"Watch this," Matt said. Using the mouse, he hovered the cursor over one of the icons and a series of numbers popped up.

"I'll be damned," I said. "Latitude, longitude, altitude, and IP address. Sweet."

"Keep watching. The real magic starts soon."

We waited a minute and nothing happened. Two minutes. Then more icons appeared, globes like before, but colored red, not blue and green like the others. I leaned over and drove the mouse to hover the cursor over one of the red globes, and got the same type of location data as I'd seen on the blue and green globes. "How's it doing that?" I said.

"Every device has an encrypted RF transceiver. They talk to each other. And since we have a good number of devices with GPS lock, and thus known locations, the devices that don't have a GPS signal can triangulate their position based on the radio signals from the ones that do. Pretty slick, huh?"

"Slicker than gorilla snot," I said, and extended a fist for a bump-five.

"As more devices establish location, the accuracy goes

up. Within an hour, this map will be accurate to within a couple feet. Now, with that done, you guys got any food around here?"

CHAPTER 50

NICHOLS BEGGED OFF FOR LUNCH, saying he had to run a couple errands. I would've figured he'd find Matt interesting to talk to, given his fairly famous status. I guess not everybody is as big a nerd as me. We went to Rings of Saturn, which had settled into the number-one spot on my list of SPACE eateries. After a visit to the Saladium Sector, we made the rounds and chose a quiet booth in the Titan Habitat.

"Been fighting any megalomaniacs lately?" I said.

Matt shook his head. "Just government bureaucrats and corporate egos."

"How's married life?" I said. He had met a Mississippi girl named Jana during the chaotic week he'd spent there while battling the aforementioned psycho, and she was something special. I had read a news article about them getting married a few months back.

He grinned. "I like it. A lot."

"You know she's way too hot for you, right?"

"No debate from me on that."

"What's she doing with herself now that you transplanted her to the other side of the country?"

"Travels with me quite a bit, hangs out with Norman the rest of the time. I think she's getting bored with it, though. She'll tell me soon that she wants to go back to work."

"Norman?"

He nodded and talked around a mouthful of butter-slathered Renduvian Roll. "My chocolate lab."

"Ah," I said.

"Still living on the land with your horse?"

"Most of the time. I did build an addition on the side of my lab. A little bedroom for me and a stall for Johnny, for when the caseload is too heavy to come and go."

"Speaking of cases, how'd you get this one?" he said.

"My brother's a lawyer. His firm had done some kind of contract work for them, I think. Not sure just how it went down, but somehow he knew they were looking for somebody, put in a couple calls."

"Where's he?"

"Houston. Listen, Matt, there's another angle to this case, something I stumbled onto."

He looked up from his plate, raised his eyebrows.

"I gotta ask you to keep this between us," I said.

"You got it. What's up?"

I told him about the rape videos. When I finished, I said, "Can't get it out of my mind."

Matt had stopped eating. "Who could?"

"A couple of those girls are younger than my daughter. I can't stop thinking, what if it was her? What would I do if I found out somebody knew about it and didn't want to get involved because it might sully a corporate image?"

"So, what are you gonna do about it?"

"Not sure yet," I said. "But something, and soon."

CHAPTER 51

NEW YORK

S.A. Courtney Meyer

SPECIAL AGENT COURTNEY MEYER LOOKED ACROSS the conference table and tried to wrap her mind around this turn of events. After eighteen months of trying and failing to get something on the Sultanovich family, she had reached a breakthrough last night with the computer expert working for SPACE. Truth be told, his threat had rippled chillbumps from her stem to her stern. But his first report had shown up this morning.

Now she was looking at a trio of witnesses who had simply strolled into the bureau's New York field office at 26 Federal Plaza and said they wanted to "make deal" for information on Max Sultanovich. When it rains, it pours.

She knew the two men were who they claimed to be, although she had not connected the portly Crimean,

Maslov, to the Sultanovich operation. Zuyev was a long-time foot soldier and looked the part with his broad Slavic face, pitted with old scars that looked a bit like acne, except they were fewer and larger. The knife scar across his forehead was fairly recent and didn't help his severe case of ugly.

The girl—Christine Gamboa was the name she gave—was straight out of left field, an unknown. She looked spent and scared. She also could not have looked more out of place than she did right now, sandwiched between Fat Boy and Dogface, and Meyer instantly distrusted her for it. When a girl who looked like this one was running with underworld characters twice her age, the reason wasn't hard to deduce.

Meyer started with her: "Miss Gamboa, how do you know these men?"

"I don't know Mr. Zuyez at all, since I just met him today. As for Sasha—Mr. Maslov—he's a client."

Meyer had expected Gamboa to sound like a gum-smacking bimbo, but that's not what she got. Her tone, her eyes, her manner were all intelligent and articulate. "What kind of client?"

"I'm an executive host at a casino."

"Executive? What exactly do you do?"

"I facilitate wonderful experiences for our most discerning clients."

That was straight from some brochure, and Meyer didn't appreciate the bounce and sass with which it was delivered. "Listen, honey, I'm not someone you want to get cute with. Got it?"

Gamboa picked up the business card Meyer had given her, looked at, then laid it back on the table. "Miss Meyer—"

"It's Special Agent Meyer."

"You know what? I don't care if it's Queen Meyer. Don't call me 'honey' or any of the other condescending tags I'm sure you have tucked away. I haven't committed any crimes. I'm here to help you and hopefully to find a way out of this mess I wandered into."

Meyer stared at her, deciding on the approach she'd take from here with the little size-four bitch who was way too full of herself. In an even tone, she said, "Can you please elaborate on your client relationship with Mr. Maslov?"

The Crimean burst to his feet, looking at Zuyev and spouting a stream of what Meyer assumed was Russian. Then he turned to her. "I am very rich gambler. Casinos like rich gamblers. Chrissy take care of me at casino, okay? She get food I like, seats to shows I like, these things. Okay? Now we stop the stupid and talk about cold killer Max Sultanovich or not?"

Meyer blew out a long breath. "Please sit down, Mr. Maslov."

His big face was red, eyes bulging, tiny crimson veins on his nose almost glowing. But he did ease back down into his chair. Meyer said, "I'm listening. What do you have to tell me about Maxim Andreyovich Sultanovich?"

"We can to tell you everything about Max, but first we make deal, yes?"

"Sure, we can talk about a deal. After I know something about the evidence you have."

Maslov nodded, a nod of satisfaction.

She had no authority to make a deal, but she'd be happy to "talk about" it. "Well?" she said, and motioned for him to start talking.

But he wasn't listening. He was tapping at an iPhone

with those sausage fingers of his. Once he finished and put the phone away, he leaned back and crossed his arms over his chest.

"Mr. Maslov?" she said. "The evidence?"

A knock sounded on the door. Two seconds later, the door opened and a fifty-something straight off the cover of GQ walked in.

"Excuse me?" Meyer said. "Who are you?"

He strode toward her with his hand out. "Jerome Balderas, representing Mr. Maslov. And his companions, for now."

Ho-ly shit.

Meyer had never met Jerome Balderas before. In fact, she had never seen him on TV or otherwise. But she knew who he was, just like everybody else in the FBI knew who the sonofabitch was. He was the lawyer who got the case against the bureau's former director dismissed. A director who was a scumbag, whose corrupt political shenanigans had gotten good agents killed. A director who deserved to be wasting away in a federal prison right now, not golfing his time away like he was.

So much for getting anything out of Maslov on the quick, without really talking deal. She shot him a look, stood, and approached Balderas with her hand out. "We didn't expect you."

He shook her hand. "You didn't. Fortunately, my clients did. Shall we get down to it?" He placed a briefcase on the table, pulled out a chair, slickly unbuttoned his suit coat, and sat. He opened the briefcase and withdrew a small stack of documents, then slid copies to each person around the table.

Meyer picked up her copy and looked at it.

PROPOSED PRELIMINARY PROFFER AR-
RANGEMENT BETWEEN THE FEDERAL
GOVERNMENT OF THE UNITED STATES
OF AMERICA AND PARTIES ALEXANDRE
MASLOV, BENJAMIN ZUYEV, AND CHRIS-
TINE GAMBOA

In exchange for full immunity from prosecution
for all actions, past and present, along with other
considerations to be negotiated, Alexandre Maslov,
a Ukrainian national, Benjamin Zuyev, a Russian
national, and Christine Gamboa, an American cit-
izen, hereinafter collectively referred to as "the Par-
ties," agree to cooperate with the Federal Bureau of
Investigation, the Department of Justice, and other
such agencies as may be deemed pertinent, herein-
after collectively referred to as "the Government,"
with regard to the investigation and possible pros-
ecution of Maxim Andreyovich Sultanovich and
his associates, hereinafter collectively referred to as
"the Sultanovich Organization."

Such cooperation will include the disclosure of sig-
nificant evidentiary information that is highly in-
criminating to Sultanovich, and therefore of great
value to the Government. This information will re-
late to the following alleged criminal activity con-
ducted by the Sultanovich Organization:

1. A computer fraud and abuse operation head-
quartered in the United States, that targets numer-
ous computer networks operated by entities within
the public and private sectors.

2. *Racketeering activities stemming from the activities in item #1.*

3. *Money-laundering activities stemming from the activities in item #1.*

4. *Political bribery activities stemming from the activities in item #1.*

5. *Further undisclosed criminal activities conducted by the Sultanovich Organization.*

Meyer finished reading the first page, flipped to the next page, saw it was nothing more than boilerplate logistical language, along with designated areas for dates and signatures. "Mr. Balderas," she said, pointing to a signature line with her name beneath it, "I'm sure you know I don't have the authority to negotiate a deal like this. But if I did? Full blanket immunity for unknown information would be a non-starter, as it will be with my bureau superiors, not to mention the U.S. Attorney."

"Miss Meyer," he said, "I'm—"

"Special Agent Meyer."

"Of course, my apology. Special Agent Meyer, can we please skip the rote posturing and proceed?"

"Beg your pardon?"

"Do you doubt I prepared before coming here?"

"I'm certain you did," she said.

"Correct. As part of that preparation, I made inquiries to certain sources within your agency. I know that this is your case. I know of your well-deserved reputation for, shall we say"—he made air quotations with manicured fingers—"your 'aggressive tenacity.' And we both know that a recommendation from you on this particular case would carry great weight. So while you are not able to officially offer a deal, as a practical matter, you can."

Meyer looked at him, studied his smooth tan face, the flawless white smile, every hair in place. She didn't like him, but she had to respect him. His summary was on target. She could probably push through any deal she wanted on this one. What he hadn't articulated was the most important reality: If he could get a deal with her signature on it, even if it wasn't binding, he would use it to obfuscate and delay any prosecution of his clients with an unending stream of pleadings, hearings, appeals, and any other challenge he could dream up. The asshole was shrewd.

She shrugged. "I'm willing to talk, but not without a sworn statement from you and each of them"—she nodded toward "the parties"—"that says I've warned you beforehand that I don't have the legal authority to guarantee any kind of immunity for anything."

Balderas's smile widened and he reached into the briefcase. He pulled a single sheet and handed it to her. It was exactly the sworn statement she had just described. She wondered how many steps ahead of her and the bureau this guy really was.

CHAPTER 52

SPACE

MATT SAID HIS GOODBYES AND HEADED BACK to Mc-Carran International, and I returned to my workroom. By the time I got back, the network map was a thing of beauty, which is to say it was populated from top to bottom. I was now able to instantly track the physical source and destination of almost any electronic communication within the SPACE network. And it took mere minutes to see that my suspicions were right: The hacking originated within the unallocated space beneath the central tower of the SPACE complex.

Armed with architectural drawings on my tablet, I locked my computers and left the workroom. Nichols wasn't back yet, so I was alone. I took the elevator down to the casino floor; the clear, space-walk-like people mover was a fun ride, but after a few times on it, the slow speed outweighed its charm. Once I reached bottom, I navigated through the Craps Corridor, the Blackjack Belt, and finally the outer layer of gaming machines. Getting out of the casino was like ciphering a maze, but I worked my way through the airlock doors and into the great out-doors. Not at the front of the property, but the rear.

The August Nevada air was hot enough and dry enough that it felt like the atmosphere itself might catch fire at any moment. This was my first time to be at the back of the tower, so I took a look around. It was pretty much like the front, on a smaller scale. A portico with a few valet attendants around, a driveway that looked like an interstate highway, and sidewalks that fed off either side of the portico. According to the drawings, I needed to go left. I did. After a few minutes of walking, I found what I was looking for.

Veering off the main drive, a wide concrete service ramp sloped down into the basement of the tower. There were no sidewalks. I watched for about five minutes as a few service vehicles drove down and in or up and out. A Sysco food delivery truck. A van from NV Energy. A pickup pulling a trailer full of PVC pipe. Typical service flow.

I stuck close to the nearer wall so I wouldn't get run over and walked down the incline into the bowels of SPACE. When the ramp leveled out, I encountered a security guard manning a little booth that sat between the in and out lanes, both of which were blocked with a fold-down barrier arm. He eyed me as I walked up to an electronic reader and touched it with my bracelet. The reader turned green and the arm raised, and the guard returned to whatever he'd been doing. In front of me, the two-lane road went left, right, and straight ahead into a tunnel. I went straight.

The tunnel was dim, lit by sparsely placed overhead lights. Beyond the guard shack, a raised sidewalk with a handrail hugged the righthand wall, so I walked there. And walked. And walked. An inbound UPS truck passed me and about fifteen seconds later, veered off the tunnel to the right. When I got to where he'd veered, I saw a sign that said PARCEL DELIVERY ONLY, above another tunnel curving deeper inside the structure. I took a minute to study a drawing on my tablet, and continued straight ahead. As my trek continued, I passed a couple more offshoot tunnels, one on the left (LAUNDRY ONLY) and one on the right (PHYSICAL PLANT PERSONNEL ONLY).

A couple hundred yards past the last offshoot, the drive dead-ended at a cinder block wall. A large, gray, steel door sat dead center. At eye level, I saw what looked at first glance to be a peephole. When I looked closer, I decided it was a video camera. Beneath the tiny lens, a fluorescent orange sign was lettered with bold black type: ABSOLUTELY NO ADMITTANCE. The door handle was a lever style, similar to ones I'd seen often up in the tower, but made of steel instead of the glasslike material in the doors above. I grabbed the lever and pushed, and got exactly what I expected. Locked. What I didn't expect, however, was what happened next. At the exact moment a tiny LED beside the lever glowed red, so did my bracelet. That was new.

I looked at my glowing bracelet and tried to remember if it had failed to open anything else since I had been at SPACE. Nothing came to mind. Maybe the red glow was routine, a signal to make it clear you were in the wrong place. Before heading back up the tunnel, I used my tablet to take photographs of everything notable at this dead end. The door. The non-electronic, key-driven part of its lock, and the three tiny cameras. The one in the door, plus one nestled in each upper corner where concrete wall met concrete ceiling.

On my way out of the tunnel, I did the same thing for every camera I saw, and that included some really unusual ones considering that I was in a concrete service tunnel that appeared routine until you got to the dead end and its door into the unallocated space: The signs were fastened to the wall with what looked like four screws, one in each corner of the sign. Something about the first one I photographed triggered my spidey sense, though, and when I looked closer, I saw that the sign was really fastened by only three screws. The bottom left "screw" was really a tiny camera lens, exactly like the one in the big bad door. How freaking weird was that? Very.

I also shot pictures of every offshoot, every light fixture, and anything else that looked remotely notable. I recorded verbal notes for each photograph, like how many paces since the last notable feature, which side of the tunnel, and estimated height off the floor. Make every recon mission count.

CHAPTER 53

SPACE

NICHOLS WAS WAITING FOR ME when I returned to the workroom, or at least he was there, still buried in a book. I pulled up my spiffy new network map and got busy pulling all the device coordinates and their associated network addresses into a spreadsheet. That was pretty quick. The next step was not, but a lot of hours and a few learning curves later, I had what I wanted. Using the architectural drawings and the data from the network map, I had constructed a 3D wireframe model of SPACE, complete with icons representing each device on the network map. It didn't include all the individual computers, of course, just Matt's geomagic routers, but that was okay. If the model contained every computer and other connected device in this data-laden tower, it would be a useless blob of icons. As it was, it was very useful. I could rotate it, zoom in and out, and glean some excellent information.

One step to go. Using the information gathered during my recon mission, I added icons for the tunnel cameras and the big bad door, which was not represented on any of the architectural drawings.

When I looked at the time, I was surprised to see it was after 10 p.m. I had been working on this model for nearly eight hours. "Jimbo," I said, "hit the road, man. I got this."

Nichols looked up from his book and yawned. "Thanks, but I'm supposed to stay."

"If you get in trouble, I'll tell them I made you go. Now get out of there."

He threw me a little salute. "Sir, yes sir!" He stood, stretched, and left.

And that was exactly what I wanted, no chance of anyone looking over my shoulder for what I was about to do. *Carte blanche.* That's what Jacob Allen had said, and I have a theory regarding authority: Use it before you lose it.

Since I now had the key to unlock the secret backdoors in the Decker Digital routers, I could do a lot of exploration inside the SPACE data universe. According to my model, a locked steel panel I had photographed on the tunnel wall concealed a router, even though the network diagram from IT didn't show that it existed. I logged into the router and started querying. I suspected I knew what was connected to it, but I wanted to know. Soon I did. That router was the connection point for the cameras in the tunnel. Damn skippy, and a bonus to boot. I had counted six cameras in the tunnel. The router had an even dozen connected to it.

I put the video feed from the cameras on my screen

and quickly accounted for the six knowns and three of the extras. Each of the offshoot tunnels had a camera I hadn't been able to see from the main tunnel. That left three. My three amigos. Unlike the other nine, which were all looking at dimly lit sections of service tunnel, each of the three amigos was looking at a brightly lit corridor. Not a tunnel for trucks. A corridor, a hallway, for humans to walk through. In each view, the corridor was similar, raw concrete, low ceiling. I could see enough differences, however, to know that the three amigos were looking at three separate corridors. I was almost certain these corridors were inside the unallocated space. Too bad Decker Digital didn't make network cameras with built-in geomagic. No worries. I'd eventually figure it out; I had that wonderful tingle dancing all around the edges of my psyche that told me I was closing in.

In addition to the cameras' video feeds, the router also provided me with the manufacturer and model of the cameras. I jumped online and found an app on the manufacturer's website that would accept the cameras' output and record it if I so chose. I so chose, but I set it to record only when a camera detected motion in its field of view. Once that was done, I chose a viewing grid that showed me all twelve cameras on one screen. Only then did I notice that the three amigos were different in another way. Each had a tiny gear icon in the corner of its viewing pane. I clicked the gear on the first amigo and a control panel popped up with four arrows. One up, one down, one left, one right. It also had a plus sign and a minus sign. I clicked the left arrow and the view moved. The three amigos had remote pan, tilt, and zoom. And I had control of it all.

CHAPTER 54

NEAR TUNICA, MISSISSIPPI

Max Sultanovich

MAX STOOD AT THE WINDOW OF HIS SUITE and watched the first sliver of sun edge above the distant horizon. This bastard land was so flat, it looked like he could see a hundred miles. When the sun was fully risen, he went to the telephone and ordered breakfast for himself and Tatyana. A few minutes later, he heard a light knock on the door and found a USA Today newspaper slid beneath the door.

He picked it up, sat on the sofa, and unfolded it. Before reading, he brought the paper to his nose and smelled the ink, something he had done since he was a boy. According to the headlines, the Arabs and Jews were fighting. Some news that was. They could all kill each other down to the last man, woman, and child, and the world would be better off as far as he was concerned. The

American stock market had a good day. Fine by him. He made money if it went up. Made money if it went down. Some teacher was in trouble for slapping a pupil in Ohio. Give her a promotion. About half these ingrate American children needed to be slapped, punched, and kicked. When he turned the page, he saw a headline that held his attention.

FBI QUIET ON CASE INVOLVING MYSTERY CAPTIVES IN MISSISSIPPI

WASHINGTON - Aside from confirming that the investigation is now being handled directly by FBI headquarters in Washington, D.C., the FBI today offered little new information on the Mississippi case of nine women who apparently escaped captivity from a hunting lodge near Casino Center, an area that is home to numerous casinos in Tunica County. An FBI spokesman would say only that the investigation is ongoing. He refused to comment on the identities of either the victims or potential suspects, despite repeated questions from members of the press in attendance.

Max stood with the newspaper, crushed it into a wad, and walked across the room to drop it into a trashcan. It said nothing. This could mean they knew nothing. This could mean they knew a little or knew a lot. FBI bastards. He hated them, every one.

CHAPTER 55

SPACE

I WOULD HAVE PREFERRED TO PUT THIS UPDATE OFF until I knew more, but I went to Jacob Allen's office first thing the next morning, to get it out of the way. When I walked into his lair of leather and wood, I found not only Jacob waiting, but Brandy Palmer as well. Swell. Who doesn't enjoy dealing with a queen bitch first thing in the morning? I nodded a greeting to the two of them, then got down to business. Didn't bother sitting first. "Jacob, I've identified the source of the hacks."

Both their faces went on high alert. "Of our machines, or the broad scheme you told me about?" Jacob said.

"They're one and the same."

Palmer: "Who is it?"

"Let me rephrase," I said. "I've found the location the hacks are coming from."

Jacob: "And?"

I handed him the document I'd brought with me, which was a printout of one of the architectural drawings. I had highlighted the wireframe rendering of the unallocated space in red and slapped a bull's-eye icon on it. "There," I said, leaning over his desk and pointing to the bull's-eye.

It lasted the tiniest of moments, but for that half second or so, Jacob looked like he'd been gut-punched. Then the droopy-eyed, unflappable Jacob was back. He stared at the printout for thirty seconds without saying anything, eyes locked on the document, lips pooched out like he was prepping for a duckface selfie to post on Facebook. Then he looked to Palmer and said, "Brandy, excuse us, please."

She scrunched her eyebrows down, her lips parted. "Jacob?"

"Please, Brandy. Just go."

And in a huff of drama and Botox, she was gone.

"For some reason," I said, "this area of the building seems shrouded in mystery. Nobody knows what it is, what it's for, who's in there. I know what's happening from there, but if you want me to really get to the bottom of this, I need information."

Jacob raised his hound-dog eyes to mine. Puffed his cheeks out. Exhaled. "This," he said, with a stab at the bull's-eye on the document, "this is a time-bomb. It's been sitting down there, ticking, ticking, ticking, and now it's about to blow a mountain of bullshit all over us, all over *me*."

He stood, leaned over his desk, hands on his beautiful blotter, eyes down. A good two minutes passed. When you need answers, the best strategy is often to keep your mouth shut and let the other person fill any awkward silence, so I said nothing, although I did sit down in one of his leather wingbacks. When he finally stood upright, he walked over to a credenza that had a crystal bar service on top. He set aside two glasses, pulled the top from a decanter, and poured. I could smell the Scotch from my seat. I hate Scotch, just like I hate every other kind of whiskey. No, that's not true. I hate Scotch much worse than other kinds. But when he returned and handed me the glass, I took it.

I needed information and wasn't about to break the flow of what was happening. Because of what I had heard from Bert Addison, the facilities manager who didn't know what was in the bowels of the facilities he managed. Because of what I'd seen with my own eyes in the tunnel. Because my gut told me this case was all about this unallocated space. Because I had expected Jacob Allen to clam up or freak out or something when the subject was broached. Most of all, because once I start a case, I *must* solve it.

Jacob and his once-again pooched lips eventually made it back to his chair and sat. After a deep draw from his glass, he removed a coaster from a holder on the desk. Put the coaster on the desk. Carefully situated the glass atop it as if he were handling nitroglycerin instead of a foul-smelling liquor.

"Sam," he said, "this goes no further, understood?"

"That's a given."

He gave a little nod, took another drink, repositioned the glass on the coaster. "In addition to my duties as general counsel, I own…a small minority stake in the company."

I took a sip of the liquid crap, said nothing, waited.

"I got that stake by working my ass off to put this

deal together, securing investors, handling the logistics. I spent five years on it before anyone ever heard of SPACE." He took another drink.

I waited.

He continued: "It took three years to build this place, so we're talking almost ten years of my life tied up here. Anyway, I had everything lined up. The money. The designs. Every damned thing there was. I had already struck the deal to buy this land, had paid millions for an option to keep it off the market until all our funding was in place."

This time, he didn't sip when he picked up the glass. He killed it. I pretended to sip mine, unable to stomach another swallow of the rot.

"At the last minute, when we exercised the option and were ready to close the deal on the land, ready to start building, the bullshit started."

Jacob looked up at me. I raised my eyebrows in anticipation, urging him on without words, which might distract.

"The land was owned by a European holding company based in Frankfurt, or so all the paperwork said, all the title searches, all the research. When it was time to sign the deal, though, guess who turned out to be the real money behind this 'German' holding company?"

I picked up the start of a slur in his words, not much, but enough that I thought he was now on a roll. Safe to engage. "Not the Germans?"

"Hell, no," he said. "Ukrainians. Scratch that. One Ukrainian. Any guess what the most corrupt country on the planet is, Sam?"

"Ukraine?"

"You got it. We're at the closing, I mean literally sitting around the conference table, me with a cashier's check in front of me for forty-six million dollars, ready to slide it across the table. In walks this old husk of a man, looks old enough to have drunk Stolichnaya with Marx. Guess what he said?"

I shrugged and faked another sip, threw in a little slurp to make it sound good.

Jacob stood, headed back to the credenza. "I need another drink. And you are not going to believe this shit."

CHAPTER 56

NEW YORK

Courtney Meyer

"Tom, I was on the phone and swapping emails with Balderas until three a.m. This is the best we can do, and it's worth it." She took another sip of coffee, held eye contact with her boss, Special Agent in Charge Thomas Belt.

"I don't know, Court. If these guys are legit—"

"Everything checks out. I think they are, for the most part."

Belt raised an eyebrow. "The most part?"

"Gamboa, the woman, she's hiding something, but that's covered in the agreement. If we find out she lied, her immunity is null and void."

"Letting them walk is a huge give," Belt said. "Sounds like Maslov and Zuyev are up to their eyeballs in this thing, and, Christ, Zuyev's record in Eastern Europe reads like a horror movie. I'd like to know just how the hell he was ever allowed to set foot on American soil."

"It's not like we're used to making deals with shining examples of the human race, Tom."

She stayed focused on Belt. He was the key. Not the little weenie of an Assistant U.S. Attorney who had sat there for the whole meeting without uttering a word. Meyer couldn't even remember his name. Belt had the clout to make the deal happen, and everybody in the room knew it.

Belt steepled his fingers, elbows on his desk, propped his chin on the steeple. "And the girl?"

"Christine Gamboa," Meyer said. "No record, nothing, I think she's incidental."

"Maybe," Belt said. "But why is she here?"

"She's scared, hanging with Maslov, hoping he can protect her."

"But that's my point, Court. Why does she need protection?"

Meyer shrugged. "She won't give details without the deal, only that she stumbled onto information that put her in danger."

Belt wheeled back from his desk, stood, and stretched. "It smells like a pig in a poke to me, but if you're convinced, I'll go along with it." He paused and looked at Weenie. "What do you think?"

Weenie straightened his tie and cleared his throat. "Well, I see one major problem."

Screw my deal up and you'll be the one with a major problem when I toss your scrawny ass out that window. "What's that?" Meyer said.

"Let's pretend it all goes as planned. You get great evidence, build an airtight case against Sultanovich."

"That's my plan."

"What are you going to do with it? The old man is in Kiev. What makes you think Ukraine will hand him over? For that matter, who knows who's actually making the calls over there? The Ukrainians? Or Putin? He's not exactly our closest friend at the moment."

Now she had him. "It's irrelevant," she said. "Max Sultanovich landed in Memphis last night. He's in the presidential suite at the Magnolia Star Casino, just outside Tunica, Mississippi."

CHAPTER 57

SPACE

Jacob killed another hefty glass of the liquor before continuing, and by then the slur was pronounced. "This old man—his name is Maxim Sultanovich—nodded to one of the gaggle of lawyers on their side of the table, and this guy pulled out copies of a new purchase agreement and slid them around the table. I asked for an electronic copy so I could quickly find the changes. Guess what those changes were?"

I shrugged. "No idea, but I'm betting they didn't favor your side of the equation."

"That's putting it mildly, Sammy. You mind if I call you Sammy?"

Okay, he was fully lit. "Not at all."

"Good, because I feel like I can talk to you, Sammy."

"I appreciate that, Jacob. I try to be a good listener." Truth? I worked *hard* to become a great listener. Hearing and interpreting tiny details has saved my life more than once.

Jacob went on: "The changes he made are to this day the most bizarre thing I've ever seen in a real estate transaction. Hell, in any transaction! You see this damned space you've got highlighted, this 'mystery area' nobody knows anything about?" This came with three knuckle-raps on the document.

I nodded.

"He refused to sell *that exact space*. The thousand or so acres around it? No problem! Mineral rights? No problem! Hell, get this, Sammy: He didn't even have a problem selling the ground and sky above that space. Just that one narrowly defined area, which is underground. That's it!"

My face no doubt registered confusion. I picked up the document and looked at it for a moment, then laid it back on the desk. "He only wanted to keep that little rectangle of ground, and even then, he just wanted the portion of it that runs from twenty feet below ground, down to forty feet below ground? That's what you're saying?"

"Bingo! Is it not the dumbest bullshit you've ever heard in your life?"

"It's way up there on the list. I assume you went along with it?"

"Had no choice," Jacob said. "Oh, and he also demanded that the space be built out to his specs, and that we give him free everything in the way of service. Power. Internet. Infrastructure."

"And let me guess," I said. " No one is allowed to enter the area?"

Jacob pointed a wavering finger at me. "Gonna start

calling you Bingo Boy, 'cause you just hit another one, Sammy."

Brandy Palmer

It felt like forever, but the hillbilly finally left Jacob's office. Palmer walked back into the inner office and found the lawyer sitting behind his desk with a drink glass in one hand and an almost-empty liquor decanter in the other. "Jacob?" she said. "Are you drunk?"

He looked up at her as if he hadn't heard her come in and didn't particularly care that she had. He raised the decanter to eye level and squinted at it. "I'd offer you a drink, but I want it all for me."

She stared at him, her brain trying to make sense of this scenario and failing. "What in hell are you doing, Jake?"

"It's all gonna come down on my ass." He picked up the decanter again. "Or more likely on my head, I suppose. Hard for something to fall straight onto the ass, wouldn't you agree?" He burst out laughing.

"What's coming down? Tell me what's going on, Jake!"

"It's that old bastard. That old commie bastard. I knew it, knew it all along." He looked like he was about to cry.

Palmer walked around the desk and took both the decanter and glass from him. She took them to the credenza, then returned to Jacob and took his face between her hands. "Jake, what are you talking about?"

"Sammy. He's my only hope, you know?"

"Sammy? Are you talking about Flatt? I warned you at the beginning not to hire that countrified hick. What has he done? "

He burst out laughing again. "Done? He'll save me,

you'll see. You'll s—" His head flopped straight back. He was out.

Palmer pulled her phone from her purse and started to dial. Changed her mind. Put the phone back, dug around, came out with another one, a basic little flipphone. She dialed a number from memory and put it to her ear. A few seconds later, she said, "Not sure yet, but we may have a problem."

CHAPTER 58

SPACE

I OPENED THE SURVEILLANCE APP that had recorded
the cameras in the tunnel and the unallocated space
overnight. I told the app to show me the segments in
which motion occurred in any camera's field of view, hit
PLAY, and settled back with my cup of Jelorian Java to
enjoy the show. I watched mundane traffic in the tunnel
for the first few minutes, then a more interesting clip
made me sit up.

The view showed one of the corridors I suspected to
be inside the quasi-bunker of the unallocated space. A
male figure who looked to be in his twenties walked toward the camera and left the field of view as he passed
underneath. I backed it up and played it again. And
again. Paused the image on the frame with the best view
of his face. The image quality was excellent, at least compared to most surveillance imagery. I used a feature in

the surveillance app that let me grab a still image of the guy's face and save it to my hard drive.

More routine service vehicles in the tunnel, followed by another corridor clip. Same guy as before, no new information. At first. Then two more people—one male, one female—entered the scene. The three stopped and talked, dead center in the camera's field of view. I went back and forth until I found the frame with the best view of the second guy's face, grabbed it, saved it. Did the same with the girl. That done, I left the paused image on screen and studied it. The girl was slim, with dark hair and Slavic features, quite pretty. Both males were unremarkable. Slender, dark hair of average length, T-shirts with no logos or other identifying information. The first guy's shirt was black, the second one's lime green. No watches. No visible tattoos. Generic jeans, both blue denim. Shoes. Black Shirt was wearing white sneakers. Not Lime Green, though. He had on a pair of leather shoes with his jeans and T-shirt, light brown loafers. A little unusual, but not unheard of. The style of shoes, however, told a tale. Long, flat, tapered toes. I'd never seen a young person in the USA wearing that type of shoe. But I had seen them many times before. In Eastern Europe. Damn skippy.

CHAPTER 59

TUNICA, MISSISSIPPI

Max Sultanovich

MAX FOLLOWED HIS DRIVER-BODYGUARD up the few steps and through the door of the small government building. Red brick, squat, ugly as his withered old asscheeks, like most non-casino things he saw in this forsaken land. Inside was just as bad. Cheap tile floors. Buzzing lights in one of those ceilings made of drop-in panels so cheap they sucked up a bit when a door was opened, then settled back down when the door closed. Cheap bastards. In Kiev, government buildings were regal, strong, worthy of a country.

He stepped to a desk in the middle of a room where an American cow sat pecking at a computer. She looked up at him and squinted through spectacles that made her eyeballs look the size of golfballs. "Help you?"

"I am Max Sultanovich, come to get my son, Mikail Maximovich Sultanovich. His body."

Now her eyes looked even bigger. "What? Oh, that—him? Oh, he's not here."

"This is coroner's office of Tunica County, correct?"

"Sure, that's right, hun. But the body's not here. We don't have bodies here, for heaven's sake." The cow gave a little shiver.

"I don't understand. Why would coroner not have body?"

"Can't say as I can tell you why, but it doesn't work that way here."

"Then where can I get the body of my son?"

"Well, I expect he's over at the hospital. In the morgue. But they won't let you have him."

"I am his father. How you say—next of kin. It is my right."

"Oh, you can get him when they're done, I'm sure. It's just th—"

"Done?" Max said.

"With the autopsy, of course."

"No!" Max slammed the heel of a fist down onto the cow's desk. "You may not cut my boy."

The cow jumped, her huge breasts jiggling. "Uh, look, mister—sir—I think you need to talk to—"

But Max was not waiting to hear the rest. He was on his way out the door and down the steps, his man trotting ahead to open the car door.

Once he and the driver were inside and the car was running and ready to go, Max said, "Go to this hospital."

The hospital looked new, still had the smell of new carpet and fresh paint when Max walked through the revolving door and into the lobby. He walked straight ahead to a high counter with a uniformed man sitting behind it.

"Can I help you, sir?" the man said.

"Where is the morgue?" Max said.

The man pointed to a pair of elevators on his right. "Down to the basement level, turn left."

Max grunted and started toward the elevator with his man in tow, but they turned toward a commotion at the hospital entrance they had come through a minute or two earlier. The ruckus was a small army of police and FBI. Moving toward and around him.

"Maxim Sultanovich, freeze!" It was the leader of the little army, a man in a dark blue jacket with "FBI" in yellow letters a half-meter tall splashed across the front. He had his gun drawn and aimed at Max. So did the others, many of whom were dressed as if they were going into the battle of the century, with all their armor and helmets and other overwrought bullshit.

As Max raised his hands, he turned toward his man to tell him to cooperate, but it was too late. The simpleminded act on instinct, and this stupid bastard's instinct was to pull his own gun and take on at least a dozen assault rifles and numerous handguns, all wielded by a gaggle of testosterone maggots who had probably dreamed their whole pathetic lives of shooting someone. His man's gun never cleared its holster. Max heard the shots and watched as the bullets tore into his man's torso, each one leaving a small crater as a gout of blood erupted. He looked at Max, a look of bewilderment on his dumb face. Then he went to his knees, stayed there a few seconds, and fell face first onto the clean tile floor.

The leader advanced toward Max. "Maxim Sultanovich, you are under arrest. You have the right to remain silent. You have the right to an attorney…"

Max tuned the voice out. More men were around him now, pulling his hands behind his back, snapping hand-cuffs into place. He said nothing, offered no reaction of any kind as he was shuffled into the center of the herd of silly men. Then the herd was moving toward the door. The leader's eyes were still on Max and his lips were still moving, but Max wasn't listening. Instead, he looked the man in the eye, held the gaze for a while, then smiled.

CHAPTER 60

SPACE

I KEPT THINKING BACK ON THE MEETING with Jacob Allen. I expected him to shut me down on anything involving the unallocated space. I expected it more so after he told me the details of what it was and who owned it. Just the opposite. He almost begged me to do something, anything, to extricate him from the coming tsunami of trouble. Yes, he'd been inebriated by the end of the meeting, but that didn't matter to me. I had authorization to act. A lack of authorization doesn't necessarily stop me from acting, mind you, but having it in your pocket sure can grease the skids.

After watching all the surveillance footage recorded the night before, I had identified a total of four different people inside the unallocated space, which I started mentally calling "the bunker." Three guys, one girl. All looked to be in their twenties, and I believed all of them were most likely from Eastern Europe. Much of that belief was based on common sense, given that the owner of the space was a Ukrainian, but there were other things. The shoes I spotted earlier. Mannerisms. And with the girl, the eyes. The camera had caught a great shot of her face as she looked up while talking to one of the guys. She had classic Slavic features, especially the eyes, a pale blue so striking it looked almost metallic. Were these the hackers, or at least some of them? My gut said yes.

After some time inside the router feeding the bunker and the area around it, I had gotten access to the router inside the bunker, and then to the electronic lock on the bunker's steel door. Sort of. I had gotten the lock's electronic serial number. Once I had that, I compared pictures of the keypad/credential sensor I had taken with my tablet, to pictures I had shot of other access panels around SPACE. The keypad-sensor on the bunker door was different. I moved on and compared pictures of the device to similar keypads and locks on Google. The result was a short list of three potential lock makes and models. I called the first manufacturer; the serial number didn't match their numbering convention. The second one did. I was looking at an ElectroSmith PX1462 keypad with proximity sensor. It was a high-security access control device that was no doubt controlling an electric deadbolt.

Things got touchy after that. Since I had knowledge that the bunker didn't belong to my client, any attempt to circumvent the lock could be interpreted as criminal breaking and entering. Strike "could be interpreted." It would be breaking and entering. Fortunately, I was certain the people inside wouldn't be calling the police. I couldn't shake the feeling that all this was tied together, not just the hacking operation, but the rape videos, as well. And on that front? Rules and laws were of no interest to me.

CHAPTER 61

NEW YORK

Courtney Meyer

MEYER STOOD IN FRONT OF BELT'S DESK AND WAITED, anxious for her boss to get off the phone and tell her what was going on.

After another minute, SAIC Belt hung up the phone and looked at Meyer. "Sultanovich is in custody and en route to the field office in Memphis."

Meyer pumped a fist. "Yes!"

Belt said, "Get down there, Court. Now that we've committed ourselves on this thing, we need to move."

She nodded, left his office, and walked to the conference room where her informants waited. When she entered, every head turned her way. "We got him," she said.

Balderas: "Protection for my clients needs to begin immediately."

Maslov: "Max will to try to kill us as soon as he knows we are to speaking with you."

"Don't worry," Meyer said. "We have a secure apartment here in the building that will be safe until we get longer-term arrangements in place."

Zuyev said, "Where is Max now? What city?"

"Memphis, Tennessee. I'm on my way there now."

"You should know," Zuyev said, those flat eyes locked on hers, "Max will think nothing of having you killed, or a dozen of you. He is a man who is capable of anything."

Meyer felt a little ripple of goosebumps on her neck. "Thank you for your thoughts, Mr. Zuyev. I'll be fine."

Zuyev locked those dead eyes on her. "I am trying to help you."

She left the room and, for the first time since this thing had started to unfold, entertained the notion that she could really be in danger. If the stakes were as high as Maslov claimed, and if Sultanovich was as ruthless as his colleagues believed him to be, what was he capable of?

CHAPTER 62

FBI FIELD OFFICE
MEMPHIS, TENNESSEE

Max Sultanovich

MAX SAT IN A STRAIGHT-BACKED METAL CHAIR, posture erect. His hands were still locked in handcuffs, but at least they were in front of him now, resting on a small wooden table in the interrogation room. He had been exactly this way for more than three hours, had seen no one, heard no one, although he knew the bastards were watching him through the mirror on the wall facing him. He looked at the mirror now, stared into his own eyes, and waited.

He heard a series of soft beeps, then a click, and the door opened. The man who had arrested him entered, carrying a manila file folder, and sat in the chair across the table from Max.

The man placed the folder on the table, opened it, and removed a single sheet of paper. Then he removed an ink pen from his shirt pocket and laid it across the document. "Mr. Sultanovich, I'd like to ask you some questions. Before we begin, I need you to sign this document, indicating that you understood the rights that have been explained to you. There has been some discussion as to whether you, as a foreign national, are entitled to those rights, but I'd like to see you afforded those rights."

Max said nothing. He watched as the man rotated the document to face Max, then smoothly slid it and the pen across the table to him.

"Will you sign the waiver, sir?"

"I will consider your document." Max looked down as if he were reading the paper, then raised his eyes back to the man and said, "If you do something for me first."

"What would that be?"

"Are you a married man?"

"Beg your pardon?"

"Married. Do you have a wife?"

"I don't see how that's relevant, but yes."

"Good. I will sign this document right after your wife sucks my fat Ukrainian cock." Max's mouth broke into a slow, thin smile.

The FBI man's face colored like a beet. His nostrils grew and quivered.

"She must swallow my seed." Still holding his gaze on the man, Max hocked up a big wad of saliva and sputum, then spat it onto the document. He leaned forward over the table. "And I want you to watch while she does it. I think you will learn much, you pathetic American cunt."

The American waited a long time before saying anything. When he spoke, his voice was controlled, flat.

"You're making a big mistake."

"It is you who has made the mistake. Now I want my lawyer."

CHAPTER 63

SPACE

AT A LITTLE AFTER 11:00 P.M., I watched the surveillance feed on my computer as a stream of people exited the bunker. No new ones entered. Workday over? It was nearly midnight when I saw that things had finally gotten quiet around and in the tunnel. I locked the computer, said good-night to Nichols, and went to my room. Things were moving in a little different direction now, and it was time to start exercising some common-sense caution. After changing into a pair of black cargo pants and a black T-shirt, I needed to take care of a pesky problem. I didn't want to be tracked with my magic SPACE credential bracelet, but I might need it to get in (or out of) somewhere if things got dicey. The bracelet tech wasn't particularly complex. Each bracelet has a tiny chip inside it, about the size of a grain of rice. It's called an RFID chip, and it contains a unique serial number. As I move about the property, thousands of RFID readers hidden in walls, doors, elevators, and a plethora of other places sense that the chip assigned to me is nearby, and logs that information in a database. That's it.

Those hidden readers can't log what they never see, and since this whole game works on radio waves, there's an easy answer. I took a coffee packet from the SPACE Refreshment Station in my room, opened it, and dumped the coffee into a filter and put it in the coffeemaker. Empty foil coffee packet in hand, I removed my bracelet and dropped it inside. Boom. RFID invisibility, thank you very much. Slid the whole thing into a pocket. Time to go.

Despite the fact that I planned to render the bunker cameras moot, I still wanted to conceal my face. I wasn't going to tamper with the footage from the casino's tunnel cameras, and I didn't want to be recognizable as I passed them. I decided against anything radical. A guy on a casino property at midnight, slinking around dressed in black and wearing a face mask, might draw exactly the wrong response. I didn't intend to be seen by anyone in the flesh, and my e-wanderings had shown me that casino security almost never looked at the tunnel cameras and didn't even have access to those inside the bunker. Still, Old Man Murphy is always lurking and never far from my mind. I decided on a compromise and put on the black SPACE baseball cap from my "SPACE Supplies" bag that had been in my room when I first arrived. I pulled it down low before entering the tunnel. I had cut a generous slot in the brim so I could keep my head down but look up through the slot and at least get a partial view ahead and above if needed.

Thanks to my electronic chicanery with the bunker door's lock, I had all twenty-eight codes capable of opening it. This, of course, suggested that since that lock went active, a total of twenty-eight people had been granted access to the bunker. I had looked at the lock's records and memorized the three most recently used codes with a lot of activity. Those would be the ones least likely to draw anyone's attention should the logs be examined.

Keeping my head angled down for the camera, I entered one of the seven-digit codes into the keypad and the LED glowed a beautiful green as a soft click sounded. I turned the lever handle and pulled the door open. Stepped inside. Closed it behind me. I was in a corridor that looked exactly like the portions of it I'd been watching through the surveillance cameras. I went left. Twenty feet later, the corridor turned right. Head down and eyes up, I stepped around the corner and saw one of the cameras I'd been watching. It was mounted high on the left wall pointed away from me, down the length of the corridor. Familiar with its view, I moved ahead. It was one of the ones I'd neutralize later, but in the worst-case scenario it would see the back of a figure in black. Big deal.

As I moved forward, I encountered doors on my right every twenty feet or so. Their doors all had conventional locks, but all were unlocked. Janitorial supplies. Empty. Empty. A big copier/printer, paper, other office supplies. Empty. Another right turn. A quick scan showed no visible cameras. A couple more empty rooms on my right, then I came to a door that was obviously more important. Big. Heavy steel. And a lock with a keypad exactly like the one on the main door. I entered the same code that had opened that main door. Success again. I stepped inside.

CHAPTER 64

MEMPHIS, TENNESSEE

Courtney Meyer

THE FBI JET TOUCHED DOWN at Memphis International Airport just shy of 10:30 p.m. Per instructions, an SUV from the Memphis field office was waiting on the tarmac when the plane taxied up to the fixed base operator, a fancy name for 'airplane service station' in Meyer's estimation, that had the current bureau contract in Memphis. No security hassle, just get out of the plane and into the vehicle. She was on her way within two minutes of the plane rolling to a stop. Within minutes, she'd finally be face to face with the man she had pursued for so long.

When they arrived at the FBI's Memphis office, she walked through the door talking: "Where can I find Agent Kline?"

A man cut from classic FBI cloth approached from

the corridor with his hand out. "David Kline. I assume you're Agent Meyer?"

Meyer nodded and shook his hand. "Any developments?"

"Nope. We let him make a lawyer call several hours ago. Nothing since then."

"Who'd he call?"

"Not sure. He dialed a cellphone registered to John Doe. Not kidding."

"Where?"

"D.C. area code."

"Got him in a mirror?" Meyer said.

"Yeah, you want to see what he looks like?"

She nodded, then followed Kline through a maze of corridors and into a room with a window looking through a two-way mirror into the interrogation room where Sultanovich was being held. He looked like the picture on her wall, just older. Not a good thing. He was gaunt, with a severe face and clear eyes, those eyes a very light and piercing shade of blue. She could see how he might have been a decent-looking man fifty years ago, but now? Max Sultanovich was one ugly, evil-looking sonofabitch. Wrinkled, papery skin stretched across a skeleton.

A light rap on the door, and a young man stuck his head in the door. "Got a guy in the lobby says he's Sultanovich's attorney."

Meyer let out a long sigh. "Let's go meet this asshole."

The three stood in Kline's office. Both Meyer's and Kline's mouths were literally hanging open. After a few seconds, Meyer got her wits about her. "You cannot be serious."

Bykov gave a little half shrug. "You see the papers."

Meyer stared at him. She wanted to rip his five-thou-sand-dollar suit off him and shove it down his throat. She looked back down to the document in her hand, a letter from the Ukrainian embassy in D.C., identifying Maxim Andreyovich Sultanovich as a "Special Envoy of Ukrainian Culture."

She looked at Bykov, then to Kline. "We need to verify this...status." She left the room and Kline followed.

As they walked down the hallway, they heard Bykov say from the doorway of Kline's office, "Excuse me? I assume Mr. Sultanovich will be released immediately?"

Meyer stopped walking and spun to face him. She jabbed a finger in the air at him. "You—"

Kline pulled her hand down and said in a whisper, "Don't. Come on." He continued walking and after a few more seconds of rapid breathing through flared nostrils, Meyer followed.

CHAPTER 65

SPACE

THIS WAS IT. The room was stark, devoid of anything cosmetic, a concrete work chamber filled with computer workstations arranged on cheap folding tables. Each workstation had a standard folding metal chair, most of which were beat to hell and back. The lights were off, the room lit only by the assorted screensavers on the computer monitors. I went to the nearest computer, sat down, and moved the mouse to clear the screensaver. As expected, I got a password prompt. The machine was running some flavor of Linux, also not a surprise. The final non-surprise was the bothersome one: the Cyrillic characters staring back at me. I didn't know enough about Russian and Ukrainian to tell the two apart, so it could have been either one. No matter. I went to work.

It took almost forty-five minutes, but it was done. I had managed to get the computer set to English, then I'd defeated the password. I was in. I leaned back and stretched, then plugged a thumbdrive into the USB port on the front of the computer and started recording information that I would need later: IP addresses, MAC addresses, and a host of other configuration information. With that data stored to the thumbdrive, I installed a spy app. It would record every keystroke made on that computer, every screen, every anything done on the machine. It was the stealthiest such app on the planet, so there was little chance of it being discovered.

Next, I had to be sure I could access this computer later, and that the spy app could covertly deliver its payload outside the bunker network. From my location inside the hackers' network, setting up that access wasn't a major challenge, and within five minutes it was complete. I switched the computer back to its original language, which had turned out to be Russian. I'd wait to be sure it went back to the screensaver that had greeted me when I got here.

While that wait ticked away, I walked the room, smartphone in hand, shooting photos of anything and everything. That done, I stepped off the room in both directions and recorded the approximate measurements that resulted. It felt like I was on a recon mission from years back. The room was smaller than I'd expected and it was hot. Rooms full of computers always are if they don't have additional cooling in place to handle the heat output of the electronics. By the time I made it back over to the workstation I'd used, it was back on the proper screensaver. Time for me to boogie and take care of the last step.

In my room, I fired up my laptop and went to work. I had previously located the surveillance computer on the bunker network, by tracing the network address the cameras "talked to." Within minutes, I had control of that computer. The perfect solution would be to insert the footage of empty corridors I had recorded the night before. Except that's movie bullshit, for a host of techno-reasons. Next best thing? Be sure they had no footage at all for the time frame of interest. Hopefully they'd shrug it off as a glitch, but even if they didn't, they still wouldn't have anything to identify me.

I studied the surveillance computer on my screen. It had two hard drives, one that ran the computer, and a separate one to store the video footage coming in from the cameras. The video storage drive had three folders, CAM-A, CAM-B, and CAM-C. Inside each folder, video was stored in files that contained fifteen minutes each. In each folder, I wiped the files containing video between 12:00 midnight and 1:30 a.m., well before I got there and well after I'd left. That done, I disconnected my laptop from the bunker network and closed the lid.

CHAPTER 66

MEMPHIS, TENNESSEE

Courtney Meyer

AFTER MIGRATING BYKOV TO AN UNOCCUPIED OFFICE far enough away that he couldn't eavesdrop, Meyer and Kline stood in Kline's office on a concall with the State Department, Meyer's boss Tom Belt in Manhattan, and the deputy director of the FBI in Washington.

"With all due respect," Meyer said, "I can't believe what I'm hearing. Sultanovich is known by law enforcement throughout the world to be the kingpin of a crime syndicate based in Eastern Europe. How can he have diplomatic immunity?"

The robotic-sounding flunky at State said, "Special Agent Meyer, I can only confirm that Maxim Sultanovich's diplomatic papers have been verified, and that does indeed grant him diplomatic immunity. He must be released."

FBI Deputy Director: "How long has he had this status?"

State robot, after some clattering on a keyboard: "Well, this is interesting."

FBI Deputy Director: "Explain."

State robot: "Two days."

Meyer: "So as soon as he knew he was coming here, he magically became a diplomat?"

FBI Deputy Director: "Are you able to tell who signed off on this status for Sultanovich?"

State robot, after more clattering and a subsequent long pause: "The president of Ukraine."

NYC SAIC Tom Belt: "Sir, pardon my language, but this is horseshit."

FBI Deputy Director: "Agreed, but I don't see what we can do about it at the moment. Agent Meyer, release the prisoner."

Meyer: "Sir, if we can just have a little time, perhaps—"

FBI Deputy Director: "Release him, Agent Meyer. And let's end this call. Goodbye."

After a series of beeps, the IN USE light on the speakerphone winked out. Seconds later, the phone rang. Kline answered, "Special Agent Kline, Memphis."

It was the deputy director. "Agents, hold while Tom is patched back in."

Moments later, Belt announced himself on the call.

The deputy director said, "Listen to me. We do have to release him, but I want him covered so tightly with surveillance that he can't turn his head without seeing our people."

Meyer said, "Sir, the moment we release him, he'll flee the country. He has a private jet at Memphis International."

"I'm aware of that, Agent Meyer. And that plane is about to encounter difficulty in obtaining clearance to take off. Let's get busy, people. We're not going to lose this guy."

Meyer delivered the news to Sultanovich that he was being released. The old man looked up at her from his seat with a leering smile. His teeth were yellow, too small for his mouth, resulting in lots of visible gums. He was as disgusting in appearance as he was in character.

"I know who you are," he said, wagging a finger toward Meyer. "You are the one who has been interfering in my business, and I think that interference will soon end."

Meyer walked to the seat at the conference table that was directly across from him, leaned forward with her palms on the table, and said with her own smile, "I'm just getting started, Mr. Special Envoy."

The smile disappeared from Sultanovich's face, leaving behind a mask of hatred. With one corner of his mouth turned up in a sneer, and vertical threads of saliva connecting his blanched lips as he spoke, he said, "You fucking cow. You march in here with your fat ass and try to play with me? You will disappear from my life. One way or the other."

She tried not to let it show, but there was no mistaking the fact that she was looking into the eyes of pure evil.

The Ukrainian embassy man, Bykov, looked mortified. "Mr. Sultanovich, I think we should—"

Sultanovich leapt from his seat with speed that belied his withered husk of a body and was in Bykov's face before anyone could blink, poking him in the chest with a bony finger. "Close your mouth, boy."

Bykov did.

Sultanovich turned back to Meyer and cracked another yellow grin, then walked out of the room without another word.

CHAPTER 67

SPACE

Daria Bodrova

DARIA WAS AT HER COMPUTER BY 7:00 A.M., as always. She was the first one in the room, as always, ready to do her job and do it well. Not because she liked it. She hated it. Not because she was well paid for it. She was not. Not even because they might kill her if she didn't do it. They might. No, it was none of these things. There was only one reason: Anya.

Daria had looked back a thousand times and wondered why it didn't occur to her that it was strange to be required to take so many tests of her computer skills, at a dating agency. No matter now. Daria could not lose Anya to these animals, and their words had been plain: Do as she was told and her sister would be returned to her safely. Make trouble, and Anya would die.

Every morning since she arrived in the United States, she left the house she shared with all the other girls, took a bus to the casino, made her way to the back of the building and down into the tunnel that eventually delivered her here, to her computer. The man Dmitry had watched over them as they worked, slapped them on the head if he decided they weren't working hard enough, screamed for no reason. Until two or three weeks ago, when Dmitry left the room with a piggish man named Mikail, and never came back. A day or two after that, the man with the dead eyes had come. He did not slap heads or scream. He only looked at you. And that was worse. Much worse.

After a few days with Dead Eyes, a new man arrived, a supposed American called Alex. This man Alex, no matter what he said or how good he spoke his English, was Slavic. Dead Eyes announced that Alex would be their new supervisor. After that, Dead Eyes was there sometimes, and sometimes he was not. Alex was there every morning at 8:00 a.m. and stayed until they left at the end of the day. He was nicer than Dmitry, and of course nicer than Dead Eyes, but how nice could he really be when he did the bidding of such criminals? Or had they taken someone precious to him, like with Anya?

Alex had noticed that Daria was there every day when he arrived, and he assigned her a chore of looking at the camera recordings from the night before, as soon as she arrived each morning. It was boring, because all the cameras ever recorded were empty cement hallways, but it wasn't difficult work. She logged on to the camera computer, ready to scan through the recordings and get it over with. What she found as soon as she connected to the computer, however, was a box flashing an error message.

WARNING - EXPECTED FILE RANGES NOT FOUND!
\VIDSTOR1\CAM-A\   12:00:00AM.VID   -
01:29:59AM.VID
\VIDSTOR1\CAM-B\   12:00:00AM.VID   -
01:29:59AM.VID
\VIDSTOR1\CAM-C\   12:00:00AM.VID   -
01:29:59AM.VID

Daria went to the file directories and looked through the file listings. The error message was accurate. The video files containing the recordings from midnight to 1:29:59 a.m. were not there. Unusual, but not surprising. Computers failed all the time. She would mention it to Alex when he arrived. After clearing the error message, she played the rest of the recordings at ten times normal speed and, as always, saw nothing. Then she moved on to the second step of her morning bore.

In addition to the mounted cameras, each computer screen in the room contained a built-in webcam. Daria suspected the webcams were there to allow their over-lords to watch them while they worked, but she had no proof of this. These cameras also had a night mode: Each webcam would activate whenever its computer entered the screensaver mode. While active, if the camera saw movement, it captured a still photo once per minute un-til the movement stopped, and saved those photos to the system drive on the camera computer. Stupid. No one was here at night in this little cement prison, so what was there to photograph?

Still, she would do as she was told, whatever she was told. For Anya. She opened the file directory where no photos were ever stored, and her breath caught in her throat. There were many photos! Of a man! With her heart beating strong and fast, she began to look through the photos.

They were all taken on the same computer, one near the door. The time stamps began at 12:23 a.m. and ended at 1:10 a.m. There were also a few others at random times, with the last one at 1:19 a.m. The man in the photos was wearing a dark shirt and a dark casino cap that was pulled low on his brow, keeping his features in shadow. The webcams were not good ones and the photos were dark and of poor quality. But there was one photo that clearly showed his face. It had been taken at 1:04 a.m. and the man was leaning back, away from the computer, stretching his arms.

The look on his face was one of satisfaction, as if he had just accomplished something important. The corners of his mouth were turned up just a little, almost a smile. His eyes were obviously looking at the computer screen, not quite in line with the camera. He had long, dark eyelashes, and despite the almost-smile on his lips, Daria thought there was something a little sad about his eyes. One thing she knew for sure: He was very handsome.

CHAPTER 68

FBI - NEW YORK

Sasha Maslov

SASHA KNEW WHEN THE FBI WOMAN walked into the room that something was wrong. Her face was wrong. He said, "Miss Agent Meyer, you do not to have Max, do you?"

She shook her head. "We're working on that, but you're safe here."

"Safe?" he said. "From Max, when Max is not inside the prison? You funny woman. Zuyev, you hear this funny woman?"

Zuyev did not smile. Sasha thought maybe Zuyev had never smiled in his life. Maybe not capable. Maybe something wrong with muscles in his face.

Chrissy said, "What happened? You said you had him?"

"Do any of you know anything about him having diplomatic status?" Meyer said.

Chrissy looked at Sasha. Zuyev looked at no one.

"Max is not the diplomat of anything, but he can say to be whatever he want to be in Ukraine. You understand me?"

"No," Meyer said. "I don't."

Sasha stood and paced, exasperated. "Politicians. All will do what Max says. He, how you to say in English, he owns them. Now you understand this?"

"Yes, got it."

Chrissy said, "What now?"

"You stay here," Meyer said. "This building is secure. We're working on the diplomatic issue. I just wanted you all to hear this from me." She turned and left.

When the door closed, Sasha looked at Zuyev. "We go now?"

Zuyev nodded. "We die here if we do not."

CHAPTER 69

SPACE

I AWOKE WITH MY DAUGHTER ON MY MIND. I lay in bed a
couple minutes to let the sleep fog clear, then picked up
my phone and texted her:

Hey, sweetie. Just thinking about you. Love you.

I ordered room service and had them deliver it in a
bag so I could take it to my workroom with me. There I
sipped coffee and ate the delicious ham, egg, and cheese
croissant while working through my email. That done, I
started the billing clock and got to work on the case.

First I made a stealthy connection to the bunker
computer I'd worked on the night before and checked for
activity. It didn't look to be in use yet. I couldn't do much,
because the last thing I needed was to set off an alarm
down there, but I didn't need to do much. I planted a tiny

script, a mini-app of sorts, that would slowly and carefully propagate the spy app throughout the computers in the bunker. It paid to still have access to an arsenal of the U.S. government's swankiest software. No, I shouldn't still have that access all these years later, but it's not my fault that some dumbass had left my username and password active on an FTP server that held some of the coolest tech on the planet, is it? Nope.

The spy app was configured to deliver its reports to me every day at midnight. When midnight rolled around tonight, I'd know how complete the propagation was by the number of reports I received.

My phone buzzed a stacatto pattern, ten quick hits, and bounced lightly on the conference table. Text message. I picked it up and saw it was from Ally: *hey dad, can u talk 2 mom abt this school thing? rather come live in the grt outdoors w/u n johnny. love u2! af*

I smiled and answered: *You hate bugs and snakes too much. Study!*

CHAPTER 70

SPACE

Daria Bodrova

DARIA SCROLLED THROUGH THE PHOTOS of the man while Alex leaned on his knees and looked over her shoulder. When she got to the one that showed his face, she stopped. She also heard Alex take a quick breath when that photo appeared. Did he know him? She sure would not ask, but that breath was very curious.

"Show me the rest," he said.

She scrolled through the rest of them and turned to look at him. His forehead was wrinkled, his face cloudy.

"Go back to the clear one," he said.

She did.

"Print thirty copies of that one."

She nodded.

Alex stood and said in a loud, commanding voice,

"Listen up!" All the keyboards in the room went silent and chairs squeaked as the workers turned to see him.

Daria wondered how one could listen up or down. So many things about English she did not understand yet.

"In a few minutes, Daria will give each of you a picture of a man. I want to know if any of you have ever seen him. Ever. I also want everybody to be alert for anything strange about your computers. Anything at all. We have been breached."

Alex paused, and the room was so quiet that Daria wondered if everyone had stopped breathing.

Then he went on. "I want each of you to stop what you're doing and immediately start a network capture on your machine. Get everything. No filters. I want it all." Alex looked at his watch. "At noon, save the captures to the server. Then do it again at end of day. Clear?"

Daria looked around and saw some confused faces. She said, "Mr. Alex, I think maybe not all understand."

"I thought everyone here spoke English?"

"Yes, but some not so well. Still learning details."

"Do you understand what I want?" he said.

"Yes."

"Explain it to them so they do, too."

Daria stood and relayed his instructions in Russian, then asked them to raise their hands if they understood exactly what they were to do. Every hand went up. She looked at Alex and nodded. "It is done."

"Good. Back to work, everybody!" he said, then walked away, pulling his mobile from his pocket as he went.

CHAPTER 71

MEMJET EXECUTIVE AIR SERVICE
MEMPHIS INTERNATIONAL AIRPORT

Max Sultanovich

RED-FACED, THE THICK BLUE VEIN above his eyebrow pulsing, Max stood on the top step of the fold-down stairway of his jet and loosed a stream of Ukrainian invective into the phone. When he looked as if his head might actually burst, he spiked the phone into the asphalt at the foot of the stairs. He descended, covered the space between the plane and the building in ten long strides, and burst through the door into the lounge of the executive aircraft facility.

Businessmen tending laptops and mobiles from plush leather chairs and sofas looked up as if they were so disturbed. Max stopped, looked around a moment, started to dare them all to fuck with him, changed his mind. He continued through the room and out the other side. Down the corridor. Into the pilots' lounge, where his two bastards sat talking and joking with other white-shirted bastards.

"Come!" he said. "We will take off right now."

The two pilots looked at each other, their monkey mouths open. Looked back to him. One said, "We still have no clearance to leave, sir."

Max took in a long, slow breath through his nostrils, switched to Russian, and with great calm said, *"Nemedlenno podnimayte svoy zad, cherez pyatnadtsat' minut moy samolyot dolzhen letet' nad zemlyoy, inache cherez pyatnadtsat' dney vy i vashy sem'i okazhetes' pod ney."* You get off your ass and get my plane off the ground in fifteen minutes, or within fifteen days you and your families will be under the ground.

Now his bastards were on their feet. He followed them through the building, outside, then pounded up the stairs into his plane. The pilots readied the outside, pulling the wheel blocks and the covers from the front of the engines.

Two minutes later, the pilots were in their seats and fingering their switches and knobs.

The MemJet ramp supervisor was on the far side of the tarmac when he saw the pilots of RF-46923, a beautiful Dassault Falcon, pulling the covers from the engines and unchocking the wheels. What the hell? Any such prep, whether for parking, storage, or departure, had to be done by MemJet personnel. That was the rule, it wasn't negotiable, and every pilot who used their facility was made aware of it with great perspicuity. Plus, this aircraft had an FAA hold on it.

As he broke into a trot toward the Falcon, the supervisor cupped his hands and shouted, "Gentlemen? You can't do that."

Neither pilot showed any sign of having heard him, though he knew they had. The trot became a run and he shouted again. Ignored again. He was still fifty feet away and both pilots were now aboard the aircraft, stowing the fold-down stairs and preparing to close the door. Realizing he wasn't going to reach the plane in time, he stopped and pulled the handheld radio from its holster, keyed to transmit, and said in an urgent tone, "Jet control, jet ramp. Jet control, jet ramp."

RADIO: "Ramp, control. I see it. Falcon four-six-niner-two-three, this is jet control. You are not unauthorized to move, sir. I repeat, you are not authorized to move. Power down your engines now, and exit the aircraft. Repeat, power down immediately and exit the aircraft."

The supervisor heard the Falcon's engines spooling up and saw the plane begin to move. The plane was parked so that they could move straight ahead; no need for a pushback. Was this really happening?

RADIO: "Ground control, this is MemJet control. We are declaring an emergency. We have an unauthorized departure in progress by a foreign aircraft that is subject to an FAA hold. Repeat, unauthorized departure in progress by on-hold aircraft."

RADIO: "MemJet control, ground control, roger on unauthorized departure. Identify aircraft, please."

RADIO: "Ground, MemJet. The airplane is a Falcon jet, tail number romeo-foxtrot-four-six-niner-two-three."

RADIO: "MemJet, ground control. Confirm that this is a romeo-foxtrot aircraft?"

RADIO: "Ground, MemJet. Confirmed. Falcon, ro-meo-foxtrot-four-six-niner-two-three."

RADIO: "Roger that, MemJet, we have it from here."

The supervisor adjusted the frequency on the radio so he could monitor all the frequencies that were about to be in use here.

RADIO: "Falcon romeo-foxtrot-four-six-niner-two-three, this is Memphis ground control. You are not authorized to taxi, repeat, you are not authorized to taxi. Stop the aircraft and power down your engines immediately, or more aggressive measures will be implemented."

Five seconds passed without reply from the Falcon. Ten. Fifteen.

RADIO: "Falcon niner-two-three, you are ordered to stop the aircraft and power down your engines immediately. Acknowledge."

The Falcon had made it to a taxiway and was picking up speed. Baker estimated it at 50 MPH and it was no more than a half mile from making a left turn onto runway 18C. Sirens were sounding now from every direction as emergency vehicles moved toward the jet. The most notable of those was a modified Armored Personnel Carrier that had turned onto the southern end of the runway, the 36C end. The bulky vehicle, covered in armored plates, had a pointed metal extension on the front that looked like a brush guard on steroids. It was this addition that turned the vehicle into a battering ram designed for this exact purpose.

Now the APC was the only thing that had any chance of stopping the Falcon, because the jet had made the turn onto the runway. Its engines screamed as the pilots pushed them to full throttle, and the nimble aircraft was accelerating quickly toward rotation speed as the APC came toward it head-on, also picking up speed. Baker watched the surreal confrontation unfold. It was close, but not enough. The gleaming white Falcon's nose rose and the aircraft left the ground, passing at least ten feet above the APC as it climbed into the hot summer sky.

CHAPTER 72

SPACE

Alex

ALEX LOOKED AGAIN AT THE PICTURE the girl had found. Then he picked up a second picture he'd been given, this one a frame from one of the thousands of surveillance cameras on this property. Same man, no doubt about it, and he'd bet money this man was involved in their loss of access to the SPACE network. He slipped the phone from his pocket and dialed the number again. This time he got an answer.

"It's me," Alex said. "We have a major problem."

Two minutes later, Alex ended the call and returned the phone to his pocket after checking the time. 12:22 p.m. He moved the mouse to wake his screen, and navigated to the folder on the server where the workers had saved the network captures from that morning. Starting with the capture from the computer that had taken the picture of the intruder, he began to pore through the mountain of network data.

Twenty minutes into his dig, he found the first confirmation of his fears. "Sonofabitch," he said to no one. Now that he had found the first tamper, he knew exactly what he was looking for on the remaining computers. He set a filter to show him only the traffic generated by the spyware app the intruder had left behind. It was already on twelve of the twenty computers on the floor. It was moving from machine to machine, duplicating itself and self-installing on the computers one by one.

How the hell was that possible? This wasn't some simple trojan. It was a sophisticated snoop that would make a record of everything that happened on a computer, and no doubt deliver the results to the asshole who planted it. None of their antivirus or antimalware scanners had picked up the slightest trace of it, and they were running superb scanners that were updated daily and supposedly capable of finding and eradicating any threat, including activity recorders like this. If Daria hadn't found that picture, they would have never known. But they did know, and now he had the advantage.

He also had a plan for how to press that advantage. He stepped out of the office and onto the workfloor, then called out, "Daria, come here."

When she arrived, he gestured for her to sit in the lone visitor's chair.

The girl looked scared. "Yes, Mr. Alex?"

"Just Alex, okay?"

She nodded.

"We have a lot of work to do this afternoon, and I need your help."

"Yes? What can I do?"

"We are going to build a trap, Daria. We're going to bait that trap, and then we're going to catch us a predator."

CHAPTER 73

FBI - NEW YORK

Christine Gamboa

"SASHA, I THINK MAYBE WE'RE SAFER HERE, in a locked apartment in the middle of an FBI building."

Sasha turned to her on the sofa and took her face in his pudgy hands. "Chrissy, you think this because you do not know Max. We must to go from here. We must to hide."

"How could he know we're here?" she said. "And even if he did, how would he get to us in here?"

"Chrissy, you must to trust Sasha. Max own people everywhere. He knows. Max is man who will kill one thousand people to kill one person."

She heard the electronic lock on the front door beep as it unlocked, and turned toward it. The young FBI employee who had been bringing them food and other requests since they were put in the apartment stepped through the door with a large pizza box in hand. Zuyev walked to him as if to take the pizza. Instead, at the last moment Zuyev picked up a heavy ceramic table lamp and hit the man in the side of the head with as much calm as a normal human being might have when picking up a newspaper. The lamp shattered and the man grunted as he went down to his knees.

Zuyev took the pizza from his hands during the fall and said, "Thank you very much."

The man looked confused for a couple seconds, then his eyes closed and he crumpled onto the carpeted floor.

"Now we go," Zuyev said.

Christine felt like she was in a dream as the cab weaved in and out of New York traffic. She wasn't worried about a car wreck. The taxi driver wanted the thousand-dollar tip Sasha had promised upon successful delivery, and he was handling the yellow Crown Vic with expertise, blowing his horn and cursing out the window at other drivers who somehow offended him. Best as she could tell, that included every driver they encountered. Plus she was wedged tightly enough in the back seat between Sasha's width and Zuyev's bones that she probably wouldn't go anywhere even if they did crash.

What scared her was everything else. Max Sultanovich had already wanted her dead. Now? He probably wanted her flayed alive or some such. Sasha had won a lot of trust from her over the past couple days, so she didn't worry about him, but that Zuyev was another story. She had looked into his eyes after he attacked the young man and did not sense a soul behind them. Then there was the fact that she was on the run from the FBI. Was it illegal to run from the FBI when you hadn't been arrested? And would the FBI honor the deal they had made, now that they had taken off? Maybe she should have refused to leave. And maybe she should have been a little more forthcoming about the full extent of her own involvement, such as it was.

Now, unbelievably, Zuyev was opening the damned pizza box. The smell of pepperoni, onions, and peppers flooded the small sweaty space and her stomach roiled. Enough. Without saying a word, she reached across Zuyev, rolled the window down, yanked the pizza box off his lap, and flung it out the window. Zuyev stared at her and she stared right back.

Sasha burst out laughing. "Yes! Yes, Chrissy! I must to marry you!"

CHAPTER 74

FBI - NEW YORK

Courtney Meyer

MEYER LOOKED IN THE RESTROOM MIRROR. No surprise there, but what a sight. Bloodshot eyes in puffy sockets. Pale face. And that hair. Good grief, that hair. She dabbed at her face with a damp paper towel, trying not to wipe off what little makeup remained, and did the best she could with the mess on her head. Time to go.

She arrived to a full conference room and walked to the end that had the wall-mounted display. "Can someone dim the lights, please?" The lights softened and she picked up the remote for her presentation. She clicked and the FBI logo on the screen faded to a picture split in vertical thirds that showed photos of Maslov, Zuyev, and Gamboa.

Someone in the room, a man, quietly said, "Wow."

She turned away from the screen and toward the room. Picked up her cup of coffee and took a sip. Looked at a young man at the far end of the room who looked like a penny that had just been struck. "Chad, and the rest of you men, can you please get your gawking at Gamboa out of the way right now?"

Nervous chuckles rippled around the table.

"All done?" she said. When the room was quiet, she went on. "Alexander Maslov, Benjamin Zuyev, and Christine Gamboa. As most of you know, these three assaulted an agent earlier today and fled from one of our in-house apartments. They were in protective custody, not under arrest. That said, Maslov and Zuyev are admitted felons, and now that they've assaulted a federal officer, all three have been classified as wanted and warrants have been issued. Their capture is a high and immediate priority."

Click. The screen switched to a photo of Sultanovich sitting in the interrogation room the night before. "Meet Maxim Sultanovich. This frail-looking old man is the head of the Ukrainian mafia and the most powerful organized crime figure in all of Eastern Europe."

"Including Russia?" someone said.

"He operates out of Kiev, but his reach is long and complex. We believe he has a personal relationship with, and the blessing of, Putin himself. So yes, including Russia."

Fresh-faced Chad said, "Where is he now?"

"He was apprehended in Mississippi yesterday and taken into custody by our Memphis field office. We were forced to release him when a legal attaché from the Ukrainian embassy presented papers showing Sultanovich to be a special envoy."

"Diplomatic immunity?" someone said.

"Yes. It's trumped-up nonsense, of course, but State gave us no support and we had to cut him loose, at least temporarily."

"Where'd he go?" someone else said.

"I'm getting to that," Meyer said. "We were able to get the FAA to put a hold on his plane while we tried to get around the diplomatic cover. An hour ago, however, his plane defied that order and took off from Memphis."

"They couldn't stop the plane? I thought airports had ways to deal with that kind of thing since nine-eleven?" Chad said.

"Homeland Security tried and failed. I understand they were attempting to ram the plane on the runway and missed getting there in time by a matter of feet."

"What now?" someone said.

Meyer took another sip of coffee. "The FAA is looking and we also have at least some support from the Air Force."

Someone gave a low whistle.

"Yeah," Meyer said. "It's a great big deal, people. Our immediate objective is to apprehend Maslov, Zuyev, and Gamboa. They're our best evidence—actually, our only evidence—against Sultanovich. We don't think they fled to avoid any potential prosecution. They came to us, and we had succesfully negotiated a deal for their cooperation."

Young Chad was full of questions. "Then why?"

"Fear of Sultanovich getting to them."

"Here?" Chad said.

"I know, I know. Secure apartment, secure building, surrounded by federal agents. So if two career criminals like Maslov and Zuyev were scared enough to run, that should give you some idea of what we're dealing with in

Sultanovich. Let's find these three, and let's do it before
Sultanovich's people do."

CHAPTER 75

SPACE

IT WAS A LITTLE AFTER ELEVEN. Less than an hour until the first batch of midnight reports should start arriving from the bunker computers. I had worked until about seven on a comprehensive report I had begun writing for Jacob Allen, one with lots of detail and data. It would take several days to put together, and on this night I was tired of it. I closed the file and sent Nichols away, told him I wanted to work on some personal things for a bit.

I opened the rape videos and all the data behind them. I studied that data, tried to find clues that would let me trace the origin of the monstrous videos beyond the anonymity of the deep web. I dug into the metadata, the hidden data buried in the code of the web pages that contained the videos. Hoped I'd get lucky and find some piece of information left behind by a sloppy tech, something that would let me get even a tenuous grip on who built the pages. Nothing. Generic pages that could have been put together by any of a countless number of people using any of a hundred different apps.

Next came the actual video files. Pictures and videos often contain a lot of hidden data, as well. It's how you can load them into some electronic photo albums and get a pretty little map with cute little pushpins showing where they were shot and when. I extracted and studied that data. No go. Every field of metadata had been stripped clean.

After stepping away for a couple minutes to grab a cup of coffee and stretch, I sat back down and pulled up my address book. After a bit of searching, I found the guy I was looking for. A professor who had done a lot of research on photographic and video evidence. He had discovered that even when you don't have the metadata, cameras leave electronic fingerprints behind. Artifacts in images that aren't visible to the human eye. Patterns in the way they process color and light that can be tied to a specific manufacturer, sometimes even a particular model. If you have the source camera, you might even get lucky and match that particular camera to images it created.

I shot the professor an email and asked if he'd be willing to take a look at a couple disturbing videos, run them through his magic algorithms, tell me what he could find. I attached a couple of the videos, along with a clear warning that they were graphic and sickening.

That done, I moved to the part of the analysis I dreaded, watching the videos. Over and over. Looking for any clues to location. Anything that might help me identify one of the girls or where she was from. An accident, a name spoken. Any peculiarity at all. After three hours of watching, I had a tiny list of notes to research, none of which were likely to yield results.

I also had an old and unwelcome friend with me at the end of the viewing session, one I had spent years burying in the deepest, most securely guarded recesses of my soul. He moved in my essence like an impossible gathering of a million black holes, sucking away all light, leaving me with only dark resolve and immutable purpose. Do my job. Mercy does not exist. Survive. Purge Earth of those who prey on the innocent. He manifested in my mind as an ethereal black mass. As he moved, as he took over my thoughts and actions, as he devoured the light, his wispy edges glowed a brilliant crimson. Then he grew stronger and stronger, devouring more and more light, the crimson edges becoming a blood-red fog that filled every crevice of my soul.

As I watched innocent girl after girl being brutalized, watched them scream and beg for mercy that never came, he grew. When I watched one young girl in particular, who reminded me of my own daughter, be savaged by these creatures, these walking wastes of flesh who were unfit to be deemed human, he grew.

He had no name, because the red fog and I were one and the same.

After watching the horrible videos the night before, I lost all interest in reports from the dungeon and instead crashed and tried to sleep. It was a night filled with fits and starts and sweats and dark dreams. When I woke the next morning—earlier than usual—I showered and dressed, then checked to see if any dungeon reports had arrived. They had, a lot of them. I'd study them later.

I ate a light breakfast and drank three cups of coffee at Rings of Saturn, then grabbed another cup to go on my way out. The weird hours and poor sleep of the past few nights had my body clock out of kilter. A few minutes of walking outdoors would fix it. After completing the maze through the casino, I exited the rear doors and hung a left. Might as well walk toward the tunnel.

The morning was cool so far, low seventies, the desert air crisp and refreshing and so clear it looked like the mountains ringing the valley were no more than a few miles away. Now that I was outside, though, it became obvious that I should have gone out the front entrance to experience the body-clock-resetting rays of Sol. The back of SPACE faced west and was of course in shadow. I walked, not wanting to trek the casino maze again. I'd just circle the tower till I hit sunshine.

I was approaching the tunnel when I saw her. She too was approaching it, but from the far side, coming toward me. My heart gave a little stutter. It was the girl from the surveillance video, the girl who had stopped beneath the camera and talked with the two guys inside the bunker. I crossed the mouth of the tunnel, felt its gentle waft of cool air, stepped onto the sidewalk on the other side. The girl was ten feet away, looking down as she walked. Five feet away, she must've sensed my presence, because she looked up.

Her reaction was instant. She literally stopped mid-step, her mouth slightly parted and her eyes wide as she looked into mine. *She recognized me.*

When she stopped, I did too. In the space of a second, I processed the fact that she recognized me: She had seen me on surveillance footage inside the bunker. No other explanation for her surprise. And if she had, others might have. She looked like she was ready to bolt, so I raised my hands, palms out. "Please," I said. "I'm a friend."

Her face and posture relaxed a bit, but barely. She said nothing, so I continued. "My name is Sam. I'd very much like to talk. You have nothing to fear from me."

She whipped her head to the left, looked behind her, to the side, then back to me. The look on her face had gone from surprise to fear. But maybe not fear of me. Fear of being seen talking to me. She stepped around me and walked at a fast clip toward the tunnel, then into it. I turned and followed. Not close enough to spook her, I hoped. I stayed about twenty feet behind her. When I saw one of the offshoot tunnels approaching, I made a guess and said, "I can help you."

There it was. The tiniest glitch in her step. I said, "Please take the tunnel to the right. There's a place we can talk. No cameras."

Her pace slowed, just a bit. Five feet from the tunnel…three…there. She turned. I followed. "There's a corridor ahead on the left. Go there."

She did and I was right behind her. No more than six feet into the corridor, a locked door formed a dead end, but that was fine. We were out of sight of anyone or any cameras. I said, "I'm Sam."

"I am Daria Bodrova. You policeman?"

"No, but I can call police later. Where are you from, Daria?"

"I live in Kiev."

Classic Eastern European pronunciation. *KEE-uhv.* I took care to speak slowly, enunciating, avoiding contractions. "You do not know me, Daria, but you can trust me. I want to help you. Do you need help?"

She nodded, and I went on. "Do you know the type of

work you are doing here?"

"I know. We stealing money."

This time I nodded. "Who are you working for?"

"I do not know. There is man we call Alex. He pretends to be American, but he is Slavic. I know when someone is from Russia, maybe Ukraine."

"Are you here against your will?"

Her face scrunched up and her head tilted a little to the side.

"Do you want to do this work?" I said.

She shook her head. "No."

"I can take you somewhere safe, right now."

This time she shook her head emphatically, and the fear returned to her face. "No, no, no!"

"Why not?"

"Anya. They kill Anya! I must work!"

I patted the air, spoke in a low, gentle voice: "Okay, okay. I understand. Do not worry. Who is Anya?"

"Sister. Anya my sister." Her accent was heavy, but her English was pretty strong, good enough that she didn't have the habit of prefacing verbs with the word 'to.' She had studied.

I said, "Do you know where Anya is?"

She shook her head.

"Do you know if she came to the United States?"

She nodded. "Yes, we come together on airplane."

"When did they take Anya?"

"In airport. They say we join later, but we do not."

"Okay. The Las Vegas airport?"

"Yes. They take Anya away in different automobile. Then I go in house here at Las Vegas. I ask many times where is Anya, but man scream on me and hit me."

"Alex hit you?"

"No. Alex come later. Was Dmitry."

"Can you tell me where the house is? Are there other girls?"

"House in street called Green Mountain, but I do not see mountain. Only flat street. Seven hundred and forty-two is number."

"And are there others?" I said.

"Many more girls. Boys also." She looked at a simple watch on her wrist. "I must go. Alex come soon."

"Okay. Can we meet later?"

"Tomorrow. I come early. I come in seven."

"Thank you, Daria. I will help you. One more question: How did you know me?"

"I see you on the recording, in room."

I nodded. "Did anyone else see the recording?"

"Alex see recording. Alex make computer cage for you. I must go now."

CHAPTER 76

SPACE

Daria Bodrova

DARIA HAD BEEN AT HER WORKSTATION about ten minutes when Alex arrived. Her insides were doing flips. What if he started talking to her? Could she behave normally? Or would he be able to tell something was wrong? And why had she talked so much, so freely, to the man named Sam, the man who had snuck into this room in the middle of the night like a bandit? Was she that desperate, so desperate as to talk to a complete stranger? And could she really trust the man? Of all the questions, she was most confident she knew the answer to that one, and it was yes. She didn't know how she knew, but yes, she believed she could trust the man Sam. Why else would she have talked to him?

"Daria," Alex said, startling her.

"Yes?" Did she flinch? Did he see it?

"Any new action on the videos?"

"No. All were normal."

"Have you checked the keylogger to see if the reports went out to the intruder last night?"

"No, I will do this now." She maneuvered through the system, Alex watching over her shoulder, her heart beating so hard and so fast that she worried if he could hear it.

"Be careful," he said. "Do it like we talked about, so he can't tell that we know."

She nodded and continued navigating to the log. "Yes, nine reports were transmitted," she said.

Alex did something he had never done. He gave a little squeeze of her neck. Then she felt and heard him kiss the top of her head.

"Good job," he said. "Very good job."

Daria fought the urge to vomit.

CHAPTER 77

SPACE

I HAD MADE DARIA WAIT WHILE I CHECKED the tunnel to be sure no one was coming, then sent her on her way to the bunker. I left the tunnel at a jog and continued the pace until I was back inside the casino. The last thing I wanted was to be seen by "Alex," and according to Daria, he would be arriving at the tunnel soon.

After a visit to my room to retrieve my laptop, I made my way to the workroom, all the while trying to process what had just happened. Through a chance meeting—maybe divine intervention was more likely—I had just gotten a huge break. I now had an inside source. I also had the invaluable knowledge that those in charge inside the bunker were aware of me, aware of my visit in the wee hours. What had Daria said? Alex made a computer cage for me? Trap. She meant trap.

A known trap is not much of a trap at all. No more

accessing the hacker computers for me. Whatever I'd find there was quickly becoming secondary anyway.

I emailed the private investigator and told him to get everything he could on 742 Green Mountain Drive, the house where Daria and the other forced tech workers were living. Then I Googled the address and checked out what I could see from the Internet myself. The house was a largish cookie-cutter situated in a cul-de-sac of a fairly new-looking subdivision, the kind with a thousand houses that all look way too much alike. Suburban America of the twenty-first century. Further searching turned up nothing useful, so I'd wait for the PI's report.

Now I had a dilemma: what to do. My instant reflex was to call the FBI agent, Meyer. They would be best equipped to deal with such a situation, and maybe such a tip would be big enough to get her off my back for good. I also had a responsibility to inform Jacob Allen, the client who was paying me and had a right to know what was going on in the bowels of the business he ran.

The problem? I wasn't sure who I could trust to react in a way that wouldn't endanger Daria or her sister or the others, who could only be described as prisoners and hostages. I liked Jacob well enough, but I also remembered how he not only didn't want to notify the police about the rape videos; he actively thwarted my attempt to involve the police. I understood his desire to keep the company brand from being associated with such a sordid situation, but I didn't agree with it. His right to know was important, but not important enough to risk this. Then there was Meyer, a cold-hearted bitch I knew I didn't trust.

In the end, the list of who I trusted to handle it was short: me.

My email notifier dinged and when I looked at my inbox, I had a reply from the professor with the fancy algorithms.

Dear Mr. Flatt,

rcvd your videos and request. "disturbing" is an understatement. ran them through my system and got results that look solid. 94.5% chance all the imagery you sent was recorded on the same camera, a canon c300 cinema. somewhat odd that a high-end camera would be used and the resulting footage compressed in such a lossy fashion. let me know if I can do more.

jcf

After sending back a thank-you email, I hopped on Amazon and looked up the C300. The camera was a new-ish model, out less than a year, which meant there were relatively fewer owners out there. I leaned back in my chair and thought about the professor's point on shooting with such quality gear, then uploading versions that had been compressed so much that the quality was indistinguishable from a low-end smartphone's output. After a couple minutes, it hit me: Maybe the deep web versions were just teasers, previews of a much higher-quality version that could be bought.

I switched to the forensic environment in which I'd watched the rape videos, a special computer setup that allowed me to view anything online without a trace of it being stored on my computer. Just having a few child porn pictures on your computer is enough to land you in prison. I sure didn't want to find myself in that situation as a result of trying to find and stop these subhumans.

It took more than two hours of sifting through the most disgusting websites imaginable—child porn, torture porn, rape porn, snuff films—but I finally scored a direct hit. The site had no name, just a long URL on the deep web that looked like gibberish. If you got to this site, either someone had given you the URL, or you'd found it via one of the deep web's unfiltered search engines. Probably with a search term like "REAL RAPE" or similar. It was laid out like a typical online store, although the aesthetics were minimal, crude by today's standards and more in keeping with online stores one would have seen in the early days of the Internet. People didn't come here for flashy graphics and a slick user experience. They came because they were the lowest form of life on the planet, the kind who derive sexual gratification from watching helpless girls brutalized. These miscreants weren't content watching twentysomething actors pretend to be fifteen-year-olds being raped. No, this scum wanted to see innocent teenagers ripped and torn body and soul, for real.

Bold text at the top of the page said AUTHENTIC-ITY OF EVERY VIDEO GUARANTEED. WATCH THESE YOUNG BITCHES SCREAM. Below the header, a grid of thumbnails showed select frames from the videos for sale. Each thumbnail had three tiny links below it: STREAM HD $55, BLU-RAY $75, and PREVIEW FREE. Clicking the preview link played the exact videos at the exact crappy quality level I had seen earlier, although they played from a different deep web address. Both the streaming and Blu-Ray links added that video to a shopping cart and went to a view of the cart that offered the choice to CONTINUE SHOPPING or CHECKOUT NOW.

Buying the streaming version would be a waste of time. These people weren't idiots, so tracking a high-def stream's origin down would yield the same results as I got when trying to find the source of the previews I'd watched. A Blu-Ray would at least provide something tangible that came from somewhere in the brick-and-mortar world. I thought about setting up a blind mailbox at one of the many services in Vegas, but decided against it. I had some Bitcoin and could pay without leaving a clue of any kind, but I didn't want this stuff shipped to me in any way, especially since I already had an FBI agent willing to throw out all scruples and notions of fair play in what she no doubt viewed as her noble quest.

I had a better idea. After working through the check-out screen and double-checking the information I'd entered, I clicked the button that said COMPLETE ORDER.

CHAPTER 78

Christine Gamboa

GIVEN THEIR PREVIOUS TRAVELS, this wasn't what Christine imagined when she learned they were taking a chartered flight to parts unknown. The Cessna had four seats, and none of them was built to accommodate Sasha, even though he managed to lodge himself in the right front seat. She was directly behind him—the pilot said she had to sit there—with Zuyev on her left. The short seatback pressed into her knees and the back of Sasha's giant head was no more than a foot from her face.

They had taken off, landed for gas, taken off, landed for gas, taken off again. Sasha declined to answer her questions about where they were or where they were going. You must to trust Sasha, Chrissy. The only thing she was sure of was that during the daylight hours, they'd always been headed generally westward. That was the case now. The sun was straight ahead, low in the sky, painting the fluffy white carpet of clouds below them a soft golden color.

She turned to Zuyev. "I have to pee. Close your eyes."

His eyelids slowly dropped, the way a doll's eyes would as you laid it back. His mouth turned up just a bit on the right side, the closest she'd seen to a smile from him. The surrealism of the situation, the confinement in the ever-more-stinky cabin as they flew, the stress and exhaustion, were all beginning to mess with her mind. She now almost believed Zuyev wasn't really a human being at all, but some macabre automaton. Sasha was some amphibian glob. She stretched to reach the pee bottle behind the back seat, got a finger through the handle, and brought it forward.

The pilot turned his head ever so quickly and their eyes met. He had done it many times, but she had gotten used to men doing that since she was about fifteen. He had bright brown eyes that seemed to always be on the verge of a smile. The grizzle on his face was dark with a flash of gray on occasion. Christine didn't know who he was or where Sasha had found him, and didn't really care.

She should've worn a dress, because getting her jeans down enough to pee in the bottle was a difficult proposition in this cocoon. She unsnapped the pants and the pilot's head did another quick swivel. This time she was ready and met his eyes with a stare that said, *Not gonna happen, buddy. What may happen, though, is me pulling your eyeballs out of your face and stuffing them in your ears.* The twinkle disappeared from the brown eyes and he turned back forward.

It took a couple minutes of hard work, but she wrestled her jeans down to her ankles and got the bottle positioned. A short time later, she snapped the lid back down and contorted enough to stow the bottle behind the seat again. After cleaning herself up, she finally got her pants up, zipped, and snapped. She gave Zuyev a jab with her elbow. "Done."

The eyes opened, a reverse of the way they'd closed. A demon doll. With the pee-wrestle over, Christine noticed that they were descending through the clouds. She watched out the window as the white shroud around them thinned to occasional wisps, then disappeared. A familiar landscape lay below the rare cover of gray clouds. They were back in Las Vegas.

CHAPTER 79

TIJUANA, MEXICO

Max Sultanovich

THE LANDING AT GENERAL ABELARDO L. RODRÍGUEZ International Airport in Tijuana, Mexico, had been routine and smooth. Max snorted as he thought about a bunch of damned Mexicans sitting around on their asses and coming up with such a name for a pathetic dump of an airport in a shithole of a country. Bastards.

Sometimes he hated that he was forced to deal with such scum, but as the cartel had promised, the airport process was hassle-free. A Mexican government official who looked like all the rest met his airplane and took him and Tatyana to a car. The car took them to a neighborhood of filth and squalor. After turning into a gravel driveway in front of a small adobe hovel, the driver motioned for them to exit the car. Yet another Mexican stood waiting in the doorway of the house, gesturing for them to come inside.

The inside of the house smelled like grease and peppers and onions and stinking Mexicans. For good reason. He counted at least a dozen of the cockroaches in the tiny front room alone, all turning their insect heads toward him and his granddaughter as they followed their guide through the stench, down a hallway and into a bedroom. The guide pulled the bed to one side and flipped up a rug to reveal a hole in the floor. A stairway was lit by a bare lightbulb hanging on a piece of flat white electrical cable. The guide stepped down into the hole and they followed.

The nasty aroma of the house gave way to the scent of cool dirt as they descended. At the bottom of the stairs, a dirt tunnel stretched into the distance. More electrical cable lay on the ground on one side, a glowing bare bulb in a socket every ten meters or so. The guide kept walking, so they did, too.

Tatyana said, "Are we almost there?"

Max patted her on the head and said nothing. He watched as the Mexican leading the way ducked beneath an occasional short wooden beam that crossed above their heads and supported a piece of plywood. Max didn't need to duck. That stretchy sonofabitch in front of them probably thought being tall made him physically superior. Max snorted at the thought, trudging forward as he slipped into a daydream involving a hammer and a handsaw.

After at least a kilometer's walk, Max saw a brighter glow ahead. Then he could make out the dirt wall of the tunnel's end. When they reached it, they climbed another crude stairway built from lumber scraps. When they stepped onto the floor above, Max looked around. Like their entry point, it was a bedroom. This one had dirty clothes all over the floor, and poster pictures of more Mexicans covered the walls here and there. Mexicans grinning through ridiculous gold teeth, holding guns in arms covered in tattoo ink. Nasty bastards.

The house itself was nicer, much nicer, than the one on the other end of the tunnel. Still shit he wouldn't live in, but better than the fly-infested rotbox to the south. They followed the tall Mexican through the house and into a decent-sized living room. Did these Mexican fuckers ever do anything that didn't involve a cluster of them? Every seat in the room was taken by either a thuggish male or a whore of a female. Some stared at phones in their hands, while two of them on a big sofa writhed and shouted with game controllers in their hands. The television they stared at with their rat eyes had to be two meters wide. It was absurd, just like all of these animals.

Max walked to a window at the front of the room and pulled apart a couple slats of the blinds to peek outside. Neat green lawns. The house across the street had a flag on an angled rod sticking out from the porch, its red, white, and blue rippling in a slight breeze on a sunny day. A fat bastard sat jiggling on a green lawn mower as it went back and forth across the grass. God bless America.

CHAPTER 80

FBI - NEW YORK

Courtney Meyer

MEYER SETTLED INTO HER OFFICE CHAIR with a printed copy of the report she had received from Computer Boy, Sam Flatt, ready to really dig into it for the first time. As expected—she had researched her target, after all—it was well written and had the feel of being accurate on the technical front. And now that she'd had some time for the adrenaline of the case to subside, for the first time she felt a twinge of regret over the way she'd coerced his cooperation. She didn't have kids, had never married. Maybe she couldn't appreciate the full gravity of going at someone through his kid, but in her calm, quiet office, what she had done started to feel very wrong. There was his unexpected threat, too, but that didn't really bother her. She'd been threatened by everyone from drug dealers to pedophiles to full-blown mafia gangsters, so in retrospect, some computer nerd's rant hardly registered. Her conscience did, however; that's not the kind of agent she was.

She pushed through the reverie and focused on the report. Interesting. He was brought in because SPACE was being hacked. Meyer hadn't seen that one coming. Her interest in SPACE had been based on the fact that the land the casino sat on had been bought from Sultanovich. In fact, the real estate records showed that Sultanovich still retained ownership of some tiny part of the land, which had piqued her interest. The money-laundering possibilities of a casino were huge, and the connection was something she couldn't ignore.

Her plan had been to co-opt Flatt, just to see if she could get any kind of inside scoop on the company and whether any ongoing business relationship existed with Sultanovich. It had been the ultimate long shot, really. Her assumption had been that they hired him to search for an embezzler, or to check out allegations of some employee looking at kiddie porn, something like that. That's the kind of thing the FBI's computer forensic nerds looked at day in and day out, at least according to the ones she'd talked to. Computer Boy was working on something much different.

Then the report got very interesting: Christine Gamboa was a person of interest in the affair. Meyer's pulse quickened and her brain sped up. Now she had a nexus between Flatt's work and the Sultanovich case. Coincidences do happen, but everything about this screamed that this was not the case here. No way. Time to fire up a new pot of coffee.

CHAPTER 81

SPACE

I COULDN'T STOP THINKING ABOUT DARIA and her predicament. And that of the others in her situation, but Daria now had a flesh-and-blood face in my mind. I needed a brainstorm partner but had none. Couldn't trust Meyer. Wasn't sure I could trust Jacob Allen. And this was too much to trust Nichols with. Truth is, now that I was having to do more and more of my work on the sly, Jimbo Nichols was starting to be a bit of a disruption. I could only send him on so many errands before raising his antennae, so I worked while he sat at the end of the table reading his book.

As I pondered the facts, it again occurred to me that the rape videos could be connected to the business going on in the bunker. This wasn't the first time I thought about this, but now I was entertaining it as a significant possibility. Before now, I had thought of the videos as something Gamboa had watched on the deep web, but could the connection be more entwined? Was there more to the bunker business than stealing mountains of e-cash? Why was Daria forced to work in the hackroom, while her sister was used as the hostage? What about the other workers? Why were they chosen? I needed more info from Daria.

In the meantime, I needed info on those who owned Canon C300 video cameras. Canon wouldn't be handing over their customer data, not without a subpoena or court order, something I had no access to at this point. I might be able to break into their databases, but doing something like that without leaving a trail of digital evidence behind was tricky business. I don't mind skirting a law on occasion when the need is urgent, but opening myself up to felony charges isn't at the top of my list.

I jumped online and searched for forums where people were discussing the C300, and felt a little surge of positive energy at the small number of results. After combing through them for several hours, however, I had nothing. I moved from the web to the deep web and my search for **discussion AND c300** yielded exactly one hit. I clicked into the forum. I looked through the list of topics and quickly saw a thread for **C300 lighting,** but when I tried to click into the discussion, I got a dialog box telling me I had to be registered to view content. With a sinking feeling, I clicked REGISTER. Three fields into the registration process, my fears were confirmed. Registration required an existing member to vouch for you, a common requirement on deep web forums where underworlders hang out.

No other options came to mind, so after a couple more minutes of considering the pros and cons, I jumped to a deep web forum I did have access to. After logging in, I created a new topic called **NEED SPECIAL TALENT IN WASTE MANAGEMENT.** In the message field, I entered, **URGENT NEED. DM HERE.** With that done, I clicked POST.

I wheeled my chair back, hit something. When I turned around, I nearly jumped out of the chair. James Nichols had been standing behind me. "Damn, Jimbo!" I said. "What the hell?"

He backed away, hands up, palms out. "Whoa, Sam. Sorry, man. Just finished my book and was curious as to what you were working on. That's all!"

CHAPTER 82

FBI - NEW YORK

Courtney Meyer

Meyer was making notes in the margins of Flatt's report when her door opened without a knock. A fresh-faced analyst stood in the doorway with an excited look on his face.

"Agent Meyer," he said. "We just picked up something in the op center I think you'll want to see."

Then he was gone. Meyer stowed the report inside its folder and made quick tracks to the room where a half dozen of the most junior people in the building sat and watched screens for alerts related to their work, or scoured emails, or fielded phone calls from around the country. Fresh Face was at the front of the room, pointing to a large display panel.

The screen showed a picture of a business jet, and

Meyer knew it at a glance. It was the jet Max Sultanovich was in when it narrowly escaped the runway in Memphis.

"Where?" she said.

"Tijuana," said Fresh Face.

"When?"

"Little less than an hour ago."

"How'd we get this?" Meyer said.

"Dassault."

"What the hell is Dassault?"

"Sorry," Fresh Face said. "Manufacturer of the aircraft. We asked them to run any geotracking they had. Since it was a fairly new plane, it had telematics which—"

"Fine, I get it," Meyer said. "What else do we have?"

"Not much. We should have been able to query the database and get the names of pilots, passengers, you name it, but when I run this tail number, I get nothing."

"How's that possible?"

Fresh Face shrugged. "Mexico?"

Meyer was a half-second from telling him that Mexico was a country and not an answer to her question, but she reconsidered. Given the nature of Mexico, a corrupt hovel of a country run by drug cartels, Fresh Face's answer was probably on target. "Good work," she said. "Keep digging, and email me anything you find, the instant you find it."

Fresh Face nodded and returned to his seat and his computer.

Meyer headed back toward her office. As she passed through the little cube farm populated by admins, she spotted her favorite. "Jenny," she said without slowing down, "I need a chopper on the roof yesterday, and a bureau plane waiting with its motors running when I hit JFK. Oh, and get State involved."

"Destination?" Jenny said.

"Tijuana."

CHAPTER 83

SPACE

Daria Bodrova

STILL AT HER DESK EVEN THOUGH all the other workers had left for the day, Daria grew more uncomfortable by the moment being alone with Alex. Whatever his reason for telling her to stay late, it could hardly be good. She had been terrified all day that he knew, that somehow she had acted strangely and now Alex had found out about her meeting with the American.

She tried not to flinch when she felt his hand on her neck. Not a casual touch. He was rubbing, massaging her neck.

"Why so jumpy?" Alex said.

Obviously, her attempt had failed. She said nothing.

"And so tense," he said, his fingers kneading the base of her neck on either side.

A day earlier, the thought of what was happening would have mortified her. Now, disgusting though it still was, there was also relief flooding through her body and mind. Being touched by this man, and no doubt he planned to do more than touch, was awful, but it was so much better than being discovered. What would he do then? What would his superiors do? Not just to her, but to poor Anya. *I can do this. I can do this. For Anya, I can do this.*

CHAPTER 84

SPACE

My phone rang and the screen said SPACE. "Sam Flatt,"
I said when I answered.

"Sam, Hank Dobo here."

"Hey, man. What's up?"

"We've ID'd the slot players. Gonna email you what
we have on them, just wanted to give you a heads-up."

"Great. I'll watch my inbox."

I ended the call, and seconds later the email appeared
in my inbox. I clicked the message, then opened the PDF
attachment. The first page was just the SPACE logo. The
second had three photographs, the two women and one
man I had identified on video as the beneficiaries of the
rigged high-dollar slots. The various disguises they had
used during their slot play were nowhere to be seen here.
These were mugshots.

Page three was a dossier on the first woman. Her

name was Jennifer Randle. She was fifty-four, thick and tubby with dull gray hair that came to her shoulders. No way to say it but to say it: The woman was ugly. Her nose was fat, cheeks jowly, and she had a disturbing mole to one side of her mouth. Her background was no better, a mashup of arrests for mainly one con game or another that spanned most of the southeastern states.

Page four showed woman number two, Rebecca Light. Her one arrest had been ten years ago for a hit-and-run in which an elderly man had died after being struck by Light's car while crossing a street in Peoria, Illinois, at eight o'clock in the morning. Light had been convicted and did six years as a guest of the state of Illinois. She was forty-two. While not particularly attractive in the police photo, which was old, she was not as unpleasant to look at as her colleague.

Then came the man on page five, Jeff Tindle, who looked out of place alongside the two women. Tindle was younger, thirty years old. Handsome, a little baby-faced, but grinning like a rogue in his photo, which had been snapped by the Seattle PD. Like Light, he had a single arrest, and his was about as minor as they get while still earning you a full-on booking with photo and prints; he had been caught with a little too much weed in his pocket, a discovery made only because he smelled "strongly of marijuana" when pulled over for speeding.

I closed the file. These people were of little interest to me, just low-value pawns in the big scheme. Dobo and the police could handle them. My attention was on bigger issues.

CHAPTER 85

SAN YSIDRO, CALIFORNIA

Max Sultanovich

IF THESE AMERICAN BASTARDS AND BITCHES thought Maxim Andreyovich Sultanovich would tuck tail and run away like some mongrel, they were mistaken. They had murdered his only son. They had at least indirectly caused the deaths of his men. And now they were interfering with his business. His business, which he had spent a lifetime building. And now, thanks specifically to that FBI whore, here he sat hiding in a squalid hotel. Not just him. His granddaughter, too! He loved having her with him, business or not, but he didn't like her staying in peasant quarters like these. All the same, he wasn't going anywhere until he had settled his American affairs. All of them.

As much as it exasperated him, in order to do that, he would be forced to rely on some of the Americans in his employ until he could get suitable Slavic replacements moved here. He sat at the desk and looked through a window that had not been washed in years. Past the sidewalk that fronted the line of rooms, a gaggle of disgusting people sat around a swimming pool he wouldn't dip his cock in. He might piss in it before he left; it would be an improvement. Deciding on the immediate tasks at hand, he picked up the phone given him by the cartel baboon, flipped it open, and dialed.

The American answered. "Report," Max said. After listening for several minutes with nothing more than an occasional grunt in reply, he said, "No. There is no time for these games. This must end, and I will end it." He closed the phone, stood, and paced the small room, scowling as he pondered.

Tatyana sat on the bed, legs crossed, leaning back against the headboard as she worked some game in her hands. Max walked over, bent, and kissed her on the top of the head. She stayed focused on her game. Max smiled and patted her perfect little head, then returned to the desk and sat. A fat American man walked by the window, shirtless, his pasty white chest something that could pass for tits on many a woman. Max so wanted to go outside, walk up behind the gelatinous morphodite, and shove knives into his kidneys, one in each hand. No time for play today, however.

He reopened the phone and dialed the number for one of his men in New York who operated a restaurant in Little Odessa. The man was dumber than a bowl of borscht, but he was loyal and he would know who to call. When he answered the call, Max spoke about a minute in Ukrainian, then said, "Sam Flatt." Then he closed the phone and laid it back on the desk.

CHAPTER 86

TIJUANA, MEXICO

Courtney Meyer

AFTER MORE THAN TWO HOURS OF WRANGLING via the State Department, the TSA, the FAA, and who knows how many Mexican agencies, the Mexican official led the way down the corridor, with Meyer close behind. When they came to a door marked DIRECCIÓN GENERAL DE AERONÁUTICA CIVIL, the airport police official swiped a key card and they stepped into a dimly lit room. Meyer looked around and estimated a dozen people in the room, all staring at computer screens showing the feeds from surveillance cameras.

The official scanned the room until he spotted the person he was looking for, then gestured for Meyer to follow. They reached the workstation of a skinny girl who looked to be in her mid-twenties. The official spoke to her in Spanish and the girl typed and clicked her way through a maze of screens until she hit the right one. She looked back to the official, who nodded, and the girl clicked PLAY.

Meyer leaned forward and watched as Sultanovich's jet came into view. The airplane was coming straight toward the camera, which was obviously mounted on the outside wall of the private jet service facility the pilots had chosen. A worker in coveralls stood with his back to the camera, motioning the jet forward with handheld orange batons. The quality of the video was sharp, the colors vibrant in the sunlit recording. As the jet came closer to the camera, Meyer saw that it was streaked with rivulets of dirt, not the shiny jewel it had been when it powered its way out of Memphis. Had they landed in a field somewhere? Flown through a dust storm?

The tarmac guide crossed his batons and the Falcon stopped. Less than a minute passed before a white SUV with government plates entered the frame and pulled close to the jet.

"What agency is that?" Meyer said.

The airport policeman leaned closer and squinted. "Customs."

"Would they normally meet a plane like this, this quickly?"

He shrugged. "Maybe if someone important is on the plane. Or someone rich." He looked at Meyer and rubbed his thumb and index finger together.

Moments later, the door of the airplane opened and a stairway folded out and down. A beautiful little girl walked down the steps, followed by Max Sultanovich. The driver and passenger doors on the SUV opened and two uniformed men stepped out. Meyer looked to the police official. "Customs?"

He nodded.

The men then opened the rear doors on the SUV. Sultanovich got in on the left, the little girl on the right. The men closed the doors, returned to the front seats, and the vehicle left the frame in a hurry.

Meyer turned to the official again. "Did that look normal to you?"

He gave her the universal thumb-finger money rub again. "That looked rich to me."

CHAPTER 87

SAN YSIDRO, CALIFORNIA

Max Sultanovich

HE PREFERRED TO STAY OUT OF SIGHT in the dreadful box of a hotel room, but Tatyana needed dinner and the idea of room service in this dump was a joke. After a brief walk on a grimy sidewalk littered with bottles and food wrappers and condoms, they arrived at a place called Waffle House. He didn't like the looks of the place, but Tatyana pulled him that way and he followed.

Once they were inside and seated in a booth, a skinny old crow who may have had a total of five teeth in her head walked over and handed them menus. "Coffee?" she said.

"Yes, strong coffee, please," Max said. "Orange juice and milk for Tatyana."

"Coffee just comes one way. I think it's pretty strong but I—"

"Fine, fine, just bring." Max dismissed her with a flip of his hand.

The crow looked offended but moved away with a little grunt. He leaned over toward Tatyana. "What would you like to eat?"

She didn't speak—she rarely did—but she pointed to a picture of a waffle. Max nodded. When the crow returned with the coffee and Tatyana's juice and milk, he placed their order and sat back to wait. He looked around at the assortment of human trash with their dirty caps and blue jeans, or shorts and sandals, or that one absurdity wearing a cowboy hat. He probably thought he was the actor John Wayne.

Then the crow was headed back. Could this bitch not merely leave him in peace? When she got there, she surprised him by handing a small box of crayons and a coloring sheet to Tatyana. Her little face lit up.

"You like to color, honey?" the crow said.

"Da. Spasybi," Tatyana said with a big smile.

"Huh?" the crow said.

"Speak in English, Tatyana."

"Thank. You," Tatyana said, enunciating the two words with care.

"Aw, now ain't that the cutest thing?" The crow turned to Max and said, "What language was she talking?"

"Ukrainian," Max said. "Native tongue."

"Y'all from the Ukraine, huh?"

Max seriously wanted to leap to his feet and choke the crow until she stopped twitching, as he always wanted to do when some stupid American said "the Ukraine." He restrained himself and nodded.

"Well, I'll just declare." Then she leaned down close enough that Max could smell stale cigarette on her breath and said, "Not from around here myself. I'm an Alabama gal."

After all he had tolerated from America and Americans over the past days, this invasion of his personal space pushed Max right to the limit of his sufferance with this hag. He could feel the vein over his eye throbbing, his nostrils flaring as he drew his mouth into a tight little wad. With his last gram of forbearance, he said, "Yes, very nice." And with fortuitous timing that may have saved the crow's life, his phone rang.

Max flipped it open, put it to his ear, and said, "Yes." After some listening, he smiled. A little more listening, then he said, *"Da, sdelayte eto." Yes, do it.*

CHAPTER 88

SPACE

MY ALARM SOUNDED AT SIX O'CLOCK. I pressed a button to open the drapes and early-morning sunlight flooded the room. I turned on the shower and waited a few seconds as the glowing water morphed from blue to purple to pink to red, then stepped into the stream and let the heat chase the sleep away. Once I was clean, awake, and shaven, I killed the water and the body dryer spun up. Thirty seconds of swirling warm air later, I was done. Teeth brushed. Check. Out of longtime habit, I started to dress tactical black for my upcoming rendezvous, but remembered this was a daylight meeting in which looking normal would be the best way to not be noticed. I pulled on a pair of chinos and a FLATT FORENSIC logo shirt, then headed to breakfast.

As I walked through the casino, I looked at the number of people still plunking chips down on tables and pushing buttons on machines, people who had obviously been at it all night. Saggy stubbled faces, red eyes, and crumpled clothing told the tale. On a weekday morning, well before seven, there they were, feeding the coffers of the SPACE Corporation like mind-numbed minions.

When I reached the entrance to Rings of Saturn, the hostess said, "Good morning, Sam!" She was a black lady of about fifty who apparently never stopped smiling, and the smile was always real, the kind that brightened your soul a bit just by seeing it.

"Hey, Rose," I said. "They got the good stuff in here this morning?"

"You know it!"

I extended my fist for our ritual knuckle-bump to celebrate the good stuff, winked at Rose, and headed in. After loading up my plate, I found my favorite booth, said a prayer of thanks for the good stuff, and ran through my mental checklist of things to ask Daria this morning.

At 6:45, I left the buffet and ran the rest of the casino gauntlet to the rear exit. At 6:55, I was in the offshoot tunnel's alcove where we had talked the day before. A couple minutes later, I saw Daria approaching. Her walk was fast, her head on a nervous swivel. She really was a beautiful young woman, glossy dark hair on fair skin, and those striking Slavic eyes. Eyes that showed such vulnerability and fear. It wasn't fair, and it could not be allowed to stand.

I slipped a finger into my shirt pocket and touched the RECORD button on a small digital recorder. "Hi, Daria."

"Hello."

"Are you sure no one followed you?"

She nodded. "I not see no one."

"Good. I need to ask you some questions."

She nodded again. "You ask and I tell you. I also bring this." She withdrew a folded sheaf of yellow papers from her purse and handed them to me.

I unfolded the papers and saw that it was a stack of three pages taken from a legal pad. I flipped through them and said, "This is good, Daria. Very helpful." She had handwritten a ton of information about her and her predicament. I should've thought yesterday to ask for exactly this. No matter. She was more on top of it than I was.

"To save time," I said, "if I ask you a question that you already answered here"—I tapped her paper summary—"tell me you already answered, okay?"

"I tell you."

"Who started all this? Who did you talk to in Ukraine to arrange the trip to America?"

She pointed at the papers. "In story."

Her English was a little less careful today, but I had zero problem getting her meaning. I nodded. "Are there guards at the house where you stay? Someone watching you?"

"Sometime yes."

"How many?"

"Only the one. Is woman, not nice."

"Do you know her name?"

Daria shook her head.

"Is she Ukrainian?"

"No. Is American. Gray hair. Ugly woman with large bottom."

"Have any of you tried to escape when no one was watching you?"

She shook her head quickly. "No, we afraid."

"Are they holding family members of the other work-ers hostage?"

She tilted her head a little to the side, forehead creased.

"Like Anya," I said. "Are other workers afraid because the bad people have their brothers or sisters?"

Understanding, she nodded. "Some, yes. Maybe four or five."

"What are the others afraid of? What keeps them from running away?"

"Family at home. These people kill family at home."

"In Ukraine?"

"Ukraine, Russia, Moldova, maybe other places. I not sure."

"Okay, I understand. Do you know the names of any of the other workers?"

"Some," she said. "In story."

I chewed on my bottom lip and thought for a mo-ment. "Are you safe inside, when you work? Does anyone strike you, hit you?" I pointed in the general direction of the bunker.

Daria flinched and her eyes flooded in an instant. There was my answer. "Is it Alex?"

"Alex…yesterday he make me stay after others leave. He want me to make sex with him."

Now the tears were streaming, although her face re-mained otherwise resolute, almost defiant. "I'm sorry, Daria. He will be punished. I promise."

She wiped at her eyes and nodded.

"Have you seen anyone else, anyone other than Dmi-try and Alex and the ugly woman?"

She nodded and pointed at the papers again. "I put all in story."

"Great. You are doing great. Do you remember the

exact date you left Ukraine? Where you flew to? When
you arrived in the United States?"

"In story. I must to go now."

"Okay, can we meet tomorrow?"

"I will to be here in seven o'clock."

I reached over and squeezed her shoulder. "It's gonna
be okay, Daria. I *will* help you."

CHAPTER 89

SPACE

AFTER RETRIEVING MY PORTABLE SCANNER from my workroom, a.k.a. makeshift lab, I went back to my hotel room. I wanted to get Daria's summary into the computer so it would be part of my case dataset. I made high-quality scans of each sheet, then ran those images through a handwriting recognition package. The software wasn't perfect, but it was leaps and bounds ahead of where the tech had been just a few years ago, and it was good enough for what I was doing here. Within a half hour, I had scanned, converted, and corrected the data. I had only skimmed her summary thus far, so I sat down at the desk to read it in detail.

My name is Daria Bodrova. On 10 August me and sister Anya go to UNITED AGENCY FOR BRIDES AND MODELS in Kiev. Agency man name Vlad tell us that we go to America on 10 August to be models. We go to Boryspil Airport and fly to London and we go from London to Los Angeles in California. In Los Angeles agency man meet us when we leave plane. He not say name. He tell us to get on different airplane. He tell us suitcases come later. We get on different airplane and fly to Las Vegas in Nevada at night 11 August. When we leave airplane in Las Vegas we see two men at suitcase line. One man holds sign with my name and Anya's name. This man tell Anya must go with him. Other man tell me go with him. I am afraid now because we go from airport in different automobiles.

Other man bring me to house at Las Vegas in street GREEN MOUNTAIN #742. Other mens and womens inside this house. Some from Ukraine. Some from Russia. Some I do not know where from. I ask bring me to Anya and man tell me I see Anya tomorrow. On tomorrow, I do not see Anya. All mens and womens go in bus at large hotel name Space. Bus drive in road under hotel. We go inside strange room with many computers. Man name Dmitry in this room. Dmitry tell we must do much special computer work. Dmitry talk to each men or women and tell something. Dmitry tell me YOU MUST DO WORK OR WE KILL ANYA!!! YOU MUST NOT LEAVE ROOM OR WE KILL ANYA!!! YOU MUST NOT LEAVE HOUSE OR WE KILL ANYA!!! Dmitry tell all mens and womens something like this so everyone is afraid and do work.

All mens and womens know much on computers. When I go in university I learn all things about databases and I make databases and I make very different databases speak with each other. Others know all things about encryptions. We know many different skills on computers. When we work Dmitry tell us what we must do. All work is I think to steal money. Much money. I know we steal money from these places:

Pay roads
Electricity companies
Water companies
Autobanks
Heating and cooking vapor companies
Gamble machines at Space hotel
Petrol stores

Maybe we steal from more different companies too. We cannot talk on our work and I do not know. Dmitry tell me and few others to make some internet stores too. Every day we work. Every night we go in house at Green Mountain. We not have weekend days. A man name Mikail start coming in our room many times. He not do nothing but sit and play with phone and laugh. This man is pig and tell to many womens in room he want to make sex with them.

One day after some weeks Dmitry leaved room then the pig Mikail leaved and we not see them again. After this, man with bad eyes is with us. Then pretend American man name Alex come. Some peo-

ples think Alex much more pleasant than Dmitry but I never believe this. Alex today wanted me to make sex with him. I did this for Anya. Alex talk on telephone every day and I believe he afraid of peoples he talking to. Woman watch us sometime in house. She never tell her name. She is American woman. She has very ugly face and very large bottom. Hair like babushka but I think she not old as babushka.

I know names of these other peoples with me:

Galina Palina
Rafik Avdeyev
Angela Belyakova
Mark Demidov
Natella Kudryashova
Larisa Polyakova

We all needing help but all afraid because they hurt family. And we all do not believe we will be free. One day a different man visited room. This man smile and say we soon be free and get much money for work we do. I think this man is Ukrainian and I think this man also tell lies.

While I sifted Daria's summary through my mind and looked for info and angles that might be helpful, I pulled up my deep web browser and logged into the board where I'd left the message earlier. Bingo. My "Waste Management" message, which was a coded shout to a particular hacker in West Memphis, Arkansas, had a reply. I also had a blinking envelope icon at the top of the screen, signaling a private message. I checked the reply to the board message first and found an entry that said only 'NFM,' an acronym for 'no further message.' It was simply a way of saying my message had been read.

I clicked into the private message. It was from the right guy. He has to be the single nerdiest, dorkiest, most cliched human being and caricature of a hacker I've ever encountered, but he's also one of the most talented anywhere when it comes to accessing protected data. His name is Jimmy Arlington. In the online world, he's known as Jimmy the Geek, and his handle here was **jgeezer.** Mine was a less creative and meaningless **4692fellow.**

FROM: jgeezer
TO: 4692fellow

Long time no see, 46! How can The Geek be of service? Msg me here or hit me up on #dw777-chat.

I brought up an IRC window, which is sort of an old-school precursor to all today's instant messaging apps, and connected to the channel Jimmy specified, confident that it would be secure if he set it up.

4692fellow: you there?
jgeezer: my man!
4692fellow: urgent need for some data
jgeezer: talk to me.
4692fellow: need all registration/sales data available from canon for model c300 camera
jgeezer: whoa! major. expensive.
4692fellow: don't care, can you do it?
jgeezer: tsk. tsk.

4692fellow: how long?

jgeezer: don't know but can start now.

4692fellow: there's more

jgeezer: ?

4692fellow: need anything and everything possible on flights from KBP to LAX on august 10, and LAX to LAS night flights on august 11

jgeezer: dude! that's auto-prison if caught!

4692fellow: you in habit of getting caught?

jgeezer: love you, dude, but that is some SERIOUS shit.

4692fellow: i can make it worth your risk

jgeezer: how so?

4692fellow: whatever your fee is in cash, plus some of the sweetest tech you've never seen

jgeezer: detail?

4692fellow: NSA keylogger, stealth install over the wire on any machine you can ping

jgeezer: BULLSHIT. NOT POSSIBLE.

4692fellow: tech is REAL and i have it right now

jgeezer: your word?

4692fellow: my word

jgeezer: if i wind up some dude's bitch in club fed, i'll kill myself just so i can haunt you, dude!

4692fellow: hurry

jgeezer: roger roger. will hit you with a monkeymail when i have something.

4692fellow: monkeymail?

But he was gone. I assumed I'd be able to recognize what he sent. I killed the chat and shut down my deep web access.

CHAPTER 90

SAN YSIDRO, CALIFORNIA

Max Sultanovich

THE SHIT HOTEL AND THE WAFFLE HOUSE had been bad, or so Max thought. That was before he got to the Greyhound bus station, which apparently served both as a transportation hub and a gathering place for the rejects of the universe. Despite being in California, ostensibly part of the United States, he was surrounded by stinking Mexicans. Everywhere he looked, Mexicans. Old ones, squalling babies, and every damned thing in between.

He held on to Tatyana's hand as they stood in the line at the ticket window. She tried to pull away, but he held firm and looked down at her. "Tanechka, no." The squirming and pulling stopped. A bastard right in front of them was wearing a sombrero. An honest-to-fuck sombrero. Who the hell wore something like that in the twenty-first century? Stupid sonofabitch.

The line moved like a geriatric tortoise. When the sombrero bastard reached the window, he and the cow selling tickets yammered and laughed and yammered and laughed, as if no one else might want to buy a ticket of escape from this hell portal. Civilizations rose and fell and still they flapped their useless gums. When Max had taken all he could, he reached up and rapped his knuckles hard on the idiot's shoulder. When he turned around, Max jutted his face forward, bared his teeth like a hyena, and snapped them at him.

"*Dios mio!*" the man said, scrambling to gather up his ticket and his change and leave, never taking his eyes off Max.

Max stepped to the window and said, "Las Vegas."

CHAPTER 91

SPACE

LESS THAN A MINUTE AFTER MY CHAT with Jimmy the
Geek ended, my phone rang. The screen said ABBY
FLATT. *Not now, Abby.* My ex-bride doesn't call that often, but when she does, that one quick question she needs
to ask somehow takes an hour. I touched DECLINE and
turned back to my computer. Almost instantly, the phone
started ringing again. Again, it said ABBY FLATT. Resistance is futile when she does this, so I picked it up,
touched ANSWER, and said, "Abby, not a great time to
talk, can we—"

She was hysterical, screaming so loudly I couldn't tell
what she was saying.

"Abby, baby, calm down so I can understand you!"

Her next words were loud but clear: "Sam, they took
her! They took Ally!" My heart pounded and my mind
spun hyperactive. Why would Meyer pull this shit even

after I started cooperating with her? Why is irrelevant. I warned the bitch.

I said, with all the calm I could manufacture amid the flood of adrenaline dumping into my system, "Abby, don't worry. I'll fix this."

"Don't worry? Fix it?" She was still screaming. "How, Sam? How, how, how are you gonna 'fix it'?"

"I'll call the immigration lawyer as soon as we hang up, and—"

"What are you *talking* about, Sam? *Lawyer?*"

"Yes, Abby, the lawyer Paul found." But even as these words were crossing my lips, my brain was reinterpreting what she was saying, and by the time all the synapses fired, she confirmed it.

"Sam," she said. "It wasn't the government! Some men snatched her! Outside the school!"

Courtesy of my work history, I have experienced a lot of dreadful moments. None of them, not one, not ever, compared to what I was feeling. "Dear God."

Now Abby's hysteria was devolving into sobs of misery. I could almost feel her body wracking with the pain.

I took a deep breath. "Where are you, baby?"

She sniffed and took a couple deep breaths. "At the school."

"Are the police there?"

"Yes."

"Las Vegas PD?"

"I don't know. Police. I think all of them."

"If you see one nearby, please hand him your phone for a minute, okay?"

After some rustling, a female voice said, "Detective Hall."

"Detective Hall," I said, "Sam Flatt here. I'm Allison's father. Can you catch me up?"

I heard a muffled and brief conversation between her and Abby, then she was back. "Allison and a couple friends were sitting on a bench on the sidewalk, outside the school, waiting for their rides. Lots of other kids around, lots of parents coming and going. Surveillance video shows a Lincoln Town Car pulling into the pickup line the wrong way; the car stops near Allison and two men emerge, grab her, then drag her kicking and screaming into the car. The car then departs in a hurry. No plates. That's all we have right this minute, but we do have clear video and we also have a ton of witnesses."

"Can you protect Abby?"

A pause. "Mr. Flatt, do you have reason to believe she's in danger? Do you have information on this situation?"

"Nothing that will help you," I said. "Can you get her safely home and put someone there with her?"

"I'm sure we can, but whatever information you have, I need."

"Thank you, Detective. I assure you I'll give every scintilla of information I have to the authorities. Can you please put Abby back on for a second?"

She didn't sound quite mollified but said, "Sure."

A moment later, Abby said, "Hey."

"Baby, the police are going to take you home and leave someone there as protection, okay?"

"Protection? For me? Why?"

"I'll explain as soon as I can. Now I need you to trust me. Please do that."

She sniffed. "I do. Please tell me our baby girl is gonna be okay, Sammy. Please tell me that." Then she broke into sobs again.

"Abby," I said, "I will find Allison. I love you."

She didn't say anything to this, then after a moment said, "The police want to talk to you again."

I touched END CALL.

I willed my body and brain to calm themselves so I could think strategically. That's what Ally needed right now, not me chasing my emotions. As my breathing slowed, I closed my eyes and envisioned the neural pathways in my brain as they transformed from a tangle of red- and white-hot electrical spaghetti, unwinding and sorting and morphing into rational routes of cooler colors. I fought back the black fog, but only for now, only because it wasn't useful at this moment. When the time came, I would not only allow the black fog to rise within my soul, I would summon it, nurture it, grow it. I would welcome its crimson edges and allow them to consume me. And then I would loose a hell on these motherfuckers they couldn't fathom in their worst nightmares.

I no longer felt any compunction about protecting my client. The importance of my career wasn't even a blip on the screen. I dialed up Agent Meyer.

"Meyer," she said when she answered.

"Agent Meyer, Sam Flatt. I need your help."

"How so, Mr. Flatt?"

"My daughter's been abducted, and I have no doubt that it's related to the case I'm working here in Las Vegas."

There was a pause of about ten seconds. To my relief, she didn't try to dismiss my theory or start talking about not jumping to conclusions. She said, "What can you tell me about the abduction?"

I gave her all the information I had, and I could hear her typing notes into her computer. Then I added, "I'm going to email you everything I've found during my investigation here. It's much more detailed than the summary I sent earlier. I can also put together a list of other things I've found that aren't documented except in my head."

"All right. I'll get the bureau resources rolling and head to Las Vegas shortly."

"Thank you," I said.

"You did right by calling me, Mr. Flatt. Our people are very good at solving kidnappings. Try to stay calm. I'm on my way."

CHAPTER 92

SPACE

ALTHOUGH I THOUGHT IT WOULD, I couldn't be certain
my carte blanche access around SPACE would remain
in place. I needed that access and went to work crafting
safeguards. Okay, "safeguards" is a bit too innocuous a
description; I created surreptitious backdoors into every
area of the SPACE data universe I could imagine a need
for: Surveillance. Gaming machines. Security. Physical
plant. Accounting. My access to the network, combined
with the deep access I had to the Decker Digital routers,
made it doable. A lot of work, but doable.

If my access ended up being curtailed, using any of
these covert gateways into the SPACE network would be
considered both unethical and illegal. Using his routers
to do so might also piss off my buddy Matt Decker. My
level of concern about any of that? Zero. Ethics, laws,
rules, and even friendship no longer mattered. Someone

had my daughter. After a couple hours, the back doors were built, operable, and stealthy. No one would be locking me out.

My email notifier dinged. I opened my inbox and saw I had another email from the professor who had so graciously agreed to help on the rape videos via running them through his algorithmic magic.

> sam, i can't stop thinking about those horrific vids. still looking for helpful info. found something, maybe of value, maybe not. been working on id'ing artifacts of power sources that feed cameras. in u.s., mains electricity typically 110V-120V and freq is 60Hz. in real world, voltage and freq vary and can be tied to certain power plants. still broad, and extracting this data is resource intensive, but maybe it would help narrow search a little? anyway, mean power fingerprint on that first vid you sent me is 122.493V at 60.29Hz. hope this helps.

I fired back a thank-you email and read his email again. After thinking about it a couple minutes, I dialed Decker's cellphone.

To my surprise, he answered, "Matt Decker."

"Matt, Sam Flatt."

"Hey, Sam. What's up, buddy?"

After giving him a quick rundown on what was going on with my daughter, and receiving stunned commiseration, I said, "Need a favor."

"Shoot."

"Your firm is still sort of running the power grid, right?"

"I wouldn't put it that way, but yeah, our CEPOCS system is still the control mechanism for the U.S. grid. Why?"

"I need a list of the mean voltages and frequencies for power plants."

"Which ones?"

"All of them."

He whistled and said, "Let me think a minute on that." After a minute or so, he went on: "Getting the data shouldn't be a problem. Releasing it might be. We're under a crapload of non-disclosure agreements with the government and the involved corporations."

I said, "Damn it, Matt. I need this!" Then I explained the professor's findings and how finding the folks behind the videos would get me closer to knowing who took my daughter.

He listened without interrupting. When I finished, he said, "Let me give it a little more thought and do some checking. I'll get back to you the moment I know if I can help."

"Thanks, man. I appreciate it." I touched off the call.

CHAPTER 93

SOMEWHERE OVER COLORADO

Courtney Meyer

As the little bureau jet pushed westward, Meyer dug through the mountain of data Flatt had sent her. Much of it was over her head, but she knew enough to be impressed. This guy knew what he was doing. In fact, she had to admit that the detail and deductive reasoning in his reports far exceeded what she had seen from the FBI's own digital forensic people, who were endlessly touted within the organization as the best of the best. Maybe not.

She was flipping through the profile sheets of the people who had allegedly been the ones playing rigged slot machines. When she saw the sheet for Jennifer Randle, she froze. She had seen this woman before. Where, where, where? She pulled her laptop from its bag, positioned it on the little table in front of her, and powered it up. Once it was running, it took her several minutes to get connected to the Internet via the airplane's Wi-Fi connection, but finally she was there, wired back into the world.

The connection was slow, but she was able to connect to the network in her office and then to the bureau's internal database, which might have more information than the NCIC system that was available to every local cop everywhere. She keyed in JENNIFER RANDLE and clicked the magnifying glass to execute the search. A few seconds later, search results began to populate the screen. Slowly. As the results came in, the person's name, along with last known city and state, appeared in the list. As the search continued to run, she worked through the system options at the top of the screen and changed the results layout to include a thumbnail photo alongside the entry for each person.

Sixth on the list was RANDLE, JENNIFER - ATLANTA, GA. To the left of the info was a mugshot, the same one included in Flatt's material. There was no nice way to put it; the woman was so ugly that she was memorable. Meyer clicked on Randle's name and a detailed dossier filled the screen. Much of it was the same information that was on Flatt's profile sheet, but not all. One of her previous arrest records had intersected with the FBI, so that entry had internal case notes from the agent who had handled the case, notes that didn't feed into the NCIC network.

Randle had been arrested in Birmingham several years earlier and charged under 18 U.S. Code § 1029 with "Fraud and related activity in connection with access devices." As soon as Meyer was a paragraph into reading the case notes, she remembered. Randle and some other low-lifes had installed skimming devices and cameras on a bunch of ATMs in the Birmingham area.

When they were arrested, Meyer was working in the D.C. office as part of a group of agents targeting these skimmers. Unfortunately, it wasn't just the FBI who caught Randle. Birmingham PD had been involved on the periphery of the case, and a turf war ensued between them and the feds. In a bureaucratic pissing contest fraught with bumbling and stumbling, Randle and her fellow fraudsters had walked when it was all over. But Meyer remembered that face being on the wall in their war room for months. Now here it was again. She wouldn't walk this time.

CHAPTER 94

ORLEANS HOTEL & CASINO
LAS VEGAS

Christine Gamboa

THE DAYS AND NIGHTS WERE RUNNING TOGETHER,
melding into one never-ending nightmare of surreality,
but she thought it was two days ago that they had
returned to Vegas. Their small plane had taxied into a
hangar, where someone had been waiting with an SUV
that brought them here, to the Orleans Hotel & Casino.
They were in a suite and she had her own bedroom, but
the place was a dump. Peeling wallpaper, a big grimy
window, and a toilet that flushed about half the time.
Sasha and Zuyev sat on a sofa in the living area, hunched
over the coffee table, playing some card game. Sasha
never stopped talking and drinking and laughing. Zuyev
drank and said nothing.

With nothing to do but sleep and watch TV, she'd had far too much time for reflection. How did she get from the girl she used to be, to this? A girl with brains and looks and character and morals is what she had been once upon a time. Then the stark and ugly truth was that she had become nothing more than a well-paid whore. She glanced over at Sasha and tried to imagine the old Christine screwing him, the girl who studied day and night, the girl who wouldn't even kiss a guy on a first date. To that girl, the idea of sex with Sasha, or sex with anyone for money, or sex with anyone she didn't love, would have been so repugnant as to be unfathomable. The guilt of it had eventually consumed her when she was working at SPACE, enough so that she made the move to tech. But once you've done something, no matter how deplorable, it's too easy to do it again. Even after getting the half-million dollars for the computer work, she missed the money, so she had slipped right back into it, spreading her legs in exchange for the ridiculous "tips" that Sasha and others like him doled out. For what? A fancy apartment? A nice car? Some clothes? What did any of that matter now?

On top of it all, there was the knowledge of what was *really* going on at SPACE, knowledge even Sasha didn't have, of a reality so horrible that she sometimes wondered if she'd dreamed it. But no, she hadn't. After providing Sasha's people the access they needed to penetrate SPACE's network, she'd left herself a backdoor to keep an eye on the operation. She had seen the websites with her own eyes. It was all too real, and she was terrified to say anything or do anything about it. Put it all together, and she was about two degrees from batshit crazy.

"We need to *do* something other than sit here, Sasha!" Christine said. "What's our plan?"

Sasha's eyes never left the card game. "Chrissy, we must to hide until FBI catch Max."

"What makes you think they *will* catch him? We should go back to the FBI and get protection."

Now he laid his cards on the table, face down, and turned his big head toward her. "No. FBI cannot to protect us if Max still free."

"He's probably back on the other side of the world, don't you think?"

Sasha turned to Zuyev. "Zuyev, you think Max is where?"

Zuyev turned his dead eyes to Christine. "Max is here, United States."

"You can't know that," Christine said.

"I know him," Zuyev said. "He searches."

"For what?"

Zuyev raised a finger and pointed it at himself. Then at Sasha. And finally, at Christine, where it lingered far too long.

CHAPTER 95

SPACE

MY PHONE RANG. The screen said MATT DECKER. I answered it quickly. "Matt, what'd you find out?"

"Can't share the data out of the four centers, but I have a workaround for you."

"Talk to me."

"We own some hardware out in the field now. They're little stations that monitor power quality that's feeding the last mile."

"I don't understand," I said.

"You know what, it's not important. All you need to know is we have thousands of these little boxes out there, all over the country. They might even be a better gauge for you, since they're the closest things out there to the end users."

"Yeah, that really would be better. I don't care about what's coming out of Great Western Electric, only what the power looks like coming out of a wall socket in Joe Blow's house. How do I get the data?"

"That's the hitch. As they sit, they only measure down to a tenth of a volt and tenth of a hertz."

I felt my hope deflating. "Aww crap, th—"

"Hang on," Matt said. "I have Abdul working on it. He says the stations can measure down to the micro level if that's what we need. It's just that the current software's not set up to use that level of precision, because we've never needed it."

"Who's Abdul?"

"Abdul Abidi, my right-hand man, one of the smartest guys you'll ever meet."

"Okay."

"He's cobbling together an app right now that will get the data and then populate an online database. I gave him your email address, and as soon as he has it up and running, he'll shoot you the location of the database, login creds, everything you need."

"Bless you, brother. I appreciate this more than you'll ever know, and I'll owe you big time."

"You owe me nothing, Sam. They have your kid. Find her, and let me know if I can do anything else to help. I mean that."

"Thanks, Matt."

"Later," he said, and then he was gone.

CHAPTER 96

McCARRAN INTERNATIONAL AIRPORT
LAS VEGAS

Courtney Meyer

THE PILOT ANNOUNCED THAT landing was imminent and advised that large electronics should be shut down and stowed. Meyer was the only passenger and she ignored the silly command. If they crashed, the state of her laptop wouldn't affect the outcome one way or the other. After poring through Flatt's reports and the supporting data for most of the flight, she had spent the last half hour composing her thoughts, as well as a list of questions for Flatt. As the plane touched down, she began her final readthrough. Close enough. She closed the laptop, bagged it, and gathered up the papers around her.

She was on her feet the moment the plane came to a stop on the tarmac, her soft leather briefcase in one hand and the handle of her roller bag in the other. One of the pilots came out of the cockpit, opened the door, and folded down the little set of stairs. She descended into the late afternoon desert environment, the sun just above the western mountains painting the other business jets around them a soft amber, the air like a blast from a furnace. A black SUV was waiting no more than fifty feet away. Meyer walked toward it as the driver exited and came to meet her. When they met, she stopped briefly to shake his hand and then resumed her pace. He was part of the bureau's Critical Incident Reponse Group, a specialized sector that handled kidnappings and other intense scenarios.

Inside the truck, she pointed both her AC vents at her face and sucked in the cool air as they pulled away from the airplane and made their way along a service road that took them out of McCarran International Airport. Meyer said, "Progress on the girl?"

"Nothing tangible yet, but everything is in motion. I talked to Memphis a little while ago. They've mobilized everything they have and additional resources are being brought in from other field offices."

"Good," Meyer said.

"I'm hearing there's an Eastern European O-C element?"

She nodded. "Major enterprise, headed up by an old man named Max Sultanovich."

"The one who bugged out of Memphis on the run?"

"The one and only. The organization is run mostly out of Kiev, but with a heavy presence in Russia, Georgia, Chechnya, Moldova, you name it. Word is there's even a strong tie to Putin himself."

"What's the Vegas connection?"

"It's complex and, frankly, bizarre. Sultanovich used to own the land that the SPACE casino sits on."

"Are you kidding?"

Meyer shook her head. "How long till we get there?"

The agent pointed to his ten o'clock. Meyer leaned forward, looked out the windshield, and gasped. "Holy moly."

"Yeah, we get that a lot from people who haven't seen it before."

"I knew it was big, but that…it's…"

"Like something from a movie?"

She just nodded and continued to stare. "More like a city from the future landed in the middle of the desert."

CHAPTER 97

SPACE

About fifteen minutes after my conversation with Matt, the email from his man Abidi showed up. It contained a web address, username, and password. I popped a browser, went to the web page, logged in. It was bare-bones, but it had all the data I needed, spread across four columns: **STATION #, VOLTS, FREQ(Hz), LOCATION.** The station number was obviously an internal designator for Decker Digital. Voltage was expressed to three decimal places, frequency to two. Location was in latitude and longitude. Perfect.

The voltage and frequency values occasionally changed a bit, so the data was live. I watched it and figured out that the system was pulling a reading from each station once per minute. Now that I had the data, I sat back and thought about how to best utilize it. More accurately, I tried. My mind kept wandering to Ally, imagining her shock as those animals grabbed her. The fear. The horror. Her trying to understand why this was happening to her. What were they doing to her? Where was she right now? Locked in a room? Tied to a chair? As these thoughts spun through my mind, the blackness materialized in my mind and soul, first as scattered gossamers, wispy patches that grew until they merged into each other. No. Not now. I suppressed the black, pushed it deep. She needed my mind on what was before me right now. The black would be fuel, a cold burn.

I returned to the numbers. As a first step, I got the numbers from the professor's email and wrote them on a Post-it note: 122.493V @ 60.29Hz. Stuck to the top of my screen, that fluorescent pink square would be my rallying flag. I pictured the setting of the rape videos in my mind. A room with a bed. Beside the bed, a tripod. On top of the tripod, a Canon C300 camera. A power cable hung from the camera down to the floor and connected to an AC adapter. From the other end of the AC adapter, an electric cord emerged, laid on the floor, then up the wall where it terminated with a plug in an electrical outlet. An outlet feeding its child a diet of 122.493 volts, oscillating 60.29 times per second. Where was that outlet?

As a rudimentary first step, I searched the web page of data for any occurrence of either "122.493" or "60.29" and got no hits. Not really a surprise. These were very precise numbers that varied pretty much continuously. I looked back to the professor's email to verify my memory; the numbers were mean averages. How would the professor have calculated them? Best to ask him and be sure. I got his phone number from the email and dialed. Please answer, please answer.

He did. "Hello?"

"Professor, this is Sam Flatt."

It took him a moment to process the name. After a few seconds, he said, "Hi, Mr. Flatt. How can I help you?" His voice was refined, almost aristocratic sounding, a mismatch to his email style.

"I have a quick question about the power artifacts you found in the videos."

"Very well."

"Can you give me a basic rundown on how you calculated those averages?"

"Certainly. I measured the artifact once per second for the duration of each video, then calculated a simple mean average. Is that what you mean?"

"Exactly," I said. "Thanks so much, professor."

"My pleasure."

With the call finished, I looked back at the web page and its gently morphing columns of data. Now I knew how to approach it, and it would require one more phone call. I picked up my phone and was starting to dial when a knock sounded on the door to the conference room. A second later, the door opened and Nichols stuck his head into the room. "Someone here to see you," he said. "Says she's FBI."

CHAPTER 98

SPACE

Courtney Meyer

UNDER NORMAL CIRCUMSTANCES, even working a normal case, Meyer would have been tempted to spend some
time checking out SPACE. She had no idea anything so
futuristic, so staggering in scale and realism, even existed. But this wasn't a typical investigation.

Meyer walked with Nichols, the man who met her
when she stepped from the SUV. After what seemed miles
of walking and a brief ride on an elevator, they entered a
small vestibule that served as an anteroom to a medium-
sized conference room with glass walls. Inside the room,
a man she assumed to be Sam Flatt worked at a table arrayed with several computers. Nichols knocked on the
door to the conference room. The man inside looked up
from behind a computer screen, then stood and came

to the door. Meyer was startled: Her mental picture of Flatt had been that of, well, a nerd. The specimen headed her way was anything but. Tall and lean, he was not just handsome. He was good looking in a way that she found disarming, a little roguish but with no thug vibe.

He stepped through the door with a hand extended. "Agent Meyer, Sam Flatt."

She shook his hand, which was on the rough side, again not in keeping with her preconceptions. Meyer nodded. "I'm truly sorry about your daughter. Let's get to work on finding her."

"Yeah," Flatt said. "Let's do that." He held the thick glass door to the conference room open with a finger and gestured for her to enter, then motioned Nichols in before stepping back into the room himself. He took a seat at the head of the table and said, "Have your people found anything yet?"

Meyer shook her head. "Our investigation is being run out of the Memphis field office, and they're fully engaged. Nothing to report at this point. Have you received any demands from the kidnappers?"

"No," I said, "but I'm sure that's coming."

They spent the next half hour going through Meyer's list of questions, occasionally diverging for a discussion of some point, or for Flatt to pose a question of her. She didn't pick up anything new that struck her as significant, but she did get a lot of holes filled in and she was now convinced Flatt was right about the kidnapping being tied to what he was working on here in Las Vegas. He had a strong investigative mind and continued to impress her.

Meyer stood. "I need to make some calls, get in sync with my guys here and in New York. Is there somewhere I can work?"

"I'm sure Jimbo can find you a spot," Flatt said, pointing a finger at Nichols.

Nichols stood. "You bet. Come with me, ma'am."

As they left, she turned back and said, "I'll be back, Mr. Flatt."

He nodded. "Call me Sam."

CHAPTER 99

SPACE

I STILL REMEMBERED THE DIRTY TRICK Meyer had pulled,
but she seemed to genuinely regret that. More important,
she seemed serious about helping to find Ally. I'm not naive. She has her larger investigation in mind, as well, but
she was here now and helping, and that's what mattered
to me. My resentments could be put on a shelf.

Now that I had the room to myself for a bit, I returned to the issue of the electrical power I'd been working on when Meyer arrived. I got a phone number from
the Abidi email and called.

He answered on the first ring. "Decker Digital, this
is Abdul."

"Abdul, Sam Flatt. Got a second?"

"Sure."

"You happen to have historical data for these monitoring stations?"

"Mountains of it. What do you need?"

"Has Matt filled you in on what I'm doing?"

"He has, yes."

"Great. I need to be able to search the station logs for a range of parameters."

"Such as?"

"I have a video whose camera was powered at one-two-two-dot-four-nine-three volts, sixty-dot-two-nine hertz."

"And you want to know if logs show a station that was outputting that kind of power?"

"Almost. Those numbers are averages calculated over a duration of several minutes, so I'm thinking I'd start by searching for settings that match, plus or minus two volts, and plus or minus one hertz."

"That's doable," Abidi said. "Rather than reconfiguring the whole online system I set up for you, how about I run the search here, against the raw data? I can send you the results."

"If you don't mind, that would be fantastic."

"You got it."

"Oh, Abdul?"

"Yeah?"

"Can you include time stamps in the results?"

"Of course. Anything else?"

"Not now. Huge thanks."

"Welcome. I'll be in touch soon."

I said goodbye and ended the call. Then I did something I should have done way before that moment: I prayed.

Meyer walked back in about fifteen minutes after I got off the phone with Abdul.

"Just wanted to touch base," she said. "I'm headed to meet my team." She picked up a Post-it pad from the table and scribbled a number on it. "That's my cell. Call if you need me, or if you hear anything, okay?"

"You got it," I said.

She was barely out the door when an email arrived from Abdul.

FROM: aabidi@deckerdigital.com
TO: sflatt@flattforensic.com

Results attached, Sam. I think you'll find them interesting. BTW, I "linkified" the locations for you, so clicking the lat/lon will open a Google map showing where that station sits. Good luck!

I double-clicked the attachment, an Excel spreadsheet. When it opened, I scrolled down to see the total number of hits and was surprised to see there were only 298. They were all clustered around a period of days, several months ago. I guess that was a weird combination of voltage and frequency, for which I was thankful. Even better, the latitude/longitude values were the same on every line of the spreadsheet. I clicked one of the locations and my browser opened and started loading a Google map. My heart pounded when I saw what was loading. It was a map of Las Vegas, and the marker designating the exact location for the power monitoring station was on the Strip. When I zoomed in, my heart beat even harder. It was only two blocks from where I was sitting.

CHAPTER 100

SPACE

Courtney Meyer

STANDING IN THE DOORWAY of the meeting room Nichols had set up for Meyer was perhaps the most unprofessional-looking police officer she had ever encountered. Given the spread of her own butt over the years, she was hardly one to judge someone over a few extra pounds, but this guy was out of control. How the hell could he pass any kind of physical? He wore his pants high with a belt cinched about six inches too tight, resulting in as much belly protruding beneath the belt as above. Atop the acre of black trousers was a skin-tight black T-shirt festooned with an LVPD logo. Completing the caricature, the guy was honest-to-God standing there eating a *donut*. Flakes of sugary glaze speckled the black shirt and caked the corners of his mouth. Despite the spectacle, none of this was the problem. The problem was that he had his fat ass parked in her way and refused to move.

"Detective Huddleston," she said with all the patience and calm she could dredge up, "why are you here? And for that matter, how did you know where 'here' would be?"

Meyer would have bet money that the guy couldn't possibly make a worse presentation than he already had, but when he grinned at her, she realized she would have lost that bet. He had a mouthful of tombstone teeth that somehow managed to make his melon-sized head look undersized.

He pointed with his donut at the door. Meyer looked and saw that it said, LAW ENFORCEMENT COURTESY QUARTERS. Then he started talking around a mouthful of donut. "This is where they always stick cops. As for why I'm here, this is my town, lady. And I wanna know what the feds are doing here."

His town. "It's Special Agent Meyer, and I'm having a hard time believing you're as stupid as you look and sound." The tombstone teeth vanished behind a pound of lips. "The Federal Bureau of Investigation is conducting an investigation that has nothing to do with you."

"So you say, but until I see documentation of that or receive an order from my superiors, I'm not going anywhere."

Meyer sighed, stepped through the SPACE-logoed onlookers into the hallway, and dialed her phone.

CHAPTER 101

LAS VEGAS BOULEVARD

I EXITED THE FRONT "AIR LOCK" of SPACE and broke into a jog along the edge of the long driveway, heading toward the street. When I made the sidewalk on the street, I stopped and checked my phone. I had entered the latitude and longitude of the power monitoring station into the phone's GPS, and it pointed me north along the Strip. The Google map showed the walking distance from SPACE to the coordinates to be just over a mile and the phone showed 6,143 feet. I slid it back into my pocket and resumed my jog.

It was almost eight o'clock and the sun had dropped well behind the mountains to the west of the valley. The air was still hot, but cooling. It looked like a crystal clear evening was on the way as the peach-colored western sky faded to cerulean overhead and then a deep Pacific blue further east. I finally reached the northern edge of the

SPACE campus and pulled my phone again. I had covered about half the distance; just over 3,000 feet to go. I picked up the pace, my shoes smacking the concrete sidewalk that still radiated the heat of the desert day.

I started looking ahead, trying to figure out where exactly the power station would be situated ahead. The land immediately to the north of SPACE was empty. After that, I saw a couple of utilitarian-looking two-story buildings that had little chance of long-term survival. Someone would eventually pay a fortune for them in order to get the land beneath them. The crews and cranes would move in and some outlandish casino would take shape and climb the sky.

My next phone check showed 312 feet to go. I was passing the first building, so the second one should mark the spot. I slowed and stopped in front of the second building. Now the phone said I was thirty-two feet from my target, which made no sense. I was standing on a sidewalk with not so much as a shrub showing within anything close to the allotted distance. I looked around again, and then I saw it. Flush mounted in the sidewalk was what looked like a small manhole cover, except it was square. In the center of the cover, I saw a logo that said DECKER DIGITAL.

CHAPTER 102

SPACE

Courtney Meyer

MEYER ENDED HER CALL WITH HER BOSS, Tom Belt, and waited in the hallway for him to work the political and bureaucratic magic that would get Donut Cop out of her way. While she stood, a man wearing a SPACE SECU- RITY shirt approached and stuck his hand out.

As she shook his hand, he said, "Hank Dobo. I'm in charge of security here."

"Special Agent Courtney Meyer, FBI."

"I understand Huddleston is giving you trouble?"

Meyer nodded. "It's being handled."

"Okay. Anything I can do to help you, Agent Meyer?"

"Are you former law enforcement, Mr. Dobo?"

"No."

Meyer arched her eyebrows. "Isn't that unusual, for

an operation this size having someone in charge of security with no law enforcement experience?"

Dobo shrugged. "I can't speak to that. I can only tell you that the company thought my background qualified me for the post."

"What was that background?"

"Military."

"Something in an investigative capacity?"

"Not really." Dobo shifted his weight from foot to foot, reached up and scratched at his upper lip. "You know, I'm starting to feel like I'm being interrogated."

"Who hired you, specifically?"

"Jacob Allen. Why?"

"No reason, just curious."

Meyer heard a phone inside the office ring, followed by Donut Boy talking in low tones. Within a couple minutes, he came waddling out. He met her eyes for only a second before looking away and trundling away. Meyer extended her hand to Dobo. They shook and she said, "Thanks for your cooperation, Mr. Dobo. It's much appreciated."

CHAPTER 103

LAS VEGAS BOULEVARD

I WALKED UP THE SIDEWALK TO THE FRONT DOOR of the building. Typical commercial glass doors, beyond which sat a typical-looking commercial lobby, a small one. No signage on the building, none on the door, and I couldn't see anything in the dimly lit interior to identify the purpose or occupants of the building.

Back on the main sidewalk, I crouched to get a closer look at the cover of the power monitoring station. Not because I thought a little manhole cover was going to tell me anything useful, but because I'm a visual creature and looking at elements of a puzzle stimulates my thought processes. It worked. What was I thinking? The location of the power station itself wasn't going to tell me anything. I had gotten excited and jumped into motion for nothing. Now I'd make the right move. I looked more closely at the station cover and memorized the small number cast into the metal beneath the logo, then called Abdul.

When he answered, I said, "Abdul, Sam. Question: Can you tell me which buildings station five-five-six-eight-eight feeds?"

"It doesn't really feed, it—"

"I don't care about the technical explanation. Which buildings, or which addresses, would have the voltage-frequency combo reported by station five-five-six-eight-eight? Can you tell me that?"

"Hold a minute."

I heard him typing and a minute later he was back. "Okay, Sam. All the buildings on that circuit are on the same side of the street, the east side."

"Makes sense. I'm standing on top of the station right now, by the way."

"Okay, the station should be directly in front of a building on the west side of the street."

"It is."

"Behind that building is a major electrical substation that provides power for most of the southern end of Las Vegas Boulevard, so it—"

"The circuit, Abdul. I care only about this monitoring circuit."

I heard him draw a slow, deep breath. I was acting an ass and I knew it. Apologies could come later. "Sorry. Okay, if you stand facing east, across Las Vegas Boulevard, I count one…two…buildings to your left, and another one on your right. That's what's on five-five-six-eight-eight."

Huh?

"Wait a second," I said, "this circuit feeds buildings across the street? That's the east side of the Strip, Abdul."

"Correct, that's what I said."

Damn it.

"Thanks," I said, and punched off the call. So much for my theory that all circuits and all evidence led to SPACE. If these assholes were across the street, it didn't matter that they were close enough to see. They were in buildings I had no access to, no physical access, no electronic access, no human contacts, no intelligence. That complicated the hell out of this situation. Complexity means time, and time is something my little girl might not have.

My phone rang. The screen said PRIVATE CALLER. I answered, "Sam Flatt."

A voice that was obviously altered, deep and raspy, said, "Sam Flatt. If you want your daughter to live, return to your casino and wait for instructions. They will arrive by email, on a phone that is waiting for you at the concierge desk. Talk to no one." A beep sounded and they were gone.

CHAPTER 104

GREYHOUND BUS STATION
LAS VEGAS

Max Sultanovich

Holding firmly to Tatyana's little shoulders to guide her up the aisle, Max slowly moved them out of the bus. When they stepped off the bottom step and onto the concrete, a wave of fumes hit them. Hot rubber, burning diesel, and most of all, the stink of what was undoubtedly the most disgusting pile of humanity he had ever had the displeasure to be around. He looked at his watch and saw that it was 20:35. Ten hours to move such a distance was ridiculous. It would have been less than an hour in his airplane.

He moved Tatyana to his side and took her hand in his. He began shoving their way through the maggots and into the bus station. Once inside, the crowd thinned and he moved to an area with rows of chairs and no people. After positioning Tatyana in a seat beside him, he removed the phone from his pocket and dialed.

Phone to his ear, moments later he said, "Come now," then folded the phone shut and put it back into his pocket. He bent down to Tatyana and said, "Come, Tanechka. You want candy, my precious girl?"

CHAPTER 105

SPACE

I TOUCHED MY BRACELET TO A PAD on the concierge desk. The attendant looked at her computer, disappeared into a room behind the desk, and moments later returned with a manila envelope. I took the envelope, thanked her, and walked away.

Alone in an elevator, I looked at the envelope. No label, no markings of any kind. Not sealed with the adhesive, just the flimsy metal clasp. I bent the prongs up, opened the flap, and upended the envelope. A compact LG phone dropped into my hand. I pressed the power button and the screen lit up with a standard set of Android icons. The MAIL icon had a tiny "1" in a red circle.

The elevator doors whooshed open and I walked down the corridor to my workroom. Nichols sat in his usual spot, reading a paperback. I didn't trust the integrity of the SPACE surveillance system, and from this point forward I would behave as if the enemy was watching. There was a camera in the corner of this room, so I spoke to Nichols like normal, sat down, scribbled a note on a Post-it, and casually dropped it between him and his book as I walked by on my way back out of the room. It said: SAY NOTHING. ACT NORMAL. GO GET MEYER. NOW.

I stood in the little foyer and as he passed, I whispered, "Give her the note. Don't say anything out loud." He gave the tiniest of nods and kept walking. When he was gone, I pulled out the message phone and touched the MAIL icon. The email was short and sweet. It said, STOP INVESTIGATING NOW. Below that single line of text was a picture of Ally, sitting in a chair with duct tape across her mouth, her hands behind the chair. She looked terrified.

After Nichols was gone, I left the room and walked down the corridor toward the elevators. I had made this walk enough to know that the only surveillance camera on the route was directly outside the elevator. As I approached the elevator area, I checked the camera's orientation to be sure it was aimed as I thought it was. After verifying that, I turned around and walked back in the direction of my workroom until I reached the restrooms, which were about halfway along the route.

The men's room was on the left, the women's on the right. I went left and stepped into the men's. Even if there happened to be some kind of surveillance in the hallway that I was unaware of, there definitely wouldn't be any inside the restroom. How else might they be able to track or watch me? My phone. I thought it was secure, but couldn't take a chance. I popped the back off, and removed the battery.

For damn sure, I didn't trust the new phone they had given me, but if they were tracking it, I didn't want to tip them off, or piss them off, by pulling the battery. I slipped my hand into the pocket that held that phone and, being careful to keep my thumb and index finger over where I thought the front and rear camera lenses would be, pulled it out and looked at it. It looked stock. Being as gentle and quiet as possible, I found the tiny hole for the microphone. It was built into the glass on the front of the phone. After pondering a moment, I slipped the phone back into my pocket; if they were able to use its cameras, they'd see only black. In fact, having the phone in my pocket should provide enough masking for the microphone too, but again, I couldn't take that chance. I walked around the restroom, looking for something I could use.

There. Above the urinal. An automatic deodorizer labeled HEAVENLY SCENT was affixed to the tile wall. I pulled on it, increasing pressure until it came free with the sound of glue tearing free. It had been held in place by a double-sided adhesive strip on the back of the plastic device. Perfect. I worked a fingernail under the end of the strip and got separation from the unit, then pulled the sticky strip off. Again keeping the camera lenses covered, I slid the phone from my pocket and stuck the sticky strip over its microphone. Next I removed the phone's back cover and checked to be sure they hadn't installed any secondary electronics. Like the outside, the interior of the phone looked stock. I dropped it back into my pocket.

Now I positioned myself just inside the restroom's door, and held the door open a couple inches with my foot. I had a good view of the elevator doors, so I waited and watched.

CHAPTER 106

LAS VEGAS

Max Sultanovich

THE DRIVER PUSHED A BUTTON on a remote control that was clipped to his visor, and Max saw a garage door sliding open on a house just ahead on the right. The driver turned into the driveway and pulled the car inside the garage, then hit the button again and the garage door closed behind them.

As Max exited the car, he said to the driver, *"Prismotri za devochkoi. Pust' posidit v tihom meste."* You take care of the little girl. Keep her somewhere quiet. The driver nodded and Max walked to the door and into the house.

The American cow named Randle met him in the kitchen, grinning like an idiot. "You must be Max," she said, as if she were about to seat him at a restaurant. On second thought, no restaurant would ever hire this cow because she was ugly enough to kill the appetite. She could not, however, kill the appetite Max had right now. He was frustrated and angry and sick to death of this stinking country and its pathetic people, and these things made this particular appetite bloom.

"Show me the women," he said.

The cow bobbed her head and motioned for him to follow. They went through a short hallway and into a large open room lined with sofas on every wall. Sofas filled with women, nicely dressed, makeup applied, just as he had directed. Perhaps some could be more accurately referred to as girls instead of women. Even better. He walked over to the nearest sofa for a closer look, and worked his way around the room. Every one of the bitches looked scared. He felt his manhood swell in his trousers.

CHAPTER 107

LAS VEGAS

Anya Bodrova

ANYA KNEW WHO THE OLD MAN WAS. She had seen him on a true-crime program on television and she had even seen him once on Khreshchatyk Street. Whatever she had imagined was coming, this was worse. She sat on the sofa and looked straight ahead while he stood in front of her and sized her up like a side of beef in the Bessarabska Market. She didn't want to look him in the eye, but after he stared and stared, she looked up. His eyes were bright blue, sharp, young looking in an ancient head. A purple vein throbbed above one eye. And his mouth, oh, the mouth. It hung open in a leer, his pale old lips not quite covering the yellow teeth that seemed too small for his mouth, sized like the teeth of a child. A child from hell.

He finally moved on to leer at the girl beside her, Elena. She had been one of the stupid girls who were excited about putting on fancy clothes, thinking they were really going to be models. Elena did not seem so excited anymore. He didn't look at Elena as long as he had ogled her. Anya watched him as he moved around the room, making his way from girl to girl. When he had completed the room, he walked to the woman. Then to Anya's horror, he pointed at her. She was sure the terror covered her face, because the old man smiled with those yellow teeth, then winked at her. She felt tears fill her eyes and spill down her face.

The woman opened her mouth as if she were going to say something, then closed it. She stood for a moment, looking like she was working out a problem. Then she spoke quietly to the old Sultanovich man. At first the old man's face lit up with what looked to Anya like something you would see in the face of a wild animal. After a few moments, however, his face changed to…what was that…disappointment? He shot the hand back out, pointing a desiccated finger at Elena.

This time the woman just nodded with a little smile and did a "come here" gesture to Elena with her finger. Elena started whimpering, shaking her head and saying, "*Nyet, nyet, nyet…*" No, no, no…

Anya felt relieved that Elena was the one chosen, then felt guilty about that relief. She thought back to the day the woman had asked all of them if they had ever had sex, and the horror of the woman sticking her fingers inside the ones who claimed to be virgins, including Anya, feeling around. Elena was not a virgin. Anya was, and she had a feeling that was why the old monster had changed his selection. They were saving her for…something. Tears filled her eyes.

Sultanovich walked to their sofa with more speed than his old body looked capable of. Now his face was fierce. The purple vein had doubled in size and his mouth was drawn back in a tight sneer. Without a word, he reached down and grabbed Elena by the hair on top of her head and yanked her to her feet with such fierceness that Anya was surprised the hair wasn't pulled from Elena's scalp.

Elena yelped. The old man bent down and put his face right up to hers, the tip of his nose touching hers. He said something, more like hissed something, and Elena went silent. He released her hair, then took her by the wrist and pulled her away, following the woman as she led the way down the hallway to where all the bedrooms were located.

CHAPTER 108

SPACE

OF ALL THE TIMES FOR THE CLEANING CREW to arrive on this floor, they couldn't have chosen more poorly. They lumbered out of the elevator, four guys who looked Hispanic, wheeling mop buckets, vacuum cleaners, and big plastic garbage cans filled with supplies. Talking among themselves in loud Spanish, laughing as they spread out. The bank of elevators was situated on the outer wall of the hotel tower. When leaving the elevator, you could go left, right, or straight ahead. One guy headed left, the direction away from me, and one went straight. The other two took a right and headed my way.

As they drew closer, my spidey sense started tickling. When was the last time I had seen an all-male cleaning crew? These weren't SPACE employees, either. They were dressed in street clothes. Why would a company hire an outside cleaning crew when they had a massive housekeeping staff on the payroll? But if they weren't legit, how the hell had they gotten up here? Dobo needed to tweak some of his security procedures.

The two guys coming toward me were about fifteen feet away now. Left Guy had a large tattoo that wrapped around the side of his neck. Right Guy had something crudely inked on the tops of the fingers of his left hand, just below the knuckles. Their gait was off, too. They were trying to look casual, nonchalant, but they were too wired to pull it off.

The final confirmation came when Right Guy glanced my way. The slight openness of the restroom door had caught his eye and he looked. A microsecond after making eye contact with me, he looked away, pretending he hadn't seen me. Bullshit. When you're walking down a corridor and see someone peeking out a restroom door at you, you don't just pretend it didn't happen. It's a weird enough occurrence that you at least spend a few seconds looking. They weren't here to clean. Whatever the details were, they were here for me. I was getting too close to the bad guys and they intended to negate that risk.

I eased the door shut and backed into the restroom. If they were here to take me out or snatch me, I wouldn't have to wait long. If nothing happened within a couple minutes, they were probably dispatched to keep an eye on me. Both scenarios were unacceptable. I checked my watch and waited four minutes. Nothing. Time to force this thing and get it over with. I left the restroom and looked left, where both guys were pretending to be cleaning in the general vicinity of my workroom. One was vacuuming, while the other wiped at the glass wall that separated the anteroom of my work area from the corridor. I whistled. When they looked my way, I flipped them off with both hands and stepped back into the restroom.

Professionals at this point would call their handler or their client and report the subject acting freaky, get instructions. These weren't professionals. They were street thugs, probably gang-bangers, hired on short notice. That told me the adversary either didn't have a great deal of manpower in Vegas, or that manpower was occupied with something deemed more important than yours truly. No matter. I closed my eyes and let the black fog rise. These assholes were a part of the machine that had my daughter. That was their misfortune. I opened my eyes and backed around the corner, where a couple sinks were built on the outer wall. Beyond them, three urinals. Across from the urinals, two stalls.

The door opened and one of them said, "Hey, cabron! You need to learn some manners, you know?"

I said nothing, just listened. The electric crimson edges of the black fog were thickening, spreading through my soul. Ally flashed on the screen of my mind, just a microsecond or two, a flash of the fastest strobe. My senses were jacked, time slowing. I heard the minute squeak of rubber on tile, one person inhaling, another exhaling a split-second later. Two men. Three steps. They turned the corner abreast of each other, same order as they had been in the corridor earlier. Left Guy on the left. Right Guy on the right. Good. Right guy was the one with the tattooed knuckles, the one who looked dumber than a barrel of hair. He would be useless.

The instant Right Guy cleared the corner, I drove the heel of my hand up and into the base of his nose at a forty-five-degree angle. Heavy emphasis on the up. He was melting to the floor before my hand was fully withdrawn.

The only noise was the faint rustling of his clothes. Never knew what hit him. If the piece of shit ever understood the concept of a sharp piece of bone being driven into his brain and turning him off like a light, it would be because somebody in hell explained it to him.

Left Guy would not be so fortunate. He was the smarter one. It showed in his eyes, and it showed in the fact that he was the one who took the real responsibility of watching me when he left the elevator. He was the one who came toward my workroom with his muscle, while the others were sent into corridors in the other directions. As Right Guy's brain-dead corpse was falling to the cold tile floor, Left Guy was reflexively trying to back away. Thank you, asshole. The way you're leaning back, tipping your head back, could not be more perfect.

The opportunity was irresistible; I fist-punched him at about a quarter-strength right in the Adam's apple. The result was exactly as it always is: His hands flew to his throat as he simultaneously tried to breathe and make sense of what happened. His brown eyes bugged out, locked on me as he staggered back against the opposite wall and gasped in panic, fighting the inevitable sensation that convinced him he was suffocating, dying. He would soon wish he was dying. I'd like to say I sympathized with him, but it's against my nature to lie.

I advanced on him as he gasped and slid down the wall. Crouching to match his slide, I said, "Who sent you?"

He kept grasping and rasping, but didn't give me the answer I needed. I looked at him and asked the question again: "Who sent you?"

When he didn't answer, I reached down with my right hand and grabbed his nuts. I applied pressure, maybe a half-strength grip. His eyes flared even wider and his head cocked to the side as the intense combination of pain and nausea and incapacitation hit him. He was on the floor now. I reached into my left pocket and withdrew a lockback knife. Holding the lock to the side while I flipped it with my wrist, the blade whipped out and locked in place. As soon as I felt the snap of the blade locking into place, I stuck it through his jeans, just under the gonads in my right hand. I pressed it in far enough to pierce that tender skin between nuts and asshole and dig ever so slightly into the erector muscle.

"Who. Sent. You?" I said.

His eyes were now the size of half dollars. He said something I couldn't quite make out. I stuck the blade a quarter-inch deeper into his flesh. He made a sound halfway between a groan and a word. Another quarter-inch, and he screamed, "Russians! Russians hired us!"

"Where are these Russians?"

"Don't know, they text us."

"Where's your phone?"

"Pocket, my vest."

I released his nuts but held the tip of the knife where it was while I retrieved his phone. It was one of those with a walkie-talkie function. I said, "You talk to your two buddies on this?" I gestured with my head toward the elevators.

He nodded.

"I'm gonna push the button. You're gonna tell them to come to this restroom. Got it?"

More nodding. I held the phone to his mouth and squeezed the push-to-talk button on the side.

He rattled off the instruction in Spanish and I released the button. I said, "Thank you." Then I rammed
the knife in as far as I could. With it fully driven, I ripped
upward while staring into his eyes. Then I waited for his
friends.

CHAPTER 109

SPACE

WITH THE FOUR BODIES STASHED IN THE STALLS, I washed my hands, then used wet paper towels to clean up the pool of blood and urine that had leaked out from the leader's bifurcated crotch. I had to find out if I'd missed Meyer during any of the interruption. I left the restroom and casually walked to the workroom. Still empty. I returned to my vantage point inside the restroom, door ajar, waiting and watching.

It didn't take long. The elevator sounded its sci-fi tone and the doors whooshed open. Moments later, Meyer and Nichols were headed my way at a brisk clip. As soon as I was sure they were out of the camera's field of view, I opened the door and motioned them in.

As soon as they were inside, Meyer said, "What's going on?"

I said, "Jimbo, please guard the door and be sure we're not disturbed."

It took about ten minutes, but I explained to Meyer everything that had happened. Well, almost everything. Not the bodies in the stalls six feet away, and not the tasks I had Jimmy the Geek working on. She listened closely, asked a question now and then.

When I finished, she said, "I'll get my office working on identifying the buildings across the street, who owns them, who's in them, what they allegedly do inside. Oh, and our Las Vegas office is prepping a team to conduct reconnaisance and surveillance on the house on Green Mountain."

"I hope that's covert as hell."

"It will be. By the way, can you show me these rape videos?"

"I don't have a safe way to do that right now. Given the sophistication of the operation in the bunker, I can't be sure my computer isn't compromised. I do need a favor, though."

"What's that?"

"I need Internet access. You have a laptop?"

"Sorry, I can't loan my bureau laptop. Besides, I need to use it myself."

"Agent Meyer, all I need is a web browser to check my mail to be sure I'm not missing anything important. I have leads working."

"What leads?"

"I'll explain later if anything comes of them. Five minutes, that's all I need."

Meyer cocked her head and looked at me for about ten seconds. "Five minutes. And nothing but a browser."

I nodded and she left the restroom. I stepped outside

the restroom door, where Nichols was standing guard over our privacy. "Jimbo, can you put your hands on a laptop I can use for a while?"

He thought a minute, then said, "We have a stash of tech items we keep on hand in case a whale asks for something. I think there's a laptop or two. You need it now, I assume?"

"Yeah, if you don't mind, go see what you can find."

"You got it." He headed for the elevator.

Meyer returned and handed me a laptop that looked like it might have been the first one ever built.

"Seriously?" I said. "This is what they provide you?"

She shrugged. "It works."

I opened the lid and when the laptop came to life, I ran Internet Explorer, the only browser installed. A few seconds later, I had the web portal to my email on screen. I silently cursed as I scanned through a long list of use-less email in my inbox, and vowed to unsubscribe from a thousand mailing lists as soon as this was over. Toward the bottom of the list, I saw what I was looking for, a sub-ject that read MONKEYS RULE.

CHAPTER 110

SPACE

I OPENED THE MONKEYS RULE EMAIL, which had come from an email address composed of gibberish, and found a message that said SAME BATCHANNEL. That would be from my man Jimmy. Now I needed Nichols to reappear with a laptop that would be mine for a while, so I could talk to Jimmy and get whatever info he was able to glean.

Meyer walked back in and said, "Sorry, I know it's only been a couple minutes, but I need my laptop right now."

"Sure." I logged out of my mail server, killed the browser, and handed her the computer. "Could I ask another favor?"

"What's that?"

"Borrow your phone long enough to call and check on my ex-wife?"

She didn't argue, just pulled a Blackberry from her belt and handed it over. "Bring it to me in the workroom when you're done?"

I nodded and started dialing Abby. She answered on the first ring: "Sam, did you find out something?" She still sounded frantic, on the edge.

"Got some leads, working on them now. I also called a contact I had in the FBI and they're on it bigtime. They're the best in the world at finding and recovering victims of kidnapping. We're gonna find her, Ab."

"But what are they doing to find her, Sam? What?"

"I'm not privvy to all the particulars but I'll find out more, okay?"

"And you'll let me know?"

"I will."

We said goodbye and ended the call. I left the restroom and started down the hallway to return the phone to Meyer, then caught myself before I got in range of a camera. I walked back to the restroom and had just stepped inside when I heard the elevator tone. I looked out and and saw Nichols headed my way, and he was holding a MacBook. He handed it to me and I gave him Meyer's phone. "Hand that to Meyer for me, please. She's in the workroom."

I set up shop on the bathroom counter between the two lavatories. Fortunately, there was a power outlet within distance. I wanted to keep it charged in case I had to go mobile. It only took a few minutes to get the Mac set up for anonymity and deep web access. I downloaded an IRC chat client and loaded the room Jimmy the Geek and I had used that morning, assuming that's what he meant by SAME BATCHANNEL. *Please be there, Jimmy.* He was.

jgeezer: grew a full beard waiting for you dude

4692fellow: sorry. long story. what you got?

jgeezer: what you wanted

4692fellow: all of it?

jgeezer: roger roger

4692fellow: how you gonna get it to me?

jgeezer: will send monkeymail w/encrypted attachment, use pw v8er##ba53ball

4692fellow: got it. huge thx.

jgeezer: cash fee $5K

4692fellow: no prob, how you want it?

jgeezer: green cashola

4692fellow: will get to you tomorrow

jgeezer: sweetness

4692fellow: thx again, need the info ASAP

jgeezer: whoa dude what about my superspy software

4692fellow: sorry, forgot. crazy day. will get that to you tomorrow, too. use same pw you gave me above to open.

jgeezer: man really wanted to play tonight

4692fellow: no can do, j. tomorrow.

jgeezer: siggggggghhhh okay :(

4692fellow: later

I killed the chat and loaded a browser to get at my email. By the time I had it loaded, the email was there with a subject of POXY MONKEYS STINK. What was it with this guy and monkeys?

CHAPTER III

LAS VEGAS

Courtney Meyer

TAKING A CUE FROM FLATT, Meyer had handled her phone calls in the ladies' restroom to avoid even the potential of electronic eavesdropping. She wrapped up the final call and walked across the hall to the men's room, where she knocked on the door before entering. It was possible the guy could be using the room for its intended purpose. He was not. Flatt had turned the bathroom counter into a desk, complete with an office chair she assumed Nichols had procured from somewhere.

Meyer said, "I'm going with the recon team to the Green Mountain location. I want to be sure they understand the importance of not doing anything to spook these people before we have more information."

Flatt continued to look at a bunch of dense text and numbers on his screen. "Probably a good idea."

"Anything new to share with me?"

Flatt shook his head and kept working.

"Keep me posted."

He looked up. "Will do."

CHAPTER 112

LAS VEGAS

Max Sultanovich

THE BITCH LAY CURLED UP IN A BALL ON THE BED, whimpering like a fucking mongrel. Max looked at his naked body in the bathroom mirror. It looked like shit, a dried up husk of the man he had been. His chest muscles sagged so much that his nipples were pointed at the damned floor. But he still had the cock of a stallion, and that was worth a smile. True, it took some chemical assistance to get it into proper order, but that was fine. It had certainly sufficed to vent his frustrations and sate his appetite on the Russian cunt on the bed. After cleaning himself, he went back into the bedroom and dressed.

He arrived back in the living area to find all the girls sitting exactly where they had been, all still looking trembly and pathetic. He stared again at the one he really wanted, and felt a new swell in his crotch. He walked to the sofa and stood in front of her, just staring, saying nothing, feeling his equipment coming back to life. Not now. He bent over and leaned in, his face an inch from hers. When she was looking straight in his face, he curled his lips back and snapped his teeth at her. She drew back in a big flinch and he burst out laughing.

He stepped back and turned to the cow. "Take them back."

She looked surprised. "Now? I thought we would be staying here tonight."

Now Max moved to her and got nose to nose. "You brought them here for me. I cannot very well traipse in and out of the hotel, not safely. Perhaps you want some fucking American camera to see me? Is that what you want, you ugly bitch?"

The cow shook her head so hard he thought it might come loose. "No sir, of course not. I'll take them back right now, sir."

He leaned in and snapped his teeth at her too, just for good measure.

CHAPTER 113

SPACE

THE DATA ON CANON C300 REGISTRATIONS yielded nothing immediately useful. There were a handful of registrations in Ukraine and Russia, and a couple dozen in Las Vegas, but no recognizable names or other information. I copied out those names and their associated data like physical and email addresses, and sent it to my private investigator, asking him to find everything he could on them within the next few hours.

When I opened the other attachment, however, I found that Jimmy had left me a little bonus. In addition to the data on flights from Kiev to L.A. on August 10, and then from L.A. to Vegas on the 11th, he had included a username and password, along with an IP address and a comment that said, LAXBIGBRO. If it was what I thought it was, could I be that lucky? I entered the IP address in a browser but caught myself just before hitting ENTER.

Better to be careful. I took a few minutes to get hidden behind a chain of proxies. That done, I went back to the browser and hit the key to load that page. I got a plain white screen with a dialog box asking for username and password. I entered the ones Jimmy had sent and pressed ENTER.

Jimmy, you are a wizard and a steely-eyed missile man. I was looking at a screen with a banner across the middle of the page that said, YOU ARE ENTERING THE SUR-VEILLANCE SYSTEM FOR LOS ANGELES INTERNA-TIONAL AIRPORT. AUTHORIZED USERS ONLY. ALL ACCESS IS LOGGED. UNAUTHORIZED USERS WILL BE PROSECUTED. Sure was a good thing I'd set up the proxy chain instead of going into the site naked.

Now that I knew what I had, I jumped to the flight data. Everything was in a spreadsheet and there were several tabs, or worksheets, of different data. I started with the tab labeled MANIFEST and was shocked to see how many people traveled from Kiev to L.A. in a day. Thousands. Fortunately, I had a shortcut for plowing through this particular dataset.

I searched for Bodrova and went right to the info I needed. There on consecutive rows were BODROVA, ANYA and BODROVA, DARIA. They arrived at 7:42 p.m. on flight 6180 from London. The airline was listed as AA/BA, a codeshare between American Airlines and British Airways. The two sisters had sat in seats 23A and 23B.

Since I had access to surveillance imagery, I had a brainstorm. Looking through the other tabs in the spreadsheet, I clicked one labeled LOGISTIC. This worksheet was packed with columns of data, and I had no idea what much of it meant. What did make sense were the columns labeled ARR-GAT and BAG-CAR. A quick search for "6180" revealed that AA/BA flight 6180 had arrived at gate B6, and its baggage had been delivered on carousel #4.

I switched back to the web browser and dug into the LAX surveillance system. The interface was a clunky mess, which is par for anything the government touches. It took several minutes to figure out how to navigate the network of cameras, but eventually I was looking at a live video feed of gate B6. Now to get back to the footage from the evening of August 10.

After five minutes of increasing frustration, I accepted that there was no way to do it from the screen I was on. I jotted down the arcane six-character identifier for the camera—naming it something like "GATE-B6" would have been much too logical—and backed out to the main screen. A tiny button that almost required a magnifying glass to read sat perched in the upper right corner of the screen: SEARCH ARCHIVE.

I clicked the button, entered the date, time, and camera designator in the appropriate fields, then clicked the search icon. Finally. The screen filled with a view of the gate. Superimposed along the bottom was AUG-10 and a ticking time stamp that started at 7:40:00 p.m. After a minute or so, I could see the airliner pulling up to the jetway beyond the windows. Shortly after it stopped rolling, people began streaming from the jetway into the airport.

As the time stamp rolled through 7:51 p.m., I spotted Daria on the screen. She exited the jetway beside a girl I assumed to be her sister, Anya. The bright spot in the crappy surveillance system was the quality of the video. It was high-def and among the best I had ever seen, giving me a great view of the two young ladies as they walked toward the concourse and the camera.

I paused the playback just as they were about to turn for their walk down the concourse. They were looking at each other, Daria saying something. Whereas Daria had an earthy beauty about her, Anya looked like a model, classically gorgeous. Both girls were smiling. Despite having just stepped off a long and tiring flight, they looked excited, happy. They were in America and all their dreams were coming true. Or so they thought. I tamped the black wisps forming in my soul back down into submission. For now.

After rewinding and replaying the footage several times, I saw no one approach them, and nothing to indicate that anyone was watching them as they deplaned. I backed out to the main screen again, then navigated my way back into the live feeds, where it took a good fifteen minutes to find what I wanted. I jotted down the designator for several cameras this time, then backed out again. I really wanted to choke the moron who designed this system, then slap the crap out of the bureaucrat who approved it.

Back into the archive I went, and entered the date, time, and camera designator. And there was carousel #4, still and empty. The first passengers from flight 6180 were just arriving to await their bags. After a couple more minutes of staring at the screen, I saw Daria and Anya step off the escalator. They walked to a bank of displays, stared and pointed briefly, then walked toward #4.

That's when the large man entered the frame from the left, the direction of the doors that led outside. He was holding a small sign but his angle to the camera was such that I couldn't read the sign or see his face. I knew he was my guy, though, because he was headed straight for the girls.

I checked my notes on the cameras in baggage claim, then returned to the search screen and entered the new parameters. This time the video started rolling just before the man arrived. I had a clear view of the doors as he walked through and as he grew closer, the letters on the sign became clear: ANYA & DARIA.

Only then did I look to the man's face. I immediately paused the playback and stared. *Ho-ly shit.*

CHAPTER 114

LAS VEGAS

Courtney Meyer

MEYER CONTINUED WORKING ON HER LAPTOP as the black Bureau Suburban turned onto Green Mountain. The flow of email never seemed to stop, and she answered them as quickly as she could. Better that than putting it off and finding herself with hundreds to respond to at once. She looked up when the felt the vehicle slow to a stop. They were in a small parking lot behind a church. Another SUV was already there, along with HRT's big panel van. Meyer got out and looked around for the leader of the team that would surveil the house.

While the leader was dressed in exactly the same blackout style as the rest of his men, a minute of watching others approach and ask him questions, identified him as the agent in charge. She approached with her hand out and after the introduction and handshake were done, she said, "How far away is the house?"

He pointed in the same direction they had been traveling. "Four houses down on the right."

"Approach?"

"We got lucky. There's a railroad track that runs along the back of the houses." He hooked a thumb to point behind the church.

Meyer looked and could make out the rise of earth and a dull glint of metal in the moonlight.

The agent continued: "The back yard of the target house is unfenced, so we shouldn't have any problem with a stealthy approach."

"And you do understand the critical importance of stealth? A lot of innocent lives could depend on it, so we can't do anything that might trigger these suspects to hurt or kill these girls."

He nodded. "Completely."

"I'd like to monitor the operation."

"Not a problem. Follow me."

Meyer followed him to the panel van and then inside the back doors. The rearmost area—about half the rear space of the van—was outfitted with seating. In front of that, a bevy of high-tech equipment filled racks on either side wall and a console on the partition that separated the rear space from the cockpit. A young agent was seated at the console, looking at a series of video monitors.

The leader said, "We all wear cameras that transmit to this surveillance bank." With a nod toward the young agent, he said, "This agent will take care of you and get you set up to watch everything as it happens and if you like, he can wire you with comms to speak to me."

"Perfect," Meyer said. "How long until you go?"

He checked his watch. "Two minutes."

"Good luck."

He nodded and left the van. Console Agent said, "Have a seat and I'll get you set up."

CHAPTER 115

LAS VEGAS

Courtney Meyer

MEYER WATCHED THE TEAM ADVANCE along the railroad track toward the house. The largest monitor was displaying the leader's feed, while smaller screens showed the other five. All the cameras were in night vision mode, rendering video in shades of green. Her left ear was fitted with an insert that gave her two-way comms with the team leader, though she had no intention of speaking and interrupting his concentration.

Now they were behind the house, spread out and moving in closer. One man took each side of the house, while two covered the front and two the back. The men on the sides had the advantage of hedgerows that separated the yard from the houses next door. The leader was in front of the house, which was lit sufficiently by a pair of floodlights along the eaves to cause the camera to switch out of night vision mode. The ghostly green became a color picture with amazing clarity in such low light. He gave a hand signal and the other man on the front side moved in a crouch toward the house. When he reached it, he knelt and retrieved a black cordless drill from his gear bag, then fitted it with a long drill bit and began drilling through the cement-board siding. Meyer hoped and prayed that the drilling was quiet.

After a couple minutes, Drill Man withdrew the drill, removed the bit, and stowed it in his bag. From the bag, he pulled a case about the size of two packs of playing cards laid end to end. He opened it, removed what looked like a coil of wire, then straightened the coil and connected one end to the case itself. As Meyer watched him fiddle with the device on camera, another monitor in the console suddenly came to life. "Can you put that picture on a bigger screen?" she said.

Console Agent pressed a couple buttons and the lead agent's image was replaced by the fiber optic camera's feed. Meyer literally held her breath as she saw the view passing through the wall. Suddenly, the screen showed a carpeted floor. As Drill Man manipulated the snaky camera shaft from outside the house, more of the room came into view. It was a living room. The camera had entered the room at the left end of a sofa that was backed up to the front wall of the house.

Over the next few minutes, three more monitors came to life. She hadn't realized they were inserting multiple cameras but she was sure glad to see it. The three new cameras showed two bedrooms and one bathroom, all of which were empty. Four cameras were of course not covering the entire house—rooms were going unexplored—but the microphones on the cameras were lis-tening to a house that was largely dead quiet. The one exception was the original camera, the one in the living room. The shaft wasn't long enough to get past the sofa, so they couldn't tell who was on the sofa, but someone was because the microphone was picking up the sound of someone snoring.

Meyer's earpiece clicked and she heard the team leader's voice, just above a whisper. "Agent Meyer, can you see the cameras?"

As Console Agent had instructed, she reached to her ear and switched a tiny switch to the up position to en-able two-way comms. "I see them. Other than the person in the living room, the house looks empty."

"Roger that. Now that the cameras are transmitting, we're going to move into concealment positions and watch for activity. Hopefully the unknown in the living area will move about at some point so we can get a view."

"Understood. Standing by."

She switched the earpiece back to listen-only mode and settled in for a wait, trying to make sense of the emp-ty house. Flatt seemed certain that the workers from what he called "the bunker" left there everyday and returned to this house for the evening. So where the hell were they?

CHAPTER 116

SPACE

I WAS STILL STARING AT THE PAUSED FRAME of the surveillance video. Still trying to process the implications of what I saw. I like to think I'm a pretty sharp investigator, but I did not see this coming. My email notifier dinged and I loaded my inbox. It was from Meyer.

> Other than one person we've not yet ID'd, house is empty. Can you think of anything else Daria Bodrova might have said that would indicate an alternate location?

It was after midnight, which meant the bunker workers should be in the Green Mountain house. Unless they had some emergency work and were still slaving away in the bunker. If I had my own computer, I could've instantly brought up the bunker cameras and answered that question. And if a frog had wings, he wouldn't bump his ass all the time. It took almost ten minutes of trial and error, but working from memory I was finally able to get into the cameras. The computer room was empty. The corridors were empty. Had something spooked them into moving the workers to a new location? An idea hit me. I clicked the REPLY button on Meyer's email.

> Daria didn't mention another location, just the bunker and the GM house. Have your people made any progress on identifying the occupants of the buildings on the other side of the Strip, where the rape videos track back to? I also have new information you need. Call SPACE and ask them to ring the house phone at the fifth floor elevators. Should be secure.

I sent the email and switched back to the LAX surveillance image. There on my screen, in a crisp hi-def image, holding a sign that said ANYA & DARIA while grinning at them with his tombstone teeth, was Detective Ronnie Huddleston of the Las Vegas Police Department. Ronnie Huddleston who had blown Sam off when he took the rape videos to him.

CHAPTER 117

LAS VEGAS

Courtney Meyer

HER PHONE VIBRATED AND SAID, "Incoming email." Meyer opened the inbox and then the email, which was from Flatt. As soon as she read it, she looked up the number for SPACE and asked to be connected to the house phone Flatt had specified.

After several rings, someone said, "Hello?"

Meyer recognized the voice as Nichols. "Mr. Nichols, please tell Mr. Flatt I'm on the line."

"Hold on."

As soon as Flatt came on the line, Meyer said, "Isn't that house phone in the field of view for a camera?"

"It is, but I have to tell you something."

"What is it?"

"I heard you met the LVPD detective, Huddleston, right?"

"Yes. He's unprofessional and boorish."

"Worse than that. He's involved in all this, on the wrong side."

Meyer paused a moment, then said, "How so?"

"When Daria and Anya Bodrova got to Los Angeles, he was the one waiting for them. He's the one who gave them their tickets to Las Vegas."

Meyer paused again, trying to absorb this. "How do you know this, Mr. Flatt?"

"Call me Sam. I can't say right now, but the evidence I've seen is irrefutable. Believe this, Agent Meyer."

"Is that evidence something you can email me?"

"I can't do that. It's why we had to talk by phone instead. You're gonna have to trust me for now. If that asshole shows up, you cannot divulge anything important to him, and you cannot tip your hand that you know about him."

She drew a breath to tell him that he was in no position to dictate to an FBI agent what she could and could not do, but changed her mind. The man's daughter was missing; no need for her to create more tension. "Alright, Sam. Anything else?"

"That's all I have new for you right now. What about your people and the buildings across the Strip? Surely these people don't have that many places they can shuffle in and out of with over a dozen people without attracting a little attention."

"I haven't heard back on that, but I'll follow up soon."

"What about the house?" Flatt said. "Any development there?"

Meyer hesitated. Why was she sharing information with a civilian as if he were a part of the investigation? It violated a laundry list of Bureau regulations.

"Agent Meyer?"

Because sharing is a two-way street and this guy uncovered more in a couple weeks than we did in over a year. "Nothing n—"

"We have action," Console Agent said, pointing at the screen of the living room camera.

"Hang on," Meyer said into her phone.

On the screen, a pair of feet came into view. A man's feet in leather loafers, walking right to left across the camera's field of view. As soon as he was left of the camera's position, the view began to move. "Are those cameras remote control?" Meyer said to Console Agent.

He nodded and kept watching the screen.

The man on screen would be out of view soon, even with the camera lens tracking left. "Can't they move the camera faster?" she said.

Console Agent shook his head. "We're beta testing these cameras for the manufacturer. They're slow but we're thrilled just to have a high-res probe camera that's remote-capable at all."

Meyer reached out and tapped the screen for the bathroom camera. It was the one on the left end of the house and that's where she bet he was headed. "Make this view bigger, please."

The larger primary monitor switched to the bathroom view just as the man walked in and turned on the light. The camera had a full frontal view of him and Meyer couldn't believe her eyes. She reached up and switched her earpiece to two-way comms, then said, "This is Meyer. Be advised that the subject inside the house is our primary suspect, Max Sultanovich. Do you copy?"

The team leader's voice came back immediately in her ear. "Copy. Do you want to take him down?"

"No. Take no action. Repeat, take no action."

"Confirmed. Standing by."

CHAPTER 118

SPACE

AFTER TALKING BRIEFLY AGAIN WITH MEYER, I tried to process what I'd just heard taking place over the phone. Sultanovich, the evil seed at the center of this whole thing, was in the house. Alone. I had a strong feeling he was the one who had given the order to take my daughter. He also might know where she was, along with the other two groups of hostages he had created. He and I needed a bit of quality time together. Going there now wouldn't accomplish anything with the house surrounded by FBI agents. To get access to him, I saw two options.

One, if I stayed on Meyer's good side until he was arrested, she might let me talk to him. The problem with that was that he would be in FBI custody. It would be tough to pull off the kind of conversation I wanted to have, and even if I locked myself in the room with the bastard and got the information I needed, I'd be arrested myself and unable to help Ally.

Two, after they arrested the asshole, I could hit the transport before they made it to a detention facility. Not practical. I had no weapons and no time to plan; if it went wrong and I was caught, I'd be in the same situation: Unable to help my daughter.

There had to be another way. I paced the restroom, thinking it through. What was Meyer's play with Sultanovich? Only one thing made sense as a reason for her not to move on him immediately. She was hoping he'd lead them to the bunker workers, or Anya and whoever else was being held with her, or both. Smart move on her part, given her restraints of having to follow laws, rules, and regulations.

For the time being, I needed to forget about getting to Sultanovich, and instead concentrate on where Ally and the other hostages might be. Where would they keep her? With the bunker workers? No. They knew I'd discovered the bunker; they'd seen video of me inside it. And they would know I had seen all the computers there and could surmise that there were workers to run those computers. These bastards would put Ally with Anya and the other hostages who were being held as leverage against the computer workers.

So where the hell was that? My mind cycled through the leads I had on that. They weren't in the house on Green Mountain. That left the location where the rape videos had been recorded. That thought, combined with my belief that my baby girl was in the clutches of these sadistic animals, flipped my stomach and made my heart. I took a couple deep breaths and re-calmed myself.

The data on the electrical power was the key. That camera had been plugged into one of the buildings across the Strip when those videos were shot. That was the lair. Instead of twiddling my thumbs and waiting for the FBI to get official records on the occupants of those buildings, I went to work on Google. First I pulled up a map of the area and got the street addresses for the buildings of interest. All three buildings were part of a complex that rented various types of office space. Each one was two stories. Then I did a search for businesses located at those addresses.

I scanned through dozens of business names, clicking through to their websites, looking for anything that might stand out or connect. Toward the bottom of the third page of Google results, an entry caught my eye: THE MEADOWS MEDIA AND ENTERTAINMENT GROUP. When I clicked through to their website, I found a single page proclaiming great expertise in "videography and entertainment for the greater Las Vegas area." This was a cookie-cutter site, something thrown together just to have some kind of online presence.

Time to pay this video and entertainment mecca a visit. I opened the restroom door and asked Nichols to step inside.

CHAPTER 119

LAS VEGAS

Max Sultanovich

MAX FOUND A BLANKET IN A CLOSET and tucked it around Tatyana where she lay sleeping like a little angel on the couch, as she had been since the girls left. He sat back down and soon dozed off again himself, only to wake with a start from an outlandish dream minutes later. In the dream, Mikail was some stupid combination of alive and dead, driving a purple car that flew a meter above the ground. It was in a field of golden wheat and Mikail was trying to run Max over. Max ran, hearing the sound as the mature stalks of wheat slapped the bottom of the flying car. The slap-slap-slap got closer and closer, and just when Max was sure the car was about to take his head off, he awoke. He couldn't get peace from his worthless son even with the sonofabitch dead.

He got up and walked into the kitchen. After a bit of searching, he found some tea and put a pot of water on the stove. While he waited for it to boil, he pulled the phone from his pocket and dialed. When the other party answered, he began a conversation in Ukrainian. It went from calm to heated, Max pacing the kitchen, his face hard and red, spittle flying. After a few minutes, Max calmed and eventually wrapped up the conversation. He closed the phone and looked at the pot of water, which was now at a full boil. He laid the phone on the counter, hung a couple tea bags in his cup, and poured the water. Sniffing the aroma of the steaming cup, he returned to the sofa in the living room and picked up the laptop they had provided for him.

CHAPTER 120

OCEAN SHORES, WASHINGTON

Matt Decker

DECKER WAS HOME, getting ready to eat dinner when the phone rang. He glanced at the screen and saw it was Abdul, calling from the office. When he answered, Abdul said, "Need your thoughts on something."

"Shoot."

"Sam Flatt is acting on bad information and I can't get in touch with him. It might be important."

"What bad info?" Matt said.

"You know the monitoring data I sent him?"

"Sure."

"That data was from station five-five-six-eight-nine."

"Okay."

"Sam went looking for the actual station, wanted to lay eyes on it, I guess. He called and wanted to know which buildings were connected to that station."

"Right, so he could try to find where that video camera was when it shot some videos."

"Here's the thing," Abdul said. "When he called, he asked for the buildings tied to five-five-six-eight-*eight*, not the six-eight-*nine* station that the data came from. I think he found the station and didn't pay attention to the number."

"Where is the right one, where is six-eight-nine?"

"Twenty-five feet away. And it feeds buildings on the west side of Las Vegas Boulevard. Get this, including the SPACE building itself."

"Oh, holy hell," Decker said. "The videos might've been shot right there. He's looking at the wrong buildings altogether."

"Exactly, boss."

"Damn, Abdul. Why didn't you correct him while you had him on the phone?"

"I tried. He was agitated, kept cutting me off, eventually hung up. I've tried calling back many times, but it goes straight to voicemail. I also emailed and texted."

"Okay, keep trying to call him. I'm gonna try to track down the SPACE employee who's kind of his assistant while he's there. Let me know if you get him on the line, and I'll keep you posted."

"You got it."

CHAPTER 121

MEADOWS MEDIA - LAS VEGAS

My wristwatch gave its stacatto half-hour vibration just as I walked into the parking area under the back side of the building that housed Meadows Media. It was 12:30 a.m., and no more than a handful of cars remained. I went to the stairway door that opened into the little garage and gave it a tug. Locked. Fortunately, this wasn't a high-security building, and the contractors hadn't gone overboard on securing what was essentially a fire exit. A couple minutes with some small screwdrivers from my toolkit did the job. I pulled the door open and stepped into a concrete stairwell. On the second floor where Meadows was located, I cracked the door and looked out into an empty carpeted hallway.

It looked like every other office building in the world as I walked the hallway looking for suite 203. Most offices had solid wood doors, while an occasional suite was fronted by one or two glass doors. There was no way to tell which of the solid-door offices had someone inside right now, and I didn't see anyone inside the dimly lit glassed ones. Until I got to the one I was looking for, that is. Suite 203 fronted up to be the nicest one on the floor, which I didn't expect. Two glass doors in the middle of glass walls looked in on a well lit reception area. Not what I was expecting at all. When I pulled on the door, it opened, and a damned chime sounded that had to be audible throughout the suite.

I stepped inside and almost immediately a guy appeared through a door that led from the reception area to the deeper offices. He was tall and ripped, wearing a 'The Meadows Media' logo shirt that fit him like a latex surgical glove. This didn't feel like a porn operation, but I was here and I intended to be sure.

"What can I do for you?" He said, with a not-subtle glance at a digital clock on the wall that read 12:38.

Herein lies the problem with unplanned actions: Shit happens. Odds were a video business would be empty after midnight, yet here stood Logo Shirt. I processed the options, none of which were good at this point, and walked up to him with my right hand extended for a shake. He reluctantly took my hand. I firmed up my grip just shy of crushing, and said, "I'd like to look through your offices."

He didn't waste time looking bewildered by such a request. Instead, his angular face took on a hard sneer with his lip curled up on one side. "Fuck you," he said, dripping all the contempt he could summon.

"Thought you'd say that," I said. Still holding his right hand, I yanked him to spin him a bit counter-clockwise, then hit him with a quick left to his lower jaw on the right side of his face. I released his right hand because I expected him to fall. He didn't. He had turned his head away just as I connected, lessening the impact. He backed up a couple steps and assumed a classic MMA stance. Great.

He said, "You just made one hell of a mistake, asshole. I'm gonna fuck you up."

I blew out a sigh. "I really don't have time for this. I don't want to hurt you. Stand aside and I won't have to."

Logo Shirt blew out a great big belly laugh, then gave me a 'come here' gesture by curling his fingers.

"You've gotta be shitting me," I said. "Are you supposed to be Neo or Morpheus?"

He did it again.

"Last chance," I said.

His face reddened and contorted, and he charged. The guy was really quick, and grabbed me in a bear hug and jerked me up off my feet, then slammed me down and to his left. In an instant, he was following me down, intending to straddle me for a little ground-and-pound. As he went down, I rolled away from him and got to my feet. He sprang back up like a jack-in-the-box and I started backing up. Within a foot, I was against a wall, and there he was. He hit me two times, then a third. I shook my head and pushed him back.

Logo Shirt was fast and hard, and had obviously done a lot of training. The big problem with that, however, is that rules become ingrained. It's what makes it a civilized sport instead of brawling. I didn't have time for civilized. My baby girl was waiting for me. It was like an internal switch; once flipped, the black fog shot into my soul and erased the light where things like compassion and mercy reside. There was one goal now, one consideration, a fevered drive to do what I came to do. Logo Shirt was standing between me and that. Most unfortunate. For him.

He was two or three steps in front of me. I took those steps with perfect calm, oblivious to everything in the world except my target, his Adam's apple. I knew he was hitting me when I got close, because my target shuddered and shook in my vision. Then I was there, and everything was happening very slowly. I watched my fist as it drove into his throat, felt the muscles collapse, then the cartilage, and finally, the airway. I was stepping away even as he fell backward, his hands going to his throat as if they could somehow claw away the hideous and panicky inability to breathe he was experiencing.

Two minutes later, my exploration of the suite was complete. No porn studio here. When I got back to the reception lobby, Logo Shirt was still wheezing and holding his throat, but he was managing to breathe. He'd live.

CHAPTER 122

LAS VEGAS

Courtney Meyer

"For the third time, the call began at twelve-thir-teen and forty-two seconds, a.m., Las Vegas time!" Meyer said into the phone on the van's console. "It lasted five minutes, seventeen seconds. The authorization is alpha-six-two-nine-hotel-eight-one. Oh sure, I'd love to be on hold some more."

She turned to Console Agent and said, "On hold again. How in hell is it that these NSA geniuses can spy on the whole world but can't pull up one pre-authorized recording of a simple phone call?"

Console Agent just shrugged and resumed staring at the screens.

Meyer waited. Three or four minutes later, she perked up, listened intently for a moment, then said, "Thank you, thank you, thank you. Would you please hold a minute so I can be sure it came through?" She turned back to Console Agent and found him nodding and giving her a thumbs-up. She returned to the phone. "Thank you, we got it."

After hanging up the phone, she watched Console Agent work for a bit. He said, "Ready to hear it?"

She nodded and he pushed a button. From speakers on the console, a deep voice said, "Hello."

Sultanovich's voice, which she recognized, came next. In a foreign language.

"Damn it," Meyer said with a brisk slap of the console counter in front of her. "You have access to translators?"

Console Agent nodded and picked up the phone.

CHAPTER 123

SPACE

Brandy Palmer

"Jacob, I'm begging you, tell me what's going on," Palmer said.

Jacob Allen remained quiet as he stood at the window of his office gazing out at the lightscape spread before them in the night.

She reached out, touched him on the shoulder. "You need to talk to someone. I'm your attorney, but I'm also your friend. What is it?"

After a good minute of silence, he turned to her and said, "I've lived with this insanity as long as I can. Whatever is going on in the basement, I want to know. And I want it to end."

There had been little doubt in her mind as to what was troubling him, but hearing it still caused her stomach to churn. "You know you can't do that."

"I have to."

"Have you forgotten the agreement you signed? The agreement that all of this is built on?" Palmer stretched her arms and gestured a sphere.

Allen spun on her. "Forgotten? That document has haunted me every day since I signed it. *Forgotten?*"

"Then you know it's binding. You can't do anything about it without putting this company at grave legal risk, Jacob."

"I'm an idiot for ever going along with some mystery space in my basement."

"You did what you had to do to close the deal. And, I..."

"What?"

"I hate to bring this up, but as the attorney for this company, I have to remind you that the basement issue is not the purview of Jacob Allen, but rather that of SPACE Corporation."

"Which I run, Brandy. Me."

"For investors."

"What are you trying to say? Spit it out."

She blew out a long, slow sigh. "The investors are concerned, Jacob."

"I haven't heard a word from them."

"I have."

"Excuse me?" Allen's face reddened as he turned his body to square up and face her. "Are you talking to the investors behind my back? Is that what I'm hearing, Brandy?"

The silence was almost tangible.

"Brandy?"

She raised her hands, palms down, patting the air.

"You need to calm down."

He slammed the heel of his fist into the window hard enough that it flexed in its frame. Palmer tensed, thinking it might actually break. She realized she was subconsciously backing away from him. To put it mildly, this was a side of the docile Jacob Allen she had never seen. She watched as he turned back to the window and resumed his silent gaze for a good sixty seconds. Then he turned his head toward her and with great calm said, "Brandy, you and your firm no longer represent this company. Your services are terminated."

"You can't do that."

"I just did. Get the fuck out of my office."

The moment she left Jacob's office, Brandy Palmer dialed her phone. When the man on the other end answered, she said, "We do have a problem. Jacob is not just allowing this Sam Flatt to meddle. Now's he encouraging him."

MAN ON PHONE: "This must end."

PALMER: "Agreed. What do you want me to do?"

MAN ON PHONE: "Nothing. I will manage these two birds with one rock."

CHAPTER 124

SPACE

I was almost back to the front entrance of SPACE when the phone vibrated in my pocket. I pulled it out and saw the new-email icon. When I opened it, the first thing I saw was a new picture of Ally. She was still restrained in the chair, but now a figure wearing a black ski mask stood behind her, holding a knife to her throat.

Ally's face was contorted, her eyes liquid and spilling fat tear trails down her cheek. It was a face that said PLEASE HELP ME, DADDY. A paragraph of text sat below the photo.

IF YOU WANT KNIFE TO STAY AWAY FROM HER THROAT, FOLLOW INSTRUCTIONS. KILL JACOB ALLEN. HE DIE TONIGHT OR YOUR DAUGHTER DIE TONIGHT.

Beneath the text, another picture, this one of Jacob. It looked like a typical corporate headshot, probably from SPACE's website. It was a good ten years old, with noticeably fewer wrinkles on the sad, hound dog face.

When I thought these assholes couldn't surprise me again, they had proved me wrong. What the hell was this about? Did they really expect me to kill a man for them? Or were they yanking my chain to keep me distracted? One thing was certain: I wasn't going to play their game, either way. I was going to find these subhumans and end this. All of it.

When I stepped off the elevator on my workfloor, I stepped into a hive of police activity. Centered on the men's restroom. Great. I strolled down the hall as casually as possible, wondering where Nichols was and why he hadn't kept everyone out like I told him. Unfortunately, the gelatinous tub of lard known as Detective Huddleston saw me and scrunched up his eyes as I approached, a show of great mental effort on his face. Presumably he was trying to remember where he'd seen me. His mouth was parted just enough to expose those damned tombstone teeth. I very much wanted to remind him of my bringing the rape videos to him and him blowing the whole thing off. Then I wanted to let him know I had seen his fat ass on the LAX surveillance footage as he met Daria and Anya. Then I wanted to do all manner of other things to him. Maybe I'd get my chance before the FBI got him.

I passed on by, went to my workroom, and grabbed my laptop and a couple other items from my gear that I'd need. The more I thought about it, the more unlikely I believed it to be that they could have broken into my computer. It was well protected and I was a smart user. There was a tiny risk I was wrong, but it was a risk I had to take at this point.

This time when I passed by Tombstone in the corridor, he said, "Mr. Flatt, we need to take your statement, since I understand you've been working in this area for quite some time."

Slowing but not stopping, I looked back over my shoulder, and said, "I wasn't here tonight. Can't help you, and wouldn't have time even if I could." Back to my normal pace. I could literally feel him plodding behind me, his footfalls imparting a tiny vibration to the floor.

"I'm afraid you'll have to make time."

I pushed the elevator button and turned to face him. "Don't think so." The elevator door opened a few seconds later and I stepped inside.

He was six feet away, then three, then reaching to stop the doors as they were halfway closed. "You don't get to—"

Those sausage fingers were too inviting, curled around the edge of the elevator door. The plastic brick of my laptop's power supply weighs about three pounds. I drove the end of it into his fingers, and I didn't hold back. He jerked his hand back and his face morphed into a contortion of pain, that vast mouth opening, sucking in air to power the satisfying howl that followed. He looked like a hippo. Just before the doors closed completely, I raised my hand in a finger gun and fired it at the bastard.

CHAPTER 125

SPACE

IN MY ROOM, I did a pretty thorough five-minute scan for cameras or listening devices and found none. The next few minutes were spent activating the cheap burner phones I had grabbed from the gift shop before coming up. I plugged them up to their chargers to be sure they were topped off, then booted my laptop and went to work. Much had to be done, and time was short. Tombstone would get my room number as soon as he stopped crying about his fingers, and then he'd be on his massive way within minutes. This time he'd bring help.

Thanking the Lord that I'd taken the precaution of setting up a number of backdoors into the SPACE network, I went straight for the reservations system. I chose an empty room on the seventy-second floor and eventually figured out how to assign it to a non-existent guest. For reasons I can't fathom, the name that popped into my head was Edna Haverstein, and I went with it. Next I looked in one of my rolling suitcases and pulled an old keycard from one of its pockets. I tend to keep them when I check out, because they're handy for forensic experimentation and testing. I'd always opened my room with my bracelet, but the locks also had conventional keycard slots. Out of the main reservations database I went, and into the module that allowed desk clerks to program the electronic cards. I connected the card writer I'd retrieved from my workroom gear, and coded the old keycard for room 72195.

The next need was for Sam Flatt to disappear from SPACE's techno-tracking system. Shocker of shockers, I finally caught a break. The bracelet management system was in the same permissions module as the keycards, which meant I at least didn't have to go hunting for that. Now I needed a name and position. The human resources database was easy. I filtered it down to people assigned to the security division, sorted by employee name, and started scrolling through the long list, looking. Hoping to find two people with exactly the same name, so I could add a layer of confusion, I struck out. I did, however, find a pair who were close. Julia Gomes and Julia Gomez. I jumped back into the permissions module and with great care not to disturb the nearly omnipotent permissions my bracelet wielded on the property, I did some name-switching.

Now my bracelet was assigned to Julia Gomes and hers to Sam Flatt. Then the tedious part: I had to switch the history of movement that was assigned to our two bracelets. If the police or anyone else looked at my tracking record, they needed to see my known movements; they needed to see that Sam Flatt left the murder scene after breaking Tombstone's fingers, and high-tailed it to Sam Flatt's room. Anything else would lead them to suspect that I was using someone else's bracelet ID. I imagined Tombstone's big ass shaking the floor more than once as time kept ticking. Finally I got it done and tidied up with a little e-housekeeping.

One more task and I'd be ready to go. I hated to do this to a client who had already paid me close to a hundred grand for the few weeks I'd been here, but I had no choice. First, I found the bracelet tracking system. Then I rebooted that system's main server and quickly jumped to the surveillance network. Too bad the casino surveillance system wasn't isolated from the rest of the property, but I had noticed a while back that it wasn't. Design flaw. With a wince, I shut down SPACE's surveillance system. All of it.

The clock was ticking. With those systems down, I had a few minutes of invisibility. As soon as the servers came back up, I'd be visible on camera and my bracelet would be trackable. I didn't want my "Julia Gomes" bracelet anywhere near my room when it came back online. I threw everything I could imagine I'd need into one of my roller bags and headed out.

CHAPTER 126

SPACE

Hank Dobo, Chief of Security

"I DON'T GIVE ONE DAMN WHO HE IS or what emergency you have going on here!" Huddleston waved his bandaged hand in the air. "He assaulted a police officer, and that makes him a wanted man, so open this fucking door or we'll knock it down!"

Dobo reached up and wiped away a spray of the man's spittle that had peppered half his face. Turning to a female SPACE security officer standing behind them with a video camera, he said, "Be sure you keep the camera rolling."

The security officer nodded, and Dobo looked directly into the camera. "Hank Dobo, chief of security. Despite a critical systems failure that I was addressing on behalf of my employer, I am here because Detective Ronnie

Huddleston of the Las Vegas Police Department threatened to arrest me unless I left my station and personally assisted him. We are here at guest room one-four-zero-two-one-six, the room provided to a SPACE contractor named Sam Flatt. We object to this violation of a guest's privacy in the absence of a warrant, and I am opening this room under duress of what I believe to be an illegal coercion."

Dobo touched his bracelet to the door handle. The LED turned green. He twisted the lever and pushed the door open, then walked inside and gestured for the others to follow. It was obvious the suite was empty as soon as they entered, but Huddleston waddled around looking in every conceivable hiding place. When he finished, Dobo said, "Are you satisfied, Detective Huddleston?"

"Shit no, I'm not satisfied!"

More spittle hit Dobo. "Would it be all right if I assign one of my security officers to assist you with anything else? I need to get back to my station. The casino's frozen because of the surveillance outage, and we're losing big money."

"No! You will assist me. I'm not about to run around here with some flunky who has to make a phone call for permission every time I need something."

"I can assure y—"

The man looked like his head might literally explode. He got closer, squared up with Dobo, and said, "No, no, no, no, no," tapping one of his good fingers on Dobo's chest with each "no."

"Very well," Dobo said, "but let me give you some advice. Do *not* touch me again. Clear?"

Huddleston grunted and huffed his way toward the door. "I want to know where he is. Now."

CHAPTER 127

SPACE

SAFELY INSIDE THE ROOM of the fictional Ms. Edna Haverstein, I opened my laptop and checked my inbox. Amid another screen full of newsletters and special offers, I had two emails of interest, one from my P.I., and the other from Meyer. I opened hers first. One sentence:

> We just picked up a BOLO on you from LVPD? What in the world?

My reply was brief. I told her I had a burner phone and would call her soon. The P.I.'s email was a bit more substantive than Meyer's.

> Sam, I've attached all the reports, but only one of them looks interesting in light of the little bit you've told me about your case. And honestly?

I only stumbled onto that connection, LOL. One of the names was ALEX SOSA. Sounds Italian or something, right? Turns out that's an alias. Sorta anyway. He came here when he was grown, from Russia or somewhere like that, because his original name was ALEXANDRE ANDREYOVICH SOZONOV. He legally changed it to the more American sounding ALEX SOSA. Anyway once I had his real name I started searching and came across something curious. He didn't come here by himself. Had a brother and a sister. Brother's name was DMITRY SOZONOV and I couldn't find anything on him except he came here with the other two many years ago. Not a peep since. The sister is the connection. I don't know how you say her original name cause it's in all the databases in some weird ass letters that wouldn't copy and paste for me. You'll see what I mean if you look at her report. Anyway she changed her name too, and when I searched on her, that's when your client turned up, the Space casino. She's a lawyer and talks on her web site about them being a client of hers. Her American name is BRANDY PALMER. Anyway it's late and that's all I got for you. I'll jack the volume on my computer so it will wake me up if you need to email again.

The connection to Brandy Palmer caught me off guard but when I thought about it, it made sense. She was probably part of engineering the whole mess with the unallocated space in the bowels of SPACE. She'd had access to both sides of the equation, the criminals as well as Jacob. And Alex was the name of the guy supervising Daria and the other hackers. That tingle on the edge of my psyche when something big is breaking in a case was now way past a tingle. More like a big blue electric arc jumping around my brain.

CHAPTER 128

SPACE
SURVEILLANCE ROOM

Detective Ronnie Huddleston

HUDDLESTON PULLED A HANDKERCHIEF from his pocket and mopped the sweat off his face again. The cloth was getting saturated. And no wonder at that, given the fact that these stupid fuckers couldn't find Flatt. All the electro-magic in the world at their fingertips and still, a big fat goose egg was what he had. "Can you turn the damn air conditioning a little colder?" he said.

That Dobo looked at him like he was crazy, said, "It's sixty-five degrees. You're hot?"

Dodo would be a better name for this asshole. Huddleston held up his handkerchief and wrung out several drops of sweat. "What the hell you think?"

"Interesting, but I can't help you on that one. Computer controlled. Maybe you'll want to arrest me for that?"

"Don't be a smart-ass."

"Never."

"Thought you people had super-duper facial recognition. Why the hell can't you find this asshole?"

"Well, 'we people' lost all our surveillance for right at ten minutes. And it's still not fully operational, not synced back up with the face-rec software. Maybe we could've gotten it back up a little quicker, but I had to take you to one-forty, remember?"

Huddleston's bowels were churning. He had to find Flatt. Not just because the asshole broke his damn fingers, either. It was much more serious than that. That damn Flatt was a problem. He knew something. Twenty years of cop-sense told Huddleston that. And that just could not fucking stand, no sir. "Go back to that bracelet map," he said.

Dodo blew out a big sigh, like he was just so damn put out because he was being asked to help a law enforcement officer find a criminal. He clicked around a little bit and pointed up at the screen on the wall. "Just like last time and the time before that."

The screen showed a big blue map of the whole SPACE complex. Blinking up top, a line of red text said TAG NOT DETECTED. Huddleston pounded the counter and said, "Where *is* that sonofabitch!"

CHAPTER 129

SPACE

I DIALED MEYER. She answered on the second ring: "Meyer."

"It's Sam, Agent Meyer. How're things on your end?"

"It's still quiet here at good old nine-sixty-six Green Mountain Drive. What's going on with this BOLO?"

"Long story and it's not worth the time to tell right now," I said. "Just know that it involves a certain portly detective."

"Understand that I can't be a party to evasion of any law enforcement. Where are you?"

"I have another piece of the puzzle for you."

"Ignoring my question?" Meyer said.

"Like you said, you can't be a party to some things."

"Okay, what's the piece?"

"Two pieces, really. First, I got another email from the bad guys. It had a picture of somebody holding a knife to my daughter's throat, and instructed me to kill Jacob Allen. I've also found a connection between the Sultanovich operation and Brandy Palmer."

"Who?"

"Brandy Palmer is outside counsel for SPACE," I said. "High-powered little bitch of a lawyer."

"And how does she fit into all this?"

"That's the second puzzle piece. She's from Eastern Europe, came here with two brothers. One of them's named Dmitry. I looked back at Daria Bodrova's summary, and the original overseer of the hackers was named Dmitry, the one who vanished."

"Lots of guys named Dmitry in that part of the world."

"No doubt. But I'm pretty sure the other brother is the one who bought the video camera that was used to film those rapes."

"Holy shit," she said. "How do you know that?"

"Unimportant right now, but I'll share all of it with you later, once we find my daughter."

"Fair enough. What's this other brother's name?"

"He and his sister anglicized their names a long time ago. He goes by Alex Sosa now."

"Any idea where he is?"

"I think I know exactly where…"

It was the word "address" that triggered a momentary mind-freeze. More accurately, it's like my subconscious was screaming, Whoa, go back! Go back! What was it? Then it hit me.

Meyer said, "Sam, you there?"

"Where are you?"

"Uh…same place I've been for a couple hours now, the house on Green Mountain."

"No, exactly where?" I said.

"In the mobile command post, behind a church. Wh—"

"The address, Agent Meyer. Give me the address of the house you guys are surveilling."

"Nine-sixty-six Green Mountain Drive, Las—"

My mind raced as goosebumps popped all over me.

"That's not the address I gave you."

"What? Sam, you're losing me. Correction…you've lost me."

"Listen very carefully, Agent Meyer. The address Daria gave me was seven-forty-two Green Mountain, and that's what I gave you, not nine-sixty-six."

She went silent as it sank in. Then she got it. In perfect sync, we both said, "There are two houses."

I said, "Where'd you get the nine-sixty-six address?"

I could hear Meyer typing on a keyboard. "I sent the Green Mountain address you gave me to my office to research. They called and said it was registered to Sultanovich, and I was sure it was the right place. The search warrant they emailed me, though, is for nine-sixty-six."

"How long will it take to get a warrant for seven-forty-two?"

"I'm on it."

"Hurry!" I said.

CHAPTER 130

ORLEANS CASINO HOTEL

Christine Gamboa

On one hand, Christine was beyond relieved to be getting out of the tired, dingy hotel suite. On the other, she was confused as to the sudden impetus for going. After a couple secretive phone calls in the other room, Sasha had declared it was time, and was rushing them to move.

"What's going on, Sasha?" she said.

He was at the door, gesturing for them to hurry. "Chrissy, we must to go. We must to go now."

"Fine. Why now?"

He blew out a long noisy breath that blubbered his lips. "I am thinking Max may to know where we are."

Zuyev stood by the door, a dead-eyed, animated corpse ready to do whatever.

Christine said, "You think he's coming here?"

"Maybe he comes. Maybe he will to send other killers. We must not to wait and find out."

She nodded, and by habit, looked around to be sure she wasn't leaving anything behind in a hotel room. Then she realized that she had nothing. Nothing to take. Nothing to leave.

They left the room and rode the stale-smelling elevator to the ground floor. They walked through the casino, toward the rear of the casino, where she assumed Sasha had someone waiting with a car.

The idea came to her in an instant, but she knew she had to do it. "I have to go to the restroom," she said, and walked away from them without waiting for an answer. The moment she was out of their sight, she broke into a run.

CHAPTER 131

LAS VEGAS

Courtney Meyer

"AND YOU'RE CERTAIN BOTH HOUSES ARE JAMMED?" Meyer said into the comms headset. "No calls in or out, right?"

Team Leader responded, "Correct."

"Let's do it," she said, shifting in her seat and leaning forward to concentrate on the console screens. Two of the HRT agents remained at the 966 house where Sultanovich was. The warrant for 742 Green Mountain had just arrived, and they would hit the house hard and fast in a pure hostage rescue posture.

She turned to Console Agent and said, "How long should it take to get that translator? We still don't know what he said on that phone call."

"It's unusual to take this long. Been almost an hour.

Want me to call and rattle some cages?"

"After this is done," she said, with a nod toward the console.

The screens were all green, the four agents of immediate interest advancing on 742 along the railway behind the houses, just like they had with 966. After several minutes of bouncy green walking, they arrived. One took a prone position in the rear, facing the house from about twenty yards back. Meyer watched as the three others crept around the house, two on the right and one on the left. Soon they were converging at the front door. Team Leader gave a silent countdown from three using his fingers, and the quiet of stealth and creep was instantly replaced by a cacophony of sound and moving images.

One of the agents hit the door with a one-man door ram and the other three charged inside, Team Leader in front. Shouts of "FBI!" and "Freeze!" and "Hands in the air!" issued from the console speakers. A room light switched on and the screens, now in full color, showed a living room with two sofas against walls and three cots arranged in the middle of the room, all occupied. A female on one of the sofas was sitting up, a panicked look on her face and a paperback book in her hands. Another stood from a cot, holding what looked to be an old Nintendo GameBoy. The others were rousing from sleep. All looked bewildered and scared, and all were female. Young. Meyer guessed the range from mid-teens to mid-twenties.

Three of the agents left the living room, one straight ahead into what looked like a kitchen, one into a hallway on the left, and the other into one on the right. The kitchen and bathrooms were empty. Meyer counted four bedrooms as she tried to keep up with the fast-moving action. Each bedroom had multiple occupants and proved to be a repeat of the scene she had watched in the living room. Confusion and fright on young faces. One bedroom held five males, but everyone else in the house was female.

Now the screen still showing a green view of the rear of the house came to life. A figure was coming out of the back of the house, actually, out of the back side of the garage. The prone agent was on his feet in an instant. "Freeze! Hands in the air! You move, you die!" Now the agent was advancing toward him, his rifle visible and leading the way.

"Don't shoot! Don't shoot!" It was a man. Meyer watched a bright splotch bloom around the his crotch on the green screen. Had the agent shot him? No. The man had peed himself. Some big bad criminal he was.

She switched her attention back to the 966 screens to be sure all was quiet. It was. They had done it.

CHAPTER 132

SPACE

Detective Ronnie Huddleston

FINALLY! FLATT'S TRACKER HAD SHOWN UP on the screen. It appeared first in the employee parking area, then moved inside. The asshole had left the property. He would have stayed gone if he had any sense, but his stupidity was Huddleston's good fortune. He stood from his chair. "Let's go, Dodo."

"My name is Dobo."

Awww, little faux pas hurt the rent-a-cop's feelings. Huddleston wanted to burst forth with a gut-busting laugh, but he held it in. "My fucking bad, let's go." He hooked a thumb toward the tracking screen on the wall. "Where is that?"

"Looks like he's headed out toward the entertainment complex."

"Why the fuck would he do that?"

"Detective, I've cooperated to the best of my ability. Mind easing up on the f-bombs? Getting tiresome."

Huddleston couldn't believe his ears. Here he was trying to catch a criminal, not to mention a personal threat to Huddleston and his income, and having to put up with this candy-ass shit? He shook his head. "Whatever. Can we go?"

Dodo picked up an iPad and walked out. Huddleston followed.

CHAPTER 133

SPACE

THE BURNER PHONE RANG and I looked at its tiny screen: FEDERAL BUREAU O... I answered it. "Flatt."

"Sam, it's Court."

Court? "Sorry?"

"Courtney Meyer."

"Oh, oh, got it. Tell me you have good news."

"Your daughter wasn't there. I'm sorry."

Even though I expected that, the disappointment still hit me like a shot to the gut. I took a deep breath. "What about Daria?"

"She's safe, and fifteen others. They're pretty freaked out, worried about their families. None of them are what I'd call fluent in English, so we're having a bit of trouble getting them calmed down, making them understand that no one knows they've been rescued."

"I'm glad they're safe. Any bad players with them?"

"One man, Jeff Tindle, one of your shady slot machine players. He'll be interrogated posthaste, and he'll break quickly. The guy literally wet himself when he was being apprehended."

"What about Sultanovich?"

"We're still watching, hoping he'll make a move so we can track him to the others. Hang in there."

What was I not thinking of? What clues had I missed? Did they really expect me to kill Jacob, or was it a distraction? A new thought occurred to me: What made them think I was even capable of such a thing? As far as they knew, I was nothing more than a computer nerd. Or did they somehow know more? How? The security chief, Hank Dobo, knew at least something about my background from being in the same place at the same time in Afghanistan. The only other person I'd ever shared information with was Nichols, a drunken move of idiocy on my part. Could one of them be involved?

Too many questions I couldn't answer. Time to ground myself in things I did know. I fired up the virtual copy of Gamboa's computer that I'd copied to my laptop. It resumed to the exact state it had been in the last time I'd looked at it, which felt like a year ago even though it was a week or two max. The last thing I'd seen was the deep web page that listed all the hacking targets, the "hacking portal," as I'd come to call it. No untapped investigative value there; the feebs had the hackers themselves. I clicked the HISTORY menu in her browser and looked through the list of page titles. Even though I'd been through it, maybe something would jog a memory or spark an idea.

When I got to the hacking portal at the bottom of the list, I stared a minute. It wasn't the bottom of the list. It

was third from the bottom, and that was as far as I'd gotten. How had I left two pages unexplored? I stared at the
ceiling, cracked my knuckles, thought about the day I'd
found that page. Then I remembered. I found the hacking portal and had believed it to be the holy grail of the
investigation. That night, I went out with Nichols, acted
a fool, got way too drunk, and blabbed like a gossipy old
woman. We stayed up all night and I got very little sleep
before heading back to work. When I did resume my investigation, I followed the hacking evidence and never
went back to the rest of Gamboa's deep web history. Bottom line? I forgot it.

Both the remaining pages showed in the history list
as UNTITLED. I clicked the first one. When it loaded, I
stared, trying to wrap my mind around what I was seeing. I couldn't. Surely, for the love of God and all that is
holy in the universe, this could not be what it appeared to
be. It just could not. It wasn't possible. The more I looked,
however, the more a sickening and debilitating certainty
settled in my gut, in my very soul: It was exactly what it
appeared to be.

CHAPTER 134

SPACE

Hank Dobo

IF HE DIDN'T HAVE SUCH A SWEET GIG at this place, Dobo would've leapt on Huddleston way before now and beat the ever-loving crap out of him. When it came to obnoxious, this pathetic excuse of a detective was light-years beyond anyone Dobo had ever met. Maybe he couldn't beat his big head senseless, but he could have a little fun.

The little rail shuttles that propelled people from the center tower out through the spokes to the outlying structures were designed to hold either two or four people. They arrived every thirty seconds in sequence, a double-seater, another double, then a quad. Lather. Rinse. Repeat. A double stopped in front of them and Dobo said, "Go ahead, I'll catch the next one."

It wasn't like there was any choice. By the time Huddleston manipulated that butt down into the seat, he filled the double from wall to wall. The left armrest lit up in SPACE's cerulean blue and a contralto synthetic voice said, "Please touch credential bracelet to the lighted armrest to begin your journey."

"I got it," Dobo said. The facilities manager had taught him a neat trick. Management bracelets had the ability to double the speed of the shuttles, which were already so fast they felt like a thrill ride at a theme park. At twice that, they rivaled the brutal acceleration of a Hornet on its takeoff roll on an aircraft carrier. Dobo missed that sensation from his pilot days, and used the trick every time he rode the shuttles. With a tiny smile, he extended his hand and tapped the bracelet on the armrest four times in quick succession.

Huddleston screamed as the shuttle shot forward, kept screaming, in fact. Dobo grinned and listened to the howl as it Dopplered into the distance of the spoke. The next shuttle arrived and Dobo climbed in and quad-tapped his own armrest.

When Dobo arrived at the entertainment complex, Huddleston had just extricated himself from the shuttle. He looked pale and clammy as he wobble-waddled away. Paler and clammier than usual.

"That can't be normal," Huddleston said when Dobo approached.

"What?"

"That!" He pointed at the shuttle. "Felt like I was being shot from a fucking gun. I need to sit down."

"Hmmm," Dobo said. "Felt normal to me. We need to get going if you want to track down your fugitive." Dobo looked at the iPad. "Looks like he's a couple hundred yards to the left."

"I think I'm gonna be sick."

Dobo looked at the iPad again. "He's stationary right now. Think you can keep it together? If not, we can shuttle back to the tower and get you to the infirmary."

"Hell no. I'm never riding that thing again!" Huddleston bent over, hands on his knees for about a minute, then stood. "Let's go."

They moved at a snail's pace. Dobo tapped around on the iPad as they walked. He didn't think for a moment that they were about to find Sam Flatt, but he'd play along.

Ten minutes later, the iPad's tracking screen showed that they were within fifty feet of the bracelet. They were standing at the edge of a large cluster of tables centered in the midst of a food court. Even in the middle of the night, easily two hundred people sat eating. Dobo gestured at the area and said, "We're here. Let's interrupt his meal."

"Oh shit, not food," Huddleston said.

Dobo could've sworn the jerk was literally turning green as he rubbed a hand across an acre of belly. He fought back another smile and started threading his way between tables. The money this corporation had spent on this tracking technology astounded Dobo. Who put RFID readers in tables, for heaven's sake? Sixty seconds later, the iPad beeped. He looked at the screen and saw the tracker icon flashing red with a line of text above it that read, BRACELET LOCATED.

Only one person was in the immediate area, one of his security officers named Julia Gomes. She seemed to sense someone was looking at her and turned around with a burrito paused halfway from plate to mouth. She said, "Chief?"

"Hey, Julia."

Huddleston lumbered up with a bewildered look on his face. Dobo pointed at Julia's wrist. "There's the bracelet we've been tracking."

"What the fuck, Dobo?"

Dobo shrugged. "I don't know, man. The technology's not foolproof. You ready to head back?"

Huddleston shook his head as he pulled a chair out and collapsed into it. "You go on. I gotta rest up."

CHAPTER 135

SPACE

AT FIRST GLANCE, THE WEB PAGE looked like a standard eBay page. The same familiar color scheme, same general layout of products with their thumbnail photos and descriptive headlines. That first impression lasted seconds. At the top of the page, the jaunty logo with its primary colors had a twist: Just to the left, set at an angle in faint purple, were the letters "sh." It was no longer an eBay logo. It was a SheBay logo, and the products on the page weren't the standard fare. The "products" were women.

The more I looked, the clearer it became that girls was the more accurate description. As I scrolled down the page, they looked to be anywhere from twelve to twenty. They all had one thing in common; they were beautiful. The level of beauty varied a bit from girl to girl, but every single one was striking. The photos were professionally shot, perfectly lit, framed and angled with meticulous care.

At the top of the list was a girl who couldn't be more than fifteen. She was obviously Slavic, with pale hazel eyes that looked almost iridescent. Straight dark hair hung to her shoulders, parted on one side and pulled over in a style you might see on a schoolgirl. Her descriptive text said: GALINA, A UKRAINIAN WOMAN WHO LONGS TO MAKE YOUR DREAMS COME TRUE. I clicked her photo and her individual page loaded. A paragraph of text anchored the top of the page.

> Meet Galina, one of our featured attractions for this sale, which will be held on March 1st. A golden-eyed beauty from Donetsk, Galina is 14 years old. Her dream is to meet a successful gentleman who likes to be pampered in every way. As with all our featured attractions, this sweet girl is a tender and unspoiled lover who has never known a man. Would you like to be her teacher? Bidding starts at 250,000 Euros.

I'm not a man of fragile constitution. I've seen a lot and done a lot. Now, however, my hand had a little tremor as I reached to the touchpad on my laptop. Below the text, an array of photos of the girl filled the page. No nudes, but there were lingerie and bikini shots. High-fashion shots. Household-looking shots. Smiling. Pensive. Sad. The gamut was covered.

Once the pictures ended, I came to the "business" section of the listing, where bold red text screamed, SALE COMPLETE. PRICE 1,375,000 EUROS. Presumably on March 1st—was that this year?—this poor child had been sold as if she were nothing more than a piece of property. I had to find these bastards.

CHAPTER 136

SPACE

Christine Gamboa

SHE COULDN'T STOP NOW, couldn't pause and think about what she was doing. If she did, she'd freak, and that couldn't happen. She walked with casual purpose through the casino, as if she still worked there and had every right to go where she wanted. At the service elevator that led up into the tower, she walked in behind a SPACE employee and watched as he touched the screen for his floor. Without an employee bracelet, she couldn't choose a floor in this elevator. His selection was six floors below where she wanted to go, but it would have to do. When he left the elevator, she did too. The guy was absorbed in his phone and never gave her a glance.

Now that she was in the employees-only section of the tower, she could use the stairwell to get where she needed to be. Her legs were burning by the time she got through the six-floor climb, but she was there. She stepped from the stairwell, ran her fingers through her hair, and hoped she could work the necessary magic sans makeup and wearing sloppy clothes. She walked to the double glass doors and pushed through them into the nerve center of SPACE Security.

CHAPTER 137

LAS VEGAS

Courtney Meyer

IT HAD TAKEN ALMOST NINETY MINUTES, but Meyer finally had a transcript, in English, of Sultanovich's phone call in hand. Silently cursing the need, she dug through her purse and found the reading glasses she required more and more often. She perched them on her nose and started to read. Her hopes of a breakthrough faded. He had called a woman Meyer assumed to be his housekeeper in Kiev, Ukraine.

The call did provide a bit of illumination into the monster's psyche. He demanded that the woman give a detailed account of what she had done while he had been gone. She was apparently used to the grilling, because she recited a long list of mundane details as if she'd done it thousand times. All was well in the conversation until they got to the subject of how often she had walked Sultanovich's dog, "Little Boris." The transcript read as if she had hesitated before answering his question, and he went ballistic. He explained to her how he would kill her, kill her children, her husband, and presumably everyone she had ever known, then have them all ground into sausage for Little Boris's culinary enjoyment.

Meyer tried to mentally square such fondness for his dog with such disdain for humanity, but she didn't try long. Her experience had taught her that the quickest path to insanity was for a sane person to try to make sense of a crazy one. He eventually calmed down and the conversation returned to the banal and stayed there. She laid the transcript on the counter and picked up the comms headset. She switched to two-way comms and called for the Team Leader. He answered promptly. Meyer said, "We have a surveillance team in place now. You guys can pull out when ready."

"Roger that."

CHAPTER 138

SPACE

THE ENTIRE PAGE TURNED OUT TO BE for the sale that took place on March 1st. Galina had fetched the highest price, but according to the reported figures, none of the girls sold for less than a half-million Euros. I continued to be mortified. Knowing that slavery is alive and well in the twenty-first century is one thing, but it's so abstract and such an affront that most of us can't really grasp the reality. Seeing this site had made it nauseatingly real for me.

I clicked the browser's HISTORY menu and selected the very last page in the list, which I suspected was similar to this one. The entire screen was filled with huge red text that said, SEPTEMBER 1 SALE BEGINS AT 11:00 A.M. GMT. I calculated local time at a glance, but it wasn't necessary. The next line of huge text was a running countdown. As I watched, it changed from 2 HOURS, 0

MINUTES, AND 0 SECONDS, to ONE HOUR, FIFTY-
NINE-MINUTES, AND FIFTY-NINE SECONDS.

When I scrolled down on the page, my entire being—body, mind, soul, spirit—froze. I stared, unable to
process this new and most horrible reality that was staring me in the face: Ally, my daughter, my baby girl, was
the first girl shown. Her headline read, LAST-MINUTE
FIND! AMERICAN VIRGIN!

My stupor lasted an indeterminate number of minutes. It eventually dawned on me that my burner phone
was ringing. I answered it, my voice flat, my soul deflated
like an old balloon. "What?" It would of course be Meyer,
since no one else had the number.

"Sam, that you?" It wasn't Meyer, but Nichols.

"Yes."

"You okay?"

"No."

"What's wrong?"

"How'd you get this number?"

"From Meyer, and it took some talking, believe me.
Listen, I—"

"They're selling my baby girl."

"Selling? What are you talking about, Sam? Where
are you?"

"What do you want?"

"Matt Decker called me, said they had urgent information for you. Said somebody named Abdul had been
calling and texting you for hours."

"So what's the information?" I said.

"Don't know. Matt said tell you to check your email,
immediately."

"Okay." I pressed the END button.

I brought up my inbox and near the top I saw an email from Abdul. The subject was RESEND: INFO YOU NEED. Out of curiosity, I scrolled down and saw several more copies of it. Freaking junk subscriptions had filled up my screen and caused me to miss it. I opened the email.

> Sam, tried to call you back but your phone went to VM. You asked me for the buildings on MS (monitor station) #55688. The data for your camera came from #55689, NOT #55688. The two stations near each other. #55689, the "camera station" ties to bldgs on WEST side of LV BLVD, and Space is one of them. Thought you'd wanna know.

Now my heart was beating hard enough that I felt it in my neck, heard it in my ears. I looked at the time stamp on the email. It had come two hours ago. Damn it! Another royal screw-up on my part! What if my bullshit mistakes caused—

I willfully cut off that line of thought. No time. Those rape videos had been shot *here*. My mind shifted into operational mode. I opened the architectural drawings of SPACE and zoomed into the unallocated space where the bunker was. It had to be there, in the bowels of the building, the bowels that the Sultanovich piece of shit owned.

Leaving the drawings, I pulled up the live video feeds from the bunker. Not a soul in sight. Back to the drawings. I studied them, matching up the wireframe rendering before me with my memory of being there. And then I saw it.

CHAPTER 139

SPACE

BACK IN MY OWN ROOM, I thought about all the grief and
giggles I'd taken from Abby over the years since I left the
"service." And after I lugged it on at least a hundred business trips without ever opening it, there were times I almost gave in. Almost. Opening the suite's storage closet, I
retrieved my Maxpedition tactical bag and unzipped it on
the bed. I walked to the little wall safe, keyed in the code,
opened it, and took out my Kimber .45 and extra maga-
zines. Yeah, it's a hassle now to check a firearm every time
you fly, but that "just in case" moment had arrived. All
those times standing in line at an airline check-in counter, all the time spent arguing the law with some dumbass
counter clerk, all the grief and giggles? All worth it.

Despite the years that had passed since my final
operation, I was ready to go in under five minutes. My
heart was calm, my breathing slow, my mind emptying

of all distractions. I didn't just allow the black fog. I summoned it. I welcomed it, embraced it as an old friend. I was one with the fog. When a knock sounded on the door, I walked across the room, careful to stay away from the centerline.

I stood to the side of the door and twisted the doorknob enough for the door to open. If someone had bad intentions, now is when either they or their bullets would storm through. Instead, the door eased open about an inch, and someone said, "Flatt?"

My mind raced, looking for a match. Found it. "Dobo?" I said.

"Yep."

"Come in."

He pushed the door open, stepped through, saw the Kimber pointed at his face. "Whoa," he said, hands rising, palms out. "I'm a friend."

"Convince me," I said.

"How about lowering that cannon?"

I shook my head.

"I figured out your bracelet switch. Don't know how you did it, but I don't care. I got that fat-ass detective off you. He's stranded in the outer rim."

"Why? Why would you do that?"

"Pardon my French, but he's an ass. I don't like him and I don't trust him. Also..."

I backed up a few steps, but kept him in my sights. "Also what?"

He looked at me several seconds, then said, "I do trust you. I may not know exactly who you guys worked for— you know, over there—but stories got around. Anybody who'd do the stuff I heard? You love the same country I do. We're brothers."

I lowered the gun but didn't stow it. "So why are you here now?"

"Just wanted to warn you about Huddleston. That guy has a major woody for you."

"Yeah. No shit. You want to help me?"

Dobo nodded. "If I can, I will."

I walked toward my computer, where the wireframe drawing of the SPACE tower still glowed. "Take a look at something for me."

I sat at the desk, handling the mouse, zooming in and out of the architectural drawings of the unallocated space, while Dobo knelt beside me and studied the screen. He shook his head.

"Who would know?" I said. "There has to be another entrance to it, and I have to have it. Now."

"I want to help you, I—" Dobo's phone rang with an urgent bleating. He put it to his ear. "Dobo." I watched his lips part and his jaw go a bit slack as he listened. Finally he said, "Bring her to one-forty, two-sixteen."

"Whoa," I said as he dropped the phone back into his pocket. "Do not bring anybody to this room."

Dobo raised a hand, palm out, patting the air. "I think you'll want to hear this. A woman showed up in Security and insisted on seeing me, said she had 'life or death' information. They tried to get her to sit and wait, but that got crazy. She took her shirt off and said she'd screw the first guy who told her where I was, and if you've ever seen this woman, well—"

I couldn't believe my ears. Here I was trying to find my daughter and Dobo wanted to tell me some *soap opera cum psycho* tale? "What the hell does th—"

Dobo said, "It's Christine Gamboa, Sam."

Minutes later, I opened the door and there she was, the initial focus of my case, the investigative thread that had taken a back seat to more fruitful areas of inquiry: the impossibly beautiful Christine Gamboa. No makeup, dressed in worn-out jeans and a T-shirt, and still breathtaking. I gestured her in, then closed and relocked the door.

"What's this about?" I said.

"Who are you?" she said, then looked to Dobo in his SPACE Security garb.

Dobo said, "Christine, I don't think we've met before, but I'm Hank Dobo. This is Sam Flatt, an investigator. Whatever you have to tell me, he can hear."

"Are you sure?" she said to Dobo.

I said, "Here's what I'm sure of, Miss Gamboa. You're in my room, which makes you my guest, and if you don't have something really important to say, I'm very busy and will ask you to get the hell out."

"Okay, okay!" She turned back to Dobo. "There's something very illegal going on in the basement of this place, a big computer operation and more."

My turn: "How would you know that?"

"I'm the one who sold them the access into the SPACE network."

That's where the big pile of money in her bank account had come from. How could someone so intelligent be so stupid as to do something like that and then put the money in the bank? "What else?" I said.

"You have to understand, I had nothing to do with the other part. Nothing!"

"What other part?" I said.

"They're selling girls down there."

"They sure are," I said. "How long have you known about this and did nothing?"

"These people are scary. I was afraid, but I'm here now. I want to help."

"So far you haven't told us a single thing we didn't know, so how is it you think you can help?"

She pointed at my computer screen, still displaying the wireframe architectural drawing. "I can show you how to get inside there."

"I've been to the computer room," I said, hoping her next words would confirm what I'd finally seen on the wireframe myself.

Gamboa shook her head. "Not the computer room. The other part of the building down there."

Now she had my full attention.

Dobo was gone. Out of sight, not out of mind. He sounded sincere, and I think he was. Irrelevant. There is no trust. There is no compassion, no consideration. There is nothing now but black that glows with a thick red edge waiting to blossom and consume. The burner phone rang. Meyer or Nichols, I didn't know.

Meyer: "Sam?"

"Check your email," I said. "See what this is really all about. I know where they are. I'm ending this."

"I've seen the email, Sam, the screenshots. I have teams ready to go. Tell me where you are and we'll be there."

"No."

"You can't do this alone."

"Thank you for behaving with honor. We all make mistakes. You've corrected yours. Goodbye, Courtney."

CHAPTER 140

LAS VEGAS

Courtney Meyer

MEYER HUNG UP THE CALL, rather addled by the conversation with Flatt. Who the hell was this guy? After so many years of experience, how had she so misread, so underestimated someone? How had she been so—did she dare say it?—naive? Without government resources, he had run investigative circles around her. And not just her. How had one computer guy learned so much that she and so many man-hours of assistance had failed to find? No, "man-hours" didn't come close. She had been on this case for almost two years, with help. But no, she knew with certainty that this guy was no computer nerd with a pocket protector. She had crawled completely up his ass with background checks and, yes, he looked like nothing special, but it was...wrong. She had spent her adult life so certain of so many things. What else had she gotten…wrong?

And *did* he really know where this operation, these people, did he really know where they were? She had no reason, no evidence, to believe him. But she did believe him. She had hit him with the most despicable thing she'd ever done in her career when she threatened his daughter, the daughter who was now in the hands of evil, and yet he had just thanked her for being honorable?

She laid her phone down and looked at Console Agent. "Can I still reach the team leader on the headset?"

He nodded.

After switching to two-way comms, Meyer held one of the earpieces to her ear and pivoted the microphone to her mouth. "Take Sultanovich. Take the sonofabitch now."

CHAPTER 141

SPACE

I HUNG UP THE CALL WITH JIMMY THE GEEK and walked through the "Platinum Portal" into the VIP gaming area, head on a swivel, absorbing everything. The Chinese guy with the pained look and the bloodshot eyes, pushing a stack of brown chips—chocolate chips worth five grand each—at the dealer. The dealer saying just loud enough for the pit boss to hear, "Coloring down," and pushing back a larger stack of thousand-dollar chips—bananas.

The liver-spotted octogenarian with the twenty-five-year-old at his side, shoving five-hundred-dollar coins into a slot machine. The chick who was young and shapely with a face made pretty only by makeup, looking bored out of her mind, because she was.

A craps table with a redneck shooting and making it all too clear he was a redneck with his "hootin' and hollerin.'" At least his woman was a match; she had CRIM-

SON TIDE splayed across her chest, an elephant head in the middle with its trunk disappearing into her sagging cleavage. God bless the SEC. Hotty Toddy, Roll Tide, and throw in a pinch of LSU voodoo. Circle of Life.

The VIP elevator, the one the "common folk" never saw, was ahead and around a corner. It ferried the rich, famous and not, to the palatial suites above. A SPACE security man near the elevator glanced my way, then did a double-take, probably because of my blacked-out tactical gear, complete with Kimber on my side. The kid couldn't be much over twenty. In a show of magnanimity that surprised even me, I touched the elevator button, then turned and looked him in the eye. I gave the tiniest shake of my head and held the gaze. His Adam's apple bobbed, his eyes widened a bit, and he looked away. Good boy.

The elevator doors opened, I stepped inside, and they closed. According to the architectural drawings, this elevator only went up; the bottom of the shaft terminated here at the ground level. According to Gamboa, that wasn't so. She swore the elevator also went down. Time to find out if Hank Dobo the Hornet driver was friend or foe. I located the glowing SPACE logo above the touchscreen of floor numbers on the left, and tapped my bracelet on it four times, very quickly. According to him, if anything at SPACE had "secret" capabilities, this activated them. A single icon appeared on the screen below the existing numbers. Not a number. A large icon, a high-res graphic depicting a woman in flowing robes with a sword held high above her head. In a different situation, I might have smiled a bit at the symbology. I touched her and felt the elevator descend.

CHAPTER 142

LAS VEGAS

Courtney Meyer

MEYER HAD NOT THE REMOTEST INTENTION of letting this asshole out of her sight until he was locked behind American bars. She sat on the hard metal bench across from Sultanovich in the back of the transport van as it hummed and bounced along the Las Vegas streets. Given the hour, not to mention the east-to-west jet lag that had wracked her body and mind, she was beyond exhausted, but it didn't matter. Eighteen months. A year and a half of her life had been devoted to the pursuit of this man, and now she had him.

She opened a file folder on her lap and removed the prints she made of the screenshots from Flatt. Looking at Sultanovich with every gram of contempt she could muster, she said, "You sell human beings like they're cattle.

What kind of monster are you?"

He raised his eyes to meet hers. They were bloodshot and rheumy, not sharp and bright like they'd been earlier in Memphis. Now he looked ancient and spent. He shrugged and said, "Prostitution is legal in Nevada."

Meyer thrust the print of one of the screenshots forward, holding it by the top edge so that it faced him. "This isn't prostitution. This is slavery, and you may rest assured it's not legal anywhere in this country, you bastard."

Sultanovich looked at the page for ten or fifteen seconds. "I know nothing of this."

"Sure you don't," Meyer said. She pointed toward the front of the van. "How would you like it if that little girl riding up front—Tatyana, right?—was on a page like this? Huh? Different when it's your granddaughter, I guess? Or maybe not, with you hauling her around with you and your sorry ass. Why would you do that?"

"I know nothing, and Tatyana is no business of yours."

She put the pages back into the folder and slipped it into the briefcase beside her. "I hope they fry your decrepit old ass till your eyeballs boil."

Sultanovich lunged toward her but the chains that tethered his waist-chain to the van wall caught him. He stood there, leaning, his face jutted out, and snapped his repulsive yellow teeth at her.

CHAPTER 143

SPACE

I PREFERRED STEALTH until I sized up the opposition. As the elevator slowed, I readied myself. The fog of electric crimson filled my body and soul now, crackling through nerves and neurons. My hands were by my sides, each holding a SOG Desert Dagger. The doors parted.

A thick-necked brute dressed in a black suit and white shirt stood just outside the elevator. It took a couple seconds for his brain to process the figure before him as a threat. By the time it did, I was digging the tip of my right dagger into the soft flesh on the underside of his chin. His eyes went wide as I pushed him back against the bare concrete wall behind him. I did lightning glances left and right. It was just Thick Neck and me. I moved in within six inches of him and whispered, "How many more?"

"Two." His accent was thick, the voice tight, squeaky, and way too high-pitched for such a beast of a man.

"Where?" He tried to turn his head and I pushed the tip of the knife into the skin. "Tell me with your mouth."

"One left. One right. Little inside room."

"Thank you." I put an angle on the knife and looked into his eyes as I drove the razored steel up and back, through the throat and into his brain stem. I slid the knife free and let him fall.

I was standing in a concrete corridor that stretched left and right, the elevator at my back. It looked exactly like the others in the bunker. I should've picked up on the spatial contradiction the night I visited the hackers' computer workroom. It was far too small to consume the unallocated space depicted on the architectural drawings. But I hadn't seen it until minutes earlier. I now knew that the computer room was directly behind me, just past the concrete wall and elevator shaft. I was standing in the remainder of the unallocated space, this area totally isolated from the other rooms.

My shoes were the quietest I'd ever found, Clark Wallabees. I padded to the right, not making the slightest sound. This was a good-sized space, the corridor about sixty feet end to end. When I got to the end, I found a doorless opening on my left that led into a room. Just inside the opening—he was almost blocking it—stood another big guy in a suit. This idiot was gawking at something inside the room, paying zero attention to what was going on behind him. I rammed the knife into the back of his neck, right at the base of the skull, then caught him under his arms as he fell and dragged him backward through the opening and into the corridor, where I dropped him to the floor. Two down, one to go.

I should have been watching my own back. Something knocked me at least three feet forward. I turned and saw that the third guard had clubbed me in the back of the head with a fist the size of a ham, and now he bull-rushed me. This brute was massive, at least six-and-a-half feet and three hundred pounds. He hit me and kept driving until my back slammed into the concrete wall at the end of the corridor. It knocked the breath out of me and by the time I refilled my lungs, he pinned me to the wall by the throat and cut off my supply of air again. Then he started kneeing me in the stomach. When I tried to fend off those blows by hacking at his knees, he moved in and jammed himself right up against the front of my body.

It would have taken the Jaws of Life to pry his massive hands away from my neck. I didn't have one handy. Color faded from my vision as my brain became more and more deprived of oxygen. I would be unconscious in seconds, then dead. Although I still had a knife in each hand, both hands were now pinned between my body and his, which felt like a slab of rock. His height advantage was such that his chin was resting on top of my head, his tattooed neck mashing my face so hard that it would have been suffocating me if I weren't already being choked to death. I had one move left and I made it.

I opened my mouth as wide as I could, then bit down on his neck with everything I had left, catching him an inch or so above the hollow of his throat. The sensation of biting through flesh registered, followed by the taste of blood. The pressure on my throat released first, as his reflexive instinct was to use his hands to pull me off him. I sucked in a great gulp of air and finally—while it was probably no more than three seconds since I'd bitten, it felt much longer—the force of his torso against my hands eased.

Still anchoring his head in place with my teeth, I brought my right hand up high and drove the blade straight into his right ear, up to the hilt. He started a violent twitch that lasted much longer than I would have thought possible. Only when he went limp did I open my mouth to release him. Instead of crumpling to the floor like a cut sack of potatoes, he stayed vertical a moment, then fell straight back.

Hands on hips, I drew in deep breaths, feeling my wits return as my brain sucked in oxygen. Three down. None to go. Showtime.

CHAPTER 144

SPACE

NOT A SOUL IN THE ROOM showed the slightest aware-
ness that anything had happened. Instead, they were all
clustered toward the center of the room and facing the
back wall, talking among themselves. The crowd, which
looked to be wholly male as far as I could tell, had an
excited buzz about it, waiting for something big. I looked
around the room. In contrast to the Spartan atmosphere
of naked concrete that defined the decor elsewhere, this
room was posh. Tables loaded with food, flowers, and ice
sculptures sat along the long wall that divided the room
from the corridor.

Sticking near the wall on the right, I made my way
forward. When I was far enough up to see what was
going on, I stopped and studied the surreal scene. The
crowd was indeed all men, forty to fifty of them. On
a raised platform along the room's back wall, girls sat

on barstools. I worked my way through them and at the center of the line, there she was, my baby girl. She looked dazed, as if she had absolutely no idea what was going on. The expressions on the faces of the other girls varied from tears, to sad resignation, to defiance. Seated to Ally's immediate right, I recognized Daria's sister, Anya.

Next I studied the crowd. It was very international and, of course, very wealthy. Asians. Several Arabs dressed in the white robes popular in Saudi Arabia. Not many obvious Slavs. A few who looked American. The ages of the men ran the spectrum from twenty-somethings to octogenarians, and everything in between. And as I'd feared, a number of them had bodyguards. I couldn't believe none of them were looking at me. Every guy in the crowd seemed totally consumed with ogling the poor girls arrayed before them. This was the downside of operating in an underground bunker; the illusion of invisibility and security made them complacent, lax.

A man in a tux appeared through a door at the far end of the room and walked to the platform. He stood and patted the air with his hands, and the buzzing crowd faded to quiet. Then TuxMan said, "We will begin the sale with the beautiful Elena." He looked toward the far end of the girls and gestured to the one on the last stool. "Stand up and come to the ring, dear." He gestured to a spot beside him that had a three-foot-diameter circle painted on the floor. The girl approached, her whole body trembling in fear. According to the web page I had seen, Elena was twelve years old.

I looked back to the crowd, identifying as many of the bodyguards as possible. My plan was to enter the crowd from the back, pick a central location, and quickly pick off as many of the protectors as I could. Everything would be easier when the muscle was gone.

Then it all went to hell because I wanted to take one more look at my daughter before the melee began. When I looked at her, she happened to be looking my way. I looked into her eyes and gave a small, slow shake of my head, a desperate signal to not react. Her current mental state just wasn't capable of such subtleties.

Ally sprang to her feet and said, "Daddy!" She started moving toward me, arms outstretched.

Every eye in the room turned to me, and one of the bodyguards at the front of the crowd, one who was guarding one of the robed Arabs, grabbed Ally. By the time I had my Kimber in firing position, he was behind her with a gun to her head. She still reached forward, a look of hope on her face.

The crowd was backing away. A couple of the other bodyguards had separated from their charges and were drawn down on me from the ten o'clock and twelve o'clock positions. The strategizing and planning were done. Only action remained. Ally was at one o'clock. The only view I had of her captor was the right edge of his face and his right eye, peeking out from behind his human shield.

I shot him in the eye. The .45 RIP round was designed to fragment and fan out on impact, and his brain was now a shredded mess, switched off like a light. With zero hesitation, I pivoted to twelve o'clock, fired, to ten o'clock, fired. While their bodies were still sinking to the floor, I scanned the crowd for more threats and saw nothing immediate but kept my gun trained that way.

I said, "Ally! Girls! Let's go! Now!" Using my head, I gestured toward the door.

Ally didn't hesitate, but she also didn't go to the door

like I said. She ran to me and threw her arms around my waist. "I love you, Daddy. I knew you'd come for me."

"Love you too, sweetie." I went one-handed on the gun and extended my left hand to her. "Take that bracelet, put it on." When she'd done that, I said, "Now go, get yourself and the other girls out of here. There's an elevator in the hallway. Touch the bracelet to the call button and take the elevator to the casino. Got it?"

She nodded and started toward the door, motioning for the other girls to follow her. They passed between me and the crowd as they headed for the door. The moment my view cleared, my left shoulder exploded with pain. What the—*oh, shit.*

CHAPTER 145

SPACE

Courtney Meyer

"Mr. Dobo," Meyer said, "open that door or stand back and I'll shoot the lock until it gives. If that doesn't work, maybe I'll shoot you and take that bracelet off your arm."

Dobo sighed and touched the bracelet to the reader on the door.

Meyer entered the room and started a frantic search for anything that would lead her to Sam. His computer sat on the desk, screen open and showing what looked like a diagram of a building. She went to it and looked closer. *Damn, damn, damn.* She dug in a pocket and came out with the infernal reading glasses.

"What is this?"

"Looks like an architectural drawing of this tower," Dobo said.

Meyer stared at Dobo, then back to the screen. "You know where he went. I see it in your eyes. I know you think you're helping him, but he's in danger. He needs help."

"Not so sure about that."

"I am!" Meyer said. "He's acting on bad information! Now for the love of God, help me save him before it's too late."

A voice from the direction of the bathroom said, "I'll help you." Meyer looked and couldn't believe her eyes. It was Christine Gamboa.

CHAPTER 146

SPACE

DURING THE DISTRACTION OF THE GIRLS heading for the door, a corpulent man had entered the room through the door at the far end of the room, the same one TuxMan had used earlier. Once the girls cleared a path, the bastard had shot me.

"Everybody must to stop!" the man said.

The girls stopped walking and I saw Ally look to me for instructions I didn't yet have. Blood from my shoulder ran down my arm and fell to the floor in a steady procession of fat drops. A pit-faced man who looked to be in his late fifties or early sixties walked through the door and approached FatMan. I tried to assimilate and process what I was seeing. I failed.

I still had my gun up but I was one-handed. I knew the guy could shoot, and he already had a bead on me.

Then the situation grew stranger still: Christine Gamboa walked into the room from the corridor, the same way I'd entered. Had she followed me? But she hadn't needed to, had she? She was the one who had told me how to get here.

Gamboa looked at the man with the gun, then looked at me, then back to him. "Sasha? What are you doing?" She pointed at me. "He's one of the good guys, here to help."

"Shut up, Chrissy. He is not 'good guy.' He is big maker of much trouble for Sasha."

Gamboa tilted her head and looked at him, her mouth slightly open, eyes squinting, calculating. After a bit, she said, "Oh my God. I thought it was Max, but it was you? You're the one behind this? How could you?"

He laughed, his barrel chest and big belly shaking, but neither his eyes nor his gun left me. "Max is stupid old man. Oh, he steal much money with computers, but then he so stupid with the girls, wants only to use them as whores. He thinks is big deal to charge fifty thousand dollars to fuck virgin first time. I make this! Me, Sasha Maslov! I make millions on millions."

Even at this distance, I could tell Gamboa was tearing up. She looked devastated. "Oh God, oh God. I was such an idiot. The deal with the FBI, everything, it was all a lie. You evil, evil man."

"Ha! FBI woman with ass like Lada automobile." He started laughing again. "You know old saying, keep enemies close. Stupid woman tell us everything. But you know, Chrissy, does not to matter right now. Right now, we finish sale!"

"No!" Gamboa said. "You can't do this, Sasha! Please!"

"Sasha can. I think if you do not to like this, is maybe time to sell you, Chrissy."

I saw his finger tightening on the trigger. He was about to shoot me again. Everything around me shifted into slow motion. I was diving right, my own finger contracting on the trigger for a shot. Then Maslov pitched forward like a whale falling back into the water. Standing behind him, the pit-faced man was wiping down a leather slapstick.

He looked at the crowd and said, "Nobody move a muscle."

Then he walked toward me and said, "Reaching for ID." He slowly withdrew a small wallet from a pocket inside his jacket, then flipped it open to reveal a badge and said, "Edward Bulgakov, Interpol."

Gamboa was literally in slack-jawed shock, standing there looking at this man.

I lowered my gun and looked to the group of girls. I think every one of them was crying, including Ally. She looked up, saw me, and broke into a run. She fell into my arms—okay, more like fell into my one good arm—sobbing and saying, "Daddy, Daddy, Daddy," over and over. I just held her.

Within a couple minutes, Meyer arrived in the room like a cyclone, gun drawn. She shot a scowl at Gamboa. "That was stupid! You were supposed to stay at the elevator!"

Gamboa folded her arms over her chest and said nothing.

The Interpol agent had hung his badge on a chain around his neck, and when Meyer saw it, she had pretty much the same reaction Gamboa had. Apparently this guy had played his undercover role very well.

After the two agents introduced themselves, apparently not for the first time, I heard Bulgakov say, "These scum were here as buyers."

Someone from the direction of the crowd started saying, "Diplomatic immunity! I have diplomatic immunity!"

I looked and saw that it was one of the robed Arabs. I called Meyer over. When she got there, I whispered in her ear. She squinted her eyes and looked at me for a few seconds, then said, "Sorry, I can't leave you with a suspect."

I sighed. Two can play the pressure game, and my P.I. is very good at digging up dirt. The kind that ends FBI careers. I whispered in her ear again, this time for about thirty seconds.

Her eyes narrowed and burned, but she said nothing. Instead she nodded once and walked over to Bulgakov and said something.

Then she approached the group of hugging and crying girls. "Okay, ladies," she said, "let's get you out of here."

The girls gravitated toward her. I looked at Ally. "Sweetie, go with Agent Meyer, okay? I'll be up in a few minutes." She squeezed me in a long, fierce hug, then let go and joined the others.

Bulgakov had a gun out now and was rounding up the crowd, including a very pissed-off-looking Maslov. He stood in the opening to the corridor, and once all the girls had been elevatored up, he motioned the gaggle of human filth to exit the room. As the diplomat walked by him, Bulgakov grabbed his robe and pulled him out of the line. "You stay." Then he brought up the rear and followed the rest of them out into the corridor.

RobeMan looked smug, standing there with a semi-sneer on his face. I stood in the opening, watching the room and the corridor. In a couple minutes I saw Dobo step from the elevator. He had come to help ferry the prisoners upstairs in manageable groups. That took twenty minutes, and then it was just RobeMan and me, alone in the quiet.

I walked over to him and said, "Diplomat, huh?"

He sniffed and nodded, standing there with his chin stuck out like he was posing for a sculptor. "I demand to be released and my embassy notified immediately."

"You're an arrogant prick, aren't you?"

"How dare you sp—"

My uppercut caught him right on the bottom of his chin, and it was a good one. It had that satisfying feeling, like the thwack you get when you connect just right with the sweet spot of a baseball bat on the ball. He staggered backward, flailing around in his robe as he tried not to fall. He wound up on his knees.

I took my time walking to him. He was addled but certainly aware enough to understand that things weren't going his way. His eyes got wider as I grew closer. "Bet you intended to bid on my little girl, didn't you?"

He violently shook his head. "No, no, I had no idea what this was! I would never—"

"Shut up." He did, and I continued. "In your world, there is no justice for piles of shit like you." I slipped the Desert Dagger from its sheath on the right side of my tactical vest.

"Wh-what are you doing?"

I gave him my most charming Sam Flatt smile and said, "Welcome to my world. Let's get acquainted."

CHAPTER 147

SPACE

I REFUSED TO GO TO FBI HEADQUARTERS to give my statement, and Meyer didn't push it. Instead, after I said farewell to Nichols and thanked for all his help, I met her in Rings of Saturn, where we were situated in a quiet booth at the back of the room After I gave her my version of all that had happened—the version I was able to share—I needed some answers myself. "What will happen to Gamboa?"

Meyer blew out a long sigh. "She sold access to her employer's network for a half-million dollars. She's facing serious charges."

"No deal for testimony?"

She shrugged. "Maybe. Not my call. You know, I shouldn't be discussing any of this with you. And I *certainly* shouldn't have left you with the Saudi Arabian."

"Kind of like I shouldn't have been disclosing my client's business to you without a warrant or court order? You started the pressure game. As far as I'm concerned, we're even. I say we put it all behind us and consider it a job well done."

She puffed out her cheeks and blew out a long breath. "What I say here goes no further, right?"

"Of course not."

"If her info is good, she'll probably get off with probation."

I nodded. "What about Sultanovich and Maslov?"

"They'll never see life outside an American prison again if I have anything to do with it. Looks like Sultanovich had no idea about the sales angle. That was all Maslov."

"Speaking of those two, it had to piss you off that the Interpol agent was operating here without notifying you guys."

I could see the red rising in her face. "That's an understatement."

"Why'd he do that?"

"Claimed he was afraid the bureau was compromised, someone might blow his cover. I think he's just an undercover hot dog who wanted the bust himself."

"You think he knew about the trafficking operation?"

Meyer shook her head. "I don't think anybody knew about them selling girls, before you found it. I think the Interpol asshole was chasing the hacking and prostitution ring, no more."

"You have anything on the ones who abducted Ally? I know Sultanovich was behind it; I'm talking about the actual operators."

"We tracked the car back to a chop shop run by a Hispanic gang. We think the Eastern Europeans use them for muscle around here." Meyer looked at me over the top of her boat anchor of a laptop. "And to be clear, you're sure you know nothing at all about four Hispanic bodies in the men's room at SPACE?"

I chewed, shrugged, and shook my head.

She did a spate of typing, then looked up again. "And tell me again what happened with the Saudi?"

"There was a struggle. Bastard tried to take my knife." I slathered butter on my Renduvian Roll and took a bite. "Have you tried these rolls?"

"And in this...struggle, he was accidentally disemboweled and castrated?"

"He was a lot bigger than me, and I'd been shot. Must have been an adrenaline thing."

Meyer typed a little more, then closed the lid on her computer. She cocked her head a bit, squinted, and said, "Who *are* you?"

"Unclavius Samuel Flatt, ma'am, but you can call me Sam."

EPILOGUE

THREE MONTHS LATER

"It's CRITICAL, JIMMY. These people have been through enough," I said into the phone. "I want to be sure these Russian and Ukrainian gangsters have no records of who the families of these people are. I don't want them to go through life scared shitless."

Jimmy the Geek said, "Dude, whatever data those assholes used to have, they ain't got no more. Told you, I found that data. Dumbasses had it sitting on a hard drive in a spreadsheet. It's gone. And for the record? Just about everything else they had that was digital? That's gone, too. Once I was into their network, I cleaned house."

"All right. You rock, man."

"Where you been, by the way? I did all this freaking forever ago, the night you called me about it."

"Call it a sabbatical. This is the first time I've been in range of a cell tower. Listen, gotta go, bud."

"Later, dude."

I touched END CALL and dropped the phone back into one of the saddle bags. I stroked Johnny's neck and breathed in his beautiful equine aroma while I looked out over a spectacular scene of Colorado mountain forests turning a thousand different colors. Crystal blue lakes lay nestled in the huge valley below.

"Ready to ride, Johnny?"

Johnny snorted and tossed his head. The phone rang again and I fished it out of the old leather bag. "Hey, Abby."

"You okay?" she said. "Been months since we heard from you."

"Yeah. I'm great, Ab."

"Listen, back when those men took Ally, you said something to me, something I never answered."

"I remember."

"Sammy, I love you, too."

I smiled and said, "I know."

THE END

I need your help!

Thanks for reading *Unallocated Space*! When it's three o'clock in the morning and I'm still clattering away at the keyboard, staring at the screen through tired eyes, it's you who keeps me going. Knowing that someone enjoys these stories I make up is a wonderful feeling, and I appreciate it more than you know.

If you have just a moment more, I really need your help. Today's blockbuster authors have publishers who don't mind spending millions promoting their books, but I have something better. I have you! If you enjoy what I write, you can play a huge role in keeping the stories flowing, simply by sharing.

Readers trust other readers. Would you please leave a review on Amazon or another site where you bought the book? (Reviews are the lifeblood of today's authors.) After that, if you're a social media user, would you help spread the word? Please tell your friends, whether in person or via social media, that you found an author you enjoy. Whether it's Facebook, Twitter, Pinterest, Instagram, or maybe your own blog, I'd be eternally grateful if you'd be part of my team and help get the word out.

Happy reading!

P.S: Don't forget to sign up for my email list to stay up to date on new books and special offers! You can do it at my website: www.jerryhatchett.com

Also By Jerry Hatchett

Pawnbroker

Seven Unholy Days

Coming Soon:
Sam Flatt returns in another thrilling adventure...

Made in the USA
Coppell, TX
09 February 2020